SOLACE

Irene
ove
nev
Ire

Ire
the
apa
mu
rou
em

She
sel
wo
tha
Ad
ret

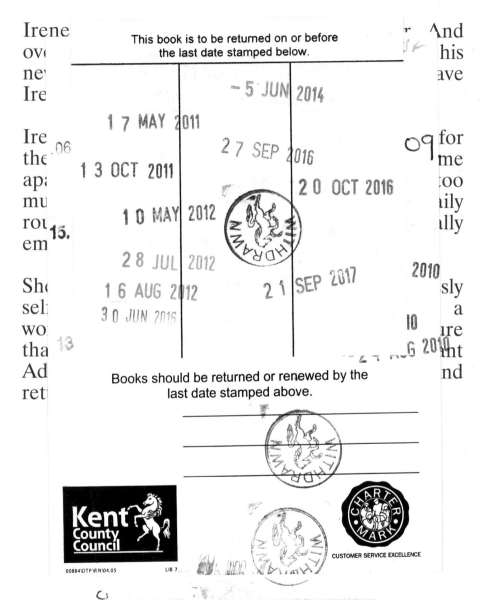

SOLACE

Nicci Gerrard

WINDSOR
PARAGON

First published 2005
by
Penguin Books
This Large Print edition published 2006
by
BBC Audiobooks Ltd by arrangement with
Penguin Books Limited

ISBN 1 4056 1296 7   (Windsor Hardcover)
ISBN 1 4056 1297 5   (Paragon Softcover)

British Library Cataloguing in Publication Data available

Printed and bound in Great Britain by
Antony Rowe Ltd., Chippenham, Wiltshire

To Edgar, Anna, Hadley and Molly

CHAPTER ONE

When did it all start? She would never know for sure, although later she would trace it, like a finger on a map following the broad river back to the invisible thread of its beginnings, to one evening in early winter. Outside, she remembered it as cold, dark, full of damp, gusty wind; the rattle of dustbin lids, the hiss of cars through puddles, the rustle of bushes, the creak of bending trees. Inside it was warm and the puddles of brightness cast by the lamps and the candles made the room seem like a deep cave in the secret heart of London. She dwelt on what might have happened until she could no longer distinguish between what she knew and what she had imagined. She illuminated the shadowy corners, poured into mysterious silences the suggestive murmur of their voices, allowed herself to picture them together: a moment when the match was struck, its cool flame licking at the dry tinder, and nobody had any idea of the conflagration to come. And if they had known, would they have stopped it? Blown out the flame, left it at that: a moment of possibility, something they would remember later, if they thought about it at all, with a rueful sense of life's precariousness.

And what about her? If Irene herself could have turned the hidden destruction of that evening back on its oiled hinge, closed it off with a neat click, would she have done so? Would she?

*   *   *

1

Everyone left late, one by one or in pairs. Irene watched them leaning over Adrian where he lay back on the sagging sofa and patting his shoulder, hugging him, kissing him and telling him it had been a treat, he'd been fabulous, brilliant. It was the start of great things, they said, not really believing it because he'd only appeared twice and the second time was as a dead body in the corner of the tv screen, his legs shockingly white and hairy. Irene saw the way he'd smiled up at them a bit drunkenly, not really believing it either but loose with alcohol and hope, watching the way Sarah's shirt was stretched tight over her pregnant stomach so that he could make out the shape of her belly button; breathing in Greg's nicotine-and-after-shave smell and the astringent subtlety of Mona's perfume.

Everyone else looked sloppy and relaxed, blurred in the firelight, worn round the edges with drink and weariness, but Irene felt vigilant and alert, made up of hard edges and precise angles. As if it were happening to her, she knew the way Adrian was feeling now. A faint, insistent headache pulsed above his left eye. Tomorrow, he would be dry-mouthed and nauseous and sour with anticlimax. He would snap at the children, cut himself shaving, stare more anxiously than ever at his hung-over face in the mirror. Now he smiled some more, feeling the skin stretch around his mouth, poured himself another glass of wine and swallowed it down in rapid gulps, ignoring Irene's anxious glance, shook Gary's hand, kissed the corner of Lisa's mouth, told everyone they didn't have to go just yet. They should stay a bit longer. He didn't want the evening to end and it to be tomorrow, the chilly pewter light of morning.

Then a child cried in the distance, a sobbing call for 'Mummy! Mu-ummeee!' Irene at once stood up, turning her back on the sprawled remainder of guests, and made her way upstairs, along the balding carpet of the corridor, into the bathroom where Clem knelt on the cold tiles, leaning over the toilet bowl and whimpering in the half-darkness. Irene crouched down and put her cool hand on her daughter's clammy forehead, murmuring soothingly. 'Poppet,' she said. 'Little love.' She heard doors open and close, voices calling goodbye. 'It'll be fine,' she said. 'Everything will be all right.' She knew she was talking to herself as well as to her daughter. She didn't really want to go back downstairs, not just yet.

So she could only imagine what happened next, picturing the scene until she almost felt that she had been there herself after all, spying from the shadows. At last just Frankie was left, sitting at the table still covered in the debris of the evening, her legs slightly apart so that Adrian could see the softness of her thighs. Her shirt was flimsy, and when she leant forward, he glimpsed the swell of her breasts. For a moment, she looked timeless to him, composed like a work of art: the medieval blue of her shirt and the creaminess of her strong bare forearms, while behind her the candles picked out the clutter of the table, the tarnished gleam of cutlery, the floppy orange curls of satsuma skin, the white plates on which bright paper napkins lay crumpled among the remainders of the meal. She picked up her wine glass and drank its last dregs. He could see the muscles of her throat working, and the red smudge her mouth left on her glass's rim. One shoe was half off. Her hair had come loose and a dark blonde strand lay across her cheek. She smiled at him. He could hear Irene's footsteps clipping busily across the bare boards of one of the rooms upstairs; a door slammed; a child's cough was loud then splintered into silence.

It was Irene who had insisted on inviting friends round to watch him in the film, which the production company had sent them on video weeks ago but which tonight was live on tv, Adrian's name appearing near the end of the credits, in smaller faster letters than those of the main parts. The *TV Times* called the film 'pointless', and privately Adrian agreed, but Irene had said they should mark the occasion nevertheless. She had asked fifteen people they knew well and a few of them had invited extras, so it ended up with twenty-two of them altogether in the small sitting room, with the table pushed back against the wall and chairs and cushions arranged around the tv screen. Irene made little crescents of puff pastry stuffed with tomato and cheese that split open in the oven and disgorged their contents, blistering darkly over the pan. She bought slabs of Cheshire with vinegary pickles, crusty baguettes that she warmed in the oven; bags of satsumas with pocked and pouchy skins and deep-filled mince pies with lattice tops, and got a crate of beer and a case of Chilean red wine, on special offer, from the off-licence. She searched out their chipped plates and assortment of glasses and tumblers to set upon the table, along with paper napkins left over from Sasha's birthday party, and candles that she pressed firmly into their glass holders. And then their friends had arrived, bringing sparkling wine,

4

popping corks at the ceiling, getting drunk enough not to notice or to care how paltry the film really was. Irene had intended it as a gesture of confidence, but it had at the same time something elegiac about it. Maybe this was the start of a new era, as their friends insisted as they raised their glasses in a hearty toast, or perhaps it was simply the undramatic coda to a career that had never taken off.

Now Irene was upstairs and only Frankie was here, her elbow splayed on the table and smiling at him, while behind her a candle flickered down, casting shadows. She stood up, swayed slightly, giggled.

'I should go,' she said. 'Look at the time. I'll be hopeless in the morning.'

'Don't leave,' he said. 'Once you've gone there's no one left and it'll all be over and what will I do with myself then? Stay. Keep me company. Have another drink.'

'No, really. I never meant to stay so late.'

'It's not late. It's only—' He stared at his watch face, squinting. The numbers swam.

'I'll call a cab, if that's OK. The underground will be closing down, and anyway I don't want to walk through Hackney at this time of night.'

'Go ahead then.' He gestured to the phone. 'I can't move.'

She punched in the numbers, gave the address, sat down by the side of the sofa, cross-legged so her skirt rode up. He looked away, looked back again.

'Ten minutes,' she said. 'Less. Tell Irene thanks.'

'She'll probably be down again in a minute—but

Clemmie's got this sickness bug . . .'

'Don't worry.'

'Pour me some more wine.'

'You're sure?' she asked, but she poured him a full glass, taking a sip herself before she handed it over. There was a red smear on the rim of the glass and he raised his head and put his lips where hers had been, took an awkward gulp, feeling his muscles untying, his thoughts unbolting, all his words fraying, coming undone.

He had never looked at Frankie properly before—his wife's oldest friend's younger sister who'd been on the outer edges of his life for more than twelve years. He could see from here that she wore no bra and her breasts were full and soft; that there were muscles in her calves and she had long ear lobes from which hung a bright jangle of metal. There was a tiny white scar in her thick eyebrows and the parting in her hair was slightly crooked. Her make-up had smudged a bit; she looked soft, blurred, full of secrets.

'I think I'm a bit drunk,' he said. If he closed his eyes now, the room would tip and he would be adrift. He kept his eyes open and took another sip.

Frankie laid her hand, very gently, on his upper thigh. 'It's your night,' she said. He looked at it for a moment, the slim fingers against his leg, the pearly nails. From upstairs came the sound of a door shutting softly. Adrian set down his wine glass and, without looking at Frankie, he put his hand on her blonde, warm head. He imagined Irene upstairs, listening outside the bedroom to make sure everything was fine the way she did every single night, her head slightly cocked and a tight, expectant expression on her face, and he tightened

6

his fingers in the tangle of hair, tugging Frankie towards him. She uncoiled her legs and knelt up, leaning over him on the sofa where he lay. He smelt the wine on her breath. He brushed a thumb against her nipple, swollen under the thin material of her shirt, and she gave a little murmur. Her hair brushed his face. Her lips parted, very slightly.

'Jesus, I want to fuck you,' he said, not moving.

They heard the footsteps on the staircase and Frankie sank back onto the floor beside him. She re-crossed her legs and pushed her hair behind her ears.

'Sorry,' said Irene, entering the room, her arms full of sheets. She'd put on a thick towelling robe, belted round the waist and rolled up at the sleeves, and washed her face. Her hair was brushed back from her thin face and she smelt of lavender soap and moisturizing cream and, faintly, vomit. 'Clemmie was sick. I had to wash her and change the sheets.'

'I should have helped you,' said Adrian. 'Sorry. You should have called.'

'Poor thing,' said Frankie. 'Can I do anything?'

'No, it's fine.' Irene looked at the two of them sitting so close together. Her husband's face was flushed. 'Do you want more coffee?'

'I'm on my way. My cab should have been here ages ago.'

And when the bell rang at the front door a few moments later Frankie pulled on her thick coat, wrapped a velvet scarf round her neck, gathered up her bag, kissed Irene goodbye on both cheeks, gripping her by her thin shoulders, and then laid one hand on the top of Adrian's thick, hot head in casual farewell.

7

'See you,' he said amiably as she left, although it was all he could do not to groan out loud, so flooded by lust and guilt that he couldn't tell the difference between them.

CHAPTER TWO

'I think that went well,' said Irene. 'Did you enjoy it?'

'Fine,' he said. 'Great. Thanks. You went to a lot of trouble for me.'

'Oh well.' She looked down at him. 'It was the least I could do.'

'Thanks,' he repeated. He looked into her candid grey eyes, with the little crow's feet, and then at her wide mouth, the faint brackets around it.

'Are you OK down there?' she said.

'Sure. Just a bit tired. Irene?'

'Mmm.'

'We should go away together sometime, like we used to. Before.'

'Bed,' she said, thinking of overdrafts, schedules, childcare, homesickness.

'I mean it. A sunny place in February, just you and me. The kids would be all right now. It's been so long. We could . . .'

'Come on,' she said and held out a hand. He took it, noticing that her nails were bitten to the quick and her wedding ring was loose on her finger.

'What about the mess?'

'Leave it. We can do it tomorrow.'

He watched her as she took off her towelling robe and hung it on the hook on the door. She was pale, with freckles on her shoulders, a mole on her hip, and prominent rib bones. She used to be slim and quick—like a flame, he'd said to her once, bowled over with love; like a wild flower—but now she was thin. He could see the sinews in her arms, and the way that her skin was slightly loose. He tried not to compare her to that other golden body, half glimpsed like a ripe fruit among the camouflaging leaves, and when Irene lay down beside him in the bed they'd shared for over a decade, he put his arms around her and held her spooned against him, feeling her vertebrae sharp as a zip against his chest.

'I still smell of sick.'

'It doesn't matter.'

He put a hand on her flat stomach, between the sharp angles of her pelvis. She held herself carefully, neither rejecting nor inviting him.

'I love you,' he said into her hair. His head was swimming; breathing deeply made him feel faintly queasy. 'You know that I love you, don't you?'

'Mmm. Me you too.'

He moved his hand lower. 'Irene?'

'Mmm?' She kept absolutely still. Her eyes were wide open and she gazed into the darkness.

'Never mind. Sleep well.'

A soft mutter came from her and he rolled onto his back, putting his arm over his eyes, feeling the walls rush towards him.

*   *   *

Irene stared out at the bedroom. She always left

9

the door slightly ajar so that she could hear the children during the night, and a fuzzy yellow blade of light from the landing lay along the carpet. She waited until she heard Adrian's breath deepen and then she got out of bed, pulled on her towelling robe, and went into the room that Clemmie and Agnes shared, their two low beds separated by a narrow gap that in their games was sometimes a river, sometimes a raging fire, sometimes an abyss that they would heroically leap across, though Agnes often missed, crashing onto the wooden floor with screams of frustration and woe. Clemmie lay with her head on a towel and a bucket beside her. She had hectic red cheeks and, when Irene laid a hand across it, a clammy forehead. The skin on her back was burning hot. A thick, sour smell hung round her.

Irene knew she wouldn't sleep now, although during the film a few hours ago she had been struck by waves of weariness, so she'd had to strain her eyes wide open and sit up straighter on her cushion, taking small nips at the glass of wine she'd made last the entire evening; nowadays, she never had more than one glass of wine with her meal, and even that she would often leave barely touched. She looked in on Sasha, then padded downstairs to the kitchen where plates were stacked up in the sink, and the table was covered with smeary glasses, empty beer bottles, balled-up paper napkins, torn-off hunks of bread.

She put Clemmie's sheets on to wash and then snapped on rubber gloves, emptied the sink of plates, and filled it with hot soapy water. She worked methodically, washing first the cutlery, then the glasses, finally the plates and bowls. She emptied the ashtrays and swilled out wine and beer bottles before putting them in the box for recycling, threw cushions back onto chairs, vacuumed the carpet, poking the nozzle into dusty corners, sucking up crumbs and dust and coloured beads that rattled down the throat of the old machine. Although her eyes were sore with tiredness she was far from sleep now, and there was a satisfaction in returning the room to its normal condition, putting things in their exact place and knowing that in the morning it would look as if nothing had happened the evening before.

It was three o'clock in the morning. She imagined all the other people who must be awake right now, making love, swallowing pills, writing poems, sobbing into their pillows, nursing newborn babies to their cracked nipples, staring at the curtains and waiting for a strip of grey dawn to appear. In the cupboard there were several boxes of teas: lemon and ginger, lemon verbena, blackcurrant, mint, camomile, something called 'tranquillity tea' which smelt dusty, like hay or old geraniums. She dropped a bag of lemon verbena into a mug and poured boiling water over it, draped the washed sheets over the radiator, then sat on the sofa in the dark living room, her legs curled up under her, cupping the mug in her chapped hands, sipping very slowly at the infusion while the fragrant steam rose into her face. Rain blew in gusts against the window and she shivered and tightened the belt on her gown.

Insomnia casts a harsh light. That evening she had finally admitted to herself, as she watched Adrian in the tv play, that she no longer believed

11

he would ever succeed as an actor and that she'd probably stopped believing it a long time ago. His face, which in person was vivid and sensual, had seemed oddly vague and unmemorable on the tv screen, like a photograph that has been overdeveloped. She saw with surprise what she hadn't properly noticed before, that his hairline was receding and his waistline thickening, his cheeks slightly jowly. She had twisted round to watch him as he watched himself. He had dropped the self-mocking grin of the early evening and his expression was solemnly attentive. She knew, with an electric jolt of pity, that he was pleased with the self that he saw; his lips half-mouthed the lines that his image on the screen spoke and he gave a tiny, sly smile. Her heart contracted. She had put out a hand to squeeze his arm, but he'd not looked up. He had no idea.

She felt hollowed-out with fatigue, panic and love. She couldn't believe she would ever feel desire for him, or anyone, ever again. But the trick, at this time of night, was not to think about it.

*   *   *

Irene had fallen asleep on the sofa and woken up with a start, chilly and stiff, just before six. For a few moments, she didn't know where she was. Indeed, she had the disconcerting sensation that she didn't even know who she was either, and that her skull contained an ocean of inchoate feelings and rolling, ceaseless memories that could belong to anyone. She lay quite still, her fingers on the rough fabric of the cushion, and waited for things to resolve and return to her. Her eyes adjusted to the gloom and she made out the armchairs, the table, the stairs dimly lit by the light from the landing upstairs. She was able to imagine what she could not see: the rug beneath her, with the threadbare patch under the table; the zigzag pattern on the cushions. She sat up, rubbed her eyes and stood up.

She had just climbed into a bath slippery with bath oil, when Agnes woke and marched into the bathroom, her feet stomping heavily on the tiles, her eyes blinking under her scraggy nest of pale hair.

'Is it morning now?' she asked.

'Just about.'

Without saying anything else, Agnes peeled off her nightdress and climbed into the water, inserting her chubby body between her mother's legs and sitting like a self-satisfied Buddha while the water came up to her chin. She picked up the bar of soap from the side, looked at it curiously, then bit into it. The soap shot from her dimpled fist but for a few seconds the expression on her face didn't change at all. Then she opened her mouth and gave a hoarse cry, while mushy tabs of soap fell from her foaming tongue and she thrashed her arms in the water.

'Oh Aggie, you've gone and done it again,' said Irene. 'Come on, out you get. We'll have to rinse it and rinse it until the taste's gone.'

She heaved herself out of the bath and lifted Agnes, still hooting dementedly, up over the bath's rim. Her wet legs swung, and her oily body slipped through Irene's grip, a plump, writhing eel.

'Spit,' she said, as she filled a plastic beaker with water. 'Get rid of it.'

'Hooooooooo.'

'Spit.'

'You woke me up. Why are you wearing no clothes?'

'Oh Clem. Sorry. Are you feeling better? You shouldn't be out of bed.'

'Hooooooo.'

'What's wrong with her? Is she ill too?'

'She's fine. Go back to bed. Spit, Aggie.'

'I had a flying dream.'

'That's nice,' said Irene distractedly, sloshing cold water down Aggie's howling mouth.

'No. I kept bumping into things. I kept bumping into windows and cows and things. It hurt.'

'That's probably because you're ill.' Irene looked at Clem intently, noticing the waxy pallor of her skin and the way her cropped hair was slightly damp and stood up in little peaks above her forehead. 'People often have funny dreams when they're ill. I used to dream I was being chased by giant ants standing on their back legs.'

'Did they have grass in their mouths?'

'What?'

'Hooooooo.'

*　　　*　　　*

By eight o'clock Irene had given breakfast to Agnes, who in the mornings only ever ate white bread with the crusts cut off and seedless strawberry jam; had taken Clem's temperature—over a hundred, and she still had that smell of wet blanket; had listened to Sasha practising for her Grade One piano exam, her skinny legs in their stripy tights pressed against the pedals, her little fingers pedantically picking out the notes and the tip of her tongue sticking pinkly out of her pursed mouth; and had looked in on Adrian who was fast asleep on his back, his hand over his eyes, one foot poking out of the duvet cover and his breath catching in the back of his throat in a rumbling half-snore. She threw his dirty laundry into the basket in the corner, then, because she didn't need to be in work till later, pulled some ancient trousers and top off the chair and some clean knickers and socks out of a drawer. He stirred, nearly woke, wrapped the duvet more firmly around him and turned his back to her. She felt a rumbling tremor of rage somewhere deep inside her but ignored it, and collected up the mugs half full of cold tea from his bedside table.

Adrian watched her from under the shield of his arm. She was wearing shapeless, faded jeans and a mustard-coloured sweatshirt that had once belonged to him, with frayed sleeves. Her hair was spiky where she'd run her fingers through it. Nowadays she wore baggy, functional clothes and never stopped moving—look at her now, picking things off the floor, wiping the smudges from the mirror. She was always in a hurry, always vigilant, never at rest; she walked on her high-arched feet as if she was about to break into a run; her eyes flickered when she spoke to him, glancing at the things she had to do. When he'd first met her, she had worn thin skirts through which you could see the shape of her slender legs and bright tops and had had long golden hair, tumbling gloriously down her back. But she'd cut it all off ten months ago, standing in the middle of the kitchen and scissoring off the locks, letting them fall in

15

flickering ribbons on the tiles, and now her face looked strangely exposed and childlike. In the summer, her freckles even spread onto her lips: he remembered the first time he had taken her face between his hands and kissed her on that wide freckled mouth and felt her smile as he kissed her. All those years ago. She had freckles on her back as well, and on her thighs among the gold down and on the backs of her rough hands and sprinkling her wrists and even a few on her knees. He looked at her, her stubborn, hunched shoulders and the way she frowned out at the saturated monochrome sky and bit the side of her nails.

'I'll get up in a minute,' he mumbled thickly. His tongue was leather.

But he lay there for several minutes longer, trying not to think about last night, which anyway seemed to him this morning as unreal and unlikely as a dream that you can't quite recall yet which lies so heavily in the mind.

CHAPTER THREE

It would be nearly three weeks before Adrian saw Frankie again. Several times, after that evening when he hadn't kissed her, he had thought about calling her, always understanding that he wouldn't. He knew her number by heart now, although he kept trying to forget it. During the week that he was employed to do the filing for Gary's company, or the Friday early evenings and Saturday mornings when he taught drama and singing to middle-class prepubescent girls who thought they

16

wanted to be actresses because they liked being the centre of attention, or whose mothers had detected a 'talent' in them, or in the hours when he idled round the house and watched daytime tv and opened just one more can of beer, he would imagine what it would be like, to hold the receiver against his ear and hear the breath of her voice. Perhaps she'd be baffled: 'Adrian? Oh yes, that Adrian.' Or cold with disapproval. Hot with embarrassment. Or maybe a man would answer and ask him to leave a message. But sometimes in his mind he would allow her to be husky and eager . . . Of course, even as he laid his hand on the phone, he knew it was ridiculous, dangerous and wrong to consider it; he broke into a sweat just toying with the impossible idea of it. He thought of Irene with her cropped hair and her shabby jeans and waited for her to return from work, pushing her bike with Aggie perched on its seat, and the other two running beside her. Everyone liked Irene; she was fierce and loyal and dogged; she spoke her mind and you could trust her. But they didn't know how she managed to juggle everything: her work, the children, and—their voices would drop conspiratorially—*you know, everything*. Dear Irene, they would say. Poor Irene.

*   *   *

Irene used to be a primary school teacher, but now she taught dyslexic children and, more rarely, dyslexic adults. She worked in a large cold room on the first floor of a large grey house in the north of London, belonging to the Quakers. The room had a bar fire, a blackboard on the wall, a box of shabby cast-off toys under the table and a bay window that overlooked an unsatisfactory park where litter and dead leaves were blown up by the wind. Over the years she had become familiar with the people who walked through the park, or who sat on the two benches with their sandwiches and books. She knew the woman who was tugged through it by her two red setters straining at their leashes; the tramp with the flaming face and boiled blue eyes who arrived on the dot of eleven every day with his supermarket trolley full of bulging plastic bags, and sat motionless on the furthest bench, staring fixedly at the stunted rose bushes as if he had learnt how to protect himself from people's disgusted glances by turning himself into just another shabby object in the urban landscape; the thin, dark man in spectacles who every lunch hour came with his newspaper, his plastic container of salad and a green apple that he would polish on his trouser leg before biting into it.

On Monday mornings, she commonly did assessments of new pupils that the educational psychologist had sent to her from the local comprehensives, asking them to write down simple spellings, telling them to repeat lists of numbers, or to isolate sounds in a word. She would watch as they struggled over the tasks, wrestling with their pens, forming wrenched and tortured approximations of letters that toppled down the page, fighting to arrive at meaning through the obscuring fog in their heads, their faces screwed up in agonized concentration. On the other days, apart from Friday mornings, she would teach, usually two children at a time. There was often no one but them in the old house, and sometimes,

18

when the children were bent over their work sheets, there was a heavy, soporific quality to the silence. The scratch of pens, the click of counters, faint rustle as pages were turned; a child fidgeting in his seat, scratching his hot, bewildered head.

She normally stopped work at half past five in the afternoon and it took her twenty-five minutes to pack her teaching tools into the pannier, pull on her yellow waterproof jacket and bike along the busy roads to the childminder—cars hooting and exhausts belching out yellow smoke—and then walk the short stretch home; maybe a bit longer in the winter, when the darkness and cold made the journey feel more of an effort, and water from the puddles would spray up round her wheels, splattering her legs with mud and seeping into her shoes.

In the spaces in her days—Wednesday midday, for instance, when she had over two hours free, or Friday mornings, often an extended Tuesday lunchtime—she would frequently go to the cinema three minutes' walk from her work. It wasn't a gleaming multiplex with blank external walls and, inside, dozens of screens and automated ticket machines and self-service buckets of popcorn, but an independent cinema that had seen better days, with little choice of movies. Its furry red seats were balding at the edges, there were stains on the carpet, and the woman behind the glass screen near the entrance was old and scruffy as well, with sagging breasts, a faint moustache on her upper lip and bleached hair framing a creased, pouchy face. Her name was Elspeth; she chewed gum incessantly and sometimes she let Irene in free, especially when she arrived halfway through the show, which she regularly did, or when she knew that Irene had seen the film before, maybe several times—like *Sixth Sense* (four times), *City of Gods* and *About Schmidt* (three), *Catch Me If You Can* (two). Irene never told anyone about these outings; she even sometimes went to see the same films with Adrian or friends and didn't mention she'd seen them before. She got a strange thrill, an illicit tingle, from knowing that, for a few hours, nobody had the slightest idea where she was.

On this Wednesday—a week before Christmas, two days before the end of term, the day after she'd been up until two o'clock making chocolate biscuits and sultana scones for the school's Christmas party—Irene was on her second showing of *Adaptation*. She paid for her ticket, bought a small bar of milk chocolate and a cup of bitter, cooling coffee, and went into the auditorium. At first she thought it was empty, then she saw that there was a man in the back row, eating a sandwich and gazing at the adverts which had just begun, and so she picked a seat halfway down and on the opposite side from him. She was methodical and practised. She took off her coat and scarf, and then unlaced her boots and pulled them off too. She turned off her mobile and dropped it into her bag, then sat back in the seat, laid her coat over herself, like a blanket, and unpeeled the chocolate, eating it slowly between sips of coffee. It was warm in here, wonderfully dark, and she knew that Sasha and Clem would be eating lunch in their school hall that smelt of sweat and polish, and that the childminder would have taken Aggie to the play group where she splashed paint on giant sheets of thick white paper and learnt to sing, with all the actions, 'Three Little Monkeys Jumping on the Bed'. Everyone was safe. The music and voices that boomed out from the screen were like a comforting wall between her and the outside world, insulating her from its damp and chilly greyness. Irene waited for the tension to go out of her.

Today, she fell asleep after ten minutes. Nicholas Cage was crouched in front of a keyboard with writer's block when her eyes irresistibly closed. Her mouth was full of the taste of chocolate and her body was soft and heavy under her itchy woollen coat. The words he was speaking became a drone, as she curled herself more tightly around in her seat, laid her head on her bent arm. She gave herself up; let herself go. She woke at some point to see a man with lank hair and a toothless smile wading along in grey swampy water, and then woke again when loud shots got into her dreams and confused them and her eyes flickered onto a giant, sorrowful face, with tears rolling down his creviced cheeks.

When the credits rolled she sat upright, blinked several times to clear her vision, and stretched, yawning widely. She ran her hands through her hair, pulled her boots back on and laced them up; then she ate the final square of chocolate and rolled the foil into a crooked pellet, which she flicked under the seat in front. You always have to return to the narrow, labyrinthine self from the limitless world of sleep. She pulled on her coat and scarf and headed for the exit.

*　　　*　　　*

21

That evening, Adrian and Irene were intending to go to the party that Karen always had before Christmas, and where she served up champagne cocktails—a lump of sugar soaked in bitters, a generous dash of brandy, sparkling wine—that made everyone garrulously drunk before the end of the first glass, and foolishly drunk by the end of the second.

Adrian was downstairs with the babysitter, writing out the phone number where she could call in an emergency; it wasn't far away; they could get back in a matter of minutes. Irene was upstairs getting changed. She tried on a short black dress that was for someone younger than her, a red dress that looked all wrong, though she used to love herself in it, and an old velvet one that had a whiteish stain down the front—toothpaste? porridge?—so had to be discarded. In the end, she put on the silky flared black trousers that she always wore and over them an ivory-coloured sleeveless top with tiny embroidered flowers on it. Adrian had given it to her on her last birthday but she hadn't had the opportunity to wear it. She examined herself in the mirror, thinking it didn't look quite right somehow, it made her look scraggy and bleached-out; then, hearing Adrian call her impatiently to hurry, they were running late, shrugged. She hooked earrings through her lobes and put on red lipstick that made her mouth look like a gash in her pale face. For a moment, she stared at herself in distaste, then she scrubbed her lips bare again.

'Coming! Sorry sorry sorry,' she called again as she hurried into the bathroom. There she found Aggie, sitting in her knickers and socks on the damp bath mat with Adrian's razor in her hand.

22

She was breathing heavily, but otherwise was silent. Blood was streaming down her cheek, gushing into her open mouth and dribbling down her neck, onto her soft white shoulders. Without a word, Irene dropped to her knees beside her daughter and pulled the razor out of her grip. She put her hand beneath Aggie's chin and leant forward to inspect the damage, scrabbling behind her for tissues as she did so. There were several nicks on her upper lip and a wide scrape all the way down one cheek. Irene mopped the blood gently with the tissues, cooing something meaningless, and only when Aggie saw the sodden scarlet tissues did she start to shriek wildly.

'Hush, you're all right. You're all right.'

'I'm bleeding, Mummy, I'm bleeding and bleeding.'

'It'll stop soon. Hold still.'

'I'm all bloody and broke. Mummy. Mummy.'

Still holding tissues to Aggie's cheek, Irene cradled her. Blood soaked into her new top. She heard the television coming from the living room, the sound of Adrian's footsteps as he took the stairs two at a time, calling her name.

'Irene, we're incredibly . . . What the hell?'

'Daddy, I'm bleeding,' whimpered Aggie.

'Jesus. What happened? Is she OK?'

'She was trying to shave.'

'Jesus.' He squatted down beside them and put his hand on Aggie's head. There was even blood sculpting the ends of her hair into stiff tendrils. 'Does she need a doctor?'

'No. It's quite shallow.'

'Thank God for that.'

'You left your razor out.'

23

For a moment, his face went stonily defensive. He stood up.

'So it's my fault, is it?'

'I didn't say that. I said, *your* razor. Never mind that now.'

'Sorry,' he said through clenched teeth.

'Oh well. It was an accident,' said Irene, then ruined it by adding, 'I suppose.' She ignored Adrian's grimace, and held Aggie closer to disguise her own trembling and crumpled up a new bundle of tissues to stem the continuing flow. 'One of those things,' she said sternly, occupying the entire moral high ground.

'Sorry, Aggie my darling.' Adrian stooped down and caressed her and she curled up between them, sniffing and triumphant. 'What a brave girl you are.'

'Isn't she?'

'You've got blood all over your new top; it'll wash out, won't it? Anyway, you'll have to put something else on.'

'I think I'd prefer to stay here now.'

'Not go?'

'I wouldn't feel right.'

'We can wait until it stops bleeding—you said yourself that the cuts were shallow. You'll be OK with Carol, won't you, Aggie?'

'Don't go, Mummy,' said Aggie, working herself up to fresh sobs. 'Don't go!'

'I don't mind, honestly,' said Irene. 'I'd quite like a floppy evening with the kids. It's been a long day. You go. Send my apologies to Karen—say I'll ring her tomorrow. And there's a little present to take, on the table.'

'This is stupid and unnecessary. And anyway, if

24

anyone's staying, it should be me. It was my fault.'

'No. I want to.'

'Stay, Mummy! Don't want Carol.'

'And Karen's your friend more than mine. I'm staying.'

'Please, Adrian, just go.'

'You hardly ever go out.'

'It'd feel wrong.'

'You're proving a point here.'

'No! I'm not being a martyr, honestly. I want to stay.'

'Why would it feel wrong for you but not for me? If you won't go, then I'll stay too.'

'Don't be daft. What would be the point of that?'

Adrian knew Frankie, Karen's sister, would be there. He'd been thinking about Frankie as he'd shaved with extra care, put on his dull-pink shirt and gargled with mouthwash, stared at himself in the bathroom mirror, trying to see himself the way a stranger would.

'Please, Irene,' he said urgently. 'Please.'

'Go on with you. Have a good time.'

*   *   *

He had one champagne cocktail before he removed his coat. It took the edge off his anxiety. He went into the crowded room, with the spangly Christmas tree standing in one corner and mistletoe hanging from the lampshade, and was immediately sucked into a group of people who were arguing about refugees, but he didn't feel like having opinions this evening. He drifted across the room, drank another glass, kissed a flushed-looking Karen on both cheeks and gave her Irene's message, joined in with an impromptu rendering of 'In the Bleak Midwinter' by the Christmas tree. He saw Karen's daughter and her friend, at the edge of the room, glance at each other and roll their eyes. He rubbed his face; he knew that to them he was just another foolish middle-aged man who drank too much and flirted at parties with middle-aged women. He couldn't see Frankie, although perhaps she was in the kitchen, or sitting on the stairs. He couldn't understand why a woman he'd met several times a year over a decade or more should suddenly have the power to make his heart jump raggedly and his mouth go dry. He told himself that it would be best if she wasn't here at all, and yet he found himself drifting towards the kitchen, pretending to himself he needed another drink, one of those mince pies that Karen always served.

Frankie wasn't there, but Sarah was standing near the opened back door, both hands resting on the tight dome of her belly, and she turned a face to him that looked stricken.

'Are you all right?'

'I think—I think it's happening. All of a sudden.'

'The baby?'

'Yes. It's too early, Adrian.'

'How early?'

'Four weeks.' She gave a little wail as she spoke and bent over. He put his arm around her and she leant into him. She smelt yeasty. He saw the sweat on her forehead and beaded on her upper lip.

'Here, sit down here, that's it, and I'll find Gary. Four weeks is fine. Trust me, I'm a bit of an expert on labours, remember. Don't worry. Try and work out how often the contractions are coming.'

'Just one after the other, all the time.'

'All the time? Oh Lord. Hang on.'

He barged out of the kitchen, shouting for Gary, telling everyone that Sarah's baby was on its way, it was an emergency. Soon everyone knew. Women clustered around Sarah, giving her advice, telling her to breathe calmly, to hold on. They helped her to her feet and, bent double, she stumbled towards the door. The men bundled Gary into his coat, checked he hadn't drunk too much to drive safely, patted him on his back, handed him his car keys. Karen rushed to the fridge, where she pulled out a bottle of mineral water for them, and Mac, in a fit of tipsy generosity, wrung the rubbery stalks off the winter clematis that stood in a pot in the hall, and pushed them into Gary's hand.

'The bag,' said Gary. He clutched the flowers and gazed at them with a nonplussed air. 'The bag they tell you to pack. I haven't got it. A nightdress and spare underwear; water spray and fruit juice and coins for the phone box . . . It's not supposed to be yet . . .'

'Don't worry about the bag,' they said.

'I was going to make a special tape and get some massage oil . . .'

'Just get to the hospital. Ring us. Good luck.'

Everyone saw them out of the door, and several of them followed them onto the pavement, shouting encouragement.

'It's a labour party,' someone said and an excited laugh ran round the party.

Adrian saw them into the car, shutting the door on the sound of Sarah's sudden howl, and then he went back to the kitchen. There were a few people

27

in the garden smoking; he saw their dark shapes huddled together and the glowing tips of the cigarettes, the sudden flare of a match. For a minute, he felt quite lost and in his panic wished that Irene were here with him, for all the reasons that he sometimes wanted so badly to escape her— that she could see right through him; that with her he knew exactly who he was, and where his boundaries lay. There was a boulder on his heart, and suddenly he felt that he was about to cry. He helped himself to another glass of champagne, turned round as he lifted it to his lips, found he was staring into the face of Frankie.

She was wearing a dress the colour of a strawberry, with a capricious black ribbon at its cleavage; her lips were deep pink, and her hair was tied back, with strands artfully escaping and framing her face. He saw that she was wearing ridiculously high-heeled shoes, with a ribbon round the ankle, that made her legs look slightly knock-kneed; on her wrist she had a large digital man's watch. He couldn't stop himself making comparisons—the lush brightness of Frankie's clothes, and Irene's habitual grey and black and brown and beige; the softness of Frankie's flesh and Irene's thin and frowning face, her scrawny arms. She was only six or seven years younger than his wife, ten or eleven years younger than him, but she seemed to him to belong to a different world— one that he had left behind without even realizing it, and for which he suddenly and fiercely longed.

'Oh,' he said, nervous as an adolescent. His drink slopped over the rim of the glass. 'You're here.'

'I've been here for ages.'

28

'You should have said hello.'

She shrugged and gave an awkward laugh, fiddling with the strap on her dress.

'Frankie, we're going,' a voice said behind them. A man in a leather coat whom Adrian vaguely recognized put his proprietorial hand on her shoulder. 'I said we'd go for a meal at the Indian down the road with the others.'

'OK,' she said. 'Be with you in a minute.'

'Don't keep us all waiting, uh? Here's your coat,' he said, and slung it on the chair beside them, then left. Frankie turned back to Adrian.

'Bye then,' she said.

'Goodbye,' he said stupidly. He remembered now he'd heard something about a long-term boyfriend; an on-off relationship that Karen had told Irene—who'd told Adrian—was a matter of dissatisfaction to her younger sister. He was taken aback by the agony that bolted through him.

He set his glass down and put his hand on the table, steadying himself. She placed her hand next to his and smiled and he shifted a few inches, so his forefinger was just touching hers. Was he imagining it, or did she return the pressure? He felt as though his entire body was throbbing through that single point.

'See you then.' She withdrew her finger.

'I'd like that.'

'Me too.'

She put on her coat and pulled un-matching woollen gloves out of the pocket, one stripy and one plain; somehow that detail gave him hope, making Frankie seem more accessible. And then she was gone, leaving him breathless by the mince pies. He picked up someone else's half-empty glass

29

and drained it, feeling slightly sick.

*   *   *

Irene sat by Aggie's bed until she fell asleep. She saw how her daughter's upper lip was swollen and there was a raw red patch on her cheek that her hair stuck to. Then she went downstairs, sent Carol home, and made poached eggs on toast for the girls. They sat at the kitchen table together. Clem pierced the skin on the yolk so it welled up and puddled onto the plate; her mouth was smeared a crusty yellow. Sasha cut the toast into squares and posted the pieces neatly into her mouth.

After supper, she sat in Sasha's bedroom, reading *Moominland in Midwinter* to them for the third time. Clem crouched on the rug beside her in her boy's pyjamas; if you didn't know, you'd think she was a boy, thought Irene—her short hair, her uncompromising boy's clothes, the football posters above her bed, the scabs on her knees from where she'd fallen over in the playground, her refusal to ever cry. She had her knees drawn up under her chin, and was picking at her toenails and scowling. Sasha sat at the table by the window, drawing an intricate geometric pattern onto a sheet of paper and colouring each square in a different colour. Irene looked across at her as she read: her hair was in tidy plaits, her nightie was buttoned up to the top, her back was straight; the tip of her tongue was on her upper lip as she concentrated on her precise mesh of shapes.

'We'll buy a tree this weekend,' she said. 'We can decorate it together on Saturday.'

'All of us,' said Sasha.

30

'Yes, of course.'
'Daddy too.'
'Tell him.'
'You tell him.'
'OK, I will.'

* * *

Irene tidied the already-tidy kitchen and then put a slice of cheese onto a cracker. She poured herself half a glass of red wine and swirled it around. She ate the dry biscuit between sips of wine, and peeled herself an orange, separating it out into segments and removing all the pith. She ate it slowly, then went into the living room and watched the evening news on television: the famine, the threat of snow, a twelve-year-old girl pregnant by her thirteen-year-old boyfriend, a *Big Issue* seller who'd won the lottery, a new kind of purple carrot.

Then, suddenly in need of company, she picked up the phone and called her half-brother. Jem was five years younger than Irene and before he was born Irene had hated him with a bitter, boiling jealousy: his mother had taken away her adored father; he was the cuckoo in the nest. In her furious calculations, he was the cause of everything bad; without him, her life would have continued like a picture book painted in primary colours: there's daddy, there's mummy, there's darling little Irene in pigtails standing between them, holding each of them by the hand. Plumb in the centre of her own life.

Even when she saw him that first time—red-faced, baggy-skinned, gummy and bawling—and he had grabbed her finger in his fist and hung on for

31

dear life, her hostility had continued. She didn't want to know him. She didn't want to love him. She preferred to see her father, on the rare occasions that he turned up, all by himself, away from the unfamiliar house that reeked of nappies and talcum powder and was full of photographs of people she didn't know. She didn't want to be anywhere near her new brother who only had to make an indeterminate sound or hold his foot in his hand and stuff his toes into his mouth to reduce everyone to sentimental adoration. Nor did she want to spend time with her new stepmother who had streaked hair piled high on her head and a dirty laugh and a smell of hyacinths on her clothes.

Then—as quickly as he'd left them—her father had abandoned his second marriage too, taking just one suitcase, leaving behind shirts with fraying collars, bottles of multivitamin tablets, numerous debts and a letter that said he knew he was behaving badly and causing suffering but he had to follow his heart and he prayed for forgiveness. He followed his heart to Wimbledon, then to Dorset, and finally to America, where he still lived.

And Irene had stopped seeing Jem at all, and almost forgotten that he existed. He was a figure from her shadowy early years, a colicky baby with ginger hair, sobbing in a house Irene could barely remember, except that there were nettles and foxgloves in the tiny backyard, and a dark pantry full of tins of condensed milk and bottles of home-made wine. She barely thought of herself as someone who had a brother. After her crowded beginning, she became the only child of a valiant single mother. Just the two of them against the world, walking hand in hand down the streets to school, playing Scrabble and patience after supper, going on bed-and-breakfast holidays in Cornwall for a week every summer.

Even when there were other men around, as there often were, she still thought of it as just the two of them, because the men were transients, passing through. Their hair, brown, black, grey, in the basin and their shaving kit on the bathroom shelf; their coats slung over the back of the chair and their shoes at the bottom of the stairs; their voices floating from her mother's bedroom into hers late at night. Murmurs, giggles, shouts, sometimes drawn-out animal sobs that would make her bury her head in her pillow, put her fingers into her ears, count to a hundred. They always left in the end, scraping the chair violently on the tiled floor, slamming the door, hurling a last word up the stairs, and the house would return to its normal quiet. She and her mother would sit at the kitchen table eating boiled eggs or lamb chops to the soft tick of the clock over the door. Irene always had the feeling, during these years, that she was waiting for her real life to begin.

She'd felt guiltily euphoric, leaving her quiet home for college; even more so when after university she went to teach English to children in a village in the south of Angola. She couldn't believe how unencumbered it was possible to be. She felt strangely weightless, as if her feet were only just touching the ground.

Then when she was twenty-three her mother had been toppled by a stroke and she had come home, as she had always known she would have to do. Her life, which for the past four years had funnelled out until at last she had the dizzy sense of having no horizons, had suddenly been telescoped back into the small tidy house of her childhood. She slept in her old narrow bed, under the red and orange duvet she had chosen when she was twelve, staring at the patterns on the curtains. She sat in the kitchen under the same clock, waiting, while the whole house seemed to hold its breath. She sat by the side of the bed, holding her mother's limp, cool fingers and talking to her because the doctors had said maybe she could still hear—somewhere behind her closed eyes and her changed face, her brain might still be ticking like the old clock.

And then Jem turned up, falling in out of the summer rain. He was eighteen and had just finished his A levels. He said—sitting in the kitchen drinking tea without milk and smoking skinny roll-ups, tobacco hanging off his lower lip— that he didn't know why he had taken so long to come and find her. He had spent his childhood missing her; he'd kept a photograph of her as a five-year-old on his bedside table; he'd always felt like her younger brother and often when he was lonely he'd imagined telling her his troubles. Irene looked at him as he talked. He was tall and red-haired and clumsy, old-fashioned-looking she thought, with sharp collarbones under his grey tee-shirt, a shy, eager smile, and freckles just like her. Guilt and elation seized her. 'I should have looked after you,' she said, reaching over to take his hand in hers. 'We're each other's family.' When her mother eventually died, he had sat beside her at the funeral in a black suit that he must have borrowed because the legs were too short and the arms finished above his bony, freckled wrists.

Now he was a kind, clever man who bent over to disguise his height, stammered when he was nervous, sometimes giggled like a teenage girl, and played mad practical jokes on his friends. He translated French for a living—technical manuals, educational text books, every so often a novel—and for the past year or so had lived in the south of France with his girlfriend.

'*Oui?*'

'Jem?'

'Irene! I was just thinking of you.'

'How are you? Is this a bad time to call?'

'No. Juliet's just making me a fish soup.'

'Lucky you.'

'You should see the mess.'

'How is she?'

'She's been a bit tired lately. They work her hard at the hospital.'

'What about your work?'

'I've finally finished translating a technical manual for a steel company that specializes in giant girders to make bridges.'

'Blimey.'

'Quite. The things I know now. I don't think they're all going to come in useful. What about my nieces?'

'Good. I think.'

'You don't sound quite sure?'

'Oh well. You know how it is—there's always one you're worried about. It's like this free-floating anxiety; it'll attach anywhere. It's Sasha at the moment, because she's so bloody *good* it unnerves me. It's not natural. But then maybe I don't see what's going on with the others properly, but you can't watch them all at once, can you? Tonight

Aggie tried to shave herself with Adrian's razor. There was blood everywhere. For a minute, I thought . . . Oh, I don't know. Tell me to shut up.'

'I'm sure they're all fine,' Jem said vaguely.

'I know. But how do you stop yourself worrying? You just have to stop yourself from showing it too much.'

'When are you going to come over and see us?'

'I'd love to. You know how much I'd love to. We're such a crowd though.'

'That's OK. We don't mind. Or you could come on your own.'

'On my own?'

'It's not such a shocking idea. I'm not asking you to run away.'

She laughed. 'I miss you,' she said.

*   *   *

Jem put the phone down as Juliet came through the door, carrying the cauldron of soup. Clouds of steam rose round her face; her forearms were strong and tanned and her bare feet dusty.

'How's Irene, then?' she asked, putting the cauldron on the table and standing back.

'OK. I guess.'

'You guess?'

'Treading water.'

'She should come and visit us, get away from everything for a while.'

'That's what I keep telling her.'

'We're not treading water, are we?'

He put his hands on her shoulders and kissed her on her forehead, then her mouth.

'Treading water? No, my darling.'

36

'The soup's getting cold.'

'God, Juliet, how did I ever get so lucky?'

'Was it luck? That's not the way I remember it. I believe I chased you until you were cornered and couldn't escape.'

'I was just shy.'

'Just as well that I wasn't, then.'

'Come here.'

'The soup . . .'

'Never mind the soup.'

*   *   *

When Adrian came in, walking with the exaggerated care of someone who has drunk too much, he babbled something about Sarah going into labour. But when he looked into Irene's face he stumbled over his words. He felt that she saw straight through him, to the bubbling mess inside.

CHAPTER FOUR

The next morning Adrian got up late, after a restless night. He'd been aware of Irene sliding out of bed in the early hours and noises downstairs, and she had returned much later with cold feet. At just after six, he'd heard Aggie call out and she had groaned and buried her face in the pillow for a few seconds until Aggie had called again, insistent. She'd hissed his name a couple of times, then heaved herself out of bed once more and left the room. Adrian squirmed into the duvet, feeling the patches of warmth where she had been. There was the faint clatter of hail against the window; even from where he lay, he could tell that it was an inhospitable morning.

Gradually the house filled up with sounds—Irene singing in the shower, children's voices, a grumpy shout from Clem, Irene calling to Sasha to hurry on down, a brief squabble between Clem and Aggie, Irene's tightly controlled morning voice, the chink of cutlery on china, something clattering on the floor, lavatories flushing, the radio news, a doorbell ringing which meant the postman must have delivered a parcel that wouldn't fit through the letterbox, and outside the increasing sound of traffic, of front doors shutting and car doors slamming. At half past eight the phone rang and a few minutes later Irene came in again. He lay quite still, his eyes screwed shut, and felt her gaze like a laser beam directed onto his face.

'Adrian.' She waited. 'Adrian! I can tell you're awake.'

'Down in a minute.'

'I'll be leaving soon. Karen rang. Sarah had a baby boy last night.'

'Ah!' He opened his eyes.

'Five pounds and six ounces. Connor.'

'Connor,' he repeated. 'Nice.'

'It is, isn't it?'

'They must be over the moon.'

'Yes.' Her voice softened for a moment. 'They must.'

'Are you all right?'

'Yep.'

'No, I mean, really?'

'I'm running a bit late, that's all.'

She started pulling on clothes—black jeans, a

38

black tee-shirt, a thick zip-up cardigan in grey and pink.

'What are you doing today?' she asked.

'This and that.'

'Hmmm.'

'What?'

'What do you mean, what?'

'You made a disapproving sou

'Oh for God's sake, Adrian . .

'You do that—pretend yc   veren't doing something when we both know you were.'

'I just made a sou d. I cleared my throat.'

'Don't you think I find it difficult, not having work, while you're slaving away?'

'I just think it would be better for you if you had a bit more structure in your day, that's all. There are lots of things you can do. You could help me in the mornings for a start. And do a bit of clearing up maybe. Or—' She came to an abrupt halt.

'I get it.'

'Anyway, this is the wrong time to talk . . .'

'You only see what you want to see. Yesterday, who was it who got up? And who drove Sasha there and back from her—'

'Let's not do this.'

'That's easy for you to say once you've started it off. I know what this is really about. What you really think is I should give up on the whole fucking idea of acting and do a job like, like *Gary*.'

'I'm only asking you for help sometimes.'

'Why don't you come right out and say it, at least.' He was letting anger take over now, stoking it and relishing its self-righteous heat.

'Oh God—let's not have this conversation. I've got to go. Listen, I didn't mean to sound

39

disapproving. I'm just a bit tired. And tired of being tired all the time.' She stopped abruptly, before the anger built up again.

'Yeah.' He made an effort. 'Me too. Is it very cold outside?'

'Bitter. Wait! I'm coming!' she yelled over her shoulder as a child called.

'Irene.'

'Yes?'

'Sorry.'

'What for?'

'Just sorry. You know.'

'Yeah.'

He held out his arms and she went over and leant down and kissed him on the forehead, once and quickly, then pulled free.

*   *   *

He had a shower and shaved, nicking his cheek with his unsteady morning-after hands, and took two Paracetamol; then he had a large mug of coffee with hot milk, a glass of orange juice, toast and the last scrapings of marmalade from the jar. He opened his bank statement, which made him wince and which he crumpled up and threw into the overflowing bin. Then he walked down the street, in hail that spat against his cheeks, to the underground station and took the train to Covent Garden. Christmas lights hung along the streets; there was a huge tree in the piazza and every shop window glittered with decorations. Men and women fought their way through the weather with bulging shopping bags. Everyone seemed to be in a hurry. Everyone looked prosperous and purposeful, except the man huddled outside the tube station selling the *Big Issue*. Adrian bought a newspaper and had another coffee in a café that had sofas and armchairs downstairs. He read the paper from front to back, slowly, then, with a sudden burst of decisive speed, he got up and went into a shop he'd seen earlier and spent a ludicrous amount of money on a pair of thin leather gloves with a small button on the cuff.

Frankie was a solicitor for a firm that did house sales, divorces and wills—all the mundane traumas of ordinary life. Her speciality was conveyancing; Irene always said if they ever managed to move house, they should use her. Adrian realized, as he went through the revolving doors into the vast lobby where security guards handed out plastic passes, that she might be a decade younger than him, with a girlish giggle, but she probably earned four or five times more than him. He felt shabby, middle-aged and wretched and for a moment he thought about turning back, but even as he thought it, he was giving his name to the receptionist who was picking up the phone, punching in a number, saying to the person who answered it that a Mr Adrian Hall was downstairs to see her.

'She'll be with you in a few minutes. Take a seat.'

He perched on the edge of a large corduroy chair and read the first few pages of his paper all over again, trying to look absorbed. A tic bounced under his left eye.

'Adrian.'

There she was in a soft white shirt with belled sleeves, knee-length skirt and sensible shoes. Little studs in her ears, one silver bangle on her wrist, a whiff of elegant perfume. Infinitely more grown-up and serious than the erotic night-time vision he'd been holding in his head. Impossible.

'Hi.' He sprang up, dropping his paper to the floor. 'I just—I was passing and I saw . . .' He ground to a halt.

'Good,' she said. 'I'm glad.'

'I bought you these.' He thrust the bag containing the gloves towards her.

'For me?'

'Christmas present.'

'Oh! But they're lovely. You shouldn't have.' She pulled the gloves on and held up her hands to admire them. 'I don't know what to say.'

'Don't say anything.'

She put a hand on his arm then withdrew it.

'Thank you very much, Adrian.'

'I guess I ought to go. Christmas shopping, you know.'

'Wait,' she said.

'Yes?'

'You're just going, like that?'

'Well, I mean, you must be very busy, and so I thought I'd just, you know—'

'Adrian,' she cut in.

'Yes?'

'Why are you really here? You've never come to see me before.'

'I don't know,' he said. He bent down and gathered together the sheets of newspaper, bundling them messily together. His cheeks felt hot.

She tugged off her gloves. 'Are you sure you want to give me these?'

'Of course. Yes.' Though now he wanted to take

42

them back, take back the whole sorry episode, and leg it out of the pompous office, away from her cool stare and grown-up, daytime self.

'I ought to get back.' She paused, then added: 'Unless you want to invite me to lunch.'

'Yes. Lovely. Sure—but what if someone sees us?' he asked, and then stopped in confusion at what he was implying. She smiled at him and he saw she had one faint dimple in her right cheek.

'Wait while I get my stuff.'

'All right. But I just want to tell you something.' Oh no no no, you ought not, screamed a voice in his head. He ignored it. 'You're very beautiful. That's why I'm here, I guess.'

She didn't move yet he had the impression that she softened and the air between them grew warmer. Then she said: 'You're married to my sister's best friend.'

He made an inarticulate noise, signifying nothing.

'I'll be back in a minute.'

*   *   *

They had lunch in a dim corner of a small brasserie Frankie knew. He didn't eat much—he felt hollow yet slightly nauseous—but she demolished her meal greedily. A little splash of orange daubed her chin and her lips were shiny. He had wanted to order two glasses of house wine but she'd put her hand on his arm.

'No,' she said. 'Let's stay clear-headed.'

Adrian asked the waiter for a bottle of sparkling water and drank two glasses with trembling hands. He didn't know what he was doing here, with an unfamiliar woman and blood roaring in his ears and a queasy sensation in his stomach. He didn't know what to say to her; there was nothing to say, until he kissed her, because he was in a fug of terror. But he couldn't kiss her. What had he been thinking of?

He started telling her a rambling anecdote about the last audition he'd been to, then heard himself talking about the lovely, disastrous feeling when you stood in the wings, waiting to walk on stage. He had a feeling he'd told her this before, a long time ago when she was just an ordinary woman, but he couldn't remember. He couldn't remember anything. His voice, which didn't belong to him any more but to a ridiculous stranger, dribbled away and he stared at her while his breath rose raggedly in his chest.

'If I kissed you,' he said hoarsely, 'what would you do?'

'I don't know until it happens.'

So he leant forward over his plate, feeling as if he was sliding towards the edge of a high cliff, and held her face in his hands, very carefully, and kissed her on her pink, full lips which opened under his. She gave a murmur deep in her throat. He drew back and tried to look at her, though he felt dizzy. She smiled widely at him: strong white teeth. Carnivorous.

'I'd say, I've wanted you to do that for years. And I'd say, you mustn't.'

It was as if a barrier—that dirty great boulder in his chest—had crumbled away and lust flooded through him, a pure transparent gush of sensation splashing through his veins, knocking his head back like someone punching him brutally on his chin. He groaned and put his hand in her hair like that first night, and he kissed her again, wanting to dissolve into her, to disappear.

'People are staring.'

'Can we go somewhere?'

'What—some cheap hotel for ten minutes?' She sat up and pushed her hair behind her ears.

'No! I didn't mean it like that. That's not how I think of you. I'm just—oh Jesus, bowled over.'

'Are you? Really?'

'Since that evening, you're all I can think about. I can't just walk away.'

She lifted his hand and kissed his palm. 'I must go, Adrian. I've got a client coming in, oh God, minus two minutes.'

'When shall I see you again?'

'I don't know. I've got to think. This isn't what I do, you know.'

'Is it your boyfriend?'

'No.' She shook her head decisively.

Adrian put a hand on her round knee and slid it up her skirt a few inches. In a few seconds, he thought, he would start to cry.

'I'll go mad,' he said. 'I promise you that I'll go mad. Let me see you this evening. Not a cheap hotel. Just for a drink or something. Just so I can have you in front of me like this again. Oh God. Just looking at you . . . I'd do anything . . . I'll tell Irene—'

She jerked away from him. 'Don't ever, *ever*, tell me what you'll tell Irene.'

'Frankie—'

'You don't get it, do you?'

'I didn't mean—'

'This was a mistake. I've got to go. I'm running

45

late.' She stood up, her chair screeching loudly.

'I'll call you,' he said desperately. 'At least let me call you.' But she was gone, clipping up the stairs away from him.

Adrian picked up the bill and stared at it. His hands seemed large and clumsy; his breath was hot in his throat. He fumbled in his wallet for the last of his cash and left a generous tip for the waiter who seemed to gaze at him with contempt as he left, pulling himself up the stairs like a drunk man, lurching back out into the street, gazing around him as if he was suddenly in a foreign land and had no idea where to go next.

*   *   *

Irene taught a woman of about her own age for an hour and a half on Thursday afternoons. Ruth was a geriatric nurse and she had only found she was dyslexic when her nephew had been diagnosed by his school, a year ago. Then she realized that the way words swam on the page wasn't normal and the difficulty she had with forming letters wasn't just clumsy incompetence; that the way she could never remember sequences—the months of the year, her times tables, telephone numbers— perhaps wasn't because she was stupid after all, 'thick' as they'd called her at school. 'I'm wrongly wired,' she said to Irene the first time they met, as if it made her happy to think of her tangled internal circuitry. 'That's all it is. Why did no one ever tell me?'

She was an eager woman who worked ferociously hard when she was in Irene's chilly first-floor room, as if by sheer dogged effort she could make up for all those years of stumbling through a mist, but that afternoon she seemed downcast and troubled, and at the end of their session Irene asked: 'Is everything all right?'

'Fine!' she said. 'I'm fine really.' Her voice slid unsteadily up the scale as she held back her tears.

'You're sure?'

'Yes.' But Irene's sympathetic tone had undone her. Tears slid down her cheeks. Irene waited as she wiped her face with a tissue and blew her nose.

'I started this morning. You know . . .'

'You started. Ah, you mean . . . ?'

'We've been trying to have a baby for ages. Well, not really ages, but it feels like ages when you're trying. It gets to be all you think about. So I just feel a bit low today. Sorry.'

She blew her nose again and mopped her eyes. Irene wondered how old she was—late thirties? Or perhaps she was less than that. She had none of the cosseted and expensive youthfulness of the middle-aged well-off. Her husband was unemployed. That she was poor and hard-working showed in the lines in her face, in the roughness of her hands, the cut of her cheap clothes. With a small stab of shame, Irene was freshly struck by the unfairness of life.

'I never dreamt I wouldn't be able to. Wesley even started getting the room ready. We even talked about names . . .'

'I'm really sorry.'

'Erin. Poppy. Daisy. Jackson. I always wanted to have a boy called Jackson, even when I was just a little girl myself.'

'It must be hard.'

'You've got children, haven't you?'

'Yes.'

'There you are. All my friends do too. They meet up at the weekends and do things together, go on outings. They talk about things like cradle cap and nursery school and they tell me how lucky I am not to feel tired all the time. Lucky! I'd like to feel tired all the time. I'd like to have no spare moment to think about myself. Sometimes I hate them.'

'Maybe you should tell them you're trying.'

'I couldn't stand the pity.'

Irene nodded and stared out of the window, where the grey sky was clearing over the London roofs. In the park, a woman was bending down to pick up her little son, who'd tripped on the path. She couldn't hear him, but she could tell by his wide open mouth that he was yelling, and his mother squatted beside him and hugged him.

'It must terrible.'

She looked at the little boy outside again, and thought of the wretchedness of missing what you've never had. Haunted by absence. Empty body, empty room, no small fist fastening round your finger, no one calling out for you in the night. Mummy, mummy, mummy: the only person in the whole wide world who would do.

*   *   *

Adrian didn't get home till late. Irene took the girls swimming after school, made them spaghetti with tomato sauce for supper, let them watch the video of *Monsters Inc.* because tomorrow was the last day of school. Then she put Clem and Aggie into a bath together and washed their hair, although Aggie screamed about the soap in her

48

eyes and the knots in her hair and how the water from the hose-shower was too cold, too hot, ow, ow, ow! After she had read to them, she left them and sat for a while in Sasha's room, tidying away clothes and sorting toys while her eldest daughter traced pictures of birds from a book. Irene looked at her pale, blunt face; her brown hair, brushed so it shone and tucked behind her ears; her small pursed lips. Her thin, bare legs were tucked underneath her. She kept everything inside herself, thought Irene. Clem and Aggie were always shouting, screaming, hooting, rushing, falling, laughing, weeping; they had no control over the feelings that coursed through them and spilled out of them. But Sasha's surface was smooth and demure, with no cracks through which her interior life showed. Sometimes Irene would ask her what she was feeling and she'd frown, thinking seriously about the question, and then shrug. 'Things,' she'd say; or 'I don't know really. Nothing.' She was an underground stream, noiseless, mysterious and cool.

Downstairs, Irene boiled some green lentils, and the steam filled the kitchen with a smell like wet dog. She made a salad, put four sausages in a medium oven. At half past eight she rang his mobile but it was switched off. At nine, she turned off the oven, leaving the sausages inside to keep warm.

She went upstairs and kissed each child goodnight once more. Sasha was lying on her back, staring at the cracked ceiling and listening to a talking tape. She murmured that she had cold feet, so Irene made her a hot-water bottle and slid it under the duvet, onto her icy toes. Aggie was asleep, clutching three Beanie Babies to her, so Irene brushed her plump cheek gently. But she put her arms around Clem and hugged her, kissing her damp forehead and her dry lips and smelling her clean hair and her soapy, sweaty skin. She left the door half-open, so light from the hall fell across their two beds, and stood for a moment, listening to the sound of Aggie's heavy breathing, the small voice from Sasha's tape.

Outside, the night sounds of Hackney were growing. Music from cars, laughter, shouts, doors slamming, footsteps pounding past the house. Through the walls, she could hear thrumming bass notes. Later, there would probably be police sirens and breaking glass as well. Irene imagined people all over London getting ready to go out, stuffing money and drugs in their pockets, picking up their keys, taking a last look at their reflections in the mirror before leaving. She'd almost forgotten what it felt like. She took a can of beer from the fridge, pulled its ring-top open and licked at the smoking tongue of foam that snaked out. Then she called Karen. They talked about the party Irene had missed, how Larry had been sick on the doorstep and how Terry and Chris had had a stand-up argument; and they talked about the baby Sarah had had, and made an arrangement to meet on Sunday. Irene could hear Mac in the background, and the piping voice of a child.

She put the phone down and then she turned on the computer that stood in the corner of the living room and wrote an e-mail to Jem. Sometimes you can write the things you can't bring yourself to say out loud: *'Adrian's out somewhere and the girls are all in bed and I'm feeling a bit down this evening. I don't know why. Nothing's quite the way I imagined it would be when I was young, when you first met me.*' She didn't send it though. She looked at the words for a few minutes, screwed up her face in self-disgust, and pressed the delete button.

Adrian came in after ten. She heard the front door open and slam shut and then the sound of him wiping his boots on the mat in the hall.

'Hi,' he called. He was carrying a couple of shopping bags and smelt of wine and smoke. 'I brought you these,' he said, and thrust a bunch of stiff orange roses into her hands before pulling off his coat which was wet from the rain. 'Sorry I'm late. Got held up. Shopping, you know how it is. Nightmare at this time of year, could hardly move for the crowds, you should have seen Hamleys, my God, the amount of money that people were spending on things, it almost made me flee. Should have done really—spent too much money on things I didn't really want to buy; always the way at Christmas. Anyway, I hope you approve of what I got.' He was talking too much, he knew that, but he couldn't stop. Words cascaded out of him and he listened to them helplessly. 'And I called in on my agent, and one thing led to another, drinks, and then I suddenly looked at my watch.' He made a cartoonish expression of surprise, and looked at his watch once again, as if to check it really was that time. 'I couldn't believe how time had rushed by. I should have called, I know, but, you know how it is, and then my mobile seemed to be in a dead zone all of its own, should get a new one sometime soon.'

'You saw Richard?'

'Yes,' said Adrian with hearty conviction. He

wasn't lying, although he felt that he was—he had seen Richard, had a few drinks, wandered round the crowded Thursday-night streets, phoned Frankie from a smoky pub and heard her voice on the answering machine, 'leave a message after the tone'. What kind of message could he leave: oh please please please please? He'd pressed his phone off and sat for a few seconds, waiting for his feeling of dislocation and dread to subside.

'Anything coming up, then?' asked Irene.

'Possibilities, just possibilities. You know how it is. We had a drink. Chatted.'

He listened to his hollow, cheery voice for a moment, picked up the wine bottle that was on the table and poured himself a hefty glass then held the bottle out towards Irene, who covered her own glass with her hand, shaking her head in refusal. He took a large swig.

'Do you want something to eat?' asked Irene. 'I made us supper, sausages and spicy lentils. We were going to have it with a video, remember? I rented *Ocean's Eleven* on my way home.'

'Oh sorry. Is it too late?' He did that mad watch-check again, and again widened his eyes incredulously. 'We can still watch it, can't we? I'm not very hungry. Had a sandwich earlier.'

'Oh.' She imagined taking the sausages out of the oven and hurling them across the room, tipping the lentils into his lap, throwing the glasses against the wall so they shattered into a thousand glinting pieces, then marching out into the open weather, letting the wind rip through her.

'You go ahead though.'

'I'm not hungry either. Not any more.'

'You should eat something. You look a bit

52

peaky. I'll have a bit too. A sausage,' he added, wondering how he would be able to eat a single mouthful.

'Are you OK?'

'Fine. Why shouldn't I be?'

'You just seem a bit—'

'A bit what?'

'Manic, maybe.'

'Probably the effect of Oxford Street. I'm fine. Completely fine. I'm sorry I wrecked our evening and left you to do everything. Were the girls OK?'

'Yeah. I took them swimming so they were tired out.'

He looked at her pale, small, angry face, her grey eyes that glared at him, and guilt grabbed him round the throat, squeezed hard. He had to stop himself from howling like a wolf, from giggling madly and putting his hands over his face to sob.

Irene put food on two plates—a blistered sausage spilling its stuffing like an old pillow, a grey sludge of over-cooked lentils—and they sat on the sofa in front of the television. Adrian poured himself another glass of wine and turned on the video. There they were, like an old married couple, eating supper in front of the tv on a Thursday night. After fifteen minutes, Irene's cropped head tipped onto his shoulder and he could hear from her breathing that she had fallen asleep. He carefully put her untouched plate onto the floor and shifted his position so that she lay against him more comfortably. She was light as a child, as a bird or a bundle of twigs.

He sat there like that for the rest of the film, though for much of the time the images on the screen were blurred and meaningless, and the ones

53

that flooded his mind were of Frankie: the perfumed fall of her hair and the smell of her peachy skin and the feeling of being turned inside out by yowling lust. His skin prickled with memory and anticipation. Irene mumbled something in her sleep and he put out a hand and stroked her coppery hair.

CHAPTER FIVE

'What happens if you're awake when Father Christmas comes?'

Irene forced the knobbly trunk of the tree they'd bought into the stand they'd sent off for years ago from a mail-order catalogue and it listed towards the window, sprinkling needles that would later work their way into the children's socks.

'I'm not sure,' she said, standing back. 'But it's a good idea to go to sleep early on Christmas Eve just in case.'

'Only babies—'

'Sasha! Here, let's hang up the things. Don't eat those chocolate reindeers; not yet anyway. I got them for the tree. I'll put the lights on; stand back a minute.'

'Only babies what?'

'Nothing, Clemmie. Let's just get this tree decorated.'

'Daddy said he was going to do it with us.'

'I know. But he had to go to his agent's Christmas party. We'll leave the fairy for him to put on the top. Aggie, don't you *dare* put that in your mouth.'

'Only babies what?'

'Sasha . . .'

'Believe—'

'I'm warning you . . .'

'She asked me. You always tell me never to—'

'Stop now. Put this on the tree. Aggie, stop that at once. Look, let's do it together. Oh shit, now look, it's everywhere. It's like there's been an explosion in a tinsel factory.'

'Believe in Father Christmas, stupid,' cooed Sasha to Clemmie.

'What!'

'Now listen to me—oh, you're stepping on the glass bauble, Aggie. Shit. You're going to pull the whole bloody tree down.'

'You shouldn't swear in front of us like that. It's rude.' Sasha pursed her lips primly.

'God, who's the parent here?'

'Mummy, there is a Father Christmas, isn't there?'

'Of course, honey. Sasha's just joking. *Aren't* you, Sasha?'

'No, I'm not.'

'Be quiet.' Irene grabbed Sasha by her forearm and leant down to her. 'Do you hear me? Don't be so mean.'

'Ow, you're hurting me, you're hurting my arm.'

'Who leaves us presents, then?'

'I'm hardly touching you, Sasha.'

'You're hurting me,' Sasha repeated coldly and Irene suddenly noticed she had a little smudge of blue eye shadow on her translucent eyelids. Then: 'Daddy. I want my daddy.'

'Who wants me?' Adrian, flushed with cold and drink, banged the door shut and swung Sasha into his arms, and she put her silky head against his cheek, smug as a cat.

'She was hurting me, Daddy.'

'Is there a Father Christmas? There is, isn't there?' Clemmie tugged at his thick coat. 'Tell her. He eats the mince pies we leave out.'

'Lift me up too.' Aggie got hold of Adrian round one leg and hung on like a koala bear. Adrian stood like a ungainly totem pole, wrapped round with children.

'Is everything all right here?' he asked Irene.

'I hate fucking Christmas.'

'Mummy! No!'

Irene looked at the crumpling, dissolving faces of her children. 'No, of course. Sorry. I'm just being stupid. I'm going to go up for a bath and when I come down I'll be cheerful again.' She stretched a smile over her face. 'OK?'

'You don't hate Christmas, do you? You love it.'

'Of course, I love it really.' She laid a hand on Sasha's head. 'Absolutely *love* it,' she repeated vigorously.

'Cross your heart and hope to die?' said Clem.

'If you insist.'

'Stick a needle in my eye?'

'Stick a needle in my eye.'

*   *   *

Over the next few days, the tree grew more clotted and baroque. Sasha made paper chains and stencilled shapes, sprayed gold and silver, to hang on its branches. Clem and Aggie ate the chocolate reindeers and left the silver foil dangling raggedly. The ancient, disintegrated fairy that Irene thought

56

she remembered her father fixing to the top of the tree when she was tiny, tipped so it looked as if it was caught in the act of falling. It was very different from the tasteful silver affair in Karen's house. Mysterious parcels arrived in the post from France, some squashy and some hard; Clem's tape of Christmas carols played over and over in children's sugary, hopeful voices; and there was the smell of baking in the kitchen—a cake lumpy with glacé cherries, ginger, sultanas and chopped nuts that they all had to stir together to make a wish; chestnuts that Irene boiled and peeled, the skin catching under her nails; cloves stuck in a ham; vanilla pods in simmering milk; coffee, spluttering over the edge of the old espresso pot in the middle of the day. Two days before Christmas Adrian made a warm punch because people were coming for drinks: cinnamon and allspice catching in the nostril. The children watched through the banisters, giggling.

*   *   *

Who had come for the drinks? Irene remembered Karen and Mac, Gary though not Sarah, a couple of out-of-work actors who swapped swashbuckling tales of failure and disaster, Polly and Leah and Kim and Max. Not Frankie. She remembered Gary telling her at great length about the colour of Connor's shit—mustard yellow—and she remembered that Polly had dyed her hair red. And she remembered Adrian walking into the garden at one point with his mobile. Or had she just made that up—the sight of him standing on the other side of the glass, under the new moon and the cold white stars, speaking urgently into his phone while inside people got drunk on mulled wine and upstairs the children jumped from bed to bed until Aggie stubbed her toe on the corner of the chest of drawers and came downstairs shrieking like a car alarm that no one could turn off?

*   *   *

'Frankie? Frankie? Can you hear me? If you can hear me, pick up the phone. Please. Pick up. Listen. I need to speak to you. I just need—I can't bear . . . Please call.'

He looked up at the lights shining out of his house. In the upstairs window, he caught sight of Sasha, brushing her hair. And through the kitchen window, he could see Irene, ladling punch into glasses, smiling at someone and nodding her head. This was his life, he thought, and he closed his eyes for a moment, then lifted up his phone again, pressed redial.

'Frankie? Frankie? Are you there?'

*   *   *

Father Christmas crept round the children's rooms, left pillowcases on the bottom of their beds (wind-up bath toys, crayons, chocolate pennies, spinning tops that played 'The Holly and the Ivy', Chinese flowers that you sprinkled over water and that blossomed into bright paper petals), drank a swig from the glass of sweet sherry she and Clem had left at the top of the stairs, then another, and poured the rest down the bathroom sink before replacing it empty on the landing; she lifted the

58

mince pie out of its foil case and ate it standing in the hallway. She read a chapter of her book, sitting by the fire whose embers still gave out a dull glow and faint heat, then slid into bed beside Adrian and kissed him on the shoulder.

'You're lovely and warm,' she said, laying a hand on his back and pushing her feet against his calves. 'Happy Christmas.'

He grunted and muttered thickly into the crook of his arm.

'Adrian?'

'Mmmph.'

'Things will get better again, you know.'

Adrian made an indeterminate sound.

'We have to be patient.' She waited and he didn't reply. 'It's about the long haul, after all,' she continued, not knowing if he could hear her. She wondered where that expression came from—was it just to do with pulling on a rope or something for a long time; or was it to do with a trip by boat, no longer hugging the shore but out on the open sea: blue water then slate-grey or tea bag-brown; a breeze and then high waves like buildings falling down on you, so you couldn't see the horizon any longer and you didn't know quite where you were heading; weathering the storms. Heave away, haul away.

'Do you remember when we moved here?' she said. A little snore came from Adrian. 'Dragging the double mattress up here? Remember?'

They'd had almost no furniture—just the stuff she'd kept when her mother died, a rocking chair and a rickety chest with lots of small drawers in it, three paintings. They'd bought a small fridge, a vacuum cleaner and a king-size mattress that they'd carried along the street in the rain, and then hauled giggling up the stairs, getting wedged in round the tight corner, him pulling backwards and her trying to manoeuvre it forwards. And when at last they'd dragged it into their room, they'd laid it out under the curtainless window and, without a word, sunk down on it together, still giggling, pulling off each other's wet clothes, tracing each other's smile with their fingers. Joy like a bird.

'Remember?' she repeated, while beside her Adrian breathed rhythmically. 'Remember?'

He grunted something; his mouth was half open and he smelt of wine and wood smoke.

'Things we should never forget,' she said to herself, pulling the duvet up a bit so his chest was covered. Funny to think that night after night they went to sleep next to each other and lay there hour after hour together, both trapped in their own secret dreams.

CHAPTER SIX

By the time Adrian's parents arrived for Christmas lunch, the children had been up for seven hours. The turkey was roasting, the vegetables were in their pans ready to cook, the pudding was tied up with muslin and string and was steaming and spitting on the hob, a new fire had been laid on top of last night's embers and lit, a few delicate petals of ash fluttering round the room, the lights on the tree were turned on—although several had been broken already, and the floor was littered with sharp pine needles and moulting tinsel. They had to get chairs and a wobbly stool from upstairs and squash together round the table, their elbows pressing against each other, legs tangling.

'So what's up on the work front?' Adrian's father asked after his second glass of wine. 'Anything happening?'

'This and that,' said Adrian. He pushed a chunk of turkey onto his fork, then speared a bit of potato and a sprout, dunked it in the gravy. 'You know how it is with acting.' He pushed the overloaded fork into his mouth.

'This and that.' His father swilled the words round his mouth, tasting them judiciously. 'This and that.'

Irene glared at him but he pretended not to notice.

'That's right.' Adrian was still chewing stolidly.

'Shall we pull our crackers?' said Irene. 'Take your elbow out of your plate, Clem.'

'Any parts then?'

'Not as such. Possibilities,' said Adrian.

'Not even panto? At this time of year I would have thought—'

'All cross your arms,' said Irene. 'That's the way. Hold that little tab there, Aggie. See? When I say go, then pull it as hard as you can.'

'I saw that friend of yours on tv the other day,' said Adrian's father, Graham. 'Some romantic comedy—he was awfully good.'

'Oh well, stuff like that,' said Adrian disdainfully.

'You mean to say, you've turned down stuff like that?'

'Crackers,' said Irene forcefully. 'One, two, three . . .'

'Anyway, he's doing well, isn't he? I'm always seeing his name. Can't he help you out? Give you a leg-up?'

'It doesn't work like that.'

'Or I could always ask around at work to see if there are any opportunities . . .'

'Pull!' cried Irene.

'You're still quite young,' said Adrian's father, carefully arranging a pink paper hat on his greying hair. 'Forty's nothing these days. You can always retrain, after all.'

'I've got a thimble,' said Sasha. 'But it's a bit big for me. I can wear it on my thumb, I suppose.'

'Knock knock.'

'Who's there?'

'Boo.'

'Boo who?'

'Ah, don't cry.'

'It must be very hard for you,' said Adrian's mother, smiling sympathetically at Irene across the table. Woman to woman.

Irene looked at Adrian, staring sullenly at his plate, like a little boy whose dignity's been punctured, and allowed her panic and anger to take hold. She put her fork and knife down, sat up straighter in her chair, her green hat skewed sideways. 'What do you mean by that?'

'Well—having to be the main earner and everything. Never knowing for sure what's going to happen. I know you cope wonderfully, but it must be hard.'

'Not at all,' said Irene. 'I'm very proud of Adrian and have complete faith in him. It's not hard at all, except for him.'

Clem tugged Adrian's sleeve. 'Why is Mummy

talking so loudly?'

'He's a wonderful actor and he's a wonderful father and it's simply a matter of time before—'

'Irene, you don't need to.'

'You should support him and have confidence. Like I do. That's what families are supposed to do.'

'Well,' said Adrian's mother. She wiped her mouth with a paper napkin. 'I was just saying it must be hard, on top of everything else. We've driven all the way from Derby for this lunch and you don't need to shout like that.'

'I was just speaking firmly,' said Irene, biting back the impulse to apologize. 'Aggie, don't do that. Eat a sprout instead.'

* * *

Later, in the small, bedraggled garden in the rain, Adrian stood with his father.

'Sorry about Irene's outburst.'

'Oh well. Women get emotional at this time of year, don't they? I'll say this for Irene: she's got spirit, hasn't she?'

'That's certainly true.'

'Val will get over it soon enough.'

'Mum was right, of course; it's been hard recently. Um—and as a matter of fact just at the moment I'm a bit strapped for cash.'

'Mmm?' His father's tone had become casual. He stared hard at the lawn and poked the soggy grass with the tip of his brogue.

'I was wondering—I hate to ask you this—if you could lend me some money. Just to tide me over. I'd be very grateful.'

'Money?' He made it sound like a foreign word

63

whose meaning he was unsure of.

'Yes.'

Both men looked down at the grass.

'How much?'

'I was thinking—I was hoping you could lend me, say, £7,000.'

'Seven thousand!'

'Yes. Or even—'

'That's a lot of money. A lot.'

'I know, I just—'

'Lend?'

'Of course.'

'Have you asked your bank?'

'Not as such.' Adrian didn't want to embark on the narrative of his recent dealings with the bank. 'But I don't think they'd be very helpful just at the moment.'

'I see. Well, I'll discuss it with your mother.' Adrian noted the phrase 'your mother' and forced his face to stay expressionless. He wasn't going to plead. 'Of course, we'd like to help you.'

'Thanks.'

'But I'm not promising.'

*   *   *

Later, Irene looked back at the week following Christmas as the last few days of a vanishing world. Yet she had felt so safe, hemmed in by domesticity. Grey and windy days outside, bare trees dipping and bending, waves of rain driving across the streets, fog blurring the horizon, and the house became like a little ship safe on its moorings.

Every morning the children crept into bed with Irene and Adrian, pushing themselves into the space between them, snuggling down into the warmth, nuzzling up to them before pattering along the bare boards to the kitchen where they'd eat white bread and raspberry jam, mini pancakes with maple syrup, squabble over imaginary games, and arrange Beanie Babies in circles around the room so they stared at each other with their bright unblinking eyes. They played happy, tedious games of Monopoly, Sasha cheating when she counted out her money and Aggie crouched under the table crunching green houses and red hotels in her sharp teeth. And every evening they cuddled on the sofa in their night clothes and ate toast and Marmite while they watched videos together: *The Snowman*, *101 Dalmatians*; the black-and-white Laurel and Hardy films that Adrian loved so much. Bowls of satsumas and branches of dates, cold turkey with baked potatoes for lunch, hot chocolate in the evenings.

A waiting time.

*   *   *

The day before New Year's Eve, Adrian opened a letter from his father. It was typed and, in awkwardly formal language, it told Adrian that they felt that in all conscience they couldn't loan Adrian the money he had asked for. After much discussion they had reached the joint conclusion that he needed to stand on his own two feet and consider his future career plan realistically. Lending him money would only postpone that, put off the inevitable, and therefore they felt it would be wrong for them to help him. They very much hoped and believed that he would understand that

65

they had thought long and hard and that they were acting in the way they felt right.

Adrian read the letter and crumpled it into a ball in his hand.

'Everything all right with them?' asked Irene.

'Seems so.' He forced a smile. 'They say thank you for Christmas dinner,' he added. He stood up. 'I'm going for a walk,' he said.

'You OK?'

'I just need to clear my head.'

'Take a coat, for God's sake. You'll catch your death.'

'It doesn't matter.'

*   *   *

Irene, piled high with washing, stood for a moment outside Sasha's room and listened to her playing with her friend Jaz. She was teaching Jaz where babies come from.

'The man puts his thingy into the woman's hole.'

'Her hole?'

'You know. Where your wee comes out. Here.' There was a brief pause, then a horrified giggle.

'That's so yucky.'

'I know, but it's true.'

'Then what?'

'Then his thingy gets hard like a gun and he shoots this stuff up her.'

'Shoots?'

'Yes. And the stuff bangs into the egg and then a baby grows.'

'My mum and dad never did that. I came out of the tummy button.'

'They did though. It takes nine months and at

66

first the baby's a pea and then it's a plum.'

'That's manky.'

'I know. But we'll do it one day too. That's what my mum says. She says, you wait!'

'I'm never.'

'I am though. I want to have a baby. I'm going to have a little boy and call him Felix. That means happy. He's going to be big and strong and have blue eyes and live to a hundred.'

Irene moved away from the door. She padded into her room and put the washing on the floor gazing at the pile of little girls' knickers and socks. A boy called Felix, called happy; that would have been nice.

*   *   *

'Jesus. I didn't see you in the dark. How long have you been out here?'

'I don't know. I don't know what time it is.'

'Half past one.'

'Hours, I guess. I just needed—I was waiting . . . Frankie . . . I've tried to call you . . . You didn't . . .'

'You're not even wearing a coat, in this weather! You must be freezing.'

'Am I? Maybe. I don't know.'

'What's happened?'

'Happened. Nothing's happened. Nothing. Frankie?'

'Come inside.'

'Your boyfriend—I can't bear to—'

'I don't have a boyfriend any more.'

'You don't have a boyfriend? I didn't know. Why don't you?'

'Here, come inside out of the cold.'

67

She led him up the stairs in the darkness. He stumbled, laid a hand flat against the wall to save himself. Frankie put an arm under his elbow and steered him into her flat.

'You're shivering. Look at you; you'll get pneumonia.'

'Frankie . . .'

'Sssh, let's get these wet things off you. I'm going to run you a bath.'

She unbuttoned his shirt and tugged it off his back, then knelt at his feet and started to undo his laces, which were stiff with cold. When she looked up at him, his face was screwed up in anguish. She straightened up.

'Oh my love,' she said and took him into her arms. He started to cry silently, tears sliding down his cheeks.

'I can't bear it,' he said. 'I can't bear it any more.'

'Ssssh. You don't have to.'

'What am I going to do?'

'Come here. Just come here.'

She gathered him into her, her thick coat wrapped around him, her scarf against his neck, his cold, sore flesh against her warm, soft body, her clothes opening up layer after layer, until it was just the silk of her skin and the satin of her hair coming loose and falling over his face, his tears drying on her breast, her arms holding him and her fingers feeling for him, finding out all the places where he hurt and healing him.

CHAPTER SEVEN

When did she know? It was a question that friends sometimes asked her later and that she often asked herself, and it always gave her a feeling of vertiginous disquiet—like looking into a slimy-sided well and not knowing how far down it went. You picked up a pebble, leant over the well's dark mouth, silent bats and dank air, and let it drop; waited for the echoing sound as it hit the water. But Irene, looking back over the plunge of months, couldn't work out at what point she had started to understand that something was happening; couldn't tell when it was that she had suspected without acknowledging her suspicions, or when she had known without properly knowing that she knew. Like a ghost in her own life, she thought: believing she was in control but actually being helpless; feeling she was doing all right, in the circumstances, when all the time she was heading for disaster; reading everything the wrong way. She could hardly bear to think of it, that time of not-knowing.

And who else had known, she wondered—what friends had found out before her and had looked at her pityingly and talked about her to their partners. Karen? After all, Karen was Frankie's sister. Had she known all along? That time they'd gone out for a meal together and Irene had talked—her cheeks burned with wretchedness when she remembered it—about how she and Adrian had been through a difficult patch over the past several months, but how basically committed they remained to each other. 'We'll grow old together,' she'd said with a slightly drunk solemnity, and 'Don't you think, once you have children, you're linked in a biological way, as if you're each other's family?' She remembered saying that, partly saying it to make it true—but had Karen known then, while she sat there nodding her sleek head, fiddling with her expensive jewellery, and smiling? Had she gone from Irene to Frankie, to hold her hand and comfort her and give her advice, encouragement, hope, help? Told Mac, in a hushed, important voice one evening, while they were undressing for bed perhaps—poor Irene, isn't it terrible, and oh God, so complicated for us, Irene's almost like my sister as well, what on earth should we do . . . ? And maybe Karen told Sarah later, while Sarah held Connor to her breast and felt so grateful for her own life. Smug with the sense of her own blessedness. And Sarah told Gary . . . But that's the way paranoia creeps in—for a moment, she let herself imagine huddles in corners, a whisper like a dry rustle in the air, that dies as she approaches, eyes looking at her and then looking away. Poor Irene.

They had seen Frankie on New Year's Eve, Irene did recall that. She had been at Megan and Larry's house, where they'd gone after having dinner elsewhere. By the time they arrived, Aggie was asleep in the car and Irene scooped her up and staggered through the crowds and up the stairs, laying her on a bed and covering her with a coat. She looked in on the main bedroom where Sasha and Clem, along with ten or so other children, were eating popcorn and watching the tv. When she came downstairs she met Frankie, who kissed her on both cheeks and wished her a happy New Year. Irene had known Frankie since she and Karen were eleven and Frankie only six, a chubby little blonde girl with a fringe and grommets in her ears who cried easily, and who used to tag after them.

'And to you too,' said Irene.

Karen had told her that Frankie and her boyfriend had finally split up at Christmas, so she felt warmly sympathetic. 'I know you've been having a hard time but I really hope next year's better for you. You're looking lovely, though.'

And it was true. She'd never really thought of Frankie as beautiful, she'd known her for too long, but this evening she had a lustrous quality. Her skin glowed and her eyes shone; her lips were full and glossy red; her hair gleamed. She was wearing leather trousers and a yellow top with a plunging neckline; around her throat was an amber pendant, smooth as an egg.

'Thanks,' said Frankie. She put her hand around the amber and smiled.

'So you're OK?'

'I'm well. Yes.'

'Good,' said Irene. 'I'm so glad.'

*   *   *

'Frankie?'

'Mmm.'

'You're wearing my present.'

'Of course. All the time. You didn't need to give me something so wonderful, you know.'

'You're wonderful. I keep thinking of last night.'

71

'Me too. I wear the shirt you left behind in bed. I can smell you on it.'

'Oh God.' For a brief moment he closed his eyes. 'You look beautiful.'

'It's because you're here.'

'I wish I could touch you.'

'Mmm. Me too.'

He moved a bit closer so their hips brushed. She stared at him and bit her lip.

'We could go upstairs,' he said. He let a thumb touch her thigh.

'You're mad. Irene's a few feet away. Your kids . . .'

'I know; I feel mad. I want to be mad. Just for a minute.'

'Tomorrow.'

'I'll die if I can't be with you soon.'

'I'll wait in all day. You don't need to tell me when you're coming. I know it's difficult for you to get away. I'll just stay in bed, in your shirt, and wait for you to come to me.'

'Jesus,' he said. 'Oh Jesus.'

*   *   *

'Happy New Year,' they said to each other, dropping the circle of hands they'd made for 'Auld Lang Syne' and turning to each other. Children, teenagers, adults; friends who had known each other for years.

Irene hugged Clem and Sasha and Aggie, who was wild with chocolate and tiredness, and then put her hands on Adrian's shoulders.

'Happy New Year,' she said softly.

'Happy New Year to you.'

'We're all right, aren't we? I know things have been difficult recently. But we're going to be all right.'

'Of course we are.' He grinned wildly at her, put his hands heavily on her waist, clumsily pulled her towards him.

They kissed each other on the lips.

*   *   *

Irene turned towards Adrian in bed. He was lying on his back, with an arm over his eyes, but she could tell by his breathing that he wasn't asleep. For a few moments she lay looking at him by the light from the hallway. Then she took a deep breath and propped herself up on an elbow, put a hand on his stomach, kissed his neck. He didn't stir.

'Adrian?' she said.

He took his arm away but his eyes remained shut. She kissed his mouth and he sighed. She moved her hand down until it rested in the coarse tangle of his pubic hair.

'Adrian?' she repeated softly. 'I want to say something, so we start the New Year properly.' He opened his eyes and made himself look at her. 'The first thing I want to say is that I do love you, you know.'

Adrian made a sound as if someone had punched him, the air going out of his body.

'And it's been a hard year,' she said. 'The hardest we've had and it's not over yet. There's no magic wand.'

He said nothing; was trapped in her eyes. She leant across and kissed him on his mouth and he

73

closed his eyes again. He couldn't bear to see her face, and the tenderness that was in it.

'That's all right,' he said at last.

'I know it's been a long time since we, you know . . .' He made an assenting noise, willing her to stop, but she continued. 'Made love. God, listen to me; why do I feel so shy and awkward? Since we fucked. And the longer it's been, the harder it's got, until it almost became impossible, if you see what I mean. It wasn't you. I just got so knotted up about it. Self-conscious. It got mixed up with everything else. I couldn't. I just couldn't.'

'I know.'

'We should have talked, shouldn't we? Before now, I mean. We shouldn't just have pretended it wasn't happening.'

'It doesn't matter.'

'Yes it does. It matters a lot.' She waited, her hand on his limp penis. 'Adrian?'

'Mmm?' He made himself sound drowsy, although in fact he was wide awake, and his heart was thumping in his chest so loud he thought she would hear it.

'It'll be all right, won't it?'

'Of course.' His voice was gruffly emphatic. 'It's not that I'm not responding. I'm just rather sleepy tonight.'

'That's OK,' she said. 'I just thought I ought to say it out loud. Little things can turn into big things without realizing, can't they?'

'Mmm,' he said.

She took away her hand and lay down beside him, her head turned into his shoulder and her breath warm on his neck. She drew up her knees and crooked them over his legs. He put a hand across her hips. That's how they went to sleep, holding each other.

CHAPTER EIGHT

She did see a look. She noticed that as it happened. From that single glance, intercepted across a room, her conscious world began imperceptibly to change.

Karen had two children and the younger, a boy called Ben, was a few months older than Clem. In January he had his sixth birthday party, to which Clem was invited—the only girl among ten or so boys, although most of the boys never realized that. She wore baggy jeans, a hoodie with frayed sleeves and scuffed trainers; her dark hair was short and spiky. After the magician, who looked like an overweight Charlie Chaplin and who sweated profusely as he pulled swathes of coloured ribbons from empty bags and blew balloons into the shapes of poodles and swans, had left, they played football on the churned lawn, Clem as ferocious as any of them. Irene was there for the whole time, piling the presents into safe corners, picking up shredded wrapping paper, helping Karen ice the birthday cake—green, for a football pitch, with piped white lines, miniature goals and footballers standing on white plastic discs, each in different postures. She spread peanut butter or honey onto sliced bread, arranged chocolate fingers on plates, ran down the road to the shop to buy sparkling lemonade.

Frankie arrived halfway through, bringing Ben's

present. She was in jeans and a pale pink jersey with a high rolled collar and wasn't wearing any make-up. Her hair was loose and tucked behind her ears and she looked tired. Irene remembered that, although not much else—not what they talked about; not whether Frankie was uneasy with her, or too friendly, or cool. The three women sat at the kitchen table with mugs of tea, sorting out party bags and watching shrubs getting trampled underfoot. Occasionally one of them would go outside to help Mac referee an argument. It started to rain, and the boys became even muddier and more boisterously quarrelsome. Irene looked at Clem, her damp hair and angry red cheeks. She was bellowing something at a boy twice her size, gesturing violently. Her chin jutted forward truculently; her hands were on her hips.

They charged in for the tea, leaving clogged shoes on the doormat and stuffing handfuls of crisps into their mouths before they even sat down. It was starting to get dark outside so Frankie drew the curtains. Parents began to turn up to collect their children, and Adrian, towing Sasha and Aggie, arrived as well, though Irene was sure she had said she would walk home with Clem afterwards and didn't need a lift. They all stood round the children at the table while Karen lit the six candles and turned off the lights. In the half-darkness, they struck up raggedly, tunelessly: 'Happy birthday to you, happy birthday to you . . .' A few sweeter voices wove through the song.

Irene looked from Sasha, opposite her, to Adrian who was standing at the end of the table behind Clem, his hands loosely on his daughter's shoulders. And as she looked his face softened and

76

became grave and tender. He smiled, beautiful in the guttering light. He wasn't smiling at her, but for a few moments she had the bewildering sensation that when she turned her head in the direction of his glance, it would be herself she would see, returning his look that was naked and intimate, like a promise.

But she just saw Karen, Mac, Frankie, other smiling mothers, a melee of muddy-cheeked children, all shouting out the song, and a space where her own face should have been. She blinked and glanced back at Adrian, but he was singing loudly and grinning towards Ben and his green cake-pitch where six candles dripped wax. The spell was broken, the candles were blown out, the lights turned back on, the cake cut into squares and handed round on pieces of paper towel. She had forgotten all about it. Or half-forgotten. It remained like a distant rumour in her mind, a chilly gust of wind that blows up before the storm.

*　　*　　*

They were well back in the term-time routine by then. They would get up while it was still half-dark, and even when it grew light it was grey and dull. Colours leaked away; pencil and charcoal on soggy paper. Houses seemed to lean in over the streets, the skies lowered and the horizon was rubbed out by fog. People didn't lift their eyes; they wrapped themselves in thick coats, pulled hats over their brows, snapped open umbrellas. But Irene, when she walked into the garden, where rain churned up the grass and bushes dripped, could see snowdrops coming up, winter aconites, the shoots of daffodils.

She examined the magnolia tree and saw the first stubby buds that would soon become a waxy candelabra.

Every morning she would wake up the girls—except Aggie, who an hour earlier would have woken her, standing at the bottom of her bed with a night-time nappy sagging heavily round her hips, smelling of sweet grass and piss. She would toast bread and spread it with honey, pour cereal into bowls, gather up damp towels and dirty knickers and balding socks, pieces of Lego that stabbed her bare feet, dolls and swords and soft toys with splitting seams, jam jars filled with blades of grass. No matter how thorough she was, it was as though chaos couldn't be held at bay. She opened cupboard doors, and jigsaw pieces showered down on her, shiny beads poured out of split plastic containers, sheets of thick white paper with drawings on drifted down from shelves and slipped behind radiators. Lavatories weren't flushed, plugs weren't pulled out of baths and sinks, crayons never put back in their cases. In Sasha's room, which in other ways was orderly, there were shreds of paper and card everywhere, little squashed models she'd painstakingly made from old shoeboxes and scraps of material. In Aggie and Clem's room, Irene battled daily with a maelstrom of possessions: sticky, plastic broken figures; soft, torn animals with bright eyes, staring up at her from wherever they lay; sheets of thick soft colouring paper covered in drawings and doodles and splashes of poster paints; mutilated cardboard boxes that they were forever in the process of turning into houses, kennels, whole new worlds; grubby socks and twisted vests under the beds;

brown, shrivelled apple cores and dried-up orange peel; strange potions of rose petals rotting in a mug.

She washed faces, brushed teeth, searched for matching socks and errant shoes, tied Sasha's hair into neat plaits or symmetrical pigtails, tugged a brush through the knots in Aggie's hair while she squirmed and screamed, checked Sasha's maths homework, dabbed disinfectant on Clem's scabby knees, rescued Aggie's pink jersey from the washing machine, tried to divert her from the fact that she'd cut her toast in half when Aggie had wanted it whole, that she'd spread the jam more thickly than Aggie liked it, heated the milk too much, too little, that Clem had finished the pack of frosted flakes, that Sasha had ignored her . . . Irene would look at her two-year-old and know, like a sailor knows a squall is riffling over the water, that a tantrum was approaching. The mutinous mouth, the eyes that glittered, the voice like a seal's bark.

Sometimes Adrian would get up as well, sit in his dressing gown at the table gazing blankly at the crossword, and then Irene would ask him, with furious politeness, if he would mop up the pool of yoghurt, put the dishes in the machine, maybe make her a cup of tea, sign the permission slip that would allow Clem to do after-school football, pick up that *bloody* pen that was rolling around on the floor waiting to be an accident, do something, anything at all, stop eating toast and drinking coffee when he could see that she was going mad with all the things that had to be done in the next ten minutes and couldn't he *see* . . . It was better if he stayed in bed, away from her glaring eyes and warrior's stance.

That early spring, he didn't get in till very late, anyway—he was rehearsing for a play that would be shown in a few weeks' time, in the upstairs room of a pub. The author was a friend and the director a colleague though most of the actors were drama school students. He said he was doing it as a favour, although they both knew he was doing it in order to keep a toe in the acting world. Irene would often be asleep when he came in. She would wake to the door shutting, food cupboards opening and slamming fast again, music playing. She would wait for him to come upstairs, the dip of the mattress, the tug of the duvet, cold skin but then the gradual heat of another body. Beer, smoke, perfume on his skin. She smelt them, although only later did she realize she'd smelt them.

One night, as he lay sleeping, she cleaned out the fridge, squatting in front of it in her dressing gown and slippers, pulling out packets of yoghurts, lettuces that had frozen to the back, browning spring onions, half a pack of feta cheese that had seen better days. The following night, on a binge even she recognized as obsessive, she defrosted the small freezer above it, hacking away slabs of ice with a sturdy knife, chipping at errant peas that were frozen to the sides, mopping up the water with kitchen roll. She sat up at three in the morning and wrote out cheques—for her credit card, for the electricity and gas, for the man who'd come round and unblocked the drains, for the man who'd replaced those tiles on the roof. Her eyes were like pebbles in her head.

Sometimes she just walked round the house, slightly dislocated by the night-time world she was occupying, where everything was dark and cold, and where time seemed suspended. She'd stand at the door of her children's rooms for minutes on end, almost in a dream herself as she watched the way their chests rose and fell, the way their lips puffed with each breath, or they made slight, bewildered expressions in their sleep, rearranging their positions, turning their heads on their pillows. One night, as she stood with her hand on the door knob, Sasha started to laugh—really laugh the way she never seemed to in her waking life, as if someone in her dream was tickling her or telling her an uproarious joke. If someone was laughing in their dreams, did that mean they were happy?

It was only when they were asleep that she saw them as completely separate creatures, far from her in their own secret worlds. She would remember how she'd snapped at Clem, held Aggie's arm so tightly she'd left a red mark, cut Sasha short in the middle of a song, and would feel ashamed of her anger and impatience. Tucking a bear worn thin with hugging under an arm, pulling a duvet back into place, she would resolve to do better tomorrow.

She was back to going to the cinema in the daytime too: *Chicago* twice, *The Pianist*, *The Hours* three times in a row, although the first time she stayed awake all the way through, flooded with sadness, and left the cinema with the restless feeling that she must change her life somehow.

She watched people closely, filing away impressions in her mind: Karen, promoted in her job, became sleeker, shinier; she had glossy hair and glossy lips and the unmistakable sheen of success about her. Her next-door neighbour to the

81

left, an old man who'd lived in Hackney all his life, seemed to have entered a suddenly foggy old age, wandering the streets in his slippers, a vague wispy smile on his folding face. Ruth came in for her lessons with a stony, shutdown face and Irene knew she had her period again. Sasha drew meticulous pictures crowded with tiny people and animals and trees; she stuck matchboxes together to make a miniature chest of drawers that she covered with wrapping paper, putting objects in each drawer—a shell, some earrings, a little pot of lip balm, a passport photograph of herself. And she watched Adrian when he held in his stomach in front of the mirror; when he cried in films; when he bought himself new shirts and hung them in the cupboard secretly, as if she wouldn't notice; when he started reading novels and listening to Mozart and Brahms instead of jazz; when he pretended to be asleep as he lay in bed.

She wrote e-mails to Jem: *'Something's wrong but I'm not sure what it is . . . Sometimes I feel this strange panic that my life's going in the wrong direction and I don't have control over it— ridiculous, I know . . .'* Delete, delete, delete.

*   *   *

Later, of course, she could see it all clearly, and despised herself for being so wilfully blind, for choosing to continue as if they were just going through a slightly rainy patch, not through a storm that changes the landscape. That time they went away for a weekend to the Peak District to visit an old school friend. At the last minute, Adrian couldn't come. He said the rehearsals had been suddenly rescheduled. He was sorry, he said aggressively and self-righteously, but what could he do. Irene drove the girls there on a Friday evening, in driving rain. Lorries sprayed water over the windscreen and headlights dazzled her. She squinted through tired eyes and drove slowly. Beside her, Sasha listened to a talking tape on headphones and behind her Clem and Aggie squabbled and asked when they'd arrive. They bought sandwiches and chocolate bars in a garage and the girls ate them and then, one by one, fell asleep, clutching crusts, mouths smeared with chocolate. She lifted them straight into their waiting beds, pulling off their shoes and jumpers, easing jeans down over their floppy bodies, and then sat up late drinking cheap wine with a throbbing head. She rang Adrian but there was just the answering machine.

'Adrian?' she said into it, for she was sure he'd be back from rehearsals by now. 'Adrian, it's me. Are you there?' And Adrian, lying in their bed, heard her voice calling up to him from the hall, but he couldn't answer. He was holding Frankie in his arms as if she were the most precious thing: it hurt him to touch her yet destroyed him to take his hands from her flesh. He put his mouth on the pulse in her throat and her hair fell across him, protecting him from the world. He rolled onto her where she lay, on Irene's side of the bed.

That night, there was a violent storm and all the children ended up with Irene. She lay awake, one arm around Sasha, the other around Aggie, while at her feet Clem lay curled like a cat. She saw through the closed curtains the flashes that lit up the sky and listened to the crackling thunder overhead. She remembered how, when she was a girl, she had lain in her mother's bed counting seconds between lightning and thunder, and she murmured to the children that everything was all right, just fine, wasn't it cosy, lying in a warm room while rain clattered and the skies boomed, and when they knew they were safe. Utterly safe.

*   *   *

Or when she sent him a card on Valentine's Day, with a childish heart inside and an arrow through it. 'From someone who loves you', she wrote in capital letters.

'Sorry, I forgot all about it this year,' he said when he opened it.

'Never mind,' she said, glaring at him with humiliation. 'It's just a stupid commercial con really. We both know that; it doesn't mean anything. Anyway, maybe that's not from me.'

'Right,' he said, attempting to laugh.

'From your secret admirer.'

'Ha!' he said.

She shouldn't have sent him a fucking card anyway. She should have just poked him in the eye. Bastard, she said in her head. Wanker. She made a face at him when he turned his back, and was alarmed at her infantile fury. Soon, she thought, she would just go off like a bomb.

*   *   *

Or there was the night he hadn't come home; how could she have just let that go? She had woken at intervals to find him absent, rung his mobile but it

84

was always turned off, then at six-thirty in the morning she sat up in bed, hearing the front door shut softly, then the noises of him downstairs, clattering a cup, turning on a tap, whistling. Fucking whistling! She threw herself out of bed, pulled on her towelling robe, yanking the belt so sharply she almost couldn't breathe, and marched downstairs, stubbing her toe on the last step.

'Where the bleeding hell were you?'

'Sorry. Like an idiot, I left my blasted key in my other jacket and by the time I realized it was late, I didn't want to wake you.'

'Oh for goodness sake, you could have rung.'

'I didn't want to wake you,' he repeated.

'How did you get in, then?'

'I found it in my jeans pocket after all,' he replied lamely.

'Oh yes. So where did you sleep?'

'At Jack's house?'

'Jack? *Jack?* Who's Jack when he's at home?'

'One of the cast,' he said vaguely. 'You don't know him.'

She snorted derisively and he looked at her calmly.

'Don't you believe me?' he asked. He wanted her to say that no, as a matter of fact she didn't. Then he would tell her and pull the house down on them both. The relief of wreckage.

She sat down in a kitchen chair and rubbed her face. Hysteria left her and she just felt tired. 'Of course I do,' she muttered. 'Of course I believe you, Adrian.'

*   *   *

85

The next day, instead of going to a film in the late morning, she cycled into Camden and bought herself a violin with the money she had been putting aside for their summer holiday. She had learnt violin for one year when she was thirteen and then given up in despair at how the sound she imagined was so far from the sound that she made—but now every time she went to the cinema she passed a busker with dreadlocks and dreamy, stoned eyes who played things like 'Scarborough Fair' and 'A Minstrel Boy' and she had been overtaken by the desire to make that kind of plangent music herself, music like a voice singing.

The violin had a hairline crack on its side, which was why it was cheaper than most of the others lining the shelves of the shop, but otherwise she thought it looked beautiful, with its blonde, grainy wood, its dull black pegs and its curves like a woman's body. The smell of rosin, the snug green felt that lined the case, released in her such childhood memories that for a moment she could almost believe herself back in the classroom, waiting for Ms Abney to ask her to play a scale. She plucked a string and felt its muted twang quiver under her finger. Upstairs, a man was trying out a cello; liquid amber notes climbed up and down the scales and then he broke into a fragment of melody.

'This is just for me,' she said aloud to herself, as she wrote out the cheque, trying not to think of her bank account.

She bought some sheet music for absolute beginners and a shiny amber disc of rosin wrapped in a soft scrap of cloth, and left the shop with a sense of excitement. Just carrying the case made her feel that something had changed about her life. Like a window opening. Like the fog lifting off hill tops and a sudden view unfurling. She imagined herself standing in the centre of a room—not one of the rooms in their own house, which were all cramped and cluttered, but a long, airy space with honey-coloured boards, white walls and quiet— and lifting the violin under her chin, drawing the bow softly along a string, hearing the note expand and feeling the bars of sunlight settling in her hair.

CHAPTER NINE

In March, when the daffodils were out all along the street, Adrian was offered another role in a two-part television drama that would be made in the summer. He rang her at work to tell her, his voice thick with excitement. At lunch Irene went out and bought a bottle of champagne—real champagne, not just sparkling wine. She cooked a chicken for supper and, after the girls were in bed, she shoved the litter of the day out of sight, swept washing into the machine, drew all the curtains and lit the candles on the table and the night lights on the mantelpiece and window ledges. She put on a silk shirt she hadn't worn for years. She stood in front of the mirror and brushed her hair, then put in earrings and smiled at herself.

He was late home. She phoned his mobile and left a message. Then another, in a politely brittle voice. After a bit, she took the chicken out of the oven and made a salad. She prowled round the children's rooms. She kicked a door violently, slammed cupboards and banged pans, though there was no one to hear her. Then, to her disgust and surprise, she found she was thumping her head on the table: bang, bang, bang. It echoed through the house, through her skull, which like an eggshell might crack open, a thick yolk of anger welling out.

She sat up numbly, feeling the throbbing subside.

'Stupid,' she said out loud. 'Bonkers. Who'd live with a bonkers woman like you?'

She stood up and to take her mind off waiting, she took her violin and went to the tiny room at the end of the house, where nobody slept and boxes of old baby clothes and books stood along the wall. She shut the door so as not to disturb the girls, tightened her bow, rubbed rosin along its length so powder fell in a fine drift, and then she played a scale. She started on the G string and climbed all the way up, trying to get the spacing correct. The bow wobbled and scraped on the bridge; the notes wavered and shrieked. The violin dug into her neck and her arms ached. Her fingers were stiff and flat. Tomorrow she would ring up the number of a teacher that Lisa had given her; she needed lessons, that was for sure. She stood up as straight as she could in the little room and drew her bow, flat and smooth, along the D string. She felt the note running through her body, and then heard the door open and shut again, a voice calling her name. It was past ten o'clock.

Adrian glowed from the cold air and the alcohol he'd already consumed; his cheeks were rosy and his lips red and he radiated energy. He apologized for being late—held up, people to see, you know how it is, yabber yabber—and lay back in the chair

88

and raised the champagne glass to his lips but he hardly touched his chicken. He hadn't shaved for a couple of days; his eyes gleamed; his hair had grown longer and fell over his collar. Irene saw that he'd lost weight since Christmas; his clothes were looser on him and his stubbly face was slightly gaunt. Irene thought he looked younger and wilder, more like the man she had fallen in love with all those years ago.

'I feel as if this could be the start of new things,' he said, pouring himself another glass, chasing his chicken around on the plate. 'At last, after all the time I've spent hanging around, going to auditions, teaching bloody Andrew Lloyd-Webber songs to spoilt pubescent girls, this could be it, Irene.'

'Yes,' she said. 'Yes. It's fabulous.' His hope was contagious, and she smiled across at him and raised her glass in a congratulatory toast. 'Well done for keeping faith.' She noticed that his hands were shaking.

'No more failure,' he said. 'Bloody, fucking failure. It eats you alive.'

And then, abruptly, his face still contorted in a grin, he started to weep. He pushed away his plate of untouched food and fat tears ran down his face and dripped off his unshaven jaw. He put his head in his hands and let himself be wrenched by spasms of grief. Pieces of words broke out between his sobs, though Irene couldn't make out what he was trying to say. For a few seconds, she sat across the table from him with her champagne glass in her hand and stared at him, then she crossed over to him and knelt by his chair.

'Adrian?'

'Oh Jesus.'

89

'What is it?' she asked, but it wasn't a real question and she didn't know if she wanted the answer. She laid her arms on his shaking shoulders and he turned towards her like a blind man. He pressed his heavy, wet face into her shoulder and she stroked his hair as if he was her child.

'Oh Irene,' he said into her neck. 'I didn't know, I didn't know . . .'

'It's all right,' she murmured, holding him against her. 'Everything's all right.'

She wiped his tears from his cheeks, and comforted him for leaving her.

*   *   *

'Sorry,' he said the next morning, drinking coffee in the kitchen, his face shaved and hair washed. 'I don't know what came over me.'

'We have to talk though.'

'Yes,' he said. He picked up the newspaper. Aggie dropped her glass of warm milk onto the tiles and her mouth opened in a howl. Clem kicked Sasha under the table because she'd taken the last waffle. Outside, their neighbour shuffled up his garden in his slippers, beaming in through the window. 'Yes, of course.'

*   *   *

He bought her blue flowers—irises and thistles—and she arranged them carefully in a glass vase and put them on top of the tinny, out-of-tune piano so that they trembled when Sasha practised her scales. He shouted at her when he couldn't find his grey shirt. He drank whisky late at night, waiting

90

until he thought she was asleep before coming into their bedroom and sliding carefully into their bed. He held her hand too tightly when they walked along the street together, so that her ring cut into her fingers. He complimented her on how she looked and bought her a bottle of expensive perfume she didn't like, silver earrings she never wore. He talked garrulously and loudly when they were together, filling in the pauses so that she wouldn't ask him. He turned his face slightly when she kissed him so their mouths didn't meet. He didn't want to kiss her; he couldn't believe he'd ever desired her.

*   *   *

She became a spy. She lifted Adrian's mobile out of his jacket pocket and, taking it into the bathroom, pressed 'Redial'. But their own phone rang and Clem snatched it up at once. 'Who is it?' she barked into Irene's ear. 'Who's there now?' In the middle of one night, she rifled through his old bank and credit card statements, without knowing what she was looking for. She looked at his e-mail messages, including the ones that had been sent and the ones that had been deleted. She watched him, standing on the other side of the door when he made calls, trying to read his face when he thought that no one was looking at him. She watched him until he became a stranger to her.

He was a stranger to himself, as well. With Irene, he had become used to being a sporadic father, a failed actor, a man approaching forty with a spreading paunch, thinning hair, dirty socks and annoying habits—someone who left cupboard doors open, flecks of toothpaste on the bathroom mirror, and nail clippings on the floor, who didn't help round the house enough, drank more than was good for him. But Frankie turned him back into an outsider and a lover; tragic and romantic and utterly wanted. She leant forward to hear stories from his childhood; gazed at him when he spoke of his hopes and his plans; trembled when he touched her; turned to liquid under his hands. How could he resist?

*   *   *

'Stand straight with your feet slightly apart.'

'Like this?'

'Fine. Now, show me how you hold the bow. No, that's completely wrong. You put your thumb under. So. Now you curve your fingers around. Not all stiff; relax them. Like a tunnel. No, relax. Look at that little finger, it's as stiff as a stick. OK, now just move your arm up and down, holding it like that. And from side to side, like a windscreen wiper. Good.'

Catherine Wattisham lived in a detached house in Islington—one of those houses with French windows giving onto green lawns, huge mirrors hanging over wide fireplaces, a smell of polish and cut flowers in the air. She wasn't at all what Irene had been expecting. She was an elderly woman with a straight back, a tweed skirt, stiff grey hair in a helmet of rigid curls. But when she picked up her violin and put it under her chin her body became suddenly supple, as if water was flowing through it, and her expression changed. She looked as if she was listening to a sound that was coming from far away and that no one else could hear—like an old sailor on the prow of a ship who knew the song of mermaids. Music rippled from her bow.

'Hold the violin by its neck—not as if you're trying to throttle it though. You're cupping it instead, cradling it. Be subtle, Irene, tender. Remember, those fingers have got to move on the strings. How will you be able to do that if you're holding onto the neck as if you're killing a goose? Now put your violin against your shoulder and under the chin, like this. You should be able to take away your hand and balance it. Everything's got its equilibrium—the bow, the violin, they should feel natural. Don't clutch so. You have to practise just holding them. Buy a shoulder pad for next week, will you?'

'Yes.'

'Can you read music?'

'Ye-es,' Irene said doubtfully. She could read music like some of her dyslexic students read words—painstakingly, letter by letter, fitting unwieldy sounds together on their tongues.

'These strings: G,D,A,E. Yes?'

'Yes.'

'Put the heel of your bow on the D and draw it all the way to its tip. Steadily. Don't move your wrist, move your elbow. Good. Now the A. Yes. Do it on all four strings. Lift your elbow or drop it to get the right position. Whole bow, remember. That's your homework. That and practising the way you hold your bow and violin.'

'OK.' She felt like a schoolgirl.

'It takes time and work. One day, you'll find you do it instinctively. Instinct comes with practice.'

'Adrian.'

'Mmm.'

'You have to tell me what's going on.'

'Nothing's going on. I'm tired, that's all. I'm in the middle of doing a play in case you haven't noticed.'

'I know, but . . .'

'And there's the film coming up. I thought you'd be pleased for me.'

'OK, that's all great, or it should be.'

'So then.'

'The other night . . .'

'I told you, the other night was just one of those things—I don't know what came over me.'

'We don't go out together.'

'I'm busy—busy at last. What do you expect?'

'More than this. I want to talk. I want you to tell me things. I want to be held and touched.'

'That's new.'

Irene flinched. 'That's below the belt.'

'OK. I shouldn't have said that. Sorry.'

'So you're saying there's nothing the matter? You're just busy and caught up with all of this?'

'Yup.'

'Really sure?' she persisted. 'I need to know. You have to tell me if something's wrong otherwise how can I do anything about it?'

'You never let up, do you?'

'What?'

'Everything has to have a meaning for you, everything has to be significant. Sometimes you should let things be—let *me* be.'

'I was simply asking you what was wrong.'

94

'Maybe it's with you that something is wrong.'

'Me?'

'You're such a fucking absolutist.'

'You used to say that as a compliment.'

'Did I?'

'Yes, you did. What's happened that everything's so changed?'

'You're the one who's changed,' said Adrian. He didn't want to look into her large grey eyes while he was speaking; he wanted to feel aggrieved. 'Look at you! You can't relax any more, not for a minute. Nothing satisfies you—nothing about me, anyway. Pick this up, ring so-and-so, look at the mess; don't eat that, drink that . . .'

'I don't . . .'

'Sometimes you look at me as if I'm some pig who's come blundering into the room, messing everything up.'

'What!'

'How do you think it feels to live with someone who's forever wanting you to turn into someone else? It's enough to send you mad.'

Irene gazed at him. She waited while her anger burned along the fuse of her remaining patience. She took a deep breath.

'Of course I've bloody changed. What do you expect? That I should be happy and carefree like I was when you met me? We were always going to be equals. That's what we said to each other. We were going to do it differently from our parents. Now look at us. I get up early in the mornings because you're always out late. I get the girls up. I get them ready for school. I tidy the house. I deliver them and I go to work myself, and by the time I arrive there I'm exhausted. And when I come back I pick

95

them up from the childminder and I do it all again. The meals. The childcare. The bloody housework. I hate housework. For years, it's been me who's earned the money and paid the bills,' she went on, wincing at what she was saying. 'I've supported you through all these years, haven't I? Encouraged you? Never told you to give up on the whole acting thing and get a job.'

'That's it, isn't it?' Adrian was flooded by a righteous indignation. Here, then, he told himself, was the real reason for his affair. His whole identity was at stake, all his dreams. Of course he had to escape. 'That's what you've always felt. That's what you've wanted all along.'

'No! Don't twist my words to suit your purpose. You know it isn't. I haven't minded—well, only sometimes when everything gets on top of me. But here's what bothers me—things are suddenly looking a bit better for you, you're going to be in this film after all; your agent's got plans. There's hope again, and I thought that would make things better between us. Easier. It's what we've been waiting for, your luck to change. What we've dreamt about. I thought you could look after me for a change. It was my turn. Instead . . .' She made a gesture, palms up.

The fight went out of Adrian. He felt tired and ashamed, and just wanted to be out of here—out of the room, out of the argument, out of himself.

'It's been hard,' he said.

'Hard.' She considered the word. Then she took the plunge. 'Are you having an affair?'

'No!' Panic almost choked him. He wanted so badly to tell her; the words were in his mouth like gritty stones. 'Don't be ridiculous. Things have just

96

been difficult.'

'OK,' she said. 'OK then. Never mind.'

CHAPTER TEN

Spring turned slowly into early summer, each day longer and brighter than the one before. Adrian went away to Prague for several weeks, filming; he phoned home occasionally but sent no letters, and when Irene suggested they all join him for a weekend, he put her off with vague excuses. He appeared in a tv commercial for an advanced razor blade which made men feel even more manly. He lost more weight and started using mouthwash. He bought himself a new suit. The phone rang for him in the middle of the day. His week was full of meetings, dinners, appointments, excuses. He crept into bed when Irene was asleep and, in the early hours of each morning, felt her slide out of it.

Early summer turned into full-blown, limp-leaved July. Irene wrote reports for her pupils. She bought sun cream, flip-flops and wide-brimmed hats for the girls and let them have ice-lollies after school and stay up late, fooled by the light into thinking it was still day. She went to end-of-term assemblies. She looked at lying holiday brochures that landed on their doormat—couples hand in hand by an azure sea where time stands still—and then chucked them in the bin.

She sniffed Adrian's shirts before putting them in the wash, making out individual odours: sweat, deodorant, soap, smoke, something fragrant, something sharp. She dug into his trouser pockets and found a crumpled tissue with a smudge of pink on it. In his jacket she found a box of matches from a brasserie in Covent Garden. On his latest credit card statement—one that he'd borrowed money from her to pay off—were several restaurants that she had never heard of. In his wallet, tucked behind the book of stamps and the AA card, was a key.

She took out the key and hid it in her own purse.

'Dear Jem,' she wrote, *'am I going mad?'*

Delete.

*   *   *

They shared a cigarette in the dark, passing it between them and watching the tip brighten and fade.

'I love you.'

'I love you too.'

'I love you so much I feel I could die of it.'

'Come here, then. Come to me. Here.'

'I don't want to go away. Two weeks without touching you.'

'I know.'

'Think of me. Don't let me out of your heart.'

'Here. Come here.'

'What am I going to do?'

'I don't know.'

'I don't know what to do.'

*   *   *

'Irene,' he said after the eleventh day of their fortnight in a boxy white house in Devon, the sea a stone's throw away and sand in all their clothes.

The children were in bed at last and they sat in the narrow conservatory with the sound of the waves breaking into their words.

'Yes.'

'We have to talk.'

'Yes.'

'I've got something to tell you.'

'I'm listening.' Her voice was stern grey; she sat up very straight in her chair, locked her knees and screwed her hands together. He was a long way off from her and she was looking through a telescope at him, as if he were already just a memory.

'You probably already know.'

'Go on.'

'When you asked if I was having an affair.'

'Yes.'

'I—I didn't tell you the truth.'

'What are you saying?'

'I didn't know how to tell you . . . I thought it would all go away . . . I'm so, so sorry.'

'Say it. Fucking say it.'

'Listen, you have to believe that I never meant to hurt you like this.'

'*Fucking say it.*'

'There's someone else.'

Irene looked at him, leaning towards her, while upstairs their three daughters slept and on the wall the clock ticked too loudly. His face was loving, as it hadn't been for weeks, months. He had new wrinkles round his eyes. She looked down at her hands wrung together on her lap. Loose wedding ring, calloused skin, blue veins. Of course he was having an affair. She swallowed hard and focused on him again but it was hard to see properly when he was so far off, this man she used to know.

'Who?' she said at last.

'Are you sure you want to . . . ?'

'*Who?*'

Into the faint sigh of waves, the name fell cleanly as a stone: 'Frankie.'

'Frankie?' For a moment, the name made no sense to her. She blinked and shook her head. 'Frankie Peveril?'

'Yes.'

'You mean, Karen's sister, Frankie?'

'Yes.'

Frankie who used to follow her and Karen around like a shadow; who used to fall over and wail. Young, blonde, sexy Frankie, who wore tight shirts over full breasts, had glossy lips, white teeth, smooth skin. For a moment, like a florid pornographic film bursting onto the screen, she saw them together: legs tangled, flesh wet, his mouth on her nipple, her hand between his legs, her head thrown back, his face screwed in that special anguish. Upstairs, they heard footsteps padding into the bathroom. They sat in silence. A lavatory flushed, the footsteps padded back again.

'How long for?'

'A few months.'

'Be specific please.' Her voice was hard and cold; stinging metal. 'When did it start?'

'Thirtieth of December,' he answered.

Irene winced; she hadn't expected him to be quite that specific. She held the date in her mind for a few seconds, feeling it set off small electric connections, then pushed it away. Later, she knew, she would pull it out and let it demolish her past. She had the distant sense that she wasn't ready for this—like an actor who hasn't learnt her lines

100

properly, she wasn't rising to the occasion. The roof should be falling in on their lives, thick dust rising around them, the screech of hopes being splintered and wrecked, the metal-on-metal whine of a tearing future. Instead, they stayed on the skin of things, speaking tight words, exchanging facts.

'Is it still going on?' she asked, cool with the unreality of it, listening to her composed voice.

He waited before replying. 'Yes.'

'The girls.'

'I know. Do you think I don't know?'

'Do you love her?'

'Irene . . .'

'Do you love her?'

'I love you too.'

There was pity in his eyes. She couldn't bear that. She felt anger crackle along her skin, lick through her veins.

'Love. You wanker, you don't know what the word means,' she said. 'You have no idea.'

'Irene, don't be like this. We need to talk calmly.'

'Ha!'

'Please.'

'Are you leaving me? Is that what you're saying?'

'No! No, of course not! I don't . . . I can't—I love you. And the children.'

His mobile phone buzzed on the table between them. He grabbed it up, looked at the name on its screen and spoke breathlessly: 'Yes, but I can't talk, I can't talk. Later.' And banged it back on the table, where it lay like a small ticking bomb between them.

'I can't believe how stupid I've been,' said Irene. 'You must have been laughing at me all this time.

101

Such a credulous fool.'

'No! It's not like that. And Frankie feels aw—'

Irene put her hands over her ears as if the name was poison that was being poured into her brain. 'Don't you dare tell me about how awful you've both been feeling all this time. Don't you fucking dare.'

*   *   *

Later that night, Irene climbed out of bed. It was very cold, very quiet. Adrian was asleep downstairs on the fold-out sofa, still dressed, an old blanket thrown over him and his feet in the socks that Father Christmas had given him sticking out at the end. His mobile was on the floor beside him. She picked it up and strode, barefooted, out of the house, into the blue moonlight. The grass was cold and damp, the sky clear. She crossed the lane and made her way onto the beach. The tide was up, dark waves sucking at the grit and sand, spitting out broken shells. She stood ankle deep in the foam and hurled the phone far out to sea, watching it turn in the air then splash into the swelling black water. She imagined it sinking to the bottom, a box full of secrets and lies, and being washed empty there till it was just another bit of salt-crusted plastic bobbing along on the dirty ocean floor.

Then she returned to the house, picked up her bow, tightened it, rubbed rosin up and down its length. She lifted her violin out of its green-lined case. At least she knew now. That was something.

She went into the conservatory and opened the door so the waves were louder and the wind licked at her bare legs. Wet feet slightly apart, back straight, the fingers of her right hand curved around the bow, the fingers of her left curled across the neck of the violin, which she tucked under her chin. She imagined herself on a stage. She pressed the heel of the bow onto the D string, and drew it along the entire length, feeling it grip and draw the music out. A perfect note. Something like excitement bubbled in her chest; something like a howl.

*   *   *

They returned to London the following day—a tense, polite journey, full of I-spy and talking tapes and ghastly silences—and when she unlocked the front door and was hit by the musty smell of absence, she knew that she had to talk to someone about it. If she didn't talk she would go mad with the rising clamour inside her.

But who should she tell? She wanted to talk to Jem, but Jem was in the south of France and she didn't want to say it down the telephone, her words translated along a wire for hundreds of miles. Karen was her oldest friend, her listener, but Karen was Frankie's sister and in Irene's mind was now grouped with the enemy. And everybody else she could think of was so tied to Adrian too. For years, they'd gone around as a couple, sharing common friends, being part of a complicated network, a maze of relationships that connected with each other. If she talked to Sarah or Lisa or Grace or any them, her words would be repeated, gathering meanings and innuendoes; they would multiply in all the separate houses and travel down the phone and through ether, echoing and rebounding.

If only her mother was still alive. But her mother had died years ago. Her mother had died and she had met Adrian—losing and finding all at the same time. She picked up the photograph of her and Adrian together, taken soon after they'd met. Strange to think that she had been this young woman who still looked like a girl, with a bright cascade of hair and freckles over her nose and forehead, her hand in his and her face lit up with excitement. She looked at his face; he looked more like his old self than she looked like hers, as if the years had carved more deeply into her while they had washed over him. She lifted the photo frame high above her head and smashed it down onto the hard floor, where it cracked apart. Then she got a dustpan and brush and swept up the pieces of glass and dropped the whole thing into the bin. Gone, before the children had even run into the house, dragging their bags, rushing from room to room to check that everything was the same as when they'd left it.

She watched as Adrian followed them, a case in each hand and the laces on his shoes trailing. Then she picked up Aggie who was coming backwards down the stairs and kissed her nose. 'Welcome home, poppet,' she said.

*   *   *

'Jem?'

'Irene! Hang on, let me turn down the music. There. How are you doing?'

'Fine,' she said. She found, sure enough, that she couldn't say the words out loud. They would

104

just bounce back off the phone's receiver and smack her in the mouth. 'I'm doing fine. I've just got back. I wanted to know how you both were.'

*   *   *

'Karen.'

'Hi! How was your holiday? I thought you weren't getting back till tomorrow. Everything OK? God, I envy you—it feels like months since we went away even though it was only two weeks.'

Irene listened for sounds of falseness, betrayal.

'Fine,' she said. 'All right.'

'It's been ages. When shall we get together?'

'Let me get sorted out here—you know how it is after a holiday. Mountains of washing, you wouldn't believe.' She laughed and heard the crack of it. 'I'll call.'

The phone rang and she snatched it up.

'Yes?'

There was a silence at the other end, a faint breathing.

She said, 'I know who you are. I know.'

The phone went dead.

*   *   *

She stood in the queue at the supermarket. I could talk to the check-out girl, she thought. Plonk down my shopping—cheese, Marmite, juice, soap powder, rice—and say: My husband's having an affair with my best friend's sister and what should I do?

Shampoo, loo rolls, free-range eggs: I don't want to be all alone again.

105

Potatoes, crisps, bean sprouts, broccoli because that's the only vegetable Aggie will eat: If I start crying, even a single tear, I'll never stop.

Pasta, apples, milk, porridge: If I start hating him, I'll never stop.

CHAPTER ELEVEN

Five days later, the school term began. Adrian and Irene dropped the children off and drove out of London, east, until they reached the flat and desolate east coast: shingle beaches, mud flats, huge grey skies and a sharp wind whistling across the sea, carrying rain. They had been walking here before, although the last time was when Sasha was a baby and Irene had carried her in a sling across her chest, her downy head just beneath Irene's chin and the bunched weight of her swinging with her steps. That time had been in the late spring. They'd held hands, discussed plans, stopped in a pub for beer and sandwiches, driven home in the long, soft shadows of the May evening. Now it was September and the snap of autumn was in the air. They pulled on their walking boots, zipped up their waterproof jackets, set off briskly along the coastal path and for several minutes they didn't speak. Yet it felt oddly companionable and sadly familiar, trudging along together, holding open gates, pulling back springy brambles, losing the path and then finding it again, noticing the same things—the heron flying overhead, the single boat on the horizon—even though they didn't mention them to each other. And they didn't squabble over the map; they were being carefully, relentlessly polite to each other, like distant acquaintances.

'What are we going to do?' said Adrian at last. He'd spent a good deal of the previous four days in bed and had red-rimmed eyes and a puffy face.

'What do you mean, *we*?' asked Irene, her voice cold.

'Irene,' he said, then stopped.

'Go on.'

'I never meant this to happen.'

'You probably didn't. But tell me this: do you now wish it hadn't happened? If you could undo it, would you?' He faltered and she stared at him. 'You don't, do you? You fucking don't.' In a corner of her mind she noted how much she was swearing nowadays; like a brawler in the navy, she would suddenly sling out salty obscenities, unrecognizably loud-voiced and sneeringly crude.

'I don't know,' he said in a low voice. 'I don't know anything.'

'Because you're in love with her.'

'Irene.'

'You're in love with her.'

'Please don't.'

'Why? Because you don't want to hurt me? Is that it? Are you in love with her?'

'All right then. Yes.'

'Have you talked to her since you told me?' He was silent. 'You have then. She's waiting, is she? Waiting to find out what you're going to do?'

'Yes.' His voice was very low, whipped away by the wind.

'I bet. Have you seen her?'

'No. Of course not. You know I've been at home. With you and the children.'

'Are you going to see her?'

'I don't know—oh God, Irene, I can't—I can't just not see her again. You don't understand. It's not just a fling.' He looked at her white, set face. 'Oh hell,' he said. 'What have I done?'

'You mean see her, as in have sex with her?'

He flinched and didn't answer.

'So you're saying you can't promise not to have sex with her again?'

'For fuck's sake, don't be so bloody functional! Can't you see I'm in torment?'

'Torment,' said Irene softly. She walked off again, her face against the wind. She wished the wind would blow harder, blow everything out of her, scour and empty her. Adrian gazed hopelessly after her, then hurried to catch up.

'Look,' he said. 'Listen. I know what I've done. And I don't want to lose you. I couldn't bear that.'

'You already have.'

'What?'

'You've already lost me,' she said. 'I'm an absolutist, remember? I'm not going to hang around waiting for things to die down between you, if that's what you're thinking.'

'No, of course not.'

'What then?'

'Just give me a bit of time.'

Her lip curled. 'To choose, you mean? Between me and her?'

'Irene, please. Don't do this. Think of the girls.'

'You've no right to say that!'

'I know, I know. But they shouldn't suffer for what we've done.'

She lifted up one hand to protest against that 'we' then dropped it again.

108

'You haven't asked me,' she said.

'What?'

'You haven't even asked me if I still want *you*.'

'I wouldn't blame you if you didn't.'

'Hmm.'

'Well?'

'I don't know,' she said. 'I haven't decided. I can't think straight. I don't know what I want any more. Just not this.'

For a moment it was as if all the heat and anger had ebbed away. They looked at each other wearily.

'You should stay somewhere else for a few days,' she said. 'I'll tell the girls you're away on a job. They're used to it—anyway, you've hardly been around much recently, have you?'

'All right. I'll ask Gary.'

'Then you can decide what you want to do. And I can think about whether I want you back,' she added. 'We can meet and talk. Maybe arrange counselling. Take it step by step, very carefully. We must know what we're doing, one way or another.'

'Yes,' he said submissively. 'Yes, of course. That's it.'

'But don't go running to her while you're deciding.' She winced at how her speech had descended into angry cliché; she was even calling Frankie 'her' as if her name would poison her. She had become a statistic: a betrayed wife, an ageing mother whose husband had gone off with a younger woman. For a second, she thought of playing the violin by the window; the feeling of horizons rolling back and a strange freedom beckoning. Was she just going to accept this as one of those things that happened in a marriage? A mundane betrayal, a tacky tragedy, a mid-life crisis that they would weather together. 'If you do that I swear to God that'll be it . . .' she said.

'Of course I won't. You don't need to ask that.'

'Promise?'

'I promise. You have my word.'

He put a hand on her shoulder as he said this but she flinched angrily.

'Don't you dare touch me,' she said.

*   *   *

Irene told the girls their father was going away for a few days; they barely looked up from their supper. When they were all in bed and he'd kissed them goodnight, goodbye for now, he packed a small bag.

'Bye,' he said, standing irresolute at the door.

'Goodbye.'

'Irene?'

'Yes?'

'You're the most wonderful mother, you know.'

She misheard him. For a second, she thought he said 'lover' and elation filled her. She was a wonderful lover. Then she realized what it was he had said. A wonderful mother: it sounded like her epitaph.

*   *   *

Richard, Adrian's agent, rang. He wanted to talk to Adrian urgently.

'I'll tell him to call you,' said Irene.

'Soon as possible, OK? Good news. Things are really on the move now.'

110

She rang up Gary, self-conscious because he probably knew everything by now.

'Gary? It's Irene.'

'Hello. How are you?' The baby was crying in the background.

'Oh, you know, up and down. Strange times,' she said in a clipped voice. 'Can I speak to Adrian, please, I've got an urgent message for him.'

'Adrian?'

'Yes.' Coldness crept through her.

'He's not here.'

'I thought he was with you.'

'He was here last night,' said Gary awkwardly. 'But I've not seen him this evening.'

'When do you expect him?'

'I think,' he gave an awkward cough. 'I think he's not coming back here tonight.'

'Oh,' said Irene. 'Thanks.'

'Irene?'

'Yes.'

'If there's anything we can—'

'Thanks.'

She banged the phone down. Everything felt strange. Her legs trembled and her stomach churned and her forehead was suddenly clammy, as if she was going to be sick. She went into the bathroom and splashed cold water over her face, waiting to feel better. Then she took off her night things and pulled on a pair of jeans and a thick jersey. She went downstairs and rang the girl who sometimes babysat.

'I've suddenly got to go out,' she said. 'An emergency. And Adrian's away. Is there any chance you can come over, just for an hour or so? Thanks.'

Irene looked up Peveril, Frances, in the telephone directory. She knew that Frankie lived in Clerkenwell, she'd been to her flat a few times, and it didn't take long to find the address. She put the pilfered key from her purse into her back pocket. When the babysitter arrived, she was waiting in her coat and gloves. She felt she would be sick if she didn't do something, at once.

She ran down the road, took the underground to Farringdon, and walked the few hundred yards to Portsmouth Road. It was just past eleven o'clock and young people were queuing up outside a club; a group of youths with shaved heads jostled past her, kicking a beer can. She stopped outside the door and, before she had time to reconsider, rang once on the bell as a kind of announcement, then pulled the key out of her pocket, unlocked the door and stepped inside. Stairs led up to the first-floor flat.

Frankie was coming down the stairs as Irene charged up. She was wearing a shirt of Adrian's, half buttoned up, but her legs were bare and her hair mussed. When she saw Irene, she stopped dead and opened her mouth, but no words came out. Irene didn't speak. She pushed past her and flung open the flat door. Clean, freshly painted, plushly carpeted, prints on the wall, everything smelling of comfort and wealth.

'Hang on,' began Frankie.

'Shut the fuck up,' hissed Irene.

'Who was it?' Adrian's voice, coming from the door across the corridor.

She threw open the door, and the light from behind her fell into the room. He was lying in the large bed, his clothes in an urgent heap on the floor and the duvet pushed down his waist so she could see the beginning of his pubic hair, a bottle of red wine open and half-drunk on the bedside table. The air smelt thickly of sweat, perfume, sex; it caught in Irene's nostrils and tipped her back to her own past and other dark rooms.

'It was me,' said Irene. She didn't recognize her own voice. She heard Frankie come into the room behind her. In the free-standing mirror next to the wardrobe, she saw herself reflected: a bony, wild woman with badly cut hair, a shabby coat, an inside-out jumper, burning eyes.

'You made a promise,' she said and started to pull off her wedding ring. As she held it between her index finger and thumb, she had a flash of recall—Adrian standing beside her in the register office, trying to push it onto her finger with shaking hands, and half laughing, half crying as he did so. 'You made a promise,' she repeated. 'And I believed you. Your word, your fucking fucking word.'

She hurled it at him, seeing it spin and gleam in the half-dark, like a little missile spinning through space. But it clinked harmlessly against the wall behind him and fell out of sight.

Adrian did something then that Irene knew she would never forget, not even when she was an old woman and all of this ugliness had faded into a story told to nobody else—he gave a little snorting laugh, as if he was amused and contemptuous of Irene's melodramatic gesture. The laugh lodged in Irene's brain, a fluttering, obscene sensation. He didn't care, she realized. He was so blinded by lust and passion that he literally did not care what she was feeling at this moment. If she started banging

113

her head against the wall; if she fell in a heap, wailing hysterically; if she cried and cried and begged him to stay with her, he wouldn't care. If she'd had a knife handy, she could have plunged it into her chest, just to make him understand what he was doing to her. Or a match and she could have set fire to herself and stood in red leaping flames in front of him: look, look, look at me now, look, you wanker, you deceiver, I'm burning, I'm dying. But maybe he still wouldn't care, just sigh at the inconvenience of her. There was nothing in the world she could do to alter her lovelessness. She felt she was gagging on her own bitter humiliation and a scream rose up in her, rushing through her body like a hot wind.

'You're just throwing us on the rubbish heap, are you?' she shouted, loud enough to make the strings of her throat hurt, a broken lute. 'Is that it? Is it? I've done so much, given so much, everything I had in me to give, I gave to you. And you're just throwing us away?'

'Not the girls,' he said softly. 'Just you.'

She heard herself give a violent, cracked yell. The next thing she knew she was on the bed, on top of his naked body, clawing at his face. She ripped a nail along his cheek and sank a fist into his neck before he caught her by the wrists and wrenched her away from him.

'Jesus,' he said in disgust. 'Look at you. Fuck.' He screwed up his face contemptuously. She noted with satisfaction that there was blood trickling down his jaw.

'I think you'd better go,' said Frankie softly. 'Come on, Irene.'

When Irene struggled to her feet, she saw that

114

Frankie's face was full of embarrassment and pity. The room seemed to tilt; the air roared in her ears.

'Don't talk to me,' she said, hard and loud. 'Don't you dare open your fat mouth. I'm here to see my husband—the man who, fool that I was, I've been supporting for years and years while he tried to make it as an actor despite the fact he can't fucking act; the man whose three little daughters are lying asleep in their beds right now, never suspecting their darling daddy's here proving his manhood by fucking his friend's randy little sister.'

'Get out,' said Adrian.

'Don't worry. You can go back to screwing. You were never very good at it anyway.'

She reached out her hand and gave the bottle on the bedside table a little shove, so the red wine poured a bloody patch onto the cream-coloured, thick-piled, smug carpet.

'Oops, silly me,' she said. 'What an ugly mess. I don't think it will ever come out, do you?'

She pulled her inside-out jersey down over her jeans and straightened her shoulders, then walked stiffly to the door, aware of both of them watching her go.

'Leave the key, will you?' said Frankie.

Irene dropped the key on the table, beside the vase of flowers and the bowl of oranges; she picked the dahlias out of the vase and wrung their necks till they snapped, then flung them, stalks dripping, onto the floor. She lifted a perfect orange and overarmed it, a puckered planet hurtling through the space and exploding through the window, leaving a lovely circle in the glass. Irene gave a delighted screech of laughter.

Then she left the flat, pulling the door softly

behind her, making it down the stairs with her chin still held high, making it into the street, one foot in front of the other, the breeze on her burning cheeks and now a few drops of rain landing in her hair. She was still giggling slightly, though her throat hurt and her chest ached.

She went home and paid the babysitter, with extra thrown in for the inconvenience, and she checked on the children, safe in their bedrooms, who'd never realized she'd been away at all.

*   *   *

It was a long night before the dawn. She sat on the sofa, her knees up under her chin and her arms wrapped around them. Just sat. The rain strengthened and blew in squalls across the garden, then died down again. Her eyes felt hard and dry, like hot coals in her skull. She stared out into the gloom. The crackling, scorching rage had gone. Her throat ached, her head throbbed, and her limbs were chilly and stiff. Time passed. It always does, even when you can't feel its movement because the minutes that are rushing past you are ones of heavy, ceaseless darkness. Like looking out of a train window at night and for a moment you think you've stopped, until you feel the tremor of the engine in your body. She clasped her knees tighter. She rocked herself gently. Time passes.

The sky lightened imperceptibly, until it was a streaked grey, with pale blue on the horizon. Somewhere a foolish rooster crowed. Somewhere a car door slammed. The street lights went off. The radiators creaked into inefficient life. Upstairs,

116

someone coughed several times.

Irene stood up. Her limbs felt rusted. She put the kettle on, splashed water over her face, and went up the stairs. She went into Sasha's room and kissed her daughter on her smooth cheek.

'Rise and shine,' she said cheerfully, pulling open the curtains. 'It's going to be a lovely day.'

*   *   *

'Dearest Jem, Adrian has been having an affair. And now he has left me.'

Short and to the point, she thought. What else was there to say?

She picked up her violin, tightened the bow, rubbed rosin up and down it, and played 'Twinkle, Twinkle, Little Star'. She hated that fucking tune.

*   *   *

'Oh God. Poor Irene. After everything.'

'Yeah. I know.'

'How do you know? Have you talked to her?'

'She sent me an e-mail. I tried to call but it's permanently engaged. She's probably taken the phone off the hook.'

'Did she say how she was?'

'No. It was a very brief message. Just that he's been having an affair and now he's left.'

'You've known for a bit that something was wrong.'

'Mmm. At least, I thought it was.'

'At least it's out in the open now.'

'I hope she'll talk about it.'

'If she will with anyone, it'd be you.'

117

'She's very proud, you know. And I've always been her baby brother—the one she protects, not the one she turns to for help.'

Juliet looked up at Jem, standing there so tall and gangly and clumsy and kind, and gave him a tender smile. He had little wrinkles round his eyes now, clearer after months in the south. Ever since she'd met him, he'd talked to her about Irene: Irene's hair, reddish like his own; Irene's job; Irene's children; Irene's charming husband who didn't adore her enough; Irene's opinions about refugees and global warming and the teaching profession and the best way to cook risotto . . . She'd been almost resentful, seeing her as a kind of rival to Jem's affections: the big sister who'd been his protective fantasy through childhood and who'd recognized the real him when no one else seemed to. Yet when they did finally meet, over a curry in an Indian restaurant—with Adrian ringing at the last minute to say he couldn't make it, and Jem talking too much and ordering a ridiculous number of dishes to cover his own awkwardness and his urgent desire that the two women should get on—her anxiety had fallen away. Irene had been warm, a bit shy, eager to like Juliet, comradely. Not formidable and glamorous and cool, the way Juliet had imagined and feared her, but little, quick, self-deprecating, nearly beautiful and nearly plain and a bit sad under the surface.

'She should turn to you for help,' Juliet said now. 'I would. I do.'

'You always must.'

They looked at each other for a few moments, then Juliet took Jem's hand, lifting it against her cheek.

'I knew as soon as I set eyes on you that you were for me,' she said. And then, before she even knew she was thinking it, added, 'We should have children ourselves soon.'

Her face flushed bright red as she said the words and she dropped her eyes.

'Juliet! I thought you said we should wait until . . .'

'I know. I just suddenly thought it would be stupid to wait. There's never a right time, is there? Now's the only right time.'

'Do you mean it? Really mean it?'

'I think I must. Look at you, I do believe you're crying.'

'I am crying. I only cry when I'm happy. Is it wrong to feel so happy when someone you love is so sad?'

'Not wrong. Strange though. Anyway, tell her she's got to come over. Her and the girls. Leave everything for a bit.'

'I've already told her.'

'Do the kids know yet?'

'I don't know. She didn't say.'

CHAPTER TWELVE

'You know that Daddy loves you very much?'

Sasha nodded solemnly then put the end of her plait into her mouth and chewed it frantically. Clem picked the scab on her knee. Aggie wriggled off Irene's lap and wandered over to the toy box, which she started to rummage through, tossing headless dolls and plastic shapes onto the floor. Irene persevered.

'But sometimes adults decide they would do better living apart.'

But oh, she was doing this all wrong! She'd discussed it with Adrian, and later with Sarah, who worked with children at the hospital, and she'd rehearsed it silently to herself late last night. Adrian sat opposite her, his hands on his knees, and nodded inanely at every word. The scratch on his cheek had nearly disappeared.

'I'm hungry,' said Clem. 'Starving.'

'Hang on, Clemmie, we're trying to tell you something.'

'Starving to death, starving to death, starving to death,' she chanted.

'I will see you just as much as before,' said Adrian, rubbing his knees as if there were grass stains on them.

'Are you splitting up?' said Sasha, still sucking her plait.

'No!' said Adrian at the same time as Irene said, 'Well, yes . . .'

'Doesn't Daddy love you any more?' said Clem. 'Is he dumping you?'

'Of course I love her! I'll always love her.' He gave a sickly smile but didn't look in Irene's direction. He couldn't seem to meet her eyes after her nocturnal visit. He always looked up and then glanced off to her right, as if something intensely important was happening just beyond her. 'But sometimes you love people and yet can't live with them.'

'We'll always be friends,' said Irene, boiling oil for blood.

'Best friends?' said Clem. 'Don't think so.'

Aggie hauled out a skipping rope and held it in a

circle behind her. 'One-two-three-ready-ready-GO,' she yelled and flung it wildly over her head, lashing Clemmie on the cheek.

'Owwwww!'

Irene hauled her onto her lap and kissed the red mark just to the side of her mouth. 'Are you OK?' she asked.

'I hate you,' Clem screamed at Aggie, who burst into tears. 'You're just a sissy little girl.'

'Where will we live?' asked Sasha, calm through the hubbub.

'Oh,' said Adrian, taken aback. 'Here.'

'Not half and half? That would be fairer.'

'I'll come and see you as much as I can,' said Adrian. Tears welled up in his eyes.

'I don't mind sharing a room with Clem and Aggie at first.'

'I bet it's because of me,' said Clem cheerily.

'What?'

'You said when I broke the window that you couldn't stand it any more.'

'No, no, no,' said Irene frantically. 'It's not you. This is nothing to do with you. You have to believe us—this is something between us. It's our fault.' She stared at Adrian: your fault, your fault, your fault, her eyes said. He gazed down at the carpet.

'Who'll look after you?' asked Sasha. 'Who'll wake you up in the mornings?'

Irene looked steadily at Adrian.

'I can look after myself, you know,' he said in a voice that was meant to sound jolly but came out loud and panicky.

'I want something to eat *now*,' said Clem. 'My tummy's rumbling. Can you hear it?' She lifted up her tee-shirt and prodded her stomach.

'All right,' said Irene, standing up. 'I'll get you all supper while you say goodbye to Daddy. He's coming tomorrow after school so you'll see him then. Give him a big hug.'

'No,' said Sasha. 'Not now. He's not going yet?'

'Give him a big hug, darling. It's not for long.'

'Daddy? Daddy?'

'Give me a hug,' said Adrian. Tears were pouring down his cheeks, into his mouth.

'Don't go yet. It's not time; later. Please, Daddy. We haven't finished reading *Wind in the Willows*.'

'Do you know what we say at school?' shouted Clemmie, her face red with fury. 'We say, go fuck your bottom in your face.'

She gave a scared, thrilled squeal and ran from the room.

There was a stunned silence, then Sasha said, 'Did you hear what she said?'

'You say goodbye,' said Irene. A howl of laughter lodged like a bone in her throat and then came splintering out. 'I'll get them supper. OK?'

'OK,' said Adrian. His face was wet and grey.

Irene fried fish fingers and heated up a tin of baked beans. She poured apple juice into three tumblers and got the ice cream out of the freezer so it could defrost a bit. She looked out of the window at the leaves swirling in the garden, at the broken threads of rain. She looked at her hands and thought, these are the hands that held, loved, promised. She clenched them so that blue ropes of veins stood up on their backs, digging her broken nails into the softness of her palms. She waited until the minute hand on the clock moved round, and then again. Adrian said goodbye.

CHAPTER THIRTEEN

There are lots of ways to measure the time.

You can do it by getting through Halloween—trick or treating with the girls, carving battlement-grins into hollowed-out pumpkins, turning on the central heating and asking the bank for a loan—and Christmas (a soldier on a march: no time to stop, no time to look at anything except the ground just in front of her; left-right-left-right, and eyes ahead, thoughts pressed hard down inside her so they wouldn't rise up and engulf her utterly) and New Year (don't think, don't turn back to last year), the grey corridor of January and February, when birds gather in black bunched shapes in bare trees and the monochrome sky presses down, and into Easter, spring at last.

Or by birthdays: Sasha's, and Irene gave her a hamster with sharp yellow teeth which bit Clem's finger when she stuck it through the bars of the cage; Clem's (an Arsenal football kit), Aggie's, Adrian's, her own. By the secondary schools she and Sasha and, once, Adrian visited together, traipsing through classrooms smelling of sweat and sawdust, looking at essays about *Jane Eyre* or First World War poets stuck to noticeboards, trying to imagine Sasha, so skinny and cautious, there among children who already looked like confident adults. By six-monthly dental check-ups. By parents' evenings. By terms and pinched holidays. By new school shoes. By teaching Clem to ride a bike without stabilizers—running skewed along the pavement, ready to catch her as she toppled.

By the imperative turn of weeks: the Saturdays when Adrian collected them at ten and brought them back at six and she was faced with the problem of longed-for, unfilled time (once she even got on an underground train and went round full circle, watching the stops until, an hour and a quarter later, she was back where she had started). The Sundays when she took them swimming and washed their hair and Aggie shrieked like a witch.

By nettles growing tall in the garden. By lawyer's bills. By the flats she visited, trudging from room to room and trying to imagine living there.

By music for the violin—from 'Twinkle Twinkle' to 'Ho Down', 'Clocks and Watches', 'Au Clair de la Lune', 'Lullaby', a tango, a waltz; formidable names like Beethoven, Mendelssohn, Elgar. Catherine Wattisham came to her house now and she stood with her arms folded watching Irene struggle as the music sheets grew darker with the keeling forests of more complicated notes, semi-quavers and slurs and sharps.

By estate agents' visits and the apparent fall in the value of the house. People tripping round the rooms that she'd spent hours tidying up, pressing fingers into damp walls, opening cupboards, staring at beloved objects till they turned shabby under their gaze.

By the dwindling amount of food in her supermarket trolley: no more red meat, no more wheat beer, no more goat's cheese, taramasalata, grapefruit, stem-ginger biscuits, marmalade . . .

By the words Aggie learnt to spell out, following the huge letters across the page with her stubby finger.

By absences—the blanks that appeared on the

walls where pictures used to hang; the rattling cavern of his wardrobe—and by things he'd left behind: it took months before they weren't turning up like stones in tilled soil, almost stopping her in her tracks. The books with his name on the front, the balled socks under the sofa, the ancient walking boots at the back of the wardrobe, the pocket notebooks with lists scribbled at the front; the school cup he'd won when he was eleven; a long scrolled school photograph and she saw his face at once, sitting in the second row to the left with that carefree, confident smile; his gardening gloves that he'd bought but never used. She came across a pink folder full of letters and, unable to resist, took the top one out. It was from her, and had been written just after they'd met. She put it down hastily, as if it were a bomb that would go off in her face. She closed the folder and put it at the back of the drawer. Don't go there.

She saw that, month by month, Adrian changed, time falling away from him, memories dropping like scales. His hair grew longer, his smell was different, his clothes were new—gradually, as the weeks and months went by, Irene ceased to recognize anything he was wearing and after a while she realized he was using unfamiliar expressions as well. It was as if she was watching him shed his old self and bit by bit turn into a person that she no longer knew.

And always in her mind was the memory of herself in Frankie's bedroom—her wild, ludicrous despair and Adrian's snigger of contempt.

'I am never going to be that woman again,' she said, standing in front of the mirror in the ladies' cloakroom, fixing a look of cool neutrality on her face before marching straight-backed and brittle as bone into the room where Adrian waited with his solicitor. 'Never again.'

*   *   *

Sometimes at night, Sasha would get out of bed. Irene would hear a thumping sound, and go to collect her daughter as she galloped round the house, rushing from room to room and banging doors. Her eyes would be wide open but she wasn't awake. Irene would lead her by the hand to the bathroom to use the lavatory. Then she would steer her back to her bed, tuck her in and sit beside her, stroking her head softly until Sasha's bright, puzzled eyes closed and her limbs relaxed.

It was like having a restless ghost in the house, thought Irene. Sasha was a ghost by night, and by day Clem was a violent boy-girl who wore football boots to school and who got into trouble for kicking teachers, pushing mud and old chestnuts into the exhaust pipes of their cars, hitting her class mates and saying 'shit' loudly in assembly. Only Aggie was consistent: a toddler who had tantrums twice a day and sometimes lay on the floor of the supermarket, in the cereal aisle or by the organic fruit and vegetables, and barked like an injured seal while people steered a wide passage round her and looked at Irene with disapproval. Once she knocked a bottle of olive oil to the floor, where it shattered and spread in a viscous puddle. Irene had picked her up and run from the scene.

*   *   *

Adrian started to take the girls 'home', where Frankie watched football on Sky with Clem, let Sasha paint her fingernails and toenails and plait her hair, ordered giant takeaway pizzas for everyone. She kissed Aggie better when she fell over. She hugged them when they left. When they came back, Irene could smell her perfume on their skin. They talked about her to Irene, only Sasha occasionally uncomfortable about it. Irene set her face into a smile, nodding enthusiastically at everything, trying not to properly hear the words that slid in as clean as an army knife, but glassy-eyed with rage and fear.

Sasha made a cushion cover at school, with lines of cross stitch, chain stitch, running stitch, in different coloured thread. 'Wow! Great,' said Irene, holding out her hand. 'It's for Frankie,' said Sasha, holding the cover to her chest and looking defiant. 'It goes with the colours in her room.'

'Great,' said Irene enthusiastically. 'She'll love it.' She imagined hurling stones through the windows of Frankie's flat, throwing boiling water over her manicured hands, setting fire to the curtains in their bedroom, running her nails down Frankie's perfect, creamy skin until little bubbles of red blood burst on it.

*   *   *

'Frankie's going to teach me how to wax my legs,' Sasha said. She was threading bright-coloured beads onto elastic.

'You're eleven!'

'Other girls do.'

'I don't care.'

'Now I know why Daddy left you,' said Sasha. 'You're just a bossy-boots with wrinkly skin. I wish I was living with Daddy and Frankie. Also, did you know that when you bite your nails like that it's worse than licking a lavatory seat.'

Irene stared at her, words boiling up inside her until she thought she would explode. Sasha gazed calmly into the mirror, furrowing her brow. She poked her index finger into a little pot of lip balm and dabbed it on her small mouth.

'There,' she said and daintily smacked her lips together.

Clemmie came across her with her head in her hands one evening, and pulled at her roughly, sharp little fingers digging into her flesh.

'Don't!' she hissed into her mother's face, her nostrils flared and her eyes glinting.

'Don't what?' asked Irene.

'Don't look like that. Smile! Not like that, smile properly, like you used to!'

Aggie every so often asked for Frankie to kiss her goodnight too. She said that Frankie never got angry with her, and smelt of roses and marshmallows.

*　　　*　　　*

At last she met up with Karen. At the restaurant she ordered cold soup, pasta and a carafe of rough house red, which at the first sip went straight to her head so that the room was full of soft edges and queasily shifting light, and she was soon saying things to Karen that she hadn't even known she'd been thinking. Words bubbled up.

'Was I happy with Adrian?' she asked, lowering

128

her spoon into the minty green sludge of the soup. 'I thought I was. If anyone had asked me, I think I would have said that I was. I would have said that, like in all marriages, we'd been through some bad times. But how do you know if you're happy? You stop asking yourself things like that after a bit, don't you? You just say: this is what I've got. Especially after you've had children together. You don't even think to yourself about what you want from life, or stand back to look at it. Not properly you don't; or I didn't, anyway. Weird, eh, not even to know if you're happy with someone. How did I get to be like that? I used to be so clear about what I wanted from life.'

She stopped for breath; picked up her wine and took a deep gulp. She wanted to get drunk, to weep and be hugged better. Wanted to shout and giggle. Wanted to run through the streets in the rain.

'Well,' began Karen, laying down her fork.

'When he left,' continued Irene, 'I was like someone who'd been in a terrible car crash, like that man we once saw when we were on a bike ride together. Remember? When we were just kids and your mum gave us a picnic and we just set off. The car was turned over in the ditch and he staggered out and there was blood all over his face and he was walking jerkily, like a marionette, but all he kept saying was that he'd lost his false teeth. That's what I was like. I just stumbled along through the days. All that mattered were the children. The children he'd fucking abandoned. But was I like that because the man I loved had left me, or because—well, I don't know. Because I'd been *left*? Because I was alone and lonely and afraid and my life hadn't turned out the way I'd meant it to? Because I'd failed.'

'You never failed,' said Karen in a sentimental voice, laying her hand over the top of Irene's.

'Failed,' Irene repeated. Then, more loudly and bellicosely, 'Failed, failed, failed.' I mustn't have more wine, she thought, even as she took a giant gulp.

'You mustn't think of it like that. He's the one who failed. Your soup's going cold.'

'It's meant to be cold. He didn't fail. Actually, that's the bloody irony of the thing. For our entire marriage he felt he was failing because his acting never took off. Everywhere he looked, his friends were doing better than him. And I was having to do the earning for both of us, though God knows I hardly earn anything. We got through all that, more or less. Then, as soon as he started being just a bit more successful, maybe turning a corner at last, he fell in love with someone else. Like he needed someone new to go with the new him, or the him he was hoping to turn into. I was just the old, ordinary, worn-out model. An old shoe. Such a cliché, isn't it?'

'It is,' agreed Karen, pouring more wine into Irene's glass and her own.

Later, before the pasta arrived, Irene suddenly said, 'Don't you loathe things like spritzing?'

'What?' said Karen. 'What are you on about?'

'You know, people who talk about spritzing themselves with perfume. I get so irritated I feel my head's going to come off—it makes me think of these glitzy women in sheer stockings and sexy black suits who are always rushing around from gym to conference room to kitchen, being all sexy and domestic.' She knew, as she said it, that she was talking about Frankie—the chic solicitor in her expensive leather shoes and dark suits, the tousled woman draped in Adrian's rumpled shirt and smelling of wine and sex. 'Then there's those people who talk about the au pair problem and the nanny problem. They're even worse. *Oh dear, the nanny doesn't iron the clothes properly blah fucking blah . . .*'

'Um, Irene—I probably do that, actually. Talk about the nanny.'

'Oh well.' Irene giggled. 'You probably do and I probably would if I could. I don't hate you, of course. But you know what I mean—women who go on about the difficulty of being—what is it?— *time-poor*. Yuck!'

'We are time-poor though. Money-rich and time-poor.'

'Bah! You may be; you're a successful business woman. I'm just a bit poor. Or poorer than you, at any rate. I keep hearing these phrases. Ahead of the curve. It makes me feel ill.'

'You seem to feel very strongly about this,' Karen said primly.

'I want us to make the world a better place; I don't want to be ahead of the fucking curve. Which is just as well, considering how I'm miles behind it. Or the other day on the tube I heard someone say that everyone needed at least £12,000 a year for holidays. They didn't say "want", they said "need". Twelve thousand pounds! How much do they think teachers earn? What about the people dying of Aids in Botswana? Or the two women I followed up the escalators in some department store and they were going on about the wedding present list.

131

I wanted to punch them. Am I talking too loudly? I am, aren't I?'

The pasta arrived and she pushed her fork into its tangle and twisted it round. 'Then there's sex.'

She said it emphatically enough for other people to turn their heads.

'What about sex?' said Karen, giggling nervously.

'Well, it's all so complicated, isn't it?'

'That's true.'

'Do you and Mac have a good sex life?'

'God, Irene. You go for months treating me like a distant acquaintance and now you're asking me about my sex life.'

'Yeah, but that's the point. We've never talked about sex, have we?'

'Haven't we? I guess not.'

'No. We've talked about everything else, but somehow it's not possible to talk about sex straightforwardly. I can't anyway and when someone I know does it, it somehow makes me cringe. It sounds fake, or boastful, or makes me feel inadequate, or prurient, or something. I don't know. I couldn't even talk about sex with Adrian, for God's sake. So what's that—you can have sex with someone but not talk about it with them? Isn't that strange? That's why girls get pregnant—they can have sex in the back of a car no problem, but can't ask the boy to put on a condom.'

Or later, pushing the half-finished pasta aside: 'He once said that he was chucking me on the rubbish heap.'

'That's unbelievably cruel.'

'I felt so humiliated, I can't describe it. I could hardly bring myself to set foot outside. I thought everyone was looking at me with this awful pity—well, they probably were. Still are. I'll always be someone who was left.'

'No!'

'It's true. Whatever happens next in my life, I was left. I wanted him and he didn't want me. He threw me over.'

'That's not the way to think of it.'

'It's hard not to. You don't know how that feels, do you? I bet no one's ever left you.'

'Well . . .' said Karen vaguely.

'No. There you are.' She pushed a forkful of pasta into her mouth and chewed. It tasted like wet cardboard in her mouth. 'I went to Frankie's flat, you know.' All of a sudden, Irene didn't feel so tipsy. She looked carefully across at Karen, who sat straighter in her chair.

'I did know, actually,' she said neutrally.

'I thought you might. What did she say about it?'

'She said—um, she said you were distraught.'

'I was crazy. Out of my mind with it.' Just the memory of that evening made Irene feel sick with shame. Only the thought of the orange curving beautifully through the air cheered her up.

'She feels very bad about it, you know.'

'Good.'

'She always liked you.'

'Does that make it better?'

'No, of course not. It makes it worse—that's the point.'

'You were like my second family when I was a teenager. I used to love the way you were this great welcoming gang, while at home it was just me and my poor mother in our quiet little house.'

'I'm sorry. I feel like it's my fault somehow.'

133

'Oh no.' The air went out of Irene, leaving her shrivelled and sad. She rubbed her face. 'It's not even really Frankie's fault. I know that. Women always blame the other woman, don't they?'

'Do you blame him then?'

'I don't know. I don't know anything any more.'

'We've all been worrying about you, you know.'

'Have you?'

'You seemed so brittle.'

'Maybe I was. But brittle people can go to pieces. Anyway, I've gone off the whole idea of men.'

'I'll remind you of that when you meet someone.'

'You'll have to wait an awfully long time.'

Walking home arm in arm, Irene said again: 'You knew, didn't you?'

'How many times do I have to tell you . . . ?'

'*You knew.*'

The atmosphere between them changed.

'Irene, please. You're behaving like a mad woman.'

'Maybe I am a mad woman.'

'What good do you think it does, hunting everything down like this?'

'Cut the crap. Just tell me you knew.'

'OK.' Karen stopped dead, took her arm out of Irene's, and looked straight at her. 'I knew. Not at first, and not the details, but yes, I knew. I knew and I hated knowing and didn't tell you because it wasn't my secret to tell and I thought it would all blow over and you wouldn't be harmed. And later, I didn't tell you because I knew you'd feel I'd betrayed you somehow by not telling you earlier. There. Does that make you feel better?'

134

'No. But at least I know. That's what I want. I don't want to be patronized and protected. I want to know.'

They walked on in silence, apart.

*   *   *

How do you change, she said to herself in the mirror—the only person she could talk to any more who would have the faintest idea what she was going on about. How do you change and grow and let the world mark you and shape you, and yet at the same time stay married? How can two people do that: choose love and yet choose freedom, choose safety and yet pursue adventure? Hmm? She stared at herself, hands on her hips and eyebrows raised. That's the big question for all of us. How? Tell me. I badly need to know. The face stared back, giving nothing away.

*   *   *

'Steve, this is Irene. Irene, Steve.'

Lisa's bright rushed introduction before she disappeared back into the kitchen made Irene's heart sink. Oh God, she'd finally agreed to come over for dinner, and here she was being introduced to a suitable fucking man: Steve with a high forehead and thick black hair and a nervous way of fiddling with the neck of his shirt. His wife had probably just run off with his best friend, and they were supposed to sit next to each other and talk about it. A furious thudding started up in her head; she could hardly breathe for the hot vexation inside her.

135

'Hi,' she said shortly.

'Hello.' He held out a hand and squeezed her fingers. 'I work with Gordon. It's very nice to meet you. I've heard of you from Karen and Mac.'

'Oh,' she said. 'Well then.'

He ploughed on stoically. 'Only good things, I assure you.'

She made an indeterminate sound and gazed around desperately. She was going to behave badly; she knew she was.

'Like, you have three wonderful daughters.'

'Yes. Well, there are three of them anyway.'

Now what? She sat on the sofa and started pushing nuts into her mouth, chewing vigorously. She could feel her jaw bones crack.

'Karen says you teach children with dyslexia.'

'Yes,' she said. It sounded very abrupt so she added, idiotically, 'indeed,' then gave a hysterical snort.

'Interesting.'

'Yes. What do you do?'

'I work with Gordon; that's how I know him. Computer programs.'

'Of course, you said. Stupid of me.' She slapped her head with her hand then put some more nuts into her mouth. 'Um, do you live near here?' she went on in a thick voice.

'No. South London.'

'Ah.' She paused and then said it again, louder: 'Aha!'

'With my two boys, some of the time at least.'

'Oh?' she said drearily. Here it came.

'Yes. But mostly alone. Their mother left last year, you see.'

'Oh dear,' she said. 'I'm so sorry.' Those were

the right words, weren't they? That was the kind of thing you should say.

'It's all right,' he said. 'It had been a long time coming. It was my fault really. I was stupid.'

'Stupid,' she repeated. She knew exactly what 'stupid' meant. She could hear Lisa banging a pan in the kitchen; Gordon saying something, then laughing.

'If only I could turn back the clock,' he went on.

'Yes.'

'Gordon says you were left too?'

'Yup,' she said curtly. 'That's me.'

'It must have been painful, with your daughters and everything.'

'You could say that.' More nuts, a gulp of wine to wash them down. She glared at him through her watery, maddened eyes.

'It's lonely, isn't it?'

'Can be.'

'Things do get better though?' He was gazing sympathetically at her, and she understood they were meant to be two victims of a disaster sharing stories.

'It's private,' she said, standing up, noticing suddenly that her shirt was on inside out; there was a faded label on its side and the buttons scratched her wrists. Oh well, who cared? 'Not something I go around sharing with whoever I sit next to.'

'I'm sorry. I never meant to pry,' he said very stiffly.

'No. You probably didn't.'

She left early, pleading a sudden migraine.

*   *   *

137

I'm in the middle, she said to herself in the middle of one wakeful night, sitting on the stairs with her chin cupped in her hands. I'm reaching the middle of my life and I'm looking forwards and looking backwards. When you're very young you hope, and when you're very old you remember. But when you're in between, you have to do both. Hope and memory, faith and loss, beginning and ending all at the same time. It's a wonder we don't all go raving mad.

*   *   *

In late May Adrian rang up, while the girls were with him, and asked her if he could take them away in the summer, to see Frankie's mother.

'But she lives in Australia now!'

'Yes.'

'But—you can't take them across the other side of the world.'

'They'd love it.'

'You've talked to them about it?'

'Well, not really talked. We mentioned it.'

'That is so underhand.'

'They just overheard us.'

'Australia! You can't be serious about this.'

'Why? We agreed at mediation that I could have them for half the summer holidays.'

'Yes, but I didn't think that meant—well, I was thinking about sharing out days and things like that, not—you know, going away. Not like that. How long for?'

'Three weeks.'

'What! You don't mean this. Adrian, Aggie's only three, for God's sake. She sometimes still

138

wears a nappy at night. She's hardly ever spent a night away from home . . .'

'She wouldn't be away from home—she'd be with me, her father.'

'It's not the same.'

'And they're very fond of Frankie, you know.' He said this with sickening compassion.

'Bah!'

'Irene, I know it's hard . . .'

'It's just not possible.' Then she added, more honestly, 'It's not fair.'

But when the girls came home talking excitedly about kangaroos and luminous fish, Irene listened to them with a feeling of dread, and then rang Adrian up once more.

'I'll think about it. OK?'

'Thank you; I knew you'd see reason . . .'

'It's got nothing to do with reason, and I'm not doing it for you, and I haven't agreed. I said I'd think about it.'

'OK.'

Two weeks later, Frankie booked five flights, to be paid for by herself and her mother, to Sydney, travelling out on Monday, 28 July, returning three weeks and two days later.

*   *   *

Dark, jittery days.

Rage spurted through Irene's veins. She was a laboratory of smoking, bubbling, frothing, hissing phials; sick-yellow and snot-green potions. Toxic, murderous, ready to explode.

CHAPTER FOURTEEN

On a Saturday morning in early July, Irene went shopping with Sasha, while Karen looked after Clem and Aggie went to her childminder's for the morning. She put all thoughts of her debts behind her and bought two large travel bags and three small backpacks for the plane journey, three wash bags with toothbrushes, miniature tubes of toothpaste, flannels. Sasha chose a summer skirt for herself, pale blue with tiny sprigs of pink flowers, and a shiny pink ribbon round the hem. They got several sleeveless tops to go with it, a cardigan, a pair of board shorts, some sandals and some tough trainers, a new pair of baggy jeans and a hoodie, blue, with green sleeves. Irene bought three waterproof jackets which could be packed into nylon bags the size of a handkerchief; three swimsuits with long arms and legs against the sun—although Sasha kept telling her it was winter in Australia, it wouldn't be that hot—and three sun hats. She got a £10 camera for Sasha and also a disposable underwater camera for when they were at the Great Barrier Reef. At W.H. Smith, they chose books with bright covers and unlined paper for each of the girls, which would serve as diaries, scrapbooks and picture books, and then stocked up on new crayons and gel pens, glue and scissors. Irene told Sasha she had to write something down about each day, so she would know all the exciting things the three of them had done.

Then they had lunch together. Sasha sat at the table behind the tall menu, swinging her bare, tanned legs. She was wearing a strappy top and some white pedal pushers and one of her friends had taught her how to put her hair into a messy bun. She looked suddenly older, thought Irene, and very self-possessed with her small, buttoned-up face and her cool grey eyes. She studied the menu and then asked for spaghetti with bacon and a banana milkshake. She said she would like to have the raspberry ice cream afterwards. Irene ordered herself a salad and a glass of sparkling water.

'Well,' she said, after the waiter had gone. 'Are you very excited?'

'I don't want to be bitten by a Box Jellyfish.'

'I don't think it's the season.'

'What will you do?'

'Goodness, I haven't really thought about it.'

'You can't go away.'

'What do you mean?'

'It'd be horrible thinking there was no one waiting for us.'

'Oh,' said Irene. 'But I have to have a life too.'

'You could go to the gym.'

'I don't belong to a gym.'

'Frankie and Daddy go to this really cool one with a pool and everything. They go every day together.'

'Good for them.'

'Except Frankie has to be careful now.'

'Does she?' said Irene, suddenly wary.

'Yes. That's what Daddy said anyway.'

'Why?'

Sasha just shrugged. Her milkshake arrived and she took a long suck at the straw then wiped her mouth with her napkin.

Irene watched her and then said, carefully: 'Do you ever want to ask me anything about . . .'

'No!'

'OK, but if you ever . . .'

'I won't.'

'OK then, my darling.'

'What about you?' asked Sasha.

'What *about* me?'

'Will you be all right when we're gone?'

'Of course I will be.'

'Sometimes when you hug me goodnight, you say you don't know what you'd do without me.'

'I don't mean it like that. It's a figure of speech. I mean, without you in the world.'

'But Mummy, I'll always be in the world.'

*   *   *

The children's departure came closer, like the wall of a great ship gradually blocking off the horizon. She couldn't see beyond it, although of course she knew what was there. The deserted sea. The great grey stretch of time, with its cold slapping waves and unimaginable depths. She had not spent more than two or three nights alone for twelve years.

*   *   *

She had an evening for her students' parents, who all arrived at the door with anxious, expectant faces. One mother kept saying tearfully: 'But will he get better?' as if her son had an illness which one day would go away. She went to Sasha's parents' evening and heard how she had become a little withdrawn; rather secretive and was refusing to choose a partner to go up to secondary school with. She said she wanted to go alone. She looked through Sasha's work. In her weekly diary, she always wrote about what she had done with Adrian and Frankie, whom she called, formally, 'my parents', not with Irene.

She went to Clem's and heard how she was disruptive in class; they'd had to deduct rather a lot of team points from her, but it didn't seem to make much difference. She fought with the boys at playtime.

She sat with Ruth at her final lesson of the term and heard how the fertility treatment hadn't worked and now they had to save up for the next round but it was so expensive and her husband didn't know if they should go through with it, but if they didn't, if they didn't . . . At this point Ruth cried into her tea and Irene put a tentative hand on her arm and told her she was sorry, so sorry.

She went to the final assembly, where Clem's class put on sunglasses and floppy hats and sang 'The Sun Has Got Its Hat On'—although that day it was raining steadily. She rearranged lessons so she could go to the sport's day, where she saw Sasha losing at the hoop race. Her face, that had been open with eagerness when she stood on the starting line, closed like a door when she reached the ribbon and looked around her and saw everyone else had finished. She saw Clem win the sack race, shooting off before the starting whistle went and bounding along in her hessian, chest out, with a purple, cheating face and gleaming eyes. She ran in the mothers' race herself, although she was absurdly nervous before it began, and came fifth out of fourteen. She went with Aggie to the

143

teddy bears' picnic in the park that her play group had organized, and sat on a prickly rug in the hot sun with other mothers as their children tottered around on the grass and pushed each other and howled while heat rash erupted on their chubby arms.

Late at night, she cooked rock cakes for the end-of-term party. Her shoulders ached; there was a band of tension wrapped like wire round her temples; her eyes were hot pebbles in her skull.

She bent over Aggie as she lay asleep in her bed and her daughter's eyes snapped open, like a doll tipped upright. She stared glassily.

'You're a bit of old rope, Mummy,' she said in a thick, frayed voice. 'Bit of old rope.'

* * *

The girls had five days between term ending and leaving for Australia. They went to the playground in the park, and for hours Irene pushed Aggie on the swings, ran in a circle with the roundabout until she could hardly breathe and her head was spinning wildly, bought ice creams. One day, they went to the outdoor swimming pool with Karen and Ben. They had a day out in Kew Gardens, where Clem ran off and hid among the palm trees for so long that Irene alerted the security guards. She cooked them comforting meals and afterwards they all sat squashed on the sofa together, watching favourite videos, Aggie hotly on her lap, with her hair tickling her cheek. Everything that was ordinary became special. Far away, she felt the tears, but they wouldn't fall. She was like a country in drought; a dry, heavy sky and a parched

144

landscape.

*　　　*　　　*

As they pushed the trolley—Aggie sitting on top of it, the rest of them pushing from behind—through the revolving doors, Irene saw Adrian. He was looking for them to come from a different direction, so for a moment she had a chance to study him. He was dressed in jeans and a baggy, olive-green tee-shirt with some emblem she couldn't read on the back. His arms and his face were tanned. He looked handsome, vigorous, utterly unfamiliar.

Then he turned and saw them. He raised his hand in greeting and Sasha and Clem ran to meet him, while Aggie, clambering down from the trolley, wailed for them to wait for her.

'Daddy!' said Sasha in an almost-sob and pressed herself against him. He lifted her up and kissed her on her lips, then swung Clem in a wide circle so her legs flew out. He bent down and hugged Aggie, pressed the tip of her nose. 'Beep,' he said and she giggled wildly. Irene stood behind the trolley and watched them.

'Hi,' he said, coming over to her. 'Thanks for bringing them. It made it much easier, what with me coming down from Scotland and Frankie . . .'

'It's OK.'

'Right, well. I'll take them from now, shall I?'

'You need their passports. Here.'

'God, yes, what am I thinking of?'

'I've put a spare pair of knickers and shorts in Aggie's backpack for the journey, just in case.'

'Fine.'

145

'And Sasha has sucking sweets for take-off and landing. She gets earache in planes.'

'Good. Do you want to, you know, say goodbye now. It'd probably be easier—Frankie's waiting by the check-in.' He gestured awkwardly.

'Right.' She turned to the children. 'You're going to have a fantastic time, I know. Give me a hug and be off with you.'

They could hardly be bothered with her. Aggie was already trying to push the trolley towards the queues and Irene had to kiss her on the top of her head. Clem gave her a brief squeeze. Sasha presented her cheek.

'They'll be fine,' said Adrian.

'Ring me sometime.'

'Yes—it might be hard though. We'll be in the middle of nowhere half the time.'

'But if there's any problem—' She sucked her high, splintering voice down to its normal pitch. 'Let me know.'

'There won't be. But if there is, you'll know at once. Of course.'

'At least when you arrive, so I know they're safe.'

'Fine.'

He started to turn but she put a hand on his arm, then dropped it at once as though she had been burned. She wanted to put her arms round his neck and drag him towards her and never let him go. She wanted to put her fingers round his neck and squeeze and squeeze until his eyes bulged in his stupid, handsome, young-again face.

'Adrian?'

'Yes.'

She stared, swallowed hard, wrenched her face back to what might be normal, who knew any

146

more? 'Take care of them.'

'Of course.'

He strode across to the trolley and pushed it away on its skewed wheels. Sasha walked beside him, her little hand laid over his large one on the handle. Clem and Aggie jostled in front of them. They pushed their way into the crowd. Now she could make out Frankie, her dark blonde head halfway along the queue. Adrian and the girls made their way across. She saw Frankie bend down to embrace them. Irene knew she must leave, yet still she stood pressed against a concrete pillar and watched them. Their five figures edged forward in the queue. Occasionally they were hidden by other people, but whenever she saw them they were talking animatedly. Adrian picked up Aggie and put her on his shoulders so she rose above the press of travellers: a chubby little girl with crooked pigtails. Sasha and Frankie were in charge of the trolley. Clemmie dipped in and out of sight. Could it really be that in an hour or so they would be in a plane, flying to Australia without her?

At last they reached the check-in and handed over their passports. They lifted their bags onto the belt and watched them disappear. Adrian lifted Aggie off his shoulders and they all walked together towards Departures. Irene stepped back further, anxious lest they see her skulking there. But though they passed not far from her, none of them looked up. Sasha was holding onto Aggie, tugging her along, and Adrian had his hand on Clem's spiky head. Frankie walked beside him. She was wearing a dark pink shirt and loose faded jeans. As Irene watched, Adrian put out his other hand and wrapped it around her shoulders. She

147

saw them smile at each other. And then she turned
away.

CHAPTER FIFTEEN

Her skin stuck to the seat of the car; sweat
gathered on her upper lip. She put on her dark
glasses, opened the windows, slid a tape of Bach's
violin sonatas in and turned the volume up. The
music fell in planes of sound into her skull,
blocking out thought; the sun slanted through the
window.

She stopped at the supermarket, putting off the
moment when she'd step into the empty house and
close the door behind her. But she didn't know
what to put into the trolley, which was
intimidatingly large; family-sized. She wheeled it
slowly up and down the aisles: four green apples,
one small loaf of wholemeal bread, six free-range
eggs, one pint of semi-skimmed milk, some freshly
squeezed orange juice which she normally never
bought because it was so expensive. She stared at
the objects at the bottom of the trolley. Now what?
She went across to the drink section and took a
bottle of whisky and a bottle of cheap wine off the
shelves.

Queuing up to pay, she stood behind a
bedraggled and scrawny young woman with a baby
in a sling, a tiny girl strapped into the child's seat in
the trolley, a dummy in her mouth, and a small boy
about Aggie's age who kept tugging at his mother's
skirt.

'Mummy,' he said. 'Mu-um.'

'Not now, Jack.' She was hauling objects out of the trolley and shoving them onto the belt: nappies, biscuits, sausages, tins of beans, oven-ready chips. Every time she stooped down, the baby half woke in the sling and whimpered. The woman looked wretchedly hot. Her hair was plastered to her forehead and there were circles of sweat under her armpits.

'But Mummy . . .' The boy gave an unmistakable, tight-legged jiggle.

'Not *now*. How many times do I have to tell you?'

'I'm desperate.'

'What?'

'I need a wee.'

'Oh God!'

'It's not my fault.'

'I asked you before if you needed a wee. Hold it, can't you?'

'Shall I take him for you?' said Irene.

'Mummy.'

'*Let me take him.*'

'Hold it!' she said to the boy, ignoring Irene. 'I'm nearly done.'

She went to the other end of the check-out to stuff her shopping into bags and sling it back into the trolley. The boy jiggled some more. He looked close to tears. Irene smiled at him encouragingly but he stared at her as if she were an object he'd never seen before and didn't recognize at all. His mother paid in cash. She handed over five ten-pound notes, then scrabbled in her purse for coins. Laboriously, she counted out four pounds, most in ten-pence and twenty-pence pieces. Then she started counting out coppers, but was still short by twenty-eight pence. She scrabbled in her purse as if the money would miraculously appear, then dug around in the bottom of her bag where she found a five-pence piece. Irene wanted to offer her the change; she couldn't bear to see the little boy crossing his legs and biting his lips, staring at his mother in desperation.

'I'll have to put back the crisps,' she said. 'That'll do it.'

The woman keyed in the reduction. The little girl in the trolley seat spat out her dummy and started to cry. The baby in the sling joined in, opening its mouth so Irene could see its pink tonsils. The boy suddenly relaxed. He ducked his head down to hide his tears and sidled up to his mother, pulling her skirt again.

'Wait!' she snapped. 'All of you. Can't you see I'm almost done?'

'I couldn't help it,' he whispered. His trousers were dark down one leg.

'Oh you haven't. I told you to bloody wait! This is the last straw, it is!'

Lifting her arm, she cuffed him round his head with the side of her hand so he staggered back towards Irene, who stepped forward to steady him, keeping a hand on his shoulder. She felt his dampness against her bare legs; she saw his tear-stained cheeks and his skinny neck and sticking-out ears. There was a high-pitched buzzing in her head; everything was happening to someone else. She was a stranger, a thin and angry woman with sweat under her armpits and a lump blocking her throat who was about to behave inappropriately. She considered herself for a moment. She didn't need to be like this, she could return to her old self right now. But it was too late.

She heard herself say, in a loud, shrill voice: 'Don't dare do that! He couldn't help it.'

The woman turned to her. Irene saw that her face was red with wretchedness and humiliation and that her angry mouth was open. She was shouting something, but Irene couldn't hear what it was she was saying.

Then her own voice came again, from a long way off: 'Do you have any idea of how lucky you are? You should always cherish precious things.'

She saw her hand, all veins and ragged nails, reaching forward and grasping the woman by her collar. She was aware that people were looking at her, but they were a massed blur in the background while overhead the lighting hummed and her head throbbed with booming, un-tuned fizzing sounds. The woman, still shouting at her, threw off her hand so it fell uselessly to her side, then yanked her son backwards and marched off with her trolley and her children.

'Are you all right?'

'What?'

'Are you all right?' The woman at the till looked embarrassed and a bit gleeful. 'Do you want to pay now? Excuse me, madam, are you all right?'

'Oh. Yes. Right.'

Irene stumbled to the till and handed over her credit card. She signed her name without looking at the amount, her signature jarring across the slip, then walked from the shop, trying to stay upright. She felt as if she was made of cheap glass, brittle and transparent. If anyone pushed against her she would shatter.

She loaded her bags in the boot, one by one,

151

their weight dislocating her arms and her legs jangling underneath her until she thought she would collapse in a pile of shards on the ground. Then she climbed into the driving seat, turned the key with spindly, clattering fingers, and headed home, driving very carefully. The wheel trembled under her hands; lights changed to red, to green, bouncing inside her eyelids. She tried to remember which pedal belonged to the accelerator, the brake, the clutch. The great yellow ball of the sun clanged in her head. She parked outside her house, took out the shopping bags and shuffled them up the path, opened the door and stepped inside, where it was cool and dark as a church.

She took off her sandals and the grainy boards comforted her stinging feet. In the kitchen, she saw that dust motes spun in the shafts of light striking through the slightly opened slatted blinds. It looked beautiful, she thought, like a painting she used to know in a different time. She put the food away, though it took so long and the clock ticked louder and louder in her head, setting off jabbing echoes. Went upstairs, dragging her feet step by step.

Closed the curtains in the girls' bedrooms, shrouding them in drugged grey light, pulled the sheets, pillowcases and duvet covers off each of the beds, and put them downstairs beside the washing machine, a soft white heap of cotton. There was a light flashing on her answering machine and she looked at it for a minute but didn't bother to listen to it.

Like a sleepwalker, she went out into the garden, where she bent to pick up the bucket and spade, the plastic mug and the headless Barbie

152

from the sandpit. Clem's wooden sword was planted firmly into a flower bed, and she drew it out and wiped the mud off on the grass as if it were blood. There was a bird singing loudly from somewhere, but she couldn't tell where the sound was coming from and when she tried to look the flat shiny blue of the sky blinded her and the clouds wheeled round so that she felt she was falling upwards.

She padded back into the kitchen, over the tiles. She picked up a tumbler off the draining board, dropped three cubes of ice into it, then unscrewed the top off the whisky bottle. She poured a generous amount over the ice. It was a glorious colour, she thought—amber like the earrings Adrian had once given her in that different world she remembered like a dream, and it glinted when she swirled it round and it burned her throat when she swallowed it. She could feel it like a narrow lane of fire flaming through her.

She walked into the living room and, from the depleted stack of CDs, picked out the *Chants d'Auvergne* and put it on. Wild female voices, like wind pouring through her. So glorious—how had she never realized how glorious it was? It hurt her in the solar plexus and behind the eyes. It hurt her deep inside herself, in a place she never knew existed until now.

She helped herself to another tumblerful of whisky and when the music was finished she took the glass upstairs, into her bedroom. She closed the curtains against the softening light and took off all her clothes; then she sat at the bottom of the bed with her drink and looked at herself in the mirror. Was that her body? She had pale brown arms and legs and a milky white stomach with a low neat scar where she'd had a Caesarean with her last birth. Oh that birth. Her beautiful, beautiful baby. Bony ankles, hollowed hips, chestnut-red pubic hair like a fuzzy arrow's head, jutting pelvis, narrow hunched shoulders with a rash of coppery freckles, thin neck beginning to show the signs of age. Long feet, long hands, poky wrists and sharp elbows. Hacked gingery hair. Was that her face? A triangular freckled face, freckles on her lips even and on her forehead up to her hairline. She stared at herself in the glass: was she really that plain, that sad, that mad?

There rose up in her mind another picture: a man and a woman and three little girls, glowing with life and excitement, passing a few feet in front of her and not seeing her where she stood pressed against the pillar.

No. This wasn't her, not this raw, dismal creature bowed over at the end of the bed. The real her was somewhere else—a soft and curving golden girl with a waterfall of coppery hair who lay in the grass with the man who would be her lover, who laughed at the table surrounded by the people she adored, who danced through the night, who said I do I do I do I do to life. I do.

Irene lifted her tumbler and hurled it against the mirror where it broke into pieces. A kaleidoscope of glass spun out from the target; pale gold liquid trickled down her thin reflected face, down the picture of her white scarred stomach. She hauled the lamp off the bedside table and, holding it by its neck, she crashed it into her naked reflection which, like a spider, scuttled towards her raising thin limbs. The lamp shattered and a web-like

154

crack grew across the glass. In her hand she held the bulb, its bare filament, and its splintered neck that bit into her palm. She stood up, swaying slightly. Drops of blood fell onto her skin like warm summer rain. Glass caught in her feet; she felt a tepid wetness and looking down saw blood seeping between her toes, a trail of blood on the rug. She went downstairs, naked, and collected the whisky bottle and then trailed back, leaving bloody footprints behind her. She lurched into the bathroom, had a pee and drank some whisky straight out of the bottle, so it didn't even touch her mouth. Then she went and lay down on her bed, the duvet pushed down past her stinging feet, the blood staining the sheet in great scarlet swathes. She closed her eyes. She closed her eyes but the pictures were all the same.

*   *   *

There was a sob. A dry racking sob like a lonely elephant bellowing; a battered seal on a rock in the ocean; some great, oily seabird shrieking far out at sea and the waves rolling endlessly past. She heard it and put her hands over her ears to block out the sound. But there it was again, again, again, hoarse and long, cracking at the edges. It filled the room and it filled her head; inside and outside was the same sound, booming and breaking, and she couldn't get away from it.

There was salt water. She tasted it in her parched mouth and it stung her skin beneath her eyes; it ran down into her neck and, when she turned, into her ears, into her hair. Floods of salt water. Where did it all come from? She would run dry. Her body would be empty of water, empty of sound. Nothing left, just a hollowed-out place.

Her sheets were wet where her feet were still bleeding.

*   *   *

She opened her throbbing eyes and it was dark outside. She closed them again, let herself drift once more into the ocean of memories. Lay tossed by them on her endless bed.

She'd met Adrian during a weekend they'd both spent in a large house just outside Exeter, to celebrate a birthday of a friend from university, whose boyfriend was a friend of Adrian's. She'd been light-headed with her mother's recent death, bereft and dizzy, appallingly relieved at her new freedom, thrillingly alive and burningly wretched. And there he was, a would-be actor full of plans, with a dazzling smile and a silver tongue. They had been conscious of each other at once, from the moment he carried her case up the stairs for her, and there had been a surreptitious thrill to the two days—sitting round the large table with a crowd of other people and looking across at each other, flushing, glancing away; lying on the lawn in the hot sun after lunch, their damp, outstretched limbs just a few inches from each other; dancing together in the early hours and at last he had kissed her, in the garden beside the copper beech tree, with music pulsing out of the open doors. He'd been freedom and family all at once; adventure and safety. He would heal her, hurl her into a new world. In a dark room at the top of the house, quietly so no one would hear, he'd lifted off her

156

dress and touched her skin with the tips of his fingers. He'd whispered in her ear that now he'd found her, he wasn't going to let her go.

Irene wrapped her own arms round her deserted body, on top of the bloody sheets. She rocked herself and little whimpers broke free of her mouth, fragments of sound like petals of dead ash in the air.

'Please please please please,' someone said, she said. 'Please.'

The sound grew louder until it was beating in waves against the inside of her skull.

*   *   *

Something was banging. She saw through half-closed lids that it was light, the washed grey light of early morning, which would brighten later into hot blue. She turned her back on the day. She let the day turn back into night.

*   *   *

Now the noise was a dribble of sound, higher-pitched and rocky, with the hint of words in there somewhere. She listened to the lament. Oh-oh-oh. That was it. Or no-no-no. Was that her voice, that querulous ladder of sound?

She needed a pee but she couldn't move. She closed her eyes and waded out once more into her dreams.

Her thick swirling dreams. Sometimes they mocked her with what she no longer had and she woke thinking she was happy and had to rediscover her misery all over again. And sometimes they reminded her of what she had lost, so that there was no escape, even in the great unbounded ocean of sleep.

She dreamt a voice calling to her, 'Mummy, mummy, mummy!' She jerked awake, and gazed around her room, which was the room she had slept in for so many years, night after night, and yet which looked so different now, ghostly and bare; stared down at the bottom of her bed half-expecting to see a child there, stretching out its arms, wanting her.

She dreamt a baby's cry that went on and on and in her dream she couldn't find where it was coming from, under the bed, in the cupboard, between the twisted sheets, but she knew she had to get to it before the crying stopped. But then the crying did stop, suddenly, just when she was close to it, and she woke to find tears rolling down her cheek.

She dreamt of bodies winding together on a bed. Whose bodies? She didn't know if she was dreaming her past or Frankie's present.

She didn't want to dream because she had no control over her dreams, anything could happen in them; she might see things she had hidden from herself; she might discover things she didn't want to know. But she didn't want to be awake either.

She lay on her bed, in the drying blood, and pictured them getting off the plane into a new and wonderful landscape. She remembered travelling with Adrian, shortly after they'd met. They'd backpacked through Europe together, sitting in coaches for days, hitching lifts, spending nights in their sleeping bags in fields off the roadside or in cheap, dark hotels in Paris, Naples, Athens, eking out their money as long as possible. She could still recall as if it were yesterday a day when they'd walked for miles along a dusty road with no cars passing and hills in a jagged rim around the horizon. They'd come to a small town where they'd bought a loaf of bread still damp and warm from the oven. They'd sat by the fountain in the main square and torn hunks off it. Moist, chewy bread and cold water in cupped hands; grimy golden skin.

'Come on, honey,' Adrian said in her dreams, holding out a hand to pull her up, smiling down at her. 'Come with me now. Come along with me.'

She held her arms towards him. Oh so happy to be here again. So very happy she could fly. Her heart was leaping in her throat; her heart was booming with joy and desire. No more dread. Everything beginning and everything possible.

CHAPTER SIXTEEN

There was a banging, then a sound of something breaking. Irene opened her eyes, dazed. There was sun shining through the curtains again; how was that possible? Was there someone downstairs? She felt dizzy in the unexpected light. Her head buzzed and hummed like a computer revving up; her swollen tongue stuck to the roof of her mouth. Were there footsteps? She blinked. Everything was unfamiliar but the same; nightmarish sameness. She lifted her hand and saw streaks of red. She smelt the ammonia-tang of urine. She'd wet her sheets like a baby. The door swung open.

'Irene? Irene!'

She tried to pull the duvet towards her to cover

her nakedness, but it was in a knotted heap at the bottom of her bed. She crossed her hands over her genitals, like a figure in a Victorian painting, and turned her face away.

'I didn't know,' she said.

'Irene, speak to me. Oh gracious, what's happened here? I'm calling an ambulance.'

'No! I'm not hurt. Please!'

She succeeded in pulling the duvet over her. Her whole body flushed hot with shame. She smelt the piss, saw the blood; the bottle of whisky half-empty on the table beside her. She saw Catherine Wattisham's stern, aghast face under her permed grey hair; her neat tweedy body amid the stinking wreckage of the room.

'What idiotic thing have you been up to?'

'I was about to get up. I've cried enough now I think. Yes, for sure.'

'Look at me. Now! I need to know you're all right. Have you taken anything?'

'Whisky,' said Irene, waving a limp hand towards the bottle.

'No pills?'

'Pills? No! I wouldn't do that. Is that what you thought? How can you think that? I just wanted to—'

'Where are you bleeding—are you menstruating?'

'What? No. Mirror broke. My feet.'

Dimly she remembered the spider in the glass. She half-raised herself and squinted towards the end of the bed. Yes, the mirror was broken, and the lamp. There were shards of glass all over the carpet. Drops of blood. There was something else too—a face in the cracked glass: a ghastly blood-smeared white face, with bleary eyes and an encrusted mouth; a crop of sticky, matted hair.

'Oh God,' she said, putting her hands over her eyes so she wouldn't have to see. 'God. I'm sorry, so sorry. I've been unbelievably stupid.'

Catherine pulled the duvet off her feet and started probing them with cool fingers. 'Yes, you certainly have,' she said. 'Hold still, there's still a bit of glass in you.'

'I'm all right now. I can manage.'

'Only a few grazes. You're lucky; it could have been far worse. How long have you been like this?'

Irene frowned. It hurt to think. 'How long? I don't know. What day is it now?'

'Thursday morning.'

'Oh no!' Irene swung herself out of bed. Her stomach lurched and the great metal ball inside her head swung and smashed against her skull. Her legs crumbled beneath her and the room tipped. She grabbed the bedpost. 'Three days! Three whole days! What if something's happened with the girls and they've tried to contact me and I wasn't here?'

'Calm down. Listen to me now, Irene. I'm going to run you a bath. While you're in it, I'll strip the bed and clear up as much of this mess as I can. Then you're going to eat a proper meal.'

'But I need to listen to the messages on the answering machine, just in case.'

'You're not doing anything until you've cleaned yourself up. I'll listen to them for you. I'm sure I can work it out.'

'Thank you,' said Irene feebly. A few final tears ran down her face. 'I don't know what to say. You must think I'm mad.'

'Hmm. We all go mad sometimes.'

161

*　　*　　*

Later, Irene remembered it in a blur: Catherine lowering her into a bath, making her drink several glasses of water. She said that the only messages on the machine were two from someone called Karen, one from Sarah, and two from a man called Jem. She could relax. Lying in the warm, soapy water with her stinging feet, the water turning pink, and listening to the sounds of cleaning going on, Irene felt as if she was a child again and her mother was bustling around next door, opening windows, pulling sheets from the bed and vacuuming the carpet, opening and shutting cupboards.

She washed her hair twice and rubbed her skin with a soapy flannel, feeling as if her skin had been peeled off her entirely. She scrubbed her nails with a brush. Then Catherine came in with a large towel and helped her out, wrapping her in its soft folds and giving her another towel for her head.

'Why are you here?' asked Irene, sitting down on her newly made bed.

'I came yesterday for your violin lesson, as arranged. I thought it was strange the curtains were all closed. You would have told me if you were going away. Then I came again today and peered through the letterbox. There was blood all over the hallway. So I broke in through your kitchen window.'

'Oh,' said Irene weakly, a little giggle forming in her chest. She couldn't imagine Catherine doing any of that—squeezing her stout, dignified body through a small gap, clambering into the kitchen

162

like a thief.

'I thought it was better than calling the emergency services.'

'Yes.'

'I made up your children's beds while I was at it, by the way. And put the bins out to be collected—I saw all your neighbours' were out so it must be collection day.'

'Thanks,' said Irene weakly.

'You don't have much in your fridge,' said Catherine. 'But there's bread that'll be all right if it's toasted and half a dozen eggs. So I'm going to scramble them, all right?'

'I feel sick.'

'I bet you do. And a big pot of coffee.'

'What time is it?'

'Just gone ten.'

'Don't you have somewhere else to be?'

'Not particularly.'

'I'll be all right you know.'

'I'm sure you will,' said Catherine briskly and left her to dress.

And it was true that Irene felt all right, although her head was light as an empty box and her body sore and hollow. She pulled aside the curtains and saw that outside the day was clear and bright, with a few white mackerel clouds on the horizon and a wind riffling through the silky green leaves. Everything looked clean, shining with promise. She looked down into the street below, where on Saturday nights crack dealers stood at the bus stop and drunk youths threw dustbin lids at windows. People were walking along in light summer clothes with open faces. She leant out of the window for a moment, hearing the sound of voices, distant music, the rumble of cars, someone calling.

She pulled on some cotton trousers that hung off her and a blue tee-shirt to match the sky, slid her feet into flip-flops, and then carefully negotiated the stairs. There was the smell of coffee and toast coming from the kitchen, and Catherine stood by the stove stirring eggs in a pan.

'I can't eat that much. I don't think I can eat anything.'

'I'm having some too.'

'Good.'

She looked out of the broken window into the garden. Yellow roses, lavender, buttercups and daisies on the uncut lawn, a dragonfly suspended a few inches from her, its wings pulsing.

'Here you are—brunch.'

They sat at the table in comfortable silence. Catherine finished her eggs in about a minute and a half, but Irene ate very slowly, chewing everything many times and washing down each mouthful with strong coffee.

'Good,' said Catherine when she'd finished. 'Do you want a violin lesson?'

'What? Now?'

'Why not?'

'I don't think—'

'Since I'm here.'

'All right then,' said Irene. 'I haven't practised much.'

'I imagine not. We'll start with scales.'

'Scales are good,' said Irene. 'Something matter-of-fact.'

She had expected Catherine to ask her about what had happened; to press her for assurances that she wouldn't do anything like it again. But

164

Catherine didn't ask her anything. She set up the music stand, tuned the violin, folded her arms and listened to Irene climbing up and down the ladder of notes with a frown on her face. 'Too sharp,' she said sternly. 'Watch that second finger of yours.' Then she put on her jacket, said she would see her next week unless she heard otherwise, and left, closing the door firmly behind her.

CHAPTER SEVENTEEN

Walking down the road, Irene marvelled at the softness of the air on her skin and the dazzle of the sun in her raw and blinking eyes. Everything seemed bright and new: the leaves that shimmered on the trees, dappling the light, the silver clouds that puffed on the turquoise horizon, the flowers in buckets outside the florist's—blazing blue delphiniums, lisianthus in floppy pink and lilac, the haze of yellow mimosa.

At the greengrocer's she stopped for a few moments to breathe in the heady scent before entering the cool, dark interior of the shop. There were open-mouthed sacks of muddy potatoes, tomatoes on the vine, purple lettuces with veined and curling leaves, baskets of small strawberries, velvet peaches, golden melons whose tops she pressed with her thumb to test their ripeness and vast green-striped water melons, some of which had been cut into thick red-pink slabs, blackcurrants mixed with tart redcurrants, gnarled organic apples, passion fruit. There were little, madly expensive baskets of wild mushrooms as

165

well—stout ceps and fluted orange chantarelles, withered black horns of plenty and white parasol mushrooms. She bent her head and sniffed in the odour of soil and decay. Joy caught her by the throat and for a moment she could hardly move or breathe for surprise and terror.

Inside the shop she bought a small bag of chantarelles, a pouch of basil leaves, two glossy nectarines, six purple plums with golden drops of juice oozing like sap out of their tops and a punnet of raspberries. At the baker's she bought a couple of crusty rolls and a square of the home-made, spicy gingerbread that Adrian used to get on Friday evenings for the family.

She walked home slowly, on coltish legs, looking about her as if she were newly released into the world, sights and sounds pouring into her brain. She still felt nauseous and the smell of garlic wafting from a kitchen or the sudden shaft of sunlight as she emerged from the shadow of a house was almost too much for her; she couldn't properly tell what delighted and what repelled her. When she got to her front door, she noticed that there was a blackbird singing from the roof, fat liquid notes pouring from its beak, and again that disturbing emotion that she'd felt in the greengrocer's halted her, so that she had difficulty turning the key in its lock. She put her shopping on the table and went straight out into the garden, where she sat on the lawn and ate one of the nectarines very slowly, catching the juice that dribbled down her chin, feeling the sun on her hair and on her arms. Then she went indoors and made herself a cup of tea which she drank with the gingerbread before wandering round the house,

166

opening windows, straightening already-straight covers in her daughters' deserted bedrooms. Downstairs, she rang a glazier and arranged with him to come round to fix the window in the early evening.

Then she answered the messages on the answering machine. First of all, Karen.

'Hello.'

'Irene. I've been trying and trying to reach you.'

'Yes, I know. I was—' She paused. 'I was all over the place.'

'Are you all right?'

'I think so. I feel odd. The girls have gone, you know.'

'I know.'

'I keep thinking I'll never see them again.'

'You will. Of course you will. It'll go in no time.'

'I guess. I'll have to think what to do with myself—I can't just sit here for three weeks waiting for them.'

'Come away with us.'

'No. I don't think so. It would be too odd—you and your family and me alone.'

'You're probably right. Have an adventure. Go and see Jem.'

'Yeah, maybe I will.'

*   *   *

Then Jem, who answered on the second ring.

'*Oui?*'

'Jem, it's me.'

'Irene. I've been trying to get hold of you. I left a couple of messages. Have you been away?'

'Not really, I just . . . I was—oh, never mind. I'll

167

tell you another time. How are you?'

'I'm OK. But I've got something to tell you.'

'Go on.'

'It's Juliet.'

'Juliet?' The air chilled around her. She waited for Jem to tell her he'd been dumped too. Then they'd just be a lonely brother and sister again. But he didn't sound as if he was going to tell her something disastrous; his voice was calm.

'She's not well. She'd been feeling run down for ages. But then . . .' He stopped.

'What is it?'

'It still feels weird to say it out loud.'

'What?'

'She's got cancer.'

'Oh Jem.'

'Breast cancer.'

'But she's too young!' said Irene. The picture of Juliet rose before her as she'd last seen her, sitting in this very kitchen with her pale, slightly asymmetrical face, her mass of dark hair, her soft full breasts under her cotton dressing gown, at home in the body which had now become her enemy. 'My age.'

'Yeah, well. She's got it anyway.'

'Oh bloody hell, I'm so sorry. When did you find out?'

'Four weeks ago now. Though we didn't know it was cancer then. It was just a lump. Lots of women get lumps and it doesn't mean anything.'

'Why didn't you tell me before?'

'We didn't tell anyone. We just wanted to live with it ourselves for a bit, if you see what I mean.'

'Did she find it early?'

'Quite early, and it'll probably be fine.'

168

'I don't know what to say. I can't imagine what you must be feeling, both of you.'

'That's the odd thing—we're fine. We're having a lovely time together—it's almost like falling in love all over again, especially when we hadn't told anyone and it was just our secret. I can't describe it properly. Maybe we're just in denial.'

He paused. 'It makes you realize what's important in life. And that's the point—we've decided to get married.'

'Have you? That's the way to do it. I'm very glad for you.'

'Yeah, me too. We'll have a little wedding—just us and four witnesses and a few of our closest friends. Then a big celebratory party and speeches and dancing and then Juliet will start chemo.'

'When is it?'

'Next Friday.'

'That soon!'

'I know it's short notice. We only decided on Sunday, though actually we had to start the proceedings three weeks ago, just in case we went ahead. All the bureaucracy, especially if you're not French. Anyway, the banns are posted in the *mairie* now. The point is, will you come over for it?'

'Of course I'll come.'

'And be a witness?'

'I wouldn't miss it for anything.'

'Mum's coming the day before. And Dad's flying over from the States.'

'*Dad*'s coming!'

'Yeah. Not just for me, I don't think—he said something about a business trip as well. God knows what business—I didn't dare ask.'

'God, I haven't seen him for years.'

'Me neither. I nearly didn't ask him, but then I thought, what the hell. He'll be diluted by the crowd anyway.'

'Mmm,' said Irene doubtfully. 'Maybe.'

'He'll be with Toni and his children.'

'His other children, you mean.'

'Yes. And all of Juliet's extended family are coming over from Dublin—all these cousins and childhood friends who'll completely outnumber us. So you see, I'll need you there. My ally.'

'I'll find out about flights at once. When do you want me to arrive, ideally?' She was already thinking ahead and her brain was frantic with the planning of small tasks and domestic details. As soon as she put the phone down, she would make a list: which airlines to try, how she'd have to contact Adrian and tell him her plans in case he needed to reach her, what to pack, what present she could buy.

And at the same time she was trying not to think ahead too much, to the time after the wedding when all images ended in a flurry of dark thoughts. She was full of questions that she wasn't going to ask. Will Juliet lose her hair? Does this mean she won't be able to have children? Is she in much pain? How does she feel about having her breast cut off from her body? How do you feel? Will she die? Does she think—like me and you, Jem—that when she dies there's nothing, that this life is absolutely all there is, nothing beyond except the great unending darkness, or is she a good Catholic girl who believes she will come face to face with her God and that dying is like crossing a threshold into another room? Is she scared, terrified, waking up in the middle of the night with loose bowels and a crazy beating heart?

'Come as soon as you can. Now. Tomorrow. Whenever. Then we can see you—and you can help us prepare. It wouldn't be the same without you. You're pretty much my only family, except Mum and Dad and they're—well, you know. It's a pity Sasha and Clem and Aggie can't be there.'

'I'll book something and call you back. Is there anything I can do? I mean, anything at all?'

'Just come and be with us. Be our witness. Wish us well.'

'I wish you well,' she said fervently. She held the receiver between both her hands as if she was praying. She wanted to say something large and important. She wanted to tell him how much she loved him and would always, always be there for him—but that would be too much like writing an obituary. 'I wish you all good things.'

*   *   *

Jem turned to Juliet, where she sat on the floor beside him, and picked up her hand, turning it over and kissing the palm.

'She's coming as soon as she can.'

'Good. I'm glad.'

'Juliet.'

'Mmmm.'

'Oh—nothing. I don't know. Just, Juliet.'

'I know. It's all right.'

*   *   *

There were no flights; none at all. Not to Montpellier, nor to Nîmes or Carcassonne or any

171

of the cities nearby. Even the expensive ones had gone. She tried on the net, and then she rang round travel companies. 'It is the summer, after all,' said one to her, and another: 'You should have booked before.'

'If it's so important, you'll just have to drive there,' said one.

Of course! She'd drive. Why hadn't she thought of that? It wouldn't take long, surely. How far was it? She'd spent holidays in France, but she'd never driven all the way through it. Anyway, it didn't matter how long it took. Work was over for the term, the children were away. If it took the entire week to drive it didn't matter. Indeed, it was like the answer to her need: this dash across France was how she would make her summer go by.

The ferries were full. She searched the net for Eurotunnel. It took less than a minute to find the site and within five minutes she had paid £123 by her credit card for a long-stay return trip, Folkestone to Calais Coquelles, going the day after tomorrow, Saturday, 2 August, in one of the last remaining slots, six minutes past four in the afternoon, arriving just thirty-five minutes later— twenty-five minutes earlier by clock time in France. She didn't have to specify when she would return, and the trains went four times an hour throughout the day.

She wrote her list and followed it methodically, ticking off each task as she completed it. Go to the bank for euros before it closed for the day; £50-worth would do for the time being. Ring Jem and tell him her travel plans and ask him to e-mail instructions for the drive into the city. Ring Catherine to put off her violin lessons. Ask Sasha's friend Kadija if she would look after the hamster for a couple of weeks or so. Cancel newspapers until further notice. Check road atlas to see approximately how long it will take to get to Folkestone. She could buy an atlas for France when she arrived there. Print out Jem's instructions. Take a deep breath and call up her father in America, who was buoyantly and undiscriminatingly cheerful in the way he always was—a wallpaper of cheerfulness to spread across the fissures in their relationship. He behaved as if they'd met yesterday, called her 'honey bun' and asked her how her gorgeous children were doing and whether Adrian had come to his senses and returned, but he didn't give her time to answer. He said he would arrive in Montpellier the day before the wedding, bringing with him wife number three and their two young children, who were about the same age as Sasha and Clem.

The following day the list continued. Mow the grass, beheading daisies and glossy buttercups, and water the pots on the patio that were withering in their cracked soil. Find passport. Buy a present for Jem and Juliet.

She got a bus into Covent Garden and wandered aimlessly down the streets and into the covered market. She considered an expensive glass plate, a wooden salad bowl with burnished swirls in the grain, a soup tureen, hand-painted mugs. There was a man on stilts juggling; his face was covered in sweat. A few feet from him a woman dressed in white, with a silvered face, stood absolutely still, but a vein bounced in her neck. A man played the trumpet in short, desperate blasts. A gypsy tried to push a sprig of lavender into her hands and cursed

173

her when she turned away and went into a bookshop. Perhaps she should buy the book on pictures of the moon—lovely black-and-white images of the glowing white rock from far off and from its cratered ground. Or the book about remarkable trees. She turned to a photograph of a vast and ancient Banyan tree in the rain forest in Australia, its trunk hollow and vaulted as a church—perhaps the children would see that. It occurred to her that throughout their lives up to now, the things they had seen were usually things she had seen too. They had shared memory banks and stories. But after this holiday with Adrian and Frankie their heads would be full of unfamiliar images. She shut the book.

Up from the bookshop was a shop selling photographs, and she went in, the door ringing as she opened and shut it. Inside, it was dim after the dazzle of the street, and cool and quiet. Images beckoned from walls and shelves—an old woman's bright eyes; a long road winding through spindly poplar trees; a child with a dirty face and on her lips a smudged slash of red lipstick; rain falling on a stagnant pool. They were all so expensive though, hundreds of pounds even without a frame. She turned to go but as she did so she saw a long, narrow photograph in the far corner and it stopped her in her tracks. Rolling red sand dunes under a darkly glowing blue sky, a blurred white sun casting shadows in lakes and pools. Irene crossed the room and stood in front of it, staring and unable to look away. She didn't know how long she stood there. It was as if the world dropped away and all that was left was this inhuman landscape, where nothing could live and the sun scorched the sand

and the sky hung above it like a shining shroud. It burned into her brain and she felt that she was empty of everything else—empty of tears, of grief, of sorrow and rage and empty even of weariness.

'Lovely, isn't it?' said a bright, sales' pitch voice behind her. She started, wrenched out of the landscape, and turned. 'The photographer's one of our new finds.'

'How much is it?' she forced herself to ask.

In its thin black frame it cost £350, about the same amount as her overdraft that she could see no way of reducing. Impossible.

'It's too much for me,' she said. 'I can't.'

Yet she couldn't bring herself to leave. She drifted round the shop, riffling through stacks of photos that leant against the white walls, pretending to consider the one of the London Eye reflected in the Thames, or the one of mist smoking off a field of corn.

'I'd consider knocking ten pounds off,' said the woman, watching her indecision.

'Well . . .'

'Call it £320, then.'

'All right,' said Irene. 'Quick, before I change my mind.'

The woman lifted the photo off the wall and wrapped it in yards of bubble wrap, Irene handed over her card, trying hard not to think about money, debts, bills, concentrating instead on the vivid afterglow of the photo in her mind. She travelled home with it carefully, cradling it to her.

There wasn't so much left to do. Pack a few things: a pair of jeans, some canvas shorts and tee-shirts, one jersey although she imagined it would be very hot; an old yellow waterproof that she balled up and stuffed into a small plastic bag, underwear, toiletries, a faded blue sun dress, trainers for the journey, sandals. Swimsuit and goggles, just in case. What should she wear for the wedding? Jem hadn't told her whether it would be in a church or a town hall and she'd never been to a French wedding, or what kind of party it would be, day or evening, smart or casual, elegant or plain rowdy. He'd just said they'd have speeches and would dance—when had she last danced, she wondered, and she imagined herself kicking off her shoes in some French hall and lifting her arms in the air, letting the music carry her. She gazed at her few dresses hanging in the cupboard. They had all been bought years ago and now looked quaint and drab. In the end she pulled out an unsatisfactory silvery-grey linen skirt and a sleeveless ruffled pink top and added it to her suitcase. Sun cream, factor thirty-five. Sunglasses. She put in a hard-backed notebook and a few pens, two books—an anthology of contemporary poetry and Dickens' *Great Expectations*—and selected some music for the car. Lucinda Williams, Aimee Mann: angry, whole-hearted women for the road.

That was it—one small case, with room to spare. Tomorrow, she could just pick it up and walk out of the house, closing the front door behind her. This wasn't like the holiday packing she'd become used to with her daughters, when she would fill bags with endless changes of clothes for cold and warm weather, wet and dry, and then still have to remember the bikes that they'd hang off the rack at the back of the car, the nappies and baby wipes, buggies and carrycots and bottles and feeder cups, the wellington boots that looked like frogs, the chapter books and picture books and books to read aloud, the drawing paper and crayons and gel pens, the games (Clem's Lego, Sasha's collection of minute dolls with their own beautifully stitched clothes, as well as snakes and ladders, Monopoly, Boggle, Uno), the football, the armbands and rubber rings, the backpacks for the journey, the treats for the car to keep them quiet, the Calpol and sticking plasters, the potty, the travel sickness pills for Clem and Aggie's bear that mustn't go in the boot . . . Like travelling with an army into unknown territory, where they might not have Coco-pops and raspberry jam.

Irene realized she was excited, full of a buzzing anticipatory energy that she hadn't felt in years. Her husband had left her, her daughters were with him on the other side of the world, and tomorrow she was going to step into her old car with the rusting sills and the passenger door that wouldn't open unless you yanked it hard, turn the key in the ignition, and set off across France to see her little brother get married. She would do it on her own, driving onto the train with men in orange fluorescent jackets shouting instructions at her, consulting the map and finding her route through foreign places, sliding her music into the tape deck and turning the volume up loud, passing euros to the men at the toll booths, filling up with petrol, stopping for the night in some hotel in a town she'd never heard of, eating alone in a restaurant and nobody facing her across the table, just the view out of the window and later a single bed with a stiff bolster.

Nobody would know who she was. There would be nobody to talk to, share thoughts and plans and laughter with. She would just hold them all inside herself and they would belong to her alone. She had not done anything like this since she had met Adrian and coupled her life to his.

It was six o'clock. In Australia, they would still be asleep unless jet lag had turned sleep on its head. She sat on her bed and closed her eyes, picturing her girls curled up and dreaming. Were they missing her? Did they ever wake up and call out for her? For one moment, she let the old desolation settle on her like fog. Then she shook her head decisively and stood up.

She had a long bath and washed her hair once more and shaved her legs. Then, to her own surprise, she went into Sasha's room and found a bottle of bright pink nail varnish for her toes. She put her cream cotton trousers back on and her bright blue shirt and stood for a moment in front of the broken mirror where she could make out distorted portions of her reflection. Her face, above her corded neck, was white and thin. With her wet hair plastered to her skull, she looked both older and younger than she actually was—a haggard woman with slightly bloodshot, staring eyes and a child in need of a square meal and an early night.

*   *   *

'Adrian? I'm glad I got you.'
   'Irene. Hi.'
   In the background she could hear Aggie crying fretfully.
   'Is she all right? What's wrong?'
   'Fine,' said Adrian. 'Frankie's just brushing her

hair. What's up?'

'I just wanted to tell you I'm going away. You won't be able to get in touch with me.'

'OK.'

'But you can leave messages on my answering machine. I'll ring every day to pick them up, just in case.'

'You don't need to ring every day.'

'I will though. Are they all OK?'

'Yes.'

'Having a nice time?'

'Yes.'

'And Aggie hasn't been too . . .'

'Irene, they're fine, all right?'

'Shall I speak to them—just to say hello?'

'I'm not sure that's a good idea. It might unsettle them.'

'Oh. Well, give them a hug from me, will you?'

'Sure.'

The whole world lay between them.

'Goodbye,' she said. The word seemed to echo long after she put the phone down.

CHAPTER EIGHTEEN

She got up before seven in the morning, woken by the birds outside the window and the sound of rain against the glass. Although she didn't have to leave until much later, she was anxious to be on her way. There wasn't much food in the house, so she made herself a large mug of milky coffee and took the punnet of soft purple raspberries from the fridge, eating them slowly, one by one, staining her fingers.

She dressed in jeans and trainers, and checked, yet again, that her passport hadn't expired and that the details of her crossing and Jem's instructions for how to get to his house were in her bag. She had a last look round the house, half drawing the curtains in the bedrooms, leaving a light on in the hallway, pouring bleach into the upstairs and downstairs lavatories. Everything felt orderly and quiet, as if she had already left and the house was standing empty, waiting for her return. She made sure the back door was locked, and the chain drawn across it, switched on the answering machine, took her jacket off the hook in the hall and picked up her bag, the picture and her violin case, into which she had put her sheets of music. Then, on an impulse, she put them down again and went to the chest in the living room, pulled open the bottom drawer, and removed the pink folder in which were the letters she had once, head over heels in love, sent to Adrian. She opened the case, and shoved the folder in. Then she left the house.

*   *   *

She got to near the terminus with hours to spare. Leaving the motorway, she headed for the coast, driving until she found a small strip of sand littered with plastic bags, pieces of polystyrene and tin cans. It was a louring day and the sky in the distance looked almost purple with approaching rain. A scummy, crooked line of seaweed marked the tide line. The wind was blowing in from the sea, which surged grey and cold in the blustery weather. On the horizon, she could see the huge

180

block of a container ship. A bit further in, a tiered ferry, heading out to sea. Little waves slapped at her feet. She took a deep breath, holding the air in her lungs. She could smell salt, fish, seaweed. Already her hair felt stiff from the spray.

Irene bent down and picked up a flat stone, tried to skim it over the choppy water, but it disappeared after one short jump. Adrian had always been good at skimming; it's a man's thing, he used to say, only half ironic. Clem and Sasha would stand beside him as he crouched down low and aimed his stone far out, away from the riffle of the waves to where it would bounce over the water while they cried out in admiration. Skimming stones, mysterious rock pools where anemones swayed and seaweed curled their miniature fronds, tepid fish and chips for supper, ice cream cones with a flake on top, rolling up trousers to paddle in the surf, tar on the rocks, sandcastles that crumbled with the tide, shells and stones that gleamed in the water but looked dull and ordinary when you got them home, French cricket, occasional transparent jellyfish just under the surface, swimsuits full of sand, the bleached skeletons of strange creatures . . . There are certain things, when you are married and have children, that you do not do alone: you don't eat out by yourself in restaurants; you don't go on your own to the theatre; you don't go to the seaside without your family.

A large raindrop landed on her cheek, then another. She pulled her jacket closer around her and walked briskly along the water's edge, back towards the car. The rain gathered strength, started pouring down, needling little holes into the wet sand. She climbed in, took off her wet jacket, turned on the ignition and the windscreen wipers. The blades cleared an intermittent semicircle of clear glass through which she caught glimpses of the grey and bucking sea. For a minute, Irene thought of turning round and heading back home again; of climbing into her bed, under the clean sheets, closing her eyes and waiting for her family to return.

*   *   *

She was in France before five, English time. She adjusted her watch forwards one hour. The rain had stopped and the sky was full of dark clouds over layers of lighter grey and streaks of watery blue. By a quarter to six, she was through customs and tensely negotiating the roundabouts and the queues of vast trucks, crouched over the wheel and remembering to drive on the right. At the first garage she pulled over, filled up with petrol and bought a spiral-bound road atlas. A few hundred metres further on, she stopped at an undistinguished supermarket and bought a small baguette, a circle of Camembert that felt soft in the middle, two tomatoes, a bottle of sparkling water and a packet of boiled sweets. She'd had nothing to eat since the raspberries that morning, and she felt tired and jittery with hunger.

She left the teeming main road and turned randomly onto a smaller one, going back towards the industrial coastline. After about five minutes, she pulled over by the gateway to a small field where dun-coloured cows were grazing peacefully and in the distance cranes hung over the skyline.

She wound down her window and let the warm, damp breeze blow into the car, then laid her picnic out on the seat beside her. She drank several gulps of warm, fizzy water, tore a chunk off the baguette and stuffed it into her mouth, then took a large bite of the Camembert that was disappointingly plasticky. She chewed slowly, then took a bite of tomato, sucking the pips from it so they didn't dribble down her chin.

Looking at the large map on the front page of the atlas, she saw she had to drive almost as far as it was possible to go in France, except for the far south-west of the country where it bordered with Spain. She turned to the page which showed distances and journey times; Montpellier wasn't marked, but to Marseilles it was 1,066 kilometres and would apparently take nine or ten hours excluding any stops. She ate another bite of bread with a wedge of cheese on top and considered her route. It could hardly be simpler, she thought; only a fool could go wrong. She would take the A26 towards Reims and then via Dijon onto the A6.

It was already nearly seven o'clock when she started off once more, and it was well past eight and in the altered light of a summer evening, when she found her way onto the A26, having taken an inexplicable wrong turn which swept her relentlessly onto the main road to Boulogne-sur-Mer, her small Renault wedged between a lorry and a car pulling a caravan, her eyes flickering nervously towards the map which lay open on the seat beside her and showed her she was going entirely the wrong way.

Finally on the A26, it started to rain again and her car windows misted over so that every so often

Irene had to lean forward to rub and clear a space in front of her. Arcs of water were spun out from the huge wheels of pantechnicons or were sprayed up from the road. Everything seemed grey and saturated. For the first few miles, it was slow going but gradually the traffic eased.

She passed signs to St Omer, and to Lille, where as a fourteen-year-old she had gone on a school exchange. All she remembered of that homesick, bewildered, practically mute week now were fragments: sitting in a small and gloomy dining room on a straight-backed chair, eating pink slices of lamb with a few green beans; playing mini-golf with her exchange while her shoes sank into the mud and the ball careered off into the long grass; drinking cool and bitter coffee out of a bowl in the morning and eating hunks of white bread with chunks of chocolate stuffed inside; spending a day in a French school and learning from the English teacher, who was French, that there was a 'whorl' in the ear—she could still hear the way he pronounced it, with a whistling 'w' and a rolling 'r'. And she remembered how she smiled all the time, from the moment she woke till the moment she went to bed, until her face felt rubbery as a squashy doll's; how she had strained to pick out, from the stream of unintelligible sounds around her, single, stable words that she could hang on to.

She slid Lucinda Williams into her tape player and the Texan voice filled the car. A bar-room-brawling, sexy-raw voice. She felt a throb of longing in her belly, between her legs.

Past signposts to Béthune, to Lens, to Arras. Lush, flat landscape dissolving in the rain. At half past nine the light was vague and Irene was aware of her tiredness. She turned off towards Cambrai, and drove down a straight road, under giant pylons, until she came to the outskirts of the town. There were several bed-and-breakfasts along the road, and a few hotels. She stopped outside one with flaking green shutters that was set back in its own small garden, and parked the car. In her rusty French, she asked the man behind the desk if there was a room free, and on being told that there was, dragged her case, photograph and violin inside. The man, who was thin, with greasy black hair combed across a bald pate, told her that if she hurried she could still have a snack in the dining room.

Her room was dark and musty, with faded floral wallpaper and net curtains across the bottom half of a narrow window. There was a tiny shower room to the side, and a tall wooden wardrobe which Irene pulled open to discover piles of blankets smelling of moth balls. She sat on the high bed and closed her eyes for a moment, feeling infinitely strange. Then she stripped off her clothes and took a shower in the weak trickle of warm water, using a flat, cracked tab of soap that didn't lather. She used the phone beside her bed to dial home: there were no messages.

Downstairs again she ordered a cheese omelette and chips with green salad on the side, and a glass of house red. She wasn't hungry any more, just tired—tired without being sleepy. There were not many guests in the dining room: by the window, an elderly woman staring spitefully at the tall glass in front of her, which was filled with scoops of variously coloured ice cream and gaily bedecked with little paper umbrellas; near the door, a portly

185

couple and their silent, shrimp-like son; and to the side of her, two middle-aged men in cheap-looking suits who were stabbing cheese onto the point of their knives and talking rapidly, jabbing fingers to make their point.

Her meal arrived. She sprinkled oil and vinegar from their separate bottles over the lettuce, then picked up a chip and popped it into her mouth. Fat and floury. She chewed a leathery mouthful of omelette, took a small sip of the thin, sharp wine. One of the men smiled across at her and raised his own glass in greeting, and she looked away in embarrassment. She should have brought her book downstairs. She prodded her omelette once more. The elderly woman left the room, her ice cream unfinished. Then the couple, their son thinly between them. She ate a few more chips, sipped at her sour wine, stopped the waiter as he passed with his arms piled high with dishes and ordered a double espresso. One of the men wiped his mouth with his napkin and got up to leave, his chair scraping across the wooden floor. The other one remained, pouring the last inch of wine into his glass and swilling it round. He lit a cigarette and held the smoke in his lungs for several seconds.

'Sorry,' he said in guttural French as he let it out again. 'Do you mind?'

Irene didn't.

'May I join you for coffee?'

She didn't know how to refuse—anyway, she'd be going upstairs soon. He sat opposite her and she allowed herself to look at his face properly for the first time. She supposed that he might be good-looking in an undramatic way. Brown eyes, thick brown hair flecked with grey, a stubbly chin, crow's feet round his eyes when he smiled; a lived-in, knocked-around face.

He tried out his bad English on her and she smiled politely, replying in her half-remembered French. He told her, swapping between languages, that he worked in printing and he was actually from Belgium, here on business and returning home tomorrow. His name was Michel; he had a wife who was a nurse, and two children, both teenage boys. They used the house like a hotel nowadays. His mother lived with them as well and that hadn't been easy. She was old and forgetful; his wife was impatient with her, and resented the extra work. But what can you do, he asked, shrugging. She's my mother, after all. He said it was sometimes a relief to travel on business. They ran out of conversation, yet still he fixed his tired brown eyes on her face.

In this new life of hers, thought Irene, she could take him upstairs to her poky room. Then tomorrow he would drive north, and she would head on south. Why not? Why shouldn't she have casual sex in an anonymous hotel before continuing her journey? It was what women did in films and books, especially French ones, where the lack of meaning took on its own kind of existential significance. She glanced across the table. He had a slight paunch, his neck was sunburned, his collar a bit grubby. She finished her coffee.

'Another?' he asked. He put his hand over hers.

No, she wouldn't have another. She wouldn't take him to her room. There was not a trace of desire in her; her flesh felt stiff and chilly and separate. The thought of him touching her, the thought of taking her clothes off in front of him and climbing under the starched sheets while he fumbled with a condom was simply impossible. She stood up and he rose also, pulling back her chair, placing his arm under her elbow.

'Goodnight,' she said kindly. 'Good luck with everything.'

He gave the slightest grimace but then nodded. It didn't really matter to him. She had just been a lonely woman sitting at the next-door table. He leant forward and kissed her on both cheeks. She smelt toothpaste.

'Good luck to you, too,' he said.

*   *   *

Sasha lay in bed. Bright blue light flooded in through her curtains and she could hear a hollow cooing of a bird. Yesterday she'd seen a flock of bright parakeets in the tree outside the hotel. Today, Frankie had said they would visit a park with kangaroos. She was going to take photographs of every different animal, then she could show them to Irene. She'd been keeping her diary, as well, writing painstakingly detailed entries for each day, sticking in airline stubs and postcards, drawing pictures, like the one of the bright blue butterfly, and the miniature tree dragon. She would write about the kangaroos and their joeys and try and make the funny feeling in her tummy go away. Sometimes, it was hard to breathe properly.

In the adjacent room, she could hear Adrian and Frankie murmuring; there was a little gurgle. Were they laughing? It didn't sound exactly like laughing. She shifted, careful not to make a sound that would wake Aggie, who'd been up half the

188

night with a tantrum that had ended only when she fell asleep; then sat up. Clem lay quite still under her sheet, but her eyes were wide open and unblinking.

'Sasha,' she hissed.

'Shhh. Yes?'

'I've been awake for hours and *hours*.'

'Me too.'

'As soon as I went to sleep I was awake again, even though we were so late.'

'It's jet lag.' Sasha tried to make her voice sound calm and reassuring, like Irene's. 'Your body clock's all wonky. It'll get better.'

'Can we get up now? What time is it?'

'I don't know. It's morning anyway.'

'No. At home, I mean. What time is it there?'

'At home it's night time.'

'I wonder what Mummy's doing now.'

'Probably sleeping.'

'Maybe she's dreaming about us.'

'It's different for grown-ups. I don't think they really dream.'

* * *

Irene brushed her teeth in front of the round, speckled mirror. She put on her flannel pyjamas and then pulled the shutters to. She tugged the sheets loose and climbed under them, laying her head on the stiff bolster. It was very quiet and very dark. For a moment, she let herself think of the girls, but they were so very far off. After the storm of her year, she had washed up here.

CHAPTER NINETEEN

Irene lay quite still, waiting to know where she was. A slit of light showed through the shutters; she could smell coffee and hear the clatter of plates. Voices drifting up from outside and under her cheek stiff, clean cotton. She sat up and in the grainy half-light saw the door to the shower, the tall cupboard, her violin and her open case; her jeans slung over the back of the chair. Memory seeped back, filling up the strange absences.

She breakfasted alone in the dining room on slightly stale baguette with a sachet of plum jam and bitter coffee, and was gone by eight. The day was pale grey, but before long it turned hazily bright. She found her way back onto the A26 and once more slid Lucinda Williams into the tape recorder. She settled back in the seat, held the steering wheel loosely between her hands. The road flowed past her.

There was a photograph that had been taken of her and Adrian when they had first got together. It was a summer photograph, and they had both been wearing baggy shorts and loose tee-shirts and were standing holding their bicycles, bulging panniers on the back and water bottles strapped to the frames, with a lane stretching behind them between an avenue of green trees. They were smiling widely; a lock of her long, unruly hair was blowing across her cheek. Their hips were just touching; their legs looked sturdy. She had always loved the picture but only now did she understand she had loved it because it had shown them setting off on their journey together.

That's how she had always thought of their relationship: a journey. Sometimes it is steep and the weather foul; sometimes you freewheel down hill and the sun's at your back and the land unfurls in front of you. Sometimes you feel free and your soul flies; sometimes you grind onwards effortfully, just keeping going through the sweat and the toil because that's what you know you must do. But you're always on it together. Pilgrims. She had never really thought you could choose to turn aside on your own, veer away down hidden paths.

Perhaps they had married too young and had children too early. Maybe it would have been better if she had had lots of relationships before falling head over heels in love with Adrian. Men sliding in and out of her bed. Secret assignations and experiments. Leaving and being left. Numerous half-loves and semi-tragedies to look back on—ah, I was a wild young woman once. But then, she had friends approaching their forties and childless, who were haunted by the fear of maybe having left it all too late. Absences, she thought, as the road ran towards her and streamed out behind her and the white sun rose hotly in the glowing sky; we all live with our different absences. The things we never did or never had or never knew; the experiences we turned away from; the doors that stayed shut; the loves we lost or left behind. The people we did not become. Absences can become like ghosts, haunting you.

St-Quentin. Laon. Reims. Chalon. Champagne country. She and Adrian had stopped near here once. She remembered nothing of it except there was a bridge and a slow wide river that they had

191

leant over together. She remembered—she thought she remembered—brown fish under the slow, clear water; a kingfisher flashing by.

A petrol station. A quick shot of espresso. Euros clinking into the outstretched hand; barriers lifting to let her pass. A grey-white sky searing outside. Troyes. A sudden flock of geese passing across her windscreen, flying in a shifting V formation with their long necks outstretched. She joined the smaller N71, and was now following the broad, beautiful Seine. Aimee Mann's nasal, heartfelt voice filling the car; something about loving, something about leaving, something about one day being happy again. She sang along with the words till they choked her. Grey chateaux on the hills in the distance. A wood, a village, a small lake, horses cantering in a field, brown cows, a sudden glimpse of children on the bank of the river, someone swimming in the shallows, pale torso gleaming. Vineyards and hills; snatched views down deepening valleys: a narrow, fast-running stream, smoke rising from a chimney, a yard where chickens scratched.

She turned off the main road, crossed the river, and soon found herself in a small, agreeably plain village whose street was lined with vast, pollarded plane trees. She wasn't hungry but she felt parched after the coffee, so she sat outside a café under a striped awning, drinking a citron pressé whose tartness made her wince. She didn't rejoin the busy road at once, but drove for a few miles along a smaller route that followed the Seine and wound through woods.

Irene examined the map. By her calculation she'd done nearly half her journey, but it was

192

already two o'clock, and she'd been driving for nearly six hours. She ate a bit of the bread, stale from yesterday, with some of the sweaty Camembert and swilled it back with a few mouthfuls of warm, flat water. A few heavy drops of rain splattered her windscreen; the scorched sky needed to break open and pour down.

The forest of Châtillon on her left. St Seine. An old grey abbey. She imagined cold flagstones, bare and empty rooms, prayers echoing in the great vaulted spaces. Out of the blue, a memory came to her from long ago, before Adrian. On holiday with four girlfriends and backpacking through France, they'd found themselves near a Cistercian monastery and on the spur of the moment entered, pulling cardigans or long-sleeved shirts over their bare shoulders, tucking hair behind their ears in an awkward gesture of respect. They had wandered round the church and then out into the cloisters, where water bubbled from a fountain and lizards ran up the walls. Then all of a sudden, they'd heard a sound, a chanting, coming from the church. Just a single male voice. And they'd all silently filed back inside to find a man in jeans standing in the aisle, singing a Gregorian plain chant. A ladder of sound, architectural and austere, climbing upwards through the still air. It had been many years since Irene had thought of that moment yet there it lay, intact in her memory and waiting to be triggered.

Memories as patches of light and foggy half-light in the close darkness that swallows up the greatest portion of our life. Is that it? Do most things fold back into our mind's inky forgetfulness and become lost for ever, or are they only dormant there, waking with the prick of recall? She didn't remember her father leaving, but she did remember him chasing her squealing round their garden with a hose, roaring 'I'm coming to get you, look out!' until she collapsed at his feet on the grass in a delicious wet heap. She remembered him pulling her out of the bath and holding her on his lap, wrapped in a towel. She didn't remember her mother crying over him when he left, but she did remember her cutting off her long chestnut hair— holding long strands of it and chopping through it with scissors until the kitchen floor was thick with shiny tresses and her mother sat, defiantly shorn and de-sexed. And now that she came to consider it, Irene thought as she approached the outskirts of Dijon, that was pretty much what she'd done a year or so ago: cut off the long orange hair that had been her glory and presented herself to Adrian cropped, androgynous. Later, of course, her mother had grown her hair back, wearing it in a loose bun that she undid at night, man after man.

Irene's feet were swollen with heat; sweat gathered under her armpits and trickled down her forehead into her eyes. The white sun burned in through the open window. She negotiated the turnings on the seething ring road and headed for the A31, signposted to Nuits St George and Chalon. She couldn't remember her first day at school, but she remembered jumping in puddles in its playground, splattering her bare calves and short white socks with mud, and she could remember viciously shoving a girl called Emily Low against the wall and hissing in her ear, 'I've gone off you.' She couldn't remember the house in Sheffield where they'd lived until she was six, but she vividly recalled the tree in her friend's garden,

194

and how she had climbed it once, scrambling up from branch to branch, blunt shoes slipping and twigs catching in her hair, dizzy with horrified excitement, until her friend's mother had come out of the house and screamed, in a voice high with fear, for her to come down; then Irene had lost her nerve and been unable to move.

She'd been a bookworm and a flat-chested tomboy until she was thirteen or fourteen, warding off the terrors of puberty. Not dolls but swords and cricket bats; not lipstick and jangly earrings but scabby knees and torn jeans and a passion for animals; not boys but books—any book she happened to come across, dictionaries and Shakespeare plays and bad poems, reading them over and over again, learning words by heart and reciting them to herself at night, lying on her bed in her room, full up and lethargic with words—and a love for solitary imaginary games in which she could be a cowboy, a knight on horseback, a pilgrim, a shipwrecked sailor, a warrior-hero, rescuing others and riding away again.

Even when she fell in love for the first time, aged sixteen, she wouldn't admit it to herself, certainly not to him. Greg, that had been his name; she pulled it from the deep well of memory and smiled. Greg with floppy hair and baggy jeans. They'd been in the school play together and she'd lost her appetite and sleep over his bland, smiling face, but held the feeling close and secret, even encouraging her friend Carly Jones to go out with him. She didn't want to enter that confusing world where boundaries between the self and the world dissolved. She hadn't had her first real boyfriend until she was seventeen going on eighteen, and even then was wary and suspicious of desire. She didn't want to lose her angular, stubborn, mutinous self. She didn't want to become her soft-hearted, lonely, abandoned mother, sobbing in her bed at night when she thought Irene couldn't hear her.

The A32 turned into the A6. Mountains in the distance; field after field of vines; stretches of purple lavender; chateaux high above the road; buzzards wheeling in the air. There was a signpost saying it was 185 kilometres to Lyons. Irene felt hot and sweaty in her jeans and trainers, and gritty with travel fatigue. Her head throbbed and her skin felt dirty. She took the first exit and, as soon as she was able, stopped the car, opening the passenger window so a hot breeze blew in. The sun was like a blow torch; she could feel it sizzling on her pale skin. She took off her trainers and socks, wriggled out of her jeans and into her shorts. She looked at the map and worked out that it was just over 300 kilometres from Lyon to Montpellier. About 500 kilometres to go and it was a quarter to four in the afternoon.

At five it started to rain: rods of water spearing the rocky, parched land, bouncing off her windscreen so she had to slow down and peer out through the downpour to see the road. She filled up with petrol and ate a croque monsieur standing at the counter, feeling the glue of melted cheese settle heavily in her stomach, then drank another cup of coffee. The rain eased and a pale turquoise broke through. She passed the lovely, steep-sided city of Lyons and imagined the people who lived there, cool behind the thick stone walls. High mountains and deep valleys; parched fields; dark green leaves hanging limply from the trees. The

196

sun sliding down her window. Her hands slipped on the steering wheel.

When she was young she thought she would be an archaeologist, or a marine biologist or an explorer—something that would take her to far-off places. She had imagined herself on lumpy camels and tough ponies, jumping out of jeeps in her khaki shorts with pockets full of implements, lying on the bow of a small deep-keeled boat, watching the swell of the sea and looking for land, standing on snowy plateaux. In a notebook that she probably still had somewhere, she had written down all the places she would go to and all the things she would see. The Sahara desert, the Amazonian rain forests, the great Pyramids, the Dead Sea, the Great Wall of China, the Barrier Reef where—she glared ahead at the road which trembled like liquid in the heat—Adrian was taking the girls in just a few days from now.

Later, she and Adrian had made their own list: they would cross America from west to east in a Cadillac; live for six months in the heart of Venice, next to the fish market and amid the pungent beauty and decay; go white-water rafting; see the midnight sun and the northern lights; go to Iceland where the sand is black and the air smells of sulphur and, so they say, you feel like you're on the very rim of the world. Of course, they'd never done any of these things. She had become a primary school teacher—just for the time being they said to each other; just till Adrian had his break, although she found she liked the work. Then she got pregnant. They'd put a deposit down on a poky little house in Hackney and struggled to make the monthly payments. The kitchen filled up with damp Babygros and rattles, pop-up books, bottles and beakers and strange, floppy-eared creatures with stitched, stubborn mouths.

Givors, Vienne, Roussillon, and from the road occasional glimpses of the Rhône flashed upon her, sometimes blue-brown and sometimes catching the sun so it looked like a river of light. She took a road off towards Serrières and stopped the car by the rise of a steep, vine-clad hillside. She opened the car and got out, stretching her limbs, balancing on the balls of her feet, breathing in deeply while the slight breeze cooled the sweat on her skin. The sun was low down and yellow as an egg yolk. The smell was of thyme, rosemary, friable leaves, things that were dry and fragrant. The air was full of the high thin melody of cicadas; it rustled with insects and the sudden movements of hidden animals among the prickly bushes and parched vegetation. A lizard flicked along the rock beside her, freezing for a moment then disappearing down a crevice. Irene drank the last of her warm water. It was past seven-thirty; she wasn't sleepy at all, but charged with a restless exhaustion that stung her eyes and cramped her shoulders and made her heart beat erratically. She would never get to Montpellier this evening, but in an hour or so would have to find somewhere to sleep the night. Then she could arrive early tomorrow.

At Valence, she took the exit and drove along a busy road towards the town. She stopped at the first small hotel that she saw, but it was full up. So too was the next, which had a dark, peeling reception area and smelt rancid. Suddenly, she was overcome by a feeling of heat and listless fatigue, and slumped back in her car seat. She couldn't bear the thought of slogging from hotel to grotty hotel in search of a bed. All that she wanted was somewhere cool, clean, quiet. Why not stay the night in the car, she thought—and having thought it, the idea was immensely appealing. She could park in the deep forest, by a stream perhaps, and stretch out on the back seat. A few hours' sleep would restore her.

First, she tracked down a yellow phone box and, having fed in euros, phoned her answering machine. There was one message from Lisa, that was all. Then she stocked up, buying a large bottle of water and a bar of chocolate and two ripe peaches from the grocery she passed; a small, still-warm meat pie from the nearby butcher's where rolls of beef, beautifully tied with string, and jars of foie gras sat behind the scrubbed counter. Finally, and on an impulse, she got a cheap bottle of local red wine, although as she drove away she remembered she had no corkscrew to open it with.

She left Valence on a minor road and wound up through wooded slopes until the town lay far beneath her and beyond it a panorama of hills and fields and distant spires scrolled away into the darkening sky. A random smaller road, winding past a single shuttered house, took her a few more kilometres up and then followed the line of the ridge, offering giddy views of empty valleys. The sun flickered low between the thick trunks of the trees and then sank beneath the horizon, turning the world suddenly grey. Here, where it was mountainous and shaded, and a fast-running stream cut a gorge into the hillside, Irene stopped her car and let the clear, pure loneliness fill her to the brim.

CHAPTER TWENTY

The darkness outside was not the botched darkness she was used to, where the dirty orange of street lamps and the grid of house lights always broke up the night. Here, there was only a dim and eerie lunar glow. Nor was the partial silence the same: no creak of plumbing, slam of car door, yowl of far-off stalking cat. Instead, under the erratic pounding of her heart, she could hear the river. It was a bubbling, implacable sound that made her feel both fearful and consoled. And with the window open, the car was filled with a baked, aromatic heat and the electrical fizz of Mediterranean insects that seemed, in her waking confusion, to be wired into the humming circuitry of her brain.

She opened her eyes and sat up stiffly from the back seat. She'd been badly bitten on the back of her knees and on her arms. There was no sign of day yet, but the night sky was clear and the moon trailed a cold radiance across the dark mass of trees and shone on the gushing water below her. She squinted at her watch, tilting it so that she could just make out that it was twenty past one. She had only slept an hour or two, and that fitfully, with the familiar razor-edged dreams snagging her awake. Someone laughing; a snickery, sly laugh licking around her brain. Children's faces swimming like pale fish in her drowning mind. Someone calling 'Mummy, Mummy' in a high-pitched, broken-backed wail. Oh, she could pick up distress a million miles away. And she had lurched out of sleep, falling upwards, with sweat trickling down her neck. Awake, she could still hear the last echoes of the hiccuping cries, and she clasped her hands together, digging her nails into her palms.

'What in the world am I doing in this place?' she said in a whisper, just to hear the sound of her own voice. 'Go back to sleep,' she told herself, more loudly. If she wept, if she screamed and howled, no one would hear her. No one in the whole world knew where she was and there was no one to whom she could talk about this feeling that had ambushed her when she woke: as if inside her things were coming loose from their foundations, breaking up like one of those detonated tower blocks folding softly in on itself, room after room, floor after floor. She pressed a hand hard against her heart, which seemed to have swollen hugely in her chest so that it was like a football just beneath the surface of her skin. She felt it skipping and lurching under her palm, a warning drum beating louder and louder, an ominous booming that must engulf her. Her stomach had turned to liquid but her throat was choked solid, as if a thrashing eel had lodged there. Her sinuses throbbed; her eyes burned. Her body was a city under siege, battened down but splitting apart, and there was an obscene fluttering and clicking in her head: trapped moths with powdery wings in the mushroomy underground of her thoughts.

Irene leant forward and fumbled for the water bottle in the front. She gulped several mouthfuls, spilling it down her chin and her neck. It was almost impossible to swallow: her throat was a closed valve. She made herself breathe deeply through the shudders that gripped her, and waited for the crouching, snarling dread to subside once more into its cave, just the tip of a tail twitching, eyes gleaming out of the terrible darkness. Always hiding there. She gave a small whimper.

'Pull yourself together now,' she said in a sharply insistent voice that she barely recognized as her own. That was no good; she didn't want to be bossed about by a no-nonsense girl guide. 'It's all right,' she said more kindly. 'This will pass. This will pass, Irene. This will pass.' Her voice sank to a croon. She wrapped her arms around her itchy, sweaty, bony body and rocked herself slightly on the seat. 'This will pass. I know I know I know.'

She waited, wrapped in her own arms. She stared into the night and watched the moon slide out from under a small cloud. Then she levered up the driver's seat and, leaning forward, opened the door. The ground was soft and mossy under her bare feet. Below her, the river gurgled. Around her the trees bent their dark branches. Somewhere in the invisible distance a car drove past. She wouldn't go back to sleep now.

Irene sat down sideways on the front seat, feet still outside the car, and picked up the unopened bottle of red wine. She turned on the overhead light, fished the car keys out from the glove compartment and jabbed at the cork, until it started to crumble inwards.

'Corked,' she said, trying to sound jaunty. 'Karen would send it back. Never mind. Here's to you, Irene.'

She tipped the bottle to drink, but the cork was blocking its neck and only when it was held strictly upside down above her open mouth did the cork shoot upwards and the wine gush out. It splashed over her cheeks, ran into her hair and ears. She spluttered and gulped the liquid; set the bottle upright outside the car. Then she took off her shirt and rubbed her face and hair with it.

'I'm all over the place,' she said out loud. Her voice had a crack in it, so she tried again, louder: 'I'm all over the place. And now,' she said, 'now I'm talking to myself as well.' She held her hands up experimentally and saw they were shaking; she clenched them into fists.

She switched on the car's internal light and, reaching into her bag, she pulled out her wallet to extract the photographs she always carried around with her though rarely looked at nowadays. Unlike a painting, a photograph must always be a *memento mori*: here is a moment that has gone, it says; here is a face that will never come again. Like this one, taken two years ago, of the whole family. Adrian was in the middle of the bunched group, the proud father. Squeezed possessively close beside him, Sasha looked very solemn, with that self-consciously noble look she adopted when she was trying to act especially grown-up; the responsible eldest child. Clem was standing to attention like a soldier; her hair stood up in a startled bristle and her cheeks were rather red. Aggie was squirming away from the camera and her face was blurred. And then . . . but Irene put the photo back in her wallet hurriedly. Not now, she thought; don't go there now, in the middle of the night, alone, in a clearing in a forest in the south of France.

Here was one of Sasha and Clem on the beach

203

at Wittering. Sasha was squatting beside a skewed sandcastle in a pair of blue shorts and a bikini top and moulding the walls with the flats of both hands; Clem, quite naked with a round white belly and sunburned shoulders, stood beside her holding aloft a large yellow spade which, a few seconds after the photo was taken, she had whacked violently onto Sasha's shoulders. Knowing that, Irene could see the approaching moment in her expression: cunning and already triumphant. Here was one of Aggie learning to walk, her legs like rubber bands and on her face a look of ferocious concentration. Moments, thought Irene. We just remember in moments, and then link them together to make up our version of a life. You have to choose the right ones to carry around in your head. She took another gulp of wine, which was pouring more smoothly now.

And here was Adrian, taken many years ago, before they'd had children. Irene examined the picture, which was curled up at its edges. He was sitting in a chair, in a garden that she could no longer remember, and there was a glass of water in front of him. His hair was quite long and thicker and fairer than it was now. On his face, which was thin and smooth with youth, there was the trace of a smile, as if he was sharing a secret. She touched his face with a finger, very gently. Had it been at her that he was looking with such intimate sweetness? It must have been, or why would she have kept the photograph all this time, tucked into a compartment in her wallet. It must have been, too, because although she did not recognize the garden or remember the occasion, she felt the moment was lodged in her memory like a gift.

Cherish precious things: the sunlight and the joy; the tiny smile passing between them. They had known each other then. What journey had taken him from that garden and that smile to the fleshy stranger lying in Frankie's bed, his naked torso, his furtive, defiant expression as he looked up at her, his serpent laugh?

Irene stared at the picture of Adrian for several minutes. Here was the man she had fallen in love with all those years ago. He was just a boy, really, all untested hopefulness and buoyant, reckless plans that he poured in her lap, laid at her feet. She stared at the smile that told her he had loved her. Yes, he had loved her. She felt the single, delicate syllable in her parched mouth: love. For months, years perhaps, they had lived on a demolition site: machines coming silently over the hill with blades already whirring; things they had built together ripped, shattered, torn splintering down; a great iron ball swinging through dreams that flew apart noiselessly; memories falling in a rubble, trampled carelessly underfoot, buried in waste, and a gritty wind blowing across the disintegrating landscape. But behind it there was this simple, restful image, of a young man in a garden smiling with love.

With a sigh, Irene slid the picture back beside the others. But something had happened; she felt it as an easing behind her ribs and her eyes, a softening. She put her hand up to her face and discovered that there were warm tears rolling down her cheeks. Good tears at last. She wiped them away with the tips of her fingers. Then she walked round to the boot and pulled out the folder of letters that she had taken from home at the last minute because she must have known she would need them. There were dozens of them written in the first six months of their relationship, some short but others several pages long, with both sides covered in her cramped and spidery scrawl. He had kept them all; perhaps when she returned home she would find their partners. One by one she held them under the small light.

*   *   *

Adrian, she had written. *When I arrived on Friday and you were standing there on the platform I felt so happy it wasn't like happiness any more, but something new. You took my bag and said, 'I've been waiting for you.' And what I want to say now, after the last two days we've spent, is that I've been waiting for you too. And now I've found you.*

*   *   *

Irene winced. She didn't need to look at the date scribbled at the top to know that she'd written the letter just a few weeks after they'd met. She remembered the weekend; the little room at the top of a long flight of stairs where he was staying for the repertory season. The square window, grimy and cracked in one corner, looking out over roofs and the church spire, the dusty wooden floor. She could still see the expression on his face when she knelt in front of him and took him in her mouth. She knew his taste, his smell, the way he put his fingers into her hair, the way he said her name, over and over, as if it were a magic incantation that could save him; save him from

206

what? Brimful of desire and just a look, just a brush of his fingers, just allowing herself to remember it later, would spill her over. So many things she had forgotten, but not that. Never that.

She pulled other letters out at random. *I didn't want to leave . . . I've never felt like this before . . . I don't care what other people think . . . Your smell's on my clothes . . .* She felt the girlish, trusting phrases enter her like soft explosions; sparks of memory illuminating her darkness. *I can't go through that again . . .* Ah yes, a memory she'd pushed down deep and only now did it poke up through the layers of the past: in the flush of their love and Adrian, addled drunk, kissing someone else at a party, shoving her up against the fence at the end of the garden, his hand on her breast and her dress riding up to her thigh. She remembered the sensation of agony, a red-hot poker against her skin. After, he'd wept and said he was a drunken idiot, a gross fool, he didn't deserve her. He'd never do it again; that's what he'd said and she had believed him.

Irene picked up another letter. *Only two weeks now.* About to go away together, biking in Italy. She closed her eyes for a moment. She heard him laugh, or was that the stream, clear and clean and full of frank delight. She saw him turn his face towards her on the pillow, in that room overlooking the gorge, and tell her she was lovely. My lovely love. She said the words out loud.

The letters stopped when they started to live together, so they contained no bickery complaints about toenails in the shower, specks of toothpaste on the bathroom mirror, whose-turn-is-it, whose-fault-is-it, no-not-tonight, what's-happened-to-you,

207

what's-happened-to-us, this-isn't-what-I-expected. They were just about hope.

When she had finished with them, Irene felt stunned, as if she'd run a long distance uphill. She turned off the car light and stared out at the night sky—except now, she saw, there was grey on its eastern horizon. She eased herself out of the car and let the breeze that had sprung up stroke her face. She walked across the mossy verge onto the crackling floor of the wood and there, near the dark rushing water, she sat on a fallen trunk, her elbows on her knees and her chin in her hands. She listened to the wind sweeping in small waves through the branches overhead, as if the tide was turning, dark waters in the sky. The panic had all gone, and in its place was a weary kind of peace. Adrian had left her and now she had to let him go. Take him back and let him go. Her love.

She didn't know how long she sat like that, watching the dawn break, feeling it break. Very slowly the sky became lighter, and as the sun rose above the scissored line of the trees, the birds flung themselves into furious song. At last, she stood up and made her way down the slope to the narrow river that rippled and bucked over the stones. She squatted down and trailed her fingers in the water, which was cool but not icy. Then she tugged off her shorts and knickers, lifted her tee-shirt over her head, and stepped off the bank. It was deeper than she'd expected, up to her thighs. She took a deep breath and pushed out for the middle of the flow, where the current was swift.

Oh, but it was glorious! Cold, fast, clean. She plunged beneath the water, which was dark because of the stone bed, and quite clear. She could see through blinking open eyes her pale body, her limbs suddenly graceful in the water, her spread hands like starfish, silver baubles of air popping on her skin; bubbles of light streaming up to the surface. She came up for breath, gasping and treading water, then struck upstream, back to where her clothes lay in a heap on the bank. She lay on her back and stared into the lightening sky. A hawk there in the clearing. Dived down again, stretched her body into an arrow flying along the river bed, following her fingers down to the bottom, down to the very depths.

This was freedom. Freedom isn't a one-night stand with a sad stranger in a cheap hotel, drowning out memories with wine and the feel of another's misery. Freedom is being all alone and coming face to face with yourself and not turning away; freedom is swimming naked and exulting in a cold river at dawn; and it's just you, just you and no one left to help you and hold you and ward off harm. And you know that this dark clarity isn't happiness or unhappiness, it's something different from anything you've ever felt before. Scary as a knife to the heart. That's freedom. That's where you will find your solace, all alone.

CHAPTER TWENTY-ONE

'Here.' Juliet put a cafetière of very dark coffee on the table in front of Irene, and a glass of freshly squeezed orange juice. 'Get this down you.'

'Lovely.'

Irene stretched her bare legs luxuriously. She'd

had a shower, washed her hair, brushed her teeth, put on her faded blue sun dress, and now she and Juliet were sitting in the garden, under the shade of a green parasol, while Jem biked to the bakery to buy fresh bread. In the distance, she could see Montpellier, its towers and spires and red-tiled roofs hazy in the hot sunlight.

'You look dreadful, like something the cat brought in.'

'Thanks very much!' Irene sipped at the burning coffee.

'I'm supposed to be the one who's at death's door,' continued Juliet quite cheerfully, 'but if a stranger came in and had to say which one of us was ill, he wouldn't hesitate.'

'It was a long drive, that's all.'

'You don't lose all that weight and have bags under your eyes and worry lines all over your face and skin like a tired mushroom just because of a long drive.'

'Hey!'

'No offence.'

'I'm fine. I've come to look after *you*, not the other way round.'

'You can forget that right now. It's bad enough with Jem rushing around treating me like I'm cut glass. I can look after myself perfectly well. You're here to come to our wedding and have a nice time.'

'Tell me first, how are you? Really?'

Juliet shrugged. 'Fine, actually. It was just a lump that was cut out. It's odd how quickly you get used to the idea of it, really. For the first week or so I woke up every morning and had this sudden lurch of terror when I remembered all over again. That's gone now.'

'Are you being well looked after?'

'Of course. I work at the hospital, remember. Everybody's falling over themselves to be helpful.'

'Do you mind me asking you about it?'

'I'd mind if you tiptoed around the subject like it was a trap that might spring shut—after all, it's pretty central at the moment. It's why you're here. It's why we're getting married. You can even say the words. Cancer,' she said loudly and emphatically. 'Death.'

'Not death.'

'Probably not death. But maybe. You have to say to yourself: maybe I am going to die. And then you have to put it away, otherwise you'll go mad thinking about it, and thinking about yourself as an invalid. I am not an invalid.'

She didn't look like an invalid either, but solid and robust. She was tanned from the summer, and her black hair sprang out in an energetic tangle round her head. She wore white cotton trousers and an orange halter-neck top round her strong shoulders. Her toes, in their sandals, had scarlet nails.

'You look gorgeous,' said Irene sincerely. 'Jem's a very lucky man.'

'That's what I keep telling him.'

'We'll be sisters.'

'We always were anyway really.'

'True.'

'So sorry about Adrian.'

'Thanks.'

'Bastard.'

'Quite right.'

'Has it been hell?'

For the first time, Irene didn't mind someone

asking her. 'Yeah,' she replied slowly. 'Kind of hell, I guess. Or I've been hell. It's getting better though.'

'Good.' Juliet grinned across the table: her slightly crooked face, her warm brown eyes. 'So you've been left by your husband and I've got cancer and here we are together.'

'Yup,' said Irene feeling suddenly and ridiculously happy.

'You have to help me choose a dress to get married in. One that will show off my *breasts*,' she added with relish.

'What's that?' said Jem, coming into the garden through the double doors. 'Look, breakfast; just out of the oven.' He spilled white rolls, still warm, onto the white tablecloth. 'I'll get the honey, shall I?'

He reappeared an instant later with a jar of honey and a pat of pale butter on a plate.

'Honey from the village,' said Juliet.

Irene took a roll and broke it in half. Inside it was piping hot, melting the butter. She trailed a teaspoon of runny honey over the top and took a bite. The warm doughy roll and the sweet liquid honey were so immensely comforting that she closed her eyes for a moment, to savour it.

'I was saying that Irene had to help me choose a dress,' said Juliet.

'Good idea,' said Jem, beaming at them. 'And then we've got the party to prepare as well. You and me mostly. Juliet's going in to work until Thursday.'

'Are you still working then?'

'Of course.' Juliet was a medical researcher, and she had come to Montpellier hospital to join a

212

team that was conducting a survey into population ageing. 'Though I'm only going in for a couple of days this week. We're at an important stage just now, collating the first batch of information.'

'Where's the party going to be?'

'Here.' Jem waved an arm at the garden. 'We just wanted to have friends and family and nothing grand.'

'It's lovely here,' said Irene, looking down the sloping, unkempt garden, sniffing in the lavender.

'Isn't it?' said Juliet. 'I won't want to leave when the study is all done and dusted. Maybe they'll offer me something permanent, then we can buy this house and settle down. Hey!' she rounded on Jem. 'Don't look so bloody tragic. It's just a lump. I can make plans, can't I? Or are you planning my funeral as well as my wedding?'

'Of course. I mean, of course not. You can make plans.'

'OK.' She turned back to Irene. 'Here are the short-term plans, anyway, just so you know what you've let yourself in for. We're going to get married at four on Friday afternoon. Just a few people will come to that, mostly the people who've travelled a long way to be here—French civil weddings are dead boring anyway. Except you have to be there, because you're one of our witnesses. Then at seven in the evening people will come here for the party.'

'How many?'

'About fifty or sixty, we think. We're not really sure. It's been rather rushed.'

'Are most of them from round here?'

'They're from everywhere,' said Jem. 'Some from here. Then you and a few friends from home—like Peter Wallis, remember? And Terence and Ellie. Then there's Dad and his lot from America. Juliet's parents from Cork, her sister and family plus about twenty of her cousins and friends from Dublin . . .'

'Six, actually.'

'Whatever. They're arriving on Thursday afternoon. The others are probably arriving on Friday morning.'

'Are most of them staying here?'

'God, no. We've only got the one extra room, and you're in that. Juliet's friends are bedding down in the living room and we've borrowed a tent and a huge blow-up lilo as well. But all our various parents are staying in hotels in Montpellier. Much better that way, don't you think?'

'Not the same hotel?'

'Mum's staying in the same hotel as Juliet's parents. They get on pretty well. They can swap stories about what we were like as babies or something. Dad's staying in a hotel on the other side of town.'

'Remember the last time we saw him, in your flat in London, and he got drunk and kept telling us how much he loved us really?'

'How could I forget? Juliet's never met him and I've only seen photographs of his kids. I never expected him to come over for this—I won't believe it till I see him standing there.'

Irene finished off her roll and reached for another, Juliet filled up her mug with coffee. A faint breeze touched her face, rippled through her tired body.

* * *

214

Her room was at the back of the house overlooking the garden. It was small, cool and dark, with bare floorboards, wooden shutters, a wide window sill on which someone had put a jam jar full of deep scarlet flowers that Irene didn't recognize, and a high and narrow iron bed pushed against the wall. Apart from that there was just a chair over which Irene could drape her clothes, and a square, unframed mirror at eye level. Irene pushed the violin and the photograph in its swathes of bubble wrap under the bed, her suitcase up against one wall, and then sat with her back against the pillows, staring dreamily out of the window. Jem and Juliet's voices floated up to her, an emphatic tone, a faint guffaw, a clink of glasses and plates being cleared from the table. The hot day drifted slowly on.

She was remembering what Jem had asked her earlier, as they sat over their late lunch. Had it been bad for a long time? She'd opened her mouth to reply and then found she didn't know what to say. Had it? Absurdly, until that moment, she hadn't really posed the question except frantically over dinner with Karen. There had been an accepted narrative format to their break-up, one which all her friends eagerly subscribed to: she and Adrian had been getting along fine, ups and downs like in any marriage but that was only to be expected after all. And then desire had ambushed him and tipped him off course. In this version, the affair had caused a sudden and violent rupture. If it hadn't been for Frankie, then they would still be together. Their break was exactly that—an accident, like a car crash which, one second earlier or later, would not have happened, would not have even been imagined.

But Jem's mild question had set her on another path. Perhaps she and Adrian had been heading for this moment for a long time, without ever realizing it. Perhaps their separation was not like a car crash, with him driving recklessly and her passive and appalled in the passenger seat, and was more like a series of wrong turnings and misdirections that they had both taken, that they were both responsible for, each one insignificant in itself, yet taking them further and further astray. The adventure of marriage had become, imperceptibly, an impasse.

In which case, thought Irene, closing her eyes, it's not just the last few months I was blind about, but the last several years. It's all about repetition, accretion—the slow build-up of trivial patterns and undredged irritation, until everything silts up. Ideas flitted through her brain and she tried to hold on to them: that she shouldn't be pitied, that she wasn't just a victim, that this was her chance, her chance to begin afresh . . . But the journey had been long and now she felt sleep wash over her; her limbs relaxed. She turned her back to the open window, pulled a plump pillow under her head and let herself forget herself for a time. Let herself go.

*   *   *

Over the next three days, Irene often wished that her week in France could remain suspended in this waiting time: the hours filled equally with idleness and purpose, the guests expected and prepared for but not yet arrived; the wedding and the party still to come; everything on the hazy blue horizon. Even when she thought of her daughters, there was no longer the stinging lash of missing.

Each morning, she would wake very early and open the shutters, lean out into the garden to breathe in the dry pungency of herbs, and see the heat already shimmering on the bleached grass. She would pull on her shorts and tee-shirt and go to the bakery for bread and pastries. Then she would come back and sit outside with a pot of coffee, sometimes reading *Great Expectations* or one of the poems in her anthology, sometimes writing down random ideas or sketches in her notebook, more often just letting thoughts and feelings drift through her mind while the sun rose higher.

Juliet, who was sullen and puffy-faced in the mornings, left for the hospital by half past eight. Jem had a translation deadline, and disappeared into his small study shortly after, though he never stayed there for long. Irene washed clothes by hand, scrubbed the smooth stone flags in the kitchen, bought food from the local shops for the day and evening, played her violin, read, took slow and meandering walks round the village and into the fields beyond, where grapes were ripening on the vines and purple mountains rose up in the distance. She sat in the narrow garden in the early evenings, sipping cold white wine and listening to the rising static of night insects. Her French got smoother. Her face lost its pinched look. Her skin became faintly honey-coloured; her freckles spread into coppery smudges across her face.

*   *   *

217

On Tuesday, she and Jem ordered the wine for the party, the long roll of best beef that Jem was going to cook and serve cold before the wedding, and then they sat under the striped awning of a café and made a list of things they had to do that they never looked at again. On Wednesday afternoon, she biked into Montpellier, through its narrow streets, past its cathedral and ancient medical faculty, and met Juliet in order to choose a dress. Juliet ended up buying two—one was blue and chic for the wedding service; the other was a long silver halter-neck.

'Wow!' said Irene when she tried it on.

'That's what I wanted to hear—right, I'll take it,' said Juliet. 'Shit, it's expensive though. Never mind. We only get married once, don't we? Oh God, or maybe some of us do it more than that,' she added.

'Don't worry.'

'Now, try this on.'

'I'm fine—I've got a long skirt to wear.'

'Orange to go with your hair.'

'I couldn't. Anyway, it's far too bright.'

'Too bright for what?'

'For me.'

'What colour's your skirt?'

'Grey.'

'Ha! Try this on. Just see what it looks like.'

'Honestly, I'm all right, Juliet. I'm not in the mood for shopping.'

'Just this one. It's my treat.'

'Nonsense.'

'You've got out of the habit of taking, haven't you? Sometimes people like to give, you know . . .'

'It's not that,' protested Irene.

'What is it then?' Juliet put her hands on her hips and stared hard at her. 'Worried that someone might just notice you? That you won't be able to hide in a corner in your grey skirt?'

'No! I don't know. I just can't . . .'

'Cinderella shall go to the fucking ball. I want to buy you a dress. It would give me pleasure.'

'I'll try it on then. But it'll look dreadful on me.'

'Let's see.'

*   *   *

She tried it on again later, when Jem and Juliet had gone to bed and she was restlessly far from sleep. She pulled the silky folds over her head and felt them fall softly around her. She stood on tiptoes in front of the mirror and stared at her head and shoulders, then climbed up on the chair and examined the rest of her in sections. Then she put the dress carefully back on its hanger and hung it from a nail on the wall. Several times during the night, when she lurched awake out of one of her dreams, she saw the dress there and thought it was a person standing quietly in the room beside her, waiting for her.

*   *   *

On Thursday morning she worked hard. She collected the beef from the butcher's and also bought three ready-cooked chickens for that evening, when all of Juliet's Irish contingent would be there, as well as two wheels of Camembert, and a dozen thick baguettes. She filled up the bike

219

pannier with tomatoes, lettuces with soil on their roots, large radishes, thin, bendy cucumbers, and a paper bag of purple figs for the wedding breakfast. On her second trip into the village, she bought two huge tarts, a bag of tea lights which she was going to put round the garden in jars, and an armful of blowsy yellow roses whose scent reminded her of home. On the third trip, she and Jem took her car into the city and collected the wine, the glasses, several bags of pistachio nuts, cashew nuts, crisps, and olives in plastic pouches, and a sack of ice that they jammed into the small freezer. She pumped up the double lilo and contemplated putting the borrowed tent up at the end of the garden, but decided she'd wait for them to arrive.

'It's been lovely,' she said to Jem.

'For me too.'

'I won't have a chance to say this properly later. I really, really . . .' She stopped. 'You know,' she said. 'Everything. I wish you both everything you want.'

'Thanks,' said Jem awkwardly. 'I know. You too.'

'I know.'

CHAPTER TWENTY-TWO

She was out when they all arrived in two taxis, carrying cases and presents and bottles of champagne and duty-free extra-dry gin, spilling out into the heat of the late afternoon with cries of greeting, exuberant hugs. She'd planned it that way, leaving the house on Juliet's bike half an hour after their plane touched down at Montpellier airport, calling over her shoulder to Jem that she'd be back soon, an hour or two at the most, better to give everybody a bit of space.

She cycled down the hill and took a small, shaded lane that wound its way through vineyards, not pausing until she was out of breath and thirsty. At a tiny village—just a squat grey church with a clock whose hands pointed to twenty past eleven, and a few run-down houses—she stopped at a bar where several men were standing around a fruit machine, smoking cigarettes, and asked for an Orangina. She drank it sitting on a bench by the small stream where ducks were grouped, making their soft querulous noises, and took her time. Now they'd surely all have arrived, even allowing for the time it takes to collect baggage. Now they'd have arranged where they would sleep, have put up the tent. Now they'd have washed, changed into fresh clothes. They'd be standing in the garden with damp hair and open-necked shirts, and Jem would be pouring cold white wine into glasses and Juliet would be doing her 'I'm not ill' act, hands defiantly on hips and thick brows sardonically raised.

*   *   *

'I'm not a bloody invalid!' said Juliet, raising a glass in salutation. She had returned home half an hour before they arrived and changed into shorts, brushed her hair out into a crackling nimbus. She surveyed her guests: her cousin Neil, who was about the same age as her and whose four-year-old daughter, Katherine, now clinging shyly to her

221

mother's skirt, was her godchild; Neil's wife, Lorrie. Then her friends she had grown up next door to: Mary, Mary's younger brother, Mickey, and taciturn Luke. These were people who—apart from Lorrie—she had known for almost the whole of her life. They had gone in different directions. Sometimes they'd lost touch; months, even years, could go by without contact. But they were more like family to her than friends. They were who she wanted around when she got married; they were who she wanted when she got ill and was scared in spite of her stalwart bravado. They were her gang.

Jem was busying himself with pouring wine and moving chairs round the table unnecessarily. He was a bit shy, she realized, and she went across to him and put her arm through his, pulled him across to her friends.

'I've known these people since I was two feet tall. I used to get to school early to bury the dead bumble bees with him'—pointing at Luke—'and we'd have funerals for them. Remember?'

'I just did what you told me.'

'You were always so bossy,' said Mary, laughing, putting a hand on Juliet's shoulder.

They had left their normal life behind—work, obligations, in some cases spouses and children—and were in carnival mood. They wore their holiday clothes—bright shirts, flip-flops, baggy shorts or skimpy dresses. Neil opened the champagne. Juliet dug out one of the bags of olives Irene had bought and handed them around. Mickey lit a cigarette and sat back in the deckchair.

'I thought your sister was going to be here,' said Neil to Jem.

'Irene. She is. She should be back any minute.'

He looked at the dusty road that snaked down the hill; saw in the distance a cyclist, crouched over the handlebars in Irene's characteristically tense posture. 'In fact, I see her now.'

*   *   *

Irene retreated to her room, saying she had to change before anything else. She felt out of place. The house, which for five days had been tranquil and safe, was suddenly full of strangers who spoke in code, tousled Juliet's unruly hair, called Jem a 'toy boy', rooted around in the fridge, chucked clothes and towels everywhere, turned the shaded garden into a playground in which they smoked, drank, shouted comments at each other, swapped stories. She pulled out her sun dress, suddenly wishing she had something a bit less old and drab to wear, and went self-consciously downstairs to join them.

Later, she would try to remember her first impressions. Neil's pale blue eyes, like the eyes of a blind man, his pleasingly crackly dry voice; Lorrie's smell of vanilla and hand cream, her long pale plait snaking down her back and tied in a blue ribbon at the end; Mary's plump and creamy face, her pointed pink shoes, her faintly secret smile—the look, Irene soon found, of a woman who is four months pregnant with her first child and has just begun to feel it move; Luke's wide-apart hazel eyes, his receding hair that was shaved close to his head and was a soft grey-brown, like moleskin; Mickey's handshake, so hard it made her wince, and his brilliant white-toothed grin which came and went suddenly, as if there was a switch inside

223

him. She was passed from one to the next, saying hello, repeating their names as they were said to her so she would remember them, trying to think of something to say that wasn't just 'pleased to meet you' yet again. She squatted down beside Katherine and asked her how old she was. Katherine stared at her and shuffled closer to Lorrie. Lorrie said she was four and three months, and Irene said: 'A bit older than my youngest, Aggie,' and suddenly felt odd to be speaking her daughter's name in this garden full of strangers.

It didn't matter what she said though. Words spilled out around her and all she had to do was smile and nod and sip her wine. What were they all going to wear tomorrow? Who was going to make a speech? What was the order of the day? Was it always this hot? They'd have to keep an eye on Katherine, and Mary was going to be as red as a tomato by the time of the party with her pasty skin. Who was going to sleep where—who had bagged the sofa and what about the tent, and who loved sleeping under canvas and who had horrible childhood memories of water dripping through the roof and damp sleeping bags and mosquito bites and cold feet and dying torches and mornings that started at five? And did they all remember . . .? And wasn't it fun . . .? And look at that huge lizard; look at that buzzard; look at that perfect view and aren't the evenings the best time of day when they're like this—soft and dry and blessed after the scorch of the day? Someone pointed at the low, diffuse clouds on the violet horizon and asked Luke what kind they were but didn't let him reply because someone else said: 'Red sky at night, shepherd's delight', that was what really mattered on the evening before Juliet and Jem got married. And they all raised their glasses again. Irene looked at Jem and saw him looking at Juliet with such tenderness she looked away.

Katherine suddenly started to cry and Lorrie lifted her up in that practised way Irene recognized, holding her like a koala bear against her chest and murmuring soothingly into her hair. Irene and Jem and Mary went into the kitchen together and took the cold, cooked chickens from the fridge, warmed the baguettes in the oven and put them in a large basket, washed lettuce leaves and chopped radishes and tomatoes. Mary made a salad dressing in a jam jar and Irene put the soft cheeses on a large plate.

They ate outside, sitting round the table with extra chairs and a stool dragged from the kitchen. Irene learnt that Mickey had two boys and was separated from his wife, who'd had an affair with his boss at the computer shop where he worked in Dublin. That Luke was a meteorologist at the university but soon was going to Boston to work. Mary was a PA, but she was going to give up when she had her baby and think about what she really wanted to do, maybe something with disturbed children. Lorrie used to work on food flavours for a multinational that she disapproved of and now she had retrained as a nurse and worked in a children's ward. Neil owned a fish shop and supplied most of Dublin's best restaurants with oysters, turbot, mackerel, salmon and cod. She learnt that on Sunday they were all setting off on holiday together, taking a boat along the Canal du Midi for a week—all except Mary, who wanted to go home to her husband and the house they were decorating, ready for the baby. Lorrie leant over and whispered something in Juliet's ear. She looked across at Irene, shrugging.

'What?' asked Irene. 'My ears are burning.'

'I was just asking Juliet if you had any plans after this.'

'Just—well, go home, I guess,' said Irene. 'I was only planning to be away a week or so.'

'You can stay here as long as you want,' said Jem. 'You know that.'

'You really, really don't want me around when you've just got married. That's not what honeymoons are supposed to be like—the bride, the groom and the groom's elder sister.'

'I don't think we'll be any different than we are now.'

'It's not that anyway,' said Juliet. 'I don't think you'd want to be around, clearing up sick.'

'I don't mind sick,' said Irene. 'And I'd do anything to help, you know that. But you two should be alone and I need to get home.'

'Anyway, what I was going to say is that there's a spare cabin on the boat,' said Lorrie. 'We booked it at the very last minute, in a kind of mad flurry, when we heard about the wedding, and they only had this huge one left. It sleeps eight or more. So if you feel like coming on holiday with a boat-load of strangers I'd be really pleased. I could do with a woman—apart from Katherine, I mean.'

'It's lovely of you to offer.'

'That means no,' said Mickey. 'I can tell.'

'But if you change your mind . . . You've got till Sunday.'

'Thanks.'

They all stayed outside long after it was dark.

Sometimes they talked and sometimes they sat in the warm silence.

She looked at Jem.

'This is better than a stag night,' he said to her.

'You shouldn't be with your fiancée the night before your wedding. It's against the rules. You should be sleeping in the tent with us,' said Mickey.

'No chance.'

'We're going to be telling ghost stories,' said Mickey. 'You don't want to miss that.'

'I want to be with my bride,' Jem said sentimentally.

Juliet gave a little snort and Irene found herself laughing—really laughing, tipping her head back and mirth rippling up from her belly and along her throat. And she thought: my God, I haven't giggled like this for years. I haven't been able to let myself go. What have I been doing all this time? The laughter caught in her throat.

'Are you all right?' asked Lorrie.

'Yes. I'm really, really fine.'

*   *   *

Mary was to sleep on the floor in Irene's tiny room, almost under the bed, though Irene tried to insist they swap places. Katherine was carried downstairs from Jem and Juliet's room, a sweaty limp bundle, and put on a mattress on the floor, banked up by pillows to stop her rolling off. Her parents took the sofa bed and outside Mickey and Luke put up the two-man tent. Irene could hear them now, talking in the garden below. She caught the faint whiff of tobacco through the window that was still open

227

behind the shutters, a rumble of laughter, occasional words and phrases. 'A man you can trust.' She hoped they were talking about Jem. 'Loving feeling.' Didn't that come from a song? Then something about sleeping on top of a sharp boulder, something about needing a pee, something about a bloody thistle, fucking mosquito, budge up, something about where's that whisky.

Beside her, Mary lay fast asleep on her back, with her arms calmly folded like an effigy, her hair brushed out and shining on the pillow, and wearing a white cotton nightdress similar to the ones Sasha preferred. They'd undressed in the room together, like girls on a sleepover, and Irene had noticed Mary's thickening waist and her heavy, blue-veined breasts with a pang of nostalgia.

'Are you excited?' she'd asked as they lay in their beds waiting for sleep.

'It's what I always wanted,' said Mary sleepily. 'It's like I've been waiting all my life for this.'

And in the half-darkness, Irene saw her put a hand under the sheet that draped her and cup it over her belly protectively.

Now Irene was listening to her deep, even breathing and the low murmurs from outside. It had been many years since she had shared a bedroom with another woman; perhaps not since she had fallen for Adrian and become part of a couple. How odd, she thought to herself, that I've spent all those years sleeping next to someone who I'll never voluntarily even touch again. He used to snore, breath catching at the back of his throat. It used to be so sweaty sleeping next to him, his hot, thickset body and his beery breath. Now the room

228

smelt of rose water and lemons and Mary was quietly plump and cottony on the floor beside her. Irene shifted to a cooler patch in the bed. It was very quiet now; the breeze that had blown up in the evening had died away, leaving behind a hushed, still darkness. Suddenly she heard a man's voice saying, quite clearly:

'Jem's sister seems very sweet, doesn't she?'

'Sweet?' replied the other—which? She didn't know them well enough to distinguish their tones. 'Sweet is *not* the word I'd use about her.'

'What word would you use?'

There was a pause. Irene strained to listen.

'She seems rather odd to me.'

Irene smiled up at the ceiling. Good. She was not sweet. Oh no. She was salty and sour and full of harsh and secret thoughts waiting to spring.

Tomorrow her little brother was getting married. Tomorrow she would see her father again.

CHAPTER TWENTY-THREE

He came across her when she wasn't expecting him. She was on her knees washing the kitchen floor, wearing her shorts and an ancient tee-shirt she'd borrowed from Jem, with the legend 'I climbed Snowdon' across the chest. Her feet were bare, with filthy soles, and she had tied a scarf that she'd found in a basket in the hall, peasant-style, round her head. Her face shone with sweat, and perspiration trickled down her breasts. Upstairs, someone was using the shower. Through the double doors, she could see that Neil and Mickey were trying to stuff the badly folded tent into its impossibly small bag while Luke was rolling up the sleeping bags, and that Katherine was sitting on the grass with Lorrie and eating last night's bread for breakfast, dipping it into a bowl of hot chocolate to soften it.

'A sight for sore eyes,' boomed a voice behind her and she started, slopping sudsy water over the floor.

At first glance, she thought that he hadn't changed at all, but then she saw that his boyish face was more florid and slacker, with red veins on his nose, new wrinkles around his eyes and lines across his forehead; that his hair was grey in new places and his belly was straining against the belt of his trousers—she could see a pale triangle of flesh beneath his shirt's last button. Behind him stood Toni. She had a look that Irene thought of as uniquely American, with boyish hips and full breasts, like two different bodies joined together to create some kind of impossible ideal. Sasha had a book like that, its pages all dissected in three, so you could turn the sections and create strange concoctions: pirates in dresses, fat men with skinny legs, a clown with the queen's head . . .

Toni's dark hair was pulled back in an immaculately mussed bun, and she wore a biscuit-coloured linen shift that showed off the tan on her legs, long painted nails, gold studs, high-heeled sandals, and a glossy, anxious smile. Behind her, hovering in the door, were two little girls with high pigtails.

'Hello, Dad,' Irene said, standing up hurriedly, scrubbing brush still in hand. 'I—er—I wasn't

230

expecting you just yet.'

'We all woke early with jet lag,' said her father. 'The kids have been up since four. And I couldn't wait any longer to see the groom—and my first lady, of course.'

He opened his arms wide. She stepped into them, letting the brush dangle by her side dribbling its dirty, soapy water down her calf, and was squashed in a bear hug. If she closed her eyes, she could have imagined herself back thirty-odd years, with that unforgettable smell of his: wine, whisky, spearmint, cigars, shaving cream. His daughters—her half-sisters, when she came to think of it—stared at her as he let her go.

'Hello, Toni,' said Irene to his wife. 'We're so pleased you could all be here. I think Jem is still in bed.'

'Look at you!' said Toni. 'What a nice sister you are, I must say. Isn't she a nice sister, honey? Slaving away while everyone else sleeps. Can't I do that for you? We're here to help in any way we can. Aren't we, Duncan, sweetie?'

She actually held out her hand, bangles clinking on her arm, for the brush. Irene looked doubtfully at Toni's elegant dress, and turned her attention to the two girls.

'You must be Coralie,' she said to the older one. 'And you're Emma.'

They nodded in unison, still stranded mutely in the doorway. They both had white socks and blue sandals, miniature v-shaped skirts. Coralie was plump and Emma skinny, with sharp knees and a wader bird's craning neck.

'Say hello,' prompted Toni.

'Hello,' they piped.

231

'Tell you what,' said Irene. 'I'm about to make coffee and put breakfast stuff out for people to help themselves to. Why don't you two go into the garden and we'll join you there. Introduce yourselves to Juliet's friends. There's another little girl,' she said to Emma and Coralie. 'But she's a bit younger than you.'

They didn't move.

'Go on,' said her father. 'We're just coming. Shoo.'

Emma's lower lip began to wobble. Coralie took her hand and tugged her across the kitchen and out through the opened doors.

'Oh look at them,' said Toni, exasperated at the way they wavered on the patio, staring out at the scene in the garden. 'How come they're so shy? Where do they get it from? Not from me.'

'I'll introduce them,' said Irene. 'Hang on.'

She put the brush into the bucket, wiped her hands down her shorts, and went into the garden. She took both girls by their hands and went across to Lorrie and Katherine. They had sweaty fingers which gripped hers fiercely. She saw how their shoes were old and scuffed and how Emma's skirt had an unravelled hem and Coralie's neck was grimy. Oh fuck, fuck, fuck, she thought—I'm feeling sorry for them.

'Hi,' she said to Lorrie. 'Have you been up for ages?'

'Bloody hours. We even took a walk into the village so we didn't disturb the whole household. We didn't wake you, did we?'

'No. Anyway, I wanted to get up early. Here, we've got some new guests who want to meet Katherine. This is Coralie, and this is Emma, just

232

arrived from America and probably completely jet-lagged and bewildered. They're my father's daughters,' she added. 'He's in the kitchen.'

'Hi, you two,' said Lorrie. They gazed at her and she looked at their tense faces, the tear stain on Emma's cheek. 'Maybe you can be ever so helpful and take Katherine down the garden to see what the men are doing. A hand each,' she added.

The three children set off, Katherine bobbing and weaving in the middle.

'Thanks.'

'It must be odd for you, being with children when your own are away.'

'It is a bit.'

The girls had reached the men. They watched as Luke waved them over and bent down to talk to them.

'Right, I'm going to make coffee and breakfast.'

'I'll help. She's OK for a bit. Neil will keep an eye on them.'

*　　　*　　　*

In the presence of his father, Jem became self-conscious and awkward; with his flushed cheeks and sudden jocose irony he was like an ungainly adolescent all over again. Irene watched him anxiously. Out of the corner of her eye, she could see the three children poking with sticks at something at the far end of the garden. Luke was sitting on the bench near them, sipping his coffee.

'What do you want for your wedding present?' asked Duncan. 'We couldn't decide, could we Toni, so we thought we should let you choose. Name it?' He shoved half a croissant into his mouth, posted a fig after it, and chewed noisily. A pip slid down his chin. 'A holiday. An object. Something for your beautiful wife.' He chuckled at Juliet, who smiled tightly.

'Remember . . .' began Toni nervously.

'Nobody asked you. I'm talking to my son here. My boy.' He sighed gustily.

'This is enough of a present, Duncan,' said Jem. 'You coming over. I never expected . . .'

'Of course I came over. Would I have missed your wedding day?'

'Well, of course it depended on your work trip fitting in with it,' said Toni. 'We could never have afforded . . .'

'What's money compared to family?'

'Have some more coffee,' said Mickey. 'Shall I fetch more croissants from the kitchen?'

Luke arrived at the table and sat beside Irene. He took a fig and turned it over in his hands, then cut it in half.

'What did I give you for a wedding present, honey?' Duncan turned to Irene.

'Um . . .'

He hadn't. He hadn't come over. He'd promised to but at the last minute he'd called to say there were unexpected problems; hitches; what a shame; his little motherless girl marrying and he wouldn't be able to give her away.

'Just hope that wastrel husband of yours didn't take it with him when he left, whatever it was.'

Irene's cheeks burned. He turned back to Jem.

'When's your mother arriving?'

'She's here already. She's—well, she's coming to lunch actually.'

'Lunch? You're having a lunch here before the

wedding?'

'Yes. We thought—that is, if you think it would be a good idea, then . . .'

Juliet watched him struggle. Then she cut in: 'Jem thought you should come in the morning and his mother and my parents for lunch. Then everyone can be at the ceremony and at the party in the evening. He thought it was easier that way— easier for all of you.'

'Absolutely,' said Toni enthusiastically. She tore a tiny flake off the croissant and put it on her tongue.

'Dear Amanda. How is she?'

'Fine.'

'Well, this will be strange,' said Duncan. 'Lives coming together today, after so many years and so much water under the bridge. Who would have thought it, eh?' He turned to Irene. 'If only your mother were here too.'

'Yes,' said Irene curtly. 'Quite.'

'Here,' said Mickey, returning with more croissants. 'And Mary's up at last. She's crouched on the living-room floor doing these very slow exercises. She looks a bit mad actually.'

*   *   *

'Why did I invite him? I must have been having a brainstorm.'

'Because he's your father and it's your wedding day.'

They were getting the lunch ready, while Juliet took her friends for a brief walk through the village.

'I always forget what he's like until I see him

again.'

'I know what you mean. Toni didn't seem very happy, did she?'

'Didn't she? She seemed OK to me.'

'No. Something's going on. Do you get the impression they're having money problems?'

'He always has money problems. He borrowed £1,500 off me a year ago. Just for a week or so, he said.'

'Ah.'

'I can never work out what job he's in.'

'It changes. Something about import-export is what he said to me.'

'Sounds like a seedy traveller out of a Graham Greene novel.'

'The little girls are sweet though. I wonder—'

'What?'

'I wonder if they're all right. Do they seem all right to you?'

'Shy, that's all. Don't worry about them—just because you haven't got yours here to worry about. Anyway, it's not a day to think about things like that.'

'Quite right. That beef must be nearly ready. We mustn't overcook it, not in France.'

'Is that enough salad?'

'Plenty. Nobody will want to eat much.'

'To be honest, I don't think I could eat anything at all.'

'Nervous?'

'Kind of. It's a big thing. You know what, I never thought I'd ever fall in love with someone who'd want to spend the rest of her life with me.' He winced sharply. 'I just want her to be all right. That's all that matters.'

The doorbell rang.

'That'll be Mum,' he said.

*   *   *

She put on her grey skirt, noticing it no longer hung loosely off her waist, her pale pink top, her stud earrings. Then she brushed her hair and slipped her feet into sandals. She could only see her face in the small mirror, but she felt that she looked like a Victorian governess. She took a scarlet flower from the vase on the window sill and snapped its stalk, then tucked it into the top of her shirt.

She looked out into the garden. The three men and Mary were playing boules and Lorrie and Katherine were sitting in the shade of the walnut tree looking at a picture book together; Katherine was wearing a stinging pink dress with a stiff wide skirt that made her look like an overcooked meringue. Jem, in his dark suit, his hair damped down, was walking up and down the grass with his mother, who was clinging to his arm to steady herself in her stiletto heels.

*   *   *

'I look like a fat middle-aged Irish peasant,' said Juliet. She stared disconsolately at herself in the mirror, sucking in her stomach and pulling back her shoulders.

'Rubbish.'

'I should never have bought this dress. It's not the kind of thing I ever wear. Look at me.'

'You look lovely.'

237

'No. I look like a dowdy executive. I wanted everything to be perfect.'

She picked up a brush and started to drag it through her tangled hair, then threw it down on the bed.

'It's no good,' she said. Her face was heavy and flushed. Her eyes filled with tears. 'Nothing's any good.'

'What do you mean?'

'Maybe he's just sorry for me.'

'How can you begin to think something so—'

'I'm nearly seven years older than him and I've had a lump in my breast cut out and maybe I'll never be able to have kids and I know he wants to be a father some day. I don't want to be a burden.'

'If ever a man was in love, Jem is. He can hardly believe his luck. It's because of you he's happy.'

'Really?'

'Really.'

'You're not just saying it?'

'Listen to me.' Irene gripped Juliet by her shoulders. 'Ever since I met him, when he was eighteen and just out of school, I've been worried about Jem because he never seemed to belong anywhere. Everyone liked him, but he was an outsider. You know. Then he met you and he changed. He's OK now. You did that.'

'I did that?'

'You know you did.'

Juliet sniffed. 'Sorry to be stupid.'

'Here.' Irene picked up the brush. 'This is one thing I am good at. Ask Aggie.'

Juliet sat for a while, letting Irene brush her hair and staring at herself in the mirror.

'I want to wear something different,' she said at

238

last, as Irene twisted her hair up and fastened it behind her head.

'What? Now, you mean?'

'Something not so—businesslike. This isn't a business meeting, it's a wedding, for God's sake.'

'OK. Let's look,' said Irene, trying not to glance at the time.

'There's nothing that's quite right.'

'What about this skirt and then your lovely white shirt with the flared sleeves?'

'Do you think?'

'Try it.'

They heard Jem's voice, calling up to them to hurry.

'Don't worry, we've got a bit of time still,' said Irene. 'There. Let's have a look at you.'

'Is it better?'

'You look gorgeous. Very romantic. Have you got a necklace or anything? This one. Let me fasten it.'

'And these earrings.'

'Juliet!' came Jem's voice again. 'Everyone's waiting. If you want to get married today, you'd better hurry.'

'Perfume,' said Juliet, and sprayed a bottle wildly over her face and down her cleavage, then squirted a bit at Irene.

'Ready?'

'Ready.'

CHAPTER TWENTY-FOUR

It was all over so very quickly. What would Irene remember, later? That Jem spoke clearly and Juliet in a rush, her words tumbling with each other. That afterwards they both cried and laughed at the same time, squeezing each other's fingers with their new gold bands. That Jem's mother cried too, surreptitiously, behind a strip of lavatory roll, dabbing carefully at her eyes to make sure her mascara didn't smudge, while on the bench behind her, her ex-husband sat with his new family, a beatific, several-glasses-of-wine smile on his face and tears in his boyish blue eyes. He'd kissed Amanda on the mouth when they met, told her she was looking marvellous, who would have guessed so many years had passed, and she'd inclined her expressionless face and turned away. That Irene's own hand shook when she signed the form. That Juliet's parents sat at the front anxiously holding hands and nodding at the incomprehensible French, and that her mother wore an enormously brimmed hat, like a flying saucer. That Jem's friends Peter Wallis and Terence Lott shared a bench at the back that creaked bitterly whenever one of them shifted his weight. That every few minutes Luke handed lemon bon-bons to the three girls to stop them fidgeting, and that Emma spent the short ceremony picking the scab off her left knee and then rubbing away the subsequent beads of blood with her licked forefinger. That Katherine fell asleep in her father's arms, so her head lolled on his shoulder and a small thread of saliva hung from her fat pink lip. That the hall smelt of camphor and beeswax. That at a certain point she had been unable to stop herself from remembering her own wedding when she'd worn a scarlet dress, no shoes and a rose in her hair.

* * *

At the pre-party party, champagne corks popped. Guests took off their suit jackets and pulled their ties loose, or kicked off their high-heeled shoes, easing their hot, aching feet on the scratchy grass. In the distance, Katherine was singing 'Ten Green Bottles' but skipping or repeating numbers randomly. Duncan held a glass in each hand. He kissed Mary on the mouth, then tried to do the same to Lorrie but she ducked her head so he found himself kissing her hairline. 'Wonderful, wonderful,' he kept saying. 'Brings everything flooding back, when we were young and foolish.' Toni followed his zigzagging course round the garden, and her daughters followed her. Jem's mother was talking animatedly to Jem's two old school friends, hands on hips and legs apart, her dark hair straying from its pinnings, her lips rubbed bare of the lipstick she'd put on for the service. Juliet changed into her silver halter-neck dress and unloosed her hair so it sprang out around her flushed face; she looked like a pagan woman, thought Irene: wild and strong. Catcalls greeted her as she came into the garden and she twirled round, the dress floating in a circle.

'Anyone who wants to change into something else had better hurry,' she said. 'Everyone will be arriving soon.'

241

'Presents first,' said Mickey. 'We've put them on the table.'

'Presents?'

'What did you expect?'

'I dunno. Just—having you here.'

*   *   *

'That's too generous,' said Juliet. 'You shouldn't have.'

Jem kissed her on both cheeks. 'Thank you,' he said into her ear. 'It's lovely.'

They turned away to the next parcel, ripping off shiny paper, greedy children at a birthday party. Irene looked back at the photograph.

'It's very empty,' she said out loud. 'I never realized quite how empty it is. Just sand and sky.' She shivered, suddenly cold under its inhuman glow.

'There's a figure, just there,' said a voice beside her: Luke. She glanced at him, his soft, tufty hair that she wanted to run her fingers over, and his wide-set caramel eyes, and for a moment wondered if he thought she was sweet, or if he thought she was odd. There was a small scar on his lip that she hadn't seen before. She followed his pointing finger and saw that on the desert's horizon, at the far left of the picture, almost out of the frame, was a speck-like figure in white, though she had to peer closely to make it out.

'So there is. I never noticed.'

'But is he on his way out of the photograph, or is he arriving? That's the question.'

'I can't tell.'

'It makes a difference though, doesn't it?'

'I suppose so,' she said. 'Yes.'

'Which would you prefer?'

'I don't know.

'I think he's arriving.'

'How do you know he's a he? Maybe it's a woman.'

'I feel it's a man.'

'That's because you're a man,' she said. 'I feel as if it's me. Me leaving.'

*   *   *

In her orange dress, in bare feet, she danced. The candles flickered and glowed along the garden, the insects hummed. She danced with Jem's tall friend Peter; with her lurching, fumbling, sodden father; with a French bacteriologist with garlicky breath and tiny feet; with a small, bald doctor who tried to talk to her about French politics as he swung round to the music; with Jem, who was a terrible dancer and trod on her toes and flung his hands wildly in the air; with Juliet's father, who was red-faced and stocky and who jogged on the spot; with Mickey several times, who grinned his white grin and held her close when the music slowed; with Luke, once, and when she looked for him later she couldn't see him although by now she had realized that he was the only person she wanted; with Coralie and Emma, in a small, bopping circle; in the middle of a conga line that weaved its way round the house, her hands on Lorrie's waist and Neil's hands on hers; with her father again, though she wanted to escape his glaring eyes and his thick voice saying: 'I made a mistake, a terrible mistake, I never should have, a mistake, oh the things we do . . .'

243

The music crackled out of the speakers that had been placed at the open windows. She stood under the walnut tree and let the breeze cool her cheeks, and watched Jem doing his mad, splay-footed dance with Toni, whose own delicately swaying movements were barely perceptible; watched Mary dancing with Luke, who at one point stopped and took her face in his hands, gazed at her for a few moments and then kissed her on both cheeks.

She held her father's forehead while he was sick into the toilet bowl, then mopped his clammy face with a damp towel. She had so adored him when she was a child and he was tall and fine and strong. His laugh had filled the house and his hero's arms had swung her free and high in the air so that for a time she had flying dreams at night. Presents had been mysteriously conjured from his pockets, promises were laid before her like coloured sweets and she had believed in them, over and over again. It had taken her a long time to realize they were so many bubbles of air, and more time still to understand that he wasn't insincere. He just said what he meant at the time and then moved on. He had the endless capacity to begin afresh, as if the past didn't stick to him, but slid harmlessly off.

After he had left, she used to lie awake at night waiting for the sound of his footsteps outside her room. She knew he would come back; how could he keep away when she was his honey, his gorgeous, his heart throb, his best love, his little princess, his sweet pea? Night after night, she would creep into her mother's room and curl up at the bottom of the bed like a cat, thinking that maybe when she woke in the morning, he'd be there, large and solid under the sheets, his long, blistered feet touching hers. She looked at him, doubled over, a dribble of vomit hanging from his chin, his blue eyes bloodshot and watering.

'Sorry,' he gasped, spluttering.

'Never mind.'

'Something disagreed . . .' he said.

'Don't worry.'

Toni found them there.

'Oh Duncan,' she said. Her voice was flat with distaste. 'Look at the state of you. Oh why in the world do you do it?'

'Party,' he said. 'Wedding. My only son. What d'you know about it? Nothing.'

Toni swung round in the doorway, her buttocks sharp under the pale blue dress, her tight shoulders hunched up. Miserably, Irene saw that her tan was fake, streaked at the back of her calves where she couldn't see properly.

'Dad,' she said urgently. 'Don't. Stop it.'

'S'OK. She's not going anywhere without me. Where would she go? She'll get over it.'

Irene had an urge to slap him across his slack cheek, to bring real tears to his eyes. She balled up the towel and chucked it under the sink, then turned to leave.

'Don't go yet,' he said. 'Don't go, Irene. I know what you think of me, all of you. But I love you, I do. And I loved your mother too.'

'Yes,' said Irene neutrally.

'We were so happy once, the three of us, weren't we? Things with Toni aren't the way—'

'Dad,' said Irene. 'This isn't the time. You shouldn't tell me about Toni.'

'You don't understand. I loved you both.'

'I know. I know.'

'You shouldn't judge me so harshly.'

'I don't judge you at all. I don't think about it any more.'

'Yes you do, I see the way you look at me. Like you despise me.'

'No.'

'You think I'm just a stupid, drunk old man.'

'That's not true.'

'You loved me once, too. You were my first little girl. When you were born . . . so tiny . . . I could always make you stop crying . . .'

Fat tears rolled down his cheeks. He put out a hand to steady himself on the sink. His shirt was half-unbuttoned and his hair stuck in strands across his forehead. Irene bit her lip—she didn't want to feel pity for him like this. She preferred the anger and contempt. And she didn't want to be standing in a bathroom that smelt of vomit and bleach, while her father reminisced about his fake past.

'Come on,' she said briskly, a girl guide. 'Jem's going to make a speech soon. We don't want to miss that.'

She hooked an arm through his and towed him listing back to the party.

Outside, there was a moon now. People were still dancing, but the music had slowed and there were ghostly figures dotted around the garden, chatting or simply looking on. Irene poured herself half a glass of wine and sat cross-legged on the grass, leaning back against the wall, feeling its roughness through the thin fabric of her dress.

'Can I join you?'

'Sure.'

Mickey lowered himself beside her.

'They look happy, don't they?'

'Mmmm.'

'This is the way to do it—dancing on a summer's evening. Nothing fancy. Sandy's parents insisted that we married in a church and then we had seventy people to a sit-down meal in this stuffy hotel with dried-out chicken breasts and lemon soufflé. It wasn't nearly as much fun.'

Irene didn't reply, just twisted her glass round by its stem.

'What was your wedding like, then?' he asked after a pause.

'Small,' she said shortly. Just them and their witnesses, and straight afterwards they'd changed into jeans, picked up their backpacks, kissed everyone goodbye and gone cycling in Portugal. But she didn't want to think about that now. She watched Lorrie and Neil standing together; Lorrie was taking animatedly, gesturing extravagantly, and Neil was watching her with a look of half-amused tenderness on his face. At one point he tucked a small snake of hair behind her ears and picked an invisible thread from her dress. She watched Jem and Juliet dance close together; Juliet's silver dress shimmered like a mermaid's scales in the moonlight. Jem stroked the back of her head and she put her face up to his, smiling.

'You should think about coming on the boat with us on Sunday.'

'It's nice of you, but . . .'

'I don't like the sound of that "but". Why not?'

'It's complicated.'

'You could just do it for a few days.'

'Well . . .'

'It'd be fun,' he said. 'And Lorrie needs another

woman. She likes you.'

'It's mutual.'

'We all do,' he added.

'Thanks.' She touched his shoulder. 'I'll think about it.'

'By the way, I've been meaning to say, that dress looks good on you.' He flashed his grin. 'By which I mean, of course, you look good in that dress.'

'Thanks,' she said again. She knew him now: he thought she was sweet. He talked too much and was a charmer—like her father; like Adrian.

Not for her. She'd had enough of easy words.

*   *   *

'Ladies and gentlemen,' called Jem. Someone tapped a spoon against a glass; conversation died away. *'Mesdames et messieurs,'* he added. *'Et maintenant je vais parler en anglais.* OK?'

Someone shouted something boisterously in French. Jem held up a hand. 'This won't take long,' he said. 'And I can always translate afterwards for anyone who doesn't understand, though that feels a bit too much like work.'

He stood on the patio holding Juliet's hand and smiled at everyone, taking in their faces. He seemed quite relaxed, thought Irene, amazed; no trace of his old stammer, no burning redness in his cheeks.

'I never knew what to call her,' he went on. 'I used to say, my girlfriend, but that made us seem like teenagers. My partner—but we're not in business together. My lover—oh God no, too explicit by half for a stammering idiotic Englishman like me. My um, er—that was the most

248

common one. Now I guess I can call her my wife, but I think it'll take me a long time to get used to that. I think I'll be surprised for the rest of my life that I have someone as kind and beautiful and clever and good for my wife.' A sentimental ripple went round the garden and Juliet's mother gave a single, rasping sob. Jem took a breath: 'Tomorrow we are going away for a one-night honeymoon, and next week I will probably spend my evenings sitting helplessly on the bathroom floor watching her being sick. And I tell you—not for one minute will I wish I was anywhere else. I'll be the luckiest man in the whole world.' He stopped abruptly and held up his glass. 'To Juliet.'

'To Juliet.'

Juliet stood forward then, stared at them all, smiled at Jem, opened her mouth and burst into tears. Everyone waited in silence and eventually she waved her hand in the air and said: 'Sorry. Thank you. Oh dear God.' She straightened her shoulders and gave a gulpy laugh: 'Actually, I'd prepared this spiel, but probably that's more or less what I wanted to say. Sorry. Thank you. Oh dear God. It seems to cover most of the bases. Now will someone please put the music back on before I start crying again.'

She stood back but then held up her hand and said in a quick, loud voice: 'No, there's one other thing. If there's something you really, really want, don't wait. Do it now.'

CHAPTER TWENTY-FIVE

Irene stood at the far end of the garden, leaning against the low wall and staring out at the stars and at the deep black of the sky that felt like a dizzying abyss hanging above her. What did she want, really really want? There was a hand on her shoulder and she turned.

'Hello,' she began.

'Irene,' said Mickey. 'I just wanted to say—oh what the hell.'

He put his hands on either side of her face and kissed her on her mouth, pulling her close and blotting out the pulsing stars and the plummeting sky. She felt his cool lips, his hot fingers on her skin, the jump of his heart against her chest. He smelt of wine and garlic and something faintly flowery, like geraniums. Nothing like Adrian; the strangeness of it shocked her. She pulled back.

'What?' he said.

'That's the first time in thirteen years or more that I've kissed anyone except my husband.'

'And? Was it OK?'

'I need to go now,' she said, smiling slightly to remove the sting. 'People will be going soon.'

*   *   *

Upstairs, Katherine and Emma were lying asleep in her bed, top to toe. She went into the bathroom and locked the door, splashed cold water over her face and looked at herself in the mirror. Her face was fuller, her eyes brighter, her hair was growing longer. Soon, she would be able to brush it behind her ears and it would cover her neck. She looked—she stared at herself for a moment—she looked more like herself at last; more like the person that she had always thought she was.

People were starting to leave. Outside in the lane, cars started up, voices called goodbye in French, in English. She returned to the garden, where the moustached bacteriologist with the garlicky breath was kissing the balding doctor and Toni was goggling at them in frank shock. Irene, grinning to herself, helped her button the bleary-eyed girls into their cardigans. Duncan was standing at the edge of the garden looking rumpled and sad.

'Our taxi's here,' said Toni. 'It's been a good party.'

'I'm glad you could come.'

'When are you leaving?' asked Toni.

'Tomorrow—or maybe Sunday. I haven't really made my plans. What about you?'

'We're going to Nice tomorrow. We have to be in Paris on Monday afternoon for Duncan's work. Then we're flying home a week later.'

'I hope you have a lovely time.'

'I've never been abroad before,' said Toni suddenly. 'We only got passports a few months ago, especially for this trip. I've been looking forward to it so much. I bought new clothes and went on this special diet. I tried to learn about the family. You and Jem. We're like, related, right? I thought . . .' She stopped.

'I hope everything goes all right,' said Irene inadequately.

'Yeah.' Toni sounded dispirited; then lifted one

251

sharp brown shoulder. 'Oh well.'

'Bye you two,' said Irene, bending down. She kissed both of the girls on the cheek. 'Thank you for helping to look after Katherine.'

'Who are you?' said Emma.

'What?'

'We don't know who you are.'

'I'm Irene.'

'Yes, but are you our aunt?'

'No, not your aunt though I can see how you'd think that.'

'Mom said you were kind-of an aunt.'

'Really, I'm your half-sister.'

They stared at her, uncomprehending.

'Ask your father,' she said, giving up. 'But not now. Tomorrow.'

*   *   *

Everyone had gone and the candles had burned down—only a few of them still guttered in the jars, giving out their last stabs of light. Now it was just the eight of them in the garden again, surrounded by the debris of the party and relaxed with each other.

'The ends of parties are always the best,' said Juliet. 'This is nice.'

'Mmm,' said Mary, stretching her arms above her head. 'But I'm going to bed now.'

'I'll move Katherine out of your way,' said Lorrie.

'We've got to put the bloody tent up again.'

'In a bit. I'm going to have my forbidden fag now.'

'Who wants something else to drink?'

252

'God, not me,' said Juliet. 'I'm floating as it is.'

'How about some of that champagne we brought with us?' said Neil.

'OK.'

Neil opened it and shared it carefully out.

'My turn to make a toast,' he said, raising his glass. 'Good luck to all of us.'

'Good luck,' they chorused, looking around at each other. Mickey stared across at Irene, and she shivered, suddenly cold in her skimpy dress and bare feet.

'Here. Have my jacket.' Luke was beside her.

'I'm fine.'

But he draped it over her shoulders, pulling it close around her.

*   *   *

'Hello, darling,' she said in a low voice, standing at the garden door with the phone while on the floor behind her Neil and Lorrie lay flung out on the mattress together, limbs entwined, half covered by a thin sheet, and on the sofa Katherine mumbled in her sleep. The standard lamp, draped in a towel to soften its light, shone on her hair that was matted on her forehead and on her shiny pink cheeks. 'Hello, my love.'

'Mummy?'

'Is it still the middle of the day there?'

'Mummy. Your voice is all echoey.'

'Can you hear me?'

'I can hear you twice.'

'Are you having a lovely time? Is everyone all right?'

'Mummy?'

'Yes.'

'Aren't you at home?'

'I'm with your uncle Jem.'

'Who's feeding my hamster then?'

Irene gave a relieved giggle. 'Kadija. She promised to take great care of him and hold him every day so he doesn't get wild.'

'Will he remember me when I get back?'

'Of course. He might be a bit shy at first. Listen, how is everyone?'

'Fine. Will I have long before I start my new school?'

'Don't worry—a couple of weeks. You can just flop around and relax and get ready.'

'I can swim under the water with the snorkel. Can I show you in the swimming pool?'

'I'd like that a lot.'

'I ate crocodile.'

'Wow!'

'It didn't taste like crocodile though.'

Irene tried to think what to say to that. She saw that Luke was sitting at the far end of the garden, smoking a cigarette. She saw its end glowing in the darkness.

'Mummy?'

'Yes.'

'I was thinking . . .'

'Tell me.'

'When we get back we could all live in the same house, maybe?'

'You mean . . .'

'I can share with Aggie and Clem. There's room. I don't mind being on the camp bed.'

'We can talk about this later. The important thing is that you're having a wonderful time with

254

Daddy and Frankie.'

'I stole your perfume, Mummy. And your lipstick. And I was the one who scrumpled up your dress and put it in the toilet.'

'I know. It doesn't matter.'

'If we all lived in the same house then it wouldn't be like this.'

'Like what?'

'You know—this funny feeling in my tummy all the time. Like I'm going to be sick, but I never am.'

'Do you get that?'

'I told Daddy and he said it was growing pains.'

'Well . . .'

'Not just now. With you too, because there's always one of you away, so I'm always wanting to be somewhere else than where I am. Do you know what I mean?'

'Yes. I do.'

'Clem wants to speak to you now.'

'Hang on, Sasha . . .'

But there was no reply, and then a few seconds later Clem's voice came on the phone.

'Hello.'

'Hello, Clemmie. It's me.'

'Who?'

'Mummy.'

'Oh.'

'Are you well?' Irene listened to Clem's heavy breathing for a few seconds. 'OK. Tell me three things you did yesterday.'

'I played.' There was another pause, and then she added: 'And I played and I played.'

'That's cheating.'

'Aggie ate a jellyfish.'

'What!'

'She put it in her mouth and bit right into it.'

'My God! Is she all right?'

'I think she thought it was a sweet or something like that.'

'But is she OK?'

'I stroked three kangaroos and held a koala bear and now I've got a photograph.'

'Blimey. Great.'

'Frankie and Daddy—'

'Can I speak to Aggie?'

'She's having a bath because she wet herself.'

'What about Daddy?'

'He's giving her the bath.'

'Oh.' Irene swallowed hard. 'Is Frankie there, just for a second?'

'Frankie!' Clem yelled. 'Mummy wants you.'

'Hello, Irene.'

'I just wanted to know—is Aggie all right?'

'Just a swollen lip and a throat that aches now because she screamed so much.'

'That's all?'

'Everything's fine.' She had a husky, sexily reassuring tone that made Irene want to gag. 'They're having a lovely time and they're mostly being terribly good and sweet, and today we're going to take them—'

'Thanks,' said Irene, cutting her short. 'I just wanted to check. Bye then.'

*   *   *

'You should have let me speak to her,' said Adrian.

'*Let* you? Hang on, you were giving Aggie a bath and she just wanted to know that everything was fine so I—'

256

'I should have spoken to her. Not you.'

'Adrian, she sounded fine. What good would it do to talk to her?'

'I feel . . .'

'What? What do you feel?'

'I feel I shouldn't have taken the girls so far away from her. I know what she must be going through.'

'It's a bit late for that. We're here. Aren't you happy here?'

'Oh Frankie, you know I am. It takes me by surprise, how happy I am—you, and the girls as well. It's just that every so often—oh shit, never mind.'

'Every so often you miss her, is that what this is really about?'

'Not miss. It's just that I was with her for so long, I guess she's a bit like a phantom limb or something. There even when she's not there. Sorry—this isn't the kind of crap you need to be hearing.'

'It's bound to be hard for a bit.'

'I hurt her so much. I keep thinking of her face the way it was at the airport, when she thought we couldn't see her. So—*bereft.*'

'I know. But you mustn't torment yourself. It does no one any good and it gets better, with time.'

'Does it?'

'I think so.'

Adrian put his hand on her stomach and looked at her ruefully.

'I hope you know what you've taken on, Frankie.'

'I always knew. From the very first moment. Eyes wide open.'

257

'What did I do to deserve you?'
'You loved me, that's what.'

*   *   *

Irene lay in her bed with the windows open and watched the shadowy figure of Luke, sitting hunched and motionless at the end of the garden, while Mary lay asleep on the floor beside her.

'I did love him very much,' she whispered to herself. 'After all, I did love him.'

The wrong man had kissed her this evening. She'd just have to stay around till the right one kissed her too.

CHAPTER TWENTY-SIX

Irene's cabin was at the front left-hand side of the lozenge-shaped boat. It had a small bunk, with a white sheet and a beige blanket on it and a shallow drawer underneath to hold her clothes, its own hand-pumped lavatory and shower, and a narrow strip of shelf. The tiny window, which opened only a few inches, was frosted except for its upper strip. When anyone walked on deck, their feet thumped over her head. Lorrie, Neil and Katherine took the largest cabin, adjacent to hers, with a double bed for them, and a fold-out single bed for Katherine. She could hear them talking together in low, conspiratorial voices; could hear when they pissed or brushed their teeth. Mickey and Luke took the two cabins at the back that looked more like cupboards with bunk beds in them than rooms, and that shared a lavatory and shower.

'Are you sure this is all right?'

'Fine,' said Mickey. 'I can put all my stuff on the top bunk and sleep on the bottom one.'

'But I thought you two would have more . . .'

'It's fine, Irene,' repeated Mickey. 'It's just for sleeping in, after all. We wanted you here.' He smiled at her and she blushed and looked away.

There was a sitting area with a collapsible table and seats that could be opened out into extra beds, and a galley kitchen with a box-like fridge and a two-ring gas hob.

'Cosy,' said Lorrie, putting milk and peaches into the fridge.

'We steer from the top,' said Neil. 'Unless it's raining, then we can do it from the sheltered lower deck.'

'But it's not going to rain, is it? It feels like it's never going to rain again. It's boiling already.'

'Make the most of it. Soon it will be November and Ireland.'

'Do we know how to steer it?'

'Luke's looking at the manual. He's good at things like that. He's the practical one.'

'I'm glad you decided to come,' said Lorrie.

'Me too,' said Irene, although now she was here she didn't know why she had changed her mind and a large part of her was wishing she had said goodbye to them this morning, and driven away. She could be alone again and going home. Away from the kiss in the garden and the disquieting, unfocused tremor of excitement she felt when she remembered it. If she had left yesterday evening, then the past few days would already be turning into memories. Instead she was trapped on a boat

259

in a small town just west of Montpellier with a group of people she hardly knew. They would all be living so close up against each other. The others were friends. They didn't mind hearing each other use the lavatory, make love, bicker. They were entirely easy with each other. But she was a stranger whom they'd met for the first time three days ago—the half-sister of their friend's new husband. Perhaps they were simply being kind to her, just feeling sorry for her—the lonely woman whose husband had fucked off and left her. If she were not here, they could wander around in their underwear, let hours of silence fill up the spaces of the days ahead.

And soon the engine would be started, the ropes untied, and the boat would be moving off, leaving her rusting car standing at the canal side for the next four or five days, and there'd be no going back.

She went to her cabin and arranged her few clothes into the drawer, her toothbrush and toothpaste into the plastic beaker in the shower room. The boat rocked slightly in the wake of a passing vessel; aqueous light rippled and glimmered on the grubby white ceiling, thin plasticky boards tacked in place. Her cabin was really just a fragile cardboard compartment, no lock on the door. Irene sat on the bed, the blanket itchy under her bare legs. She didn't want to go up on deck just yet. She wasn't quite sure what she was supposed to do up there—sit and chat with them, trying to recapture the easy intimacy of the time after the party? Read a book? Perhaps it would be a good idea to take one of the ancient yellow bikes stacked at the stern of the boat and cycle part of the way.

'Oi!' shouted a voice from outside. Mickey. 'Let's open a beer.'

'It's only eleven o'clock.'

'We're on holiday!'

'Mummy!' called Katherine from next door. 'Mummy, I need a wee.'

'OK, this is easy,' came Luke's voice. 'Who wants to know how to operate the boat? We should get moving quite soon. It would be a good idea to get through the first set of locks today and they close at five.'

The engine coughed into life and Irene could feel its faint vibration underneath her.

'Untie her then,' said Luke. 'And we're off. Neil, can you unloose her from the bows. Thanks.'

Irene sat quite still. Very slowly, the boat moved away from the towpath where it was moored. Through the top of the window, she could see trees, a red-tiled roof, a plump white cloud slowly gliding past. She remembered saying goodbye to Juliet yesterday. They'd gripped each other's hands and when she'd opened her mouth to speak, Juliet had shushed her.

'Don't,' she'd said. 'There's nothing to say. It's been wonderful.'

'It has,' said Irene. 'You've been wonderful.'

'Rubbish. Listen, I'm going to be fine. Do you hear me?'

'I know. Of course you are.'

'And so are you.'

'Of course.'

They'd gazed at each other, blinking away tears and smiling. Then Jem had taken Juliet's arm and led her to the car and the guests had been left

261

alone, feeling suddenly adrift in the house.

'Watch out, you bloody moron!' came Mickey's voice.

Irene sighed and stood up reluctantly.

She came up on deck, squinting at the flat blue of the sky and the bolts of light that flashed off the canal, making her eyes sting. There was absolutely no wind; the trees on either side were motionless, their leaves dark and limp. The water shone like great slabs of glass in front of them, although behind them, the wake of the boat chopped up the reflected sky. Ahead, a low-arched bridge was perfectly mirrored: it looked as though they would be passing through an unbroken circle of brick. Luke raised his hand in greeting to Irene. He was sitting in his shorts and dark glasses at the boat's steering wheel, turning it fractionally to the right and left, frowning in concentration. The tip of his tongue was on his upper lip. A pair of binoculars hung round his neck and he had a notebook beside him. The canal was narrower now they'd left the village mooring and the boat nosed along, almost near enough to the towpath to jump ashore.

'Beer,' called Mickey, who was sitting on a chair near Luke, looking at the map. His bright turquoise shirt was unbuttoned and he wore a blue cap jauntily askew.

'Maybe coffee first,' said Irene, feeling shy and strange among them.

'Good idea. Make some for me too, will you?' asked Luke.

'And us,' called Neil from the boat's interior. 'We're coming up soon. Lorrie's just covering every spare inch of Katherine's skin in sun cream.'

'I'll make a big pot.'

'Then you can have a go. It's easy once you get the hang of it, but you have to make constant adjustments.'

*   *   *

Irene made coffee, standing hunched in the galley. She rubbed on some of her factor thirty-five sun lotion which left her arms and face looking a dull white, like a clown before the red mouth is painted on, and then put on her hat and her dark glasses.

'Here,' she said as she re-emerged on deck. 'Five coffees, that's the one with sugar, and an apple juice for Katherine.'

'Thanks,' said Mickey, taking a sip of coffee then one of beer, making a face of mock surprise. 'My God, what do you look like?'

'Ridiculous?'

'Is this a way of putting me off?' he said in a low voice. 'Because it's not going to work.'

'I don't want to get burned, that's all.'

He had long lashes, she saw, like a girl's; a hairy chest that she turned her eyes from.

'I'm sure we'll get used to it. It's like having a cute ghost on board.'

'Drink your coffee,' said Luke. 'And then I'll show you how to steer.'

'There's nothing to show,' said Mickey. 'You just hold the wheel, like in a car. End of story.'

Irene thought she sensed a faint antagonism between them, a tiny spark that died as soon as it was struck. She turned away from them both and looked out on to the banks of the canal. There were vast and knobbly plane trees on either side, whose roots had grown down into the water,

263

making a kind of wall. They had been brutally pollarded and their branches were thick crabbed stumps, like an old man's fingers amputated at the knuckles. Their bark was smooth, and dappled a silver and grey-green.

'Look,' said Luke. 'There.'

Two herons, their long legs tucked back, their heads outstretched, flew overhead.

'I should have brought binoculars.'

'Here. Have a go with these.'

He passed them across and she took off her sunglasses and squinted through them, swinging them round to watch the herons beating their way across the blazing sky, and then pointing downwards to the swampy meadows on either side.

'Look!' she said. 'White horses, there in the distance. Lots of them. Look, before they go. Can you see?'

'So there are.' Mickey stood very close to her, much too close, following the direction of her pointing finger.

'It's what the Camargue's famous for,' said Luke, standing up and steadying the wheel with his foot, shading his eyes with his hand. 'I've been reading about it in my book. White horses, black bulls and flamingoes.'

'How beautiful. Are they wild? They look it. Watch them go.'

'I don't know.'

'Beautiful,' Irene repeated, sighing.

'Do you want to steer for a bit?'

'OK. Show me.'

'Like Mickey says, nothing to it. You only have to make small adjustments to make a difference but the boat responds slowly, so you shouldn't keep on turning it otherwise you'll tack along the canal. Anticipate. This lever here, you pull backwards for reverse. If you pull sharply and then return it to neutral, that's the way to stop if you need to. OK?'

'You sound like a teacher.'

'I am.'

'What do you teach?'

'Meteorology. Geo-chemistry. Weather.'

'Luke's a cloud man.'

'What?'

'He loves clouds,' said Mickey. 'Ever since he was a kid, he loved clouds. He used to spend hours drawing them. Maybe he still does—that notebook there's probably full of them.'

'Not many clouds here,' said Irene.

'Here,' said Luke, ignoring their words. 'Sit here.'

They changed places. Irene gripped the wheel. When she turned it, she could feel the boat's ponderous weight.

'Why do you love them?' she asked. 'Clouds, I mean.'

He shrugged. 'I always liked watching them.'

'That's it? Very informative.'

He glanced up at her, his expression impassive. 'They change their shapes all the time. They start as one thing and then they pass into another. Watch out, you're swinging too far to the left.'

'Oops!'

'That's better.'

'Can I get through that bridge ahead?' said Irene dubiously. 'It looks alarmingly narrow. Does one of you two want to do it instead?'

'Me and Mickey will stand at the bow and stern

and push you off if you hit.'

'OK.'

The boat passed safely under the low brick arch. Katherine and Lorrie came out on deck, Neil followed carrying a bag of toys which Katherine proceeded to lay out next to Irene: two floppy rag dolls with braided hair and patchwork skirts; a small box of plastic bricks with pictures painted on their sides; a large, lift-the-flap picture book; a toy phone with a rattling dial tone; a case of thick wax crayons and a pad of thick paper in red and green and blue that Katherine proceeded to open.

'What are you going to draw?'

She looked at Mickey.

'You,' she said, picking up a blue crayon that snapped when she jabbed it against the paper, the two halves spinning across the deck and over the edge. Katherine calmly watched them go and then picked up another crayon.

His face was a wobbly green circle, his hair a wild scribble of black, his eyes were huge overlapping loops, his smile was a pink bisecting slash, his legs and arms sprang out from his chin, his fingers were multiple random spikes like a collapsing bunch of twigs.

Irene steered the boat along the canal. Trees flicked slowly past on either side, stripes of shadow in her eyes. The sun was high and white, the water tea-bag brown, with small clouds of insects hovering above its surface, twigs and leaves bobbing at the side where they'd been washed by successive passing vessels. As if there was a television set turned down in the corner, she heard the voices of the others on the humming margins of her consciousness. Neil reading to Katherine,

266

the same book over and over again until the words became a meaningless incantation. Mickey telling Lorrie about the man he'd known at university who'd set fire to his house when his wife left him. The faint scrape of pen on paper as Luke wrote or drew in his notebook. The far-off echoing call of a bird coming from the land which had become flat and watery as they approached the wetlands of the Camargue. The whine of invisible insects. The voices of people on other boats as they passed by. The snatches of music coming from a café on the canal's edge, the sudden lament of wind through the thick rushes, and the steady, arrhythmic slap of water against the boat's blunt bow. The landscape poured through her, the sun and the canal and the fields that seemed to be turning to water in front of her eyes.

After an hour or so, Neil took over and she and Lorrie went into the kitchen, put cheeses and pâtés out onto a tray, warmed the baguettes they'd bought that morning in the oven, filled a jug with iced water, cut tomatoes into wedges and dressed them with olive oil, salt and black pepper. But it was too hot to eat. Irene went and lay in her cabin with her forearm over her eyes to block out the light and for a while she fell asleep, lulled by the purring engine.

She woke with a jerk. Someone was calling her name.

'Mummy, Mummy, Mummy!'

She swung her feet off her bed, bewildered, and stood up dizzily, the objects around her swimming. She laid her hand against the wall to steady herself. Where was she? Who was she?

'Mummy!'

She stared at the small frosted window, the narrow shelf beside her bed where *Great Expectations* lay, no longer crisp but dog-eared, damp and stained, the hook on the door where she'd hung the small, royal-blue towel that she'd found folded on the bed when she'd arrived. She was on a boat, far from home. The child calling was not her child. She was nobody's mother here.

CHAPTER TWENTY-SEVEN

In the glazed heat of afternoon, the landscape shimmered. Irene cycled steadily along the towpath, with Lorrie just behind her, and ahead Neil, and Katherine, sitting in the child's seat and pointing at things, her hair whipping across her cheeks.

They left the boat far behind, and so stopped at the first small village they came to, dismounted, and bought ice creams while they waited for it to appear. Neil and Katherine wandered onto the bridge a few hundred yards away where ducks were bobbing, and Lorrie and Irene sat in the shade of the trees.

'Tell me about Mickey and Luke,' said Irene casually.

Lorrie cast her a sideways look.

'Which one do you really want to know about?'

'Both!'

'OK. Let me see. Mickey works with computers. I think he's a software programmer—though I've never been quite sure what that means—'

'No. Not his cv, real stuff. You know.'

'Hmmm. Well, from what Neil says, Mickey was always the one who got into trouble when he was a kid. He's a year younger than Mary and Neil and Luke, and they were always having to cover up for him, and break up fights. A tearaway really. He used to play truant, things like that; hated school. He had girlfriends early—was always falling in and out of love. Well, you can tell by his manner, can't you? He's a bit of a lady's man.'

Her glance slid across Irene's face. Irene made a neutral sound.

'He was really cut up when his wife left—he went on a bender for months and nearly lost his job. I think it was a massive blow to his pride, but also, he adores his boys. He's a complete softie with them. I know he misses them a lot. He's always talking about them, showing you photos and things, telling you their latest triumphs, the last funny thing they said. It's very painful to witness.'

'What's she like?'

'Sandy? Not what you'd expect from previous girlfriends. Rather serious and stern and ambitious. She bossed him about quite a bit but he seemed to like it, or need it or something. Who knows what goes on in marriages.'

'How long ago did they separate?'

'It must be a couple of years now, maybe more.'

'So is he all right now?'

'I guess. He still drinks quite a bit and has the occasional wild fling. I know Mary worries.'

'Ah,' said Irene vaguely. Then, 'What about Luke?'

'Luke? Luke's a honey.'

'Is he?'

'Well, he's rather an oddball actually. He can be

269

very abrupt and off-putting, but that's only because he's shy. Shy but quite self-sufficient, I'd say. You could imagine him on a desert island, getting on fine, making a neat shelter with things he found washed up on the beach, staring at the weather. And not really minding that he was alone. But maybe that's wrong—I don't know him like Neil and Mary do.'

Irene took her sunglasses off, blew on them and said, as she rubbed them clean with the edge of her tee-shirt, 'Is he involved with anyone?'

'He and Mary went out for years. It took the rest of us by surprise, especially Mickey; he was a bit put out at first, to say the least. It almost seemed incestuous, like cousins falling in love or something. Then everyone got used to it. We thought they'd stay together, but suddenly, a year and a bit ago, it was all over—no one really knows why. And then Mary married David and straight away she got pregnant. I don't know what Luke thinks about that; he seems all right, but he's quite a secretive kind of person, so who knows. Since Mary, there's been nobody really, not that we know of. Though he's a bit of a mystery to us.' She licked the last bit of ice cream, then chucked the wooden stick into the canal. 'He's very good with children; we all hope he'll have some of his own one day.'

'Who'll have his own what?'

Neil was standing behind them, holding Katherine by her sticky hand. Chocolate was smeared round her mouth.

'I was just talking about Luke.'

'Oh, Luke. He's got his head in the clouds,' said Neil. Irene could tell this was something they always said about him.

'There's the boat,' she said.

'There's another thing about Mickey,' said Lorrie as they scrambled to their feet, waving their hands to the two men on board.

'What's that?'

'He's fallen for you.'

'Oh nonsense, Lorrie.'

'He has.'

'Only because I'm the only available woman on board.'

'Even so, he's got his sights set on you. It's obvious a mile off. You should watch out.'

The boat slowed right down and Luke chucked a rope across to them. It snaked onto the path and Irene picked it up, wrapping it round the nearest tree and passing it back. Neil, Lorrie and Katherine stepped aboard and Lorrie disappeared down below.

'I'm going to cycle on for a bit,' Irene said when Mickey reached across for her bike. 'Unless I'm needed on board, that is.'

'How about if I come with you? Luke can steer for a bit. All right, Luke?'

'We'll meet you at the series of locks then; we'll need your help for that.'

*   *   *

For about half an hour, they cycled in single file with the sun ahead. Every so often Mickey, ahead of her, would point at the white horses in the distance, the chateaux on the horizon, the bull standing near the towpath, head lowered. When they came to the lock, they leant their bikes against the bank and walked up to the top. There were

271

several locks together, like a watery staircase. They looked down, watching as the lower gates swung open for a boat, then shut again, closing them into a capsule of water. The people on board climbed with their ropes up the ladders on the lock's walls and fastened them to the fixed bollards on the towpath high above. Then water rushed into the enclosed space and the boat was slowly lifted up to the second step, where the process was to be repeated.

'It's amazing,' said Irene. 'Extraordinary.'

'Isn't it?' said Mickey. He slid an arm round her sweaty shoulder. 'I'm very glad you're here with us.'

Irene stood quite still. There was a part of her that wanted to lean into him, turn her face to his, kiss his wide mouth, let herself be held at last. To be looked at as if she was gorgeous; to be touched and feel her flesh stir; to let desire seep through her, turning her to heat and liquid. Oh it had been a long, long time. Months, years—a whole lifetime away, before the years of ice and frost and earth hard as concrete. It was summer again, summer at last; she'd waited too long in the chilly shadows. She had almost forgotten what it was like to feel herself opening out and unfurling, until now with Mickey's fingers curling round her slick shoulder, his eyes fixed on her freckled mouth, she let herself remember and felt her stomach loosen.

'Do you miss your husband much?' he asked.

She felt herself stiffen slightly. All desire left her.

'Oh I don't know,' she replied.

'When Sandy left, I got drunk every day for about six months.'

'Well, I haven't done that.'

'But that was two years ago. You get used to it. I don't think it would matter now except for the kids.'

He still had his arm around her. Couldn't he feel how wooden she was to his touch?

'Did he leave you, or was it the other way round?' he asked.

'He left me,' she said shortly. If she gave him a small shove now, he'd topple in the canal. Her hands itched. She'd take him completely unawares and he'd sail through the air in a surprised dive, and then she'd be standing alone and unencumbered again.

'Stupid man.'

'Oh well,' she said, making an enormous effort to stay amiable. 'It's always complicated, isn't it?'

'Was there another woman?'

'Yup.' She imagined him hitting the water with a tremendous splash, his turquoise shirt soaked, his dark hair plastered to his skull, his outraged face glaring at her, goggle-eyed.

'Tough for you. Did you know her?'

What gave him the right to ask such questions?

'A bit,' she forced out through clenched teeth.

He put his mouth against her burning hair. 'Irene?' he said.

'Yes?' she said politely, as if they were in a business meeting, still staring down at the slowly rising boat. 'Yes, Mickey?'

He took her chin in his hand, turned her face towards him and stared into it. Now, she thought. One shove; a punch hard in his solar plexus and he'd topple like a falling tree.

She stepped neatly out of the circle of his arms.

273

'They've nearly reached the top now. And our boat should be here any minute. We should be ready to help.'

'It's holiday,' he said. 'Just a few days before we go back to our ordinary lives.'

'I don't think so,' she said, grimacing at the predictability of it all. 'It's not the right time for me, Mickey.'

'Are you sure?'

'I'm sure. I'm sorry. It's nothing to do with you. It's me. I'm not ready for anything.'

'I'm not giving up that easily.'

*　　　*　　　*

Lorrie steered, Mickey sat at the bows of the boat, staring ahead, and Luke sat on the deck with his binoculars and his notebook. He stared through the lenses, then jotted things down in the book with a dark blue cartridge pen. In the silence of late afternoon, Irene could hear the nib scratching on the coarse paper. Over the top of her book, she looked at his dextrous fingers, his concentrated frown. When he glanced up she quickly returned to *Great Expectations*, trying to fix an interested expression on her face. In the hour she'd been sitting here, she'd read two pages.

What was he thinking of? Mary? The gathering clouds ahead of them? The long-legged birds on the water's edge? Her?

No, he wasn't thinking of her. Why would he be? She hadn't entered his radar. Mickey wanted her, kind of, and she, maybe, wanted Luke, and Luke wanted—well, she had no idea. He was a closed book. She stared down at the page, the blurring words.

'It's nearly six,' said Neil, coming up through the hatchway. 'We should stop soon.'

'There's a small town a couple of kilometres ahead,' said Luke, screwing the top back on his pen, closing his book. 'I thought that would be a good place. What do you reckon?'

'The sooner the better for us,' said Lorrie. 'Katherine needs to eat and stretch her legs.'

'She's fine at the moment with her crayons.'

'In the meantime,' said Irene, standing up. 'Why don't I pour us all some cold white wine?'

'I'll help you,' said Mickey, scrambling to his feet. His manner towards her hadn't altered since their encounter on the bank. He was still eager, gallant, but slightly nonchalant at the same time. He didn't really mind, she thought, as she followed him down the narrow steps into the living area; I'm simply a diversion. Katherine was scribbling ferociously all over her drawing book, a look of scowling intensity on her face as she randomly filled in any remaining white spaces.

'That's very bright,' said Irene, pointing at the violet and red slashes. 'What is it?'

'Daddy tickling me.'

'Oh, OK—which one is you then?'

'There,' said Katherine firmly.

'Wonderful.'

'And that's your dad there?'

'No.' Her tone was scornful. 'That's the tickle.'

'Aha! The tickle. Of course.'

She went to the fridge and opened the wine. Mickey found five glasses and a tin of pistachio nuts that he poured into a cracked white bowl.

'Irene?' he said, standing very close to her.

275

'Mmmm?'

'Everything all right?'

'Of course.'

'I just wanted to say—I'm here for you. You know that.'

'Thanks,' she replied, crackling with irritation. What a stupid phrase—'here for you'. What the fuck did that mean? Nothing. And what a stupid, smiling, handsome face.

'Friends then?'

'Friends,' she said between clenched teeth.

He took one of her hands in his and carried it to his lips, and she made herself smile at him. Luke, barefooted, jumped down the last of the steps and landed in the boat's interior a few feet from where they stood. He looked at the two of them, Irene's hand still held to Mickey's lips. His face was quite expressionless. Then he turned to Katherine, squatting beside her.

'What's that then?' he asked.

'It's a tickle.'

'Of course it is. Like this.'

Katherine squealed. Mickey waited before he dropped her hand. He gave her a giant wink. Irene glared. In a boat, you can't storm off. She edged into her tiny cabin and hid behind its membranous walls.

*   *   *

They found a small restaurant on the canal's edge. Katherine ate half her chips and one mouthful of steak haché, then fell asleep with her head in Lorrie's lap. Irene sat between Mickey and Luke. The wine and the heat made her head swim. The

276

memory of Luke looking at her and Mickey was like a dull, throbbing toothache. She tried to focus on what Mickey was saying. Something about a kind of potato you could get around here that grew by the sea and so was naturally salted. Luke was very silent. She couldn't think of anything to say to him. Halfway through the meal, she excused herself and went to the pay phone by the door, slotted in her euros and called her answering machine. She listened to her voice saying that no one was at home right now and then pressed the code for messages. Even after she had found out that Adrian hadn't called, she loitered outside the restaurant. Through the open door she could see that Neil and Mickey were laughing together, and Lorrie was saying something to Luke, leaning forward and talking earnestly. She could only see the back of his head and his shoulders. She noticed that he sat up quite straight in his chair, and that once or twice he touched Katherine's forehead with the tips of his fingers, wiping away damp locks of hair.

It was so windlessly hot she could barely breathe.

*   *   *

In the night, there was a storm. Irene lay in bed and listened to the sound over her head. It was like being in a tent, except now she could hear the clatter of rain in the canal as well as the pounding of raindrops on the deck. There was a flash of lightning across her window and a few seconds later the rumble of thunder. She heard Katherine squeal, Lorrie talk reassuringly to her. She

277

imagined the little girl crawling into the bed between her parents and being held by them, and for a moment was gripped by the old terror, steel fingers round her neck. Missing a child is physical. It throbs in the belly and the chest and blocks the throat and stings in the eyes. Like a conquering army, it invades every space of the body. Irene sat up in bed, trying to breathe normally, and waited. The rain streamed down from the tilted open window; she could hear it streaming down the deck's runnels.

After several minutes, she knew she wouldn't sleep now. She eased herself out of her bed and felt her way gingerly into the kitchen like a blind woman, arms outstretched. She groped for the overhead light, then lit the stove and filled the kettle with water, trying to make as little noise as possible. She made herself a herbal tea and sat on the sofa. Water ran in rivulets down the windows and outside it was pitch black. Her reflection looked like the face of a drowning woman.

It was oppressively hot. Putting the empty mug down, she found the torch in the cutlery drawer and opened the door to the lower deck. The rain was vertical, drenching and warm. She tipped her head back and felt it trickle down her face, her neck. Almost immediately her night clothes were wet through. She turned on the torch and climbed the ladder to the upper deck where water ran like a shallow river. When she shone the torch over the canal she could see in its spotlight the arrows of rain piercing its surface, sending up hundreds of splashy explosions. She turned the beam of the torch, seeing the rain striping through it. The trees dripped like fountains. The towpath was churned up by the rain's bullets. Small casings of mud lay strewn near the bank.

'I thought it would be you.'

She turned, sloshing in the water.

'Luke. Amazing, isn't it?'

'Mmmm.' He was wearing boxer shorts and a tee-shirt. Rain poured off his smooth head. He looked a like a diver just surfaced from the canal.

'I didn't wake you, did I?'

'Who could sleep in this?'

A lightning flash stood in the sky again like a vast, gnarled tree, its branches pointing upwards. They waited for the thunder to follow.

'It's getting further off.'

'Maybe. Do you want some chocolate? I grabbed it from the fridge.'

'OK.'

He snapped off a couple of squares and handed them across.

She wanted to say: there's nothing going on with Mickey. But how could she? He would just look at her in embarrassment, shrug maybe. She gazed up into the teeming sky, blinking as the rain hammered against her face.

'It'll be lovely tomorrow,' he said. 'There's nothing like a landscape after rain.'

'Yes.' Like me, she thought. I'm a landscape after rain. She imagined taking her shirt off and standing naked on the deck, then pushed the second soft square of chocolate into her mouth and chewed slowly, feeling sweetness slide down her throat.

'Do you fancy some whisky? Help us both sleep.'

'All right then.'

'Up here or down there?'

'Oh—up here, definitely. I couldn't get any wetter anyway.'

'Good.'

He disappeared below deck. She waited in the rushing rain. Her night clothes clung heavily to her and the water streamed across the deck, bubbling round her feet.

'Here.'

'Cheers,' she said.

He raised his glass to her. 'Cheers.'

'I've always loved storms.'

'Me too. Storms, wind, snow . . . I couldn't live in a place there wasn't weather. Rolling skies.'

'There's weather in Ireland, anyway.'

'I remember once when I was just a kid, thirteen or so, there was this freak gale where we lived—a bit like the gale you had in 'eighty-seven, except this was only in one small area. My parents were out for the evening and it was just me and my little sister. It was wild.' Irene listened, amazed: he hadn't said more than a sentence or two since she'd met him. Here were full paragraphs, without even being prompted. 'There was this horizontal rain hitting the windows,' he continued. 'Like there was an army shooting at us from the garden, and lightning so bright it lit up the whole sky. Our cherry tree was ripped up by the roots and the roof of the garden shed Dad had spent months building blew off and at one point our garden bench flew past the window. Just flew by like a bird or something. You could actually see the shape of the storm swirling around on the lawn.'

'Were you scared?'

'Terrified. But I loved it. My sister didn't.'

'I didn't know you had a sister.'

'Why would you?'

The old curt tone was back. Irene winced.

'Sorry,' he said after a pause. 'That sounded rude.' He paused again. 'She died, actually.'

'I'm very sorry.'

'Years and years ago now. A car ran her over. She was ten.'

'Sorry,' she said again. 'Really sorry.' She was about to ask him, stupidly, if he missed her a lot but stopped herself. You say things when you're ready.

'Katherine.'

'What?'

'She was called Katherine.'

'Is that why—?'

'I guess so.'

They drank their whisky. The rain was gradually easing. It was no longer just a roar of falling water in their ears, but a rapid staccato beat.

'Time to get dry,' said Luke.

'I guess.'

But she didn't follow him down at once. She stood for a few more seconds in the rain, the inky water roiling underneath her and the dark sky teeming above, and thought about the dead sister, and about Juliet, and about all the people who go too early into the plunging night.

CHAPTER TWENTY-EIGHT

The next day the sky was like scoured metal and the boat travelled through miles of salty wetlands, a waterway over water, so that there was no horizon, just a gradual dissolving of liquid marshes into the sea, into the sky. There was nothing to fix the eye, no vertical marker save for the occasional group of bushy trees and thick, bleached rushes. The world seemed flat, shapeless, never quite still but shimmering and dissolving in the scratchy silver light. They saw flamingoes standing on one pink leg in the distance, pointed out groups of swans and egrets, or buzzards circling high above them in the currents of air. They drank cups of bitter coffee and batted aside dense clouds of mosquitoes; Mickey spent much of his morning pursuing them round the boat, flattening them against the walls, leaving small dark smears of blood.

'Imagine it in winter,' said Lorrie.

'I can't decide whether it's wonderful or grim,' said Irene.

'Both.'

Irene steered while the men played poker below deck. Katherine sat under the table, yelping in outrage every time their feet nudged her. When Neil took over, Irene went to the front of the boat with Luke's binoculars, swinging her legs over the side. She wasn't really looking at anything in particular, simply staring out at the dazzling emptiness all round her.

Ahead of her, a shape rose out of the water—at first, it was just a faint cloud on the horizon, but gradually it resolved and clarified, became an island of grey stone houses with a church at the top.

'Look!' she called.

'We're coming to the lakes,' said Neil. 'Hey!' he shouted down to the others. 'We're nearly at the lakes.'

Half an hour later, the boat slid out of the mysterious, blurred emptiness of the wetlands and into the mouth of the salt lake, by the side of the thriving village. There was a small harbour where other boats were moored, a row of restaurants and bars with brightly coloured awnings and blackboards on the pavement advertising their menus, a pebble beach where children played. Fishing boats bobbed on the corrugated blue water; oyster beds spiked the distance like a bamboo plantation. As the boat headed towards the quay, the sun broke through; pale eggshell-blue cracks appeared in the sky.

'God, what a relief,' said Neil. 'Normality. I was beginning to think it would go on for ever. Let's stop here for a while and have lunch in one of those restaurants. They look as if they're still open.'

'Oysters,' said Mickey. 'A dozen oysters and a carafe of white wine.'

'Shouldn't there be an "r" in the month for oysters?' asked Lorrie.

'You sound like my bloody mother.'

'But she's right,' said Neil. 'As the fish expert here, I'd warn you that—'

'Who cares? We're on holiday. If they've got oysters, then that's what I'm having. The most sensuous food in the world.' He turned his wide smile on Irene. 'This is the life.'

Then, without warning, Mickey stripped off his shirt and ran whooping off the edge of the boat, crookedly flying through the air, arms akimbo and legs running wildly mid-air, before hitting the water with a splash, coming up into an untidy crawl.

'There are jellyfish,' said Neil. 'Should we swim if we might get stung?'

But Irene already stood on the edge of the top deck, hesitating. It suddenly looked a long way down.

'Come on, all you cowards!' cried Mickey. 'Jump.'

She took a breath and jumped, feet first, and for a moment was going straight down into the murky green, able to make out nothing except the dim crowds of jellyfish all around her, dozens of translucent lungs. Then she surfaced, mosquitoes sticking to her cheeks. She wiped them off and laughed up at the faces peering down from the upper deck.

'I want to go in,' said Katherine.

'Not from the boat—and not with those jellyfish.'

'I want to!'

'Not now. Look, Mummy's about to jump.'

Lorrie wore a red bikini and goggles; her hair was tied back in a ponytail. She raised her hands and dived into the lake, clean as a knife, leaving a small circle where her feet had disappeared.

'Mummy!'

'Look for where she comes out.'

'I want Mummy!'

Lorrie came up, lifted her hand in greeting, then turned her back on the boat and set off in a steady, straight-backed crawl. Everyone watched her go. Mickey clambered aboard again, Irene lay on her back in the water, sculling and watching the blue sky with its far-off mountains of billowing clouds. A few moments later, Neil was in the water too, swimming with a skew-kneed breaststroke after Lorrie, his head, like a retriever's, lifted eagerly out of the water.

Mickey launched himself once more into the water, hitting it with a tremendous thwack, then setting off, more energy than motion.

'Daddy!' yelled Katherine. 'Mummy! Don't leave me!'

Luke held her hand firmly. 'They'll be back soon. Watch.'

'Mummy.' She was weeping now, and tugging away from his hands.

'Listen, Katherine. Look through these binoculars. I'll hold them and you just look, like that. There. Can you see them? They're fine. The water holds them up, see? And soon they'll be back with you and you can go swimming from the shore.'

'I want them.'

'You'll have them soon.' His tone was quite patient. 'They're having a nice time.'

'I want them now!'

'I know you do, Katherine. But you have to wait a few minutes. Wait with me and we'll watch them come back again.'

Lying on her back in the green water, Irene listened to his voice, calm and grave, solicitous. She trusted it. She liked the way he was respectful to a weeping child even when he was brusque with adults; how he gave her his concentrated attention. The way he was silent, not spewing out treacherous words. Everything he said had the weight of his sincerity behind it. Last night seemed a long way off now; she should have told him there was nothing going on with Mickey. She should have stepped forward then, taken the whisky from his hand, pressed her wet body against his under the rain, put her mouth against his cool lips . . . Oh, but she'd forgotten how to do all of this. She'd lost the confidence, lost the knack. She turned over and let herself sink under the surface of the lake.

Lorrie and Neil were returning to the boat now, swimming slowly side by side, talking to each other as they came. Occasionally they stopped, trod water facing each other. Irene saw Lorrie lay her hands on Neil's shoulders; their heads were close together, two seals with sleek, blunt heads. She imagined their limbs tangling under the water in a promise of later.

'They're nearly here,' said Luke above her. 'Let's dry your eyes, shall we? Hmm?'

Katherine whimpered, a little spasmodic shudder of ebbing panic. For an instant, Irene could feel Aggie pressed against her, arms wound fiercely around her neck, plump strong body racked with sobs, wet cheek against wet cheek; damp candy-floss hair, salt tears and grassy breath. The flurry of heartbeats which are your heartbeats too. How do you ever get over the love of a child? How do you get beyond it?

Gripping the rim of the deck, she hauled herself out of the water and tumbled into the boat.

*   *   *

They swam, they had races, they persuaded Katherine, wreathed with a red rubber ring and fat yellow armbands, to walk from the beach into the lake up to her knees, where she stopped dead and refused to go in an inch further. They drank cold

286

beer and then had relay races round the boat—one adult always staying with Katherine and acting as umpire—and whoever was in Lorrie's team always won. She shone with a transfiguring sexualized vigour. Whenever he was near her, Neil couldn't resist touching her, laying his hand across her flat, wet belly, along her strong shoulders, proprietorially on her thigh.

In the late afternoon, they let the boat float in the centre of the lake, drifting idly on small currents. Mickey was tired and retired to his cabin to have a sleep. Luke went to take a shower. Irene lay on her stomach reading. The day was still warm but there was a faint cooling breeze blowing off the water and plump white clouds in the sky. She heard the shower turned off and then Luke opening drawers downstairs. She was dimly aware of Katherine's sudden, peremptory demands and of Neil and Lorrie talking occasionally in low voices. At one point she heard a faint plop, like a stone being lobbed into the lake, and looked up. She saw them kissing each other, arms loosely across the other's lap. She frowned. Where was Katherine? She stood up, looking around.

'Where's Katherine?' she called.

'She just this minute went down to the lower . . . oh my God? Oh dear God. Where is she? Neil! Where is she? Katherine, Katherine! Jesus, Katherine! Katherine!'

There was a faint ripple on the surface of the water behind them, a smudged concentric circle in the corrugated pattern of waves. Without thinking, Irene took three running strides and jumped into the water towards it. Everything was in slow motion. She was suspended between sky and lake and could see Neil and Lorrie standing on the deck, Mickey's head rising up from below, the scudding white clouds, the stretch of her arms in front of her. Could hear the sound of her ragged intake of breath and Lorrie's wild cry still tearing through the air: 'Katherine!' It seemed to go on for ever, the cry of raw pain. Her sun hat lifted from her head and flew off, spinning through the air like a sudden frisbee. She thought of standing in a meadow with Sasha and Adrian, flicking their old frisbee to each other, seeing it wheel above the tall grass. The sunlight bounced off the lake, refracted into a dozen angles.

Slap of water against her body and then she broke its barrier and was falling through sudden silence, falling through time, the present streaming away from her. For a few seconds, she could barely remember her name, or the name of the child she wanted so badly to save. Green opaque water all around her—above her, below her, and she was just a pinpoint in the great watery expanse, with showers of plankton swirling noiselessly around her and a small army of mute jellyfish dilating and contracting near her blind, groping fingers.

There was a knife with serrated blade stabbing and sawing at her tightening lungs; red bolts and flashes of pain in her head. She stared desperately into the foggy water, salt in her stinging eyes. Nothing. Nothing. Nothing.

Then, when she could stay down no longer, she saw something blue. Blue. The soles of blue jellybean sandals. She reached down, why did it take so long to move, every second stretched out into a line she had to crawl along. At last she felt a leg beneath her hand. Grasped it. Pulled and pulled. Dear God, help. Don't let this happen. A vertical body in the weeds of the lake, like a diver frozen in flight.

Up rose a tiny child, a pale face, open eyes and floating hair. She wrapped her arm around her waist, held on tight. Body screaming to breathe; mustn't breathe, mustn't pull water into gasping lungs. She felt a shudder rack her entire body with the effort of not breathing. Driving through her mind was the memory of giving birth—another child, another drowning body sucked into life. Thrashing upwards now in a tangle of limbs but where's the air, where's the surface of the world? Lungs exploding now. Soon got to take a giant, hopeless, drowning breath; water will stream in, fill up all the cavities. Black and red and purple lights shattering in her head, like coloured glass dashed against the walls of her skull, flying off in sharp, cutting fragments. And then air at last, thick and violent air ripping into her lungs, tearing them apart before she sank again. Up once more, pedalling desperately with her legs and trying to push the heavy little body out into the world, holding it aloft while she herself was submerged by the water.

Then her arms were empty. The body was gone from her. All she held was absence.

She fell back into the water. Felt a hand under her back, someone pulling her. She breathed in and felt air running through the burning passages of her body, into the collapsed space where her lungs had once been. Through her throbbing, burning eyes she saw a face. Calm face, eyes to drown in. She smiled.

'You're beautiful,' she said.

'Let's get you aboard.'

Then Mickey leant down from the boat and held out a hand.

'Is Katherine all right?' she said.

'Get aboard.'

She grasped Mickey's hand. Luke pushed her from behind, and she was landed like a thrashing fish on the hot deck.

'Katherine?' she said again.

Katherine lay a few feet from her, on Lorrie's lap. Her eyes were open. She was chalky-pale, blue around the lips, but she was breathing and whimpering slightly. Lorrie held her, pressed her to her breast. Neil crouched beside her with his hand on her matted hair.

'She should be kept warm,' said Luke. He bounded downstairs and reappeared with two thick blankets that he wrapped around the pair. Lorrie hardly looked at him; her eyes were wide and glassy.

'Are you OK?' Mickey asked Irene.

'Hang on,' said Irene. She crawled across to Lorrie and Neil, put a hand on Neil's shoulder, stared at Lorrie. 'It could have happened to anyone.'

'We weren't looking. We looked away.'

'It could have happened to anyone. Believe me. No one can be looking all the time.'

'She would have drowned.' Lorrie's voice was dull. 'You saved her. But she would have drowned.'

'Nonsense. She was in there for a few seconds.'

'Here.' Luke was back with a pile of towels. 'Strip off and dry yourself and then we're going to get a warm drink inside you.'

'Listen to me. It's important.' Irene was urgent.

'We all look away and every so often something terrible happens. There's always something that very nearly happens—a second earlier or later and it would have. All those times they nearly get run over, nearly pull the boiling water over themselves, nearly fall out of the window . . . The world's crammed full of disasters that we're a hair's breadth away from. We can't be vigilant every second of every day. We'd go mad. It's not possible. It's not human.'

'She would have drowned.'

'But she didn't. Be happy. Look at her, she's completely fine.'

'Irene,' said Neil. 'Thank you very much.'

'I didn't do anything, honestly—someone else would have jumped a second later than me—'

'You've no idea . . .' Neil covered his pale blue eyes with his hand and started to cry. Lorrie put an arm around him and they leant into each other, hands on their daughter's quivering body.

'Come on,' said Luke, and led Irene away.

She let herself be looked after by Mickey and Luke, fussed over as if it was she who'd nearly drowned. They pulled off her shirt and trousers, so that she was just in her bra and knickers, and then wrapped two towels around her and sat her in the sun on the upper deck. Mickey rubbed her hair dry and warmed her chilly fingers between his warm ones. Luke went and made tea, insisting on adding several spoonfuls of sugar. She took a sip and grimaced.

'For shock. Drink it down.'

'I'm not shocked. Katherine's shocked.'

'I've made her a mug of hot chocolate.'

'Is she all right?'

291

'She says she thought the water would just hold her up. It's what I told her when she was worrying about Lorrie and Neil in the lake. Apart from that, she's very quiet but completely OK. She'll probably fall asleep soon.'

'And Lorrie and Neil?'

'They're pretty quiet too. It's all been a bit much.'

'We should have a drink,' said Mickey.

'Good idea. It's after six now anyway.'

'There's the whisky we've hardly touched,' said Irene. 'And I think Neil brought brandy as well. That somehow seems good for things like this. You two fetch it and I'll go and get dressed.'

She hardly had any clean clothes left, so she put on her grey skirt and ruffled top. They sat round the table on the upper deck, Katherine asleep now but still tight in her mother's arms. Every few minutes, Lorrie would bend forward and kiss her forehead.

'I'm exhausted,' she said. 'I feel as if I've been up for days.' She tipped a shot of whisky down her throat, then, immediately afterwards, one of brandy, and blinked several times in surprise.

'Here's to Irene,' said Neil. 'Our hero.'

'No, really!' But she felt light-headed with relief. She drank her brandy, feeling its heat burn through her like a lit fuse. Everything around her seemed suffused with a new radiance. The sky to the west was a glorious deep-swirled pink now; below it, the water glowed and above, there were rosy banks of clouds. She smiled giddily at Luke. 'Look at the clouds,' she said.

He smiled at her but didn't look round. 'Yes.'

'What shall we eat this evening?'

'I feel a bit sick actually,' said Mickey. He had beads of sweat on his forehead and had turned a curious green colour.

'Shock,' said Irene, drinking another hot bolt of brandy and thinking suddenly of Juliet crouched by a lavatory bowl, heaving up her guts.

'Oysters,' said Neil. 'In August. I warned you.'

'Don't say that! I'll be fine. It'll pass.'

But a few minutes later he went downstairs and they heard him retching violently.

Irene knocked at the lavatory door.

'Can I do anything?'

'No,' he gasped.

'He'll be out of it for the night,' said Neil when she came back up to the deck. 'Food poisoning.'

'Horrible. Poor thing.'

'Shall we leave him to it and find somewhere to eat?'

'I'm staying here with Katherine,' said Lorrie. 'You go, Neil.'

'No way.'

'I don't mind.'

'We'll have bread and cheese and red wine. It'll be romantic, the two of us.'

'And Katherine.'

'And Katherine, of course.'

'And Mickey chucking up next door.'

'Better and better.'

Lorrie laid her hand across Neil's. 'You two go,' she said.

Irene looked across at Luke. 'Shall we?'

'Why not?'

CHAPTER TWENTY-NINE

They left the quayside and went up the hill, to the older part of the town, where they found a restaurant with a few tables on the terrace, overlooking the lake. Luke ordered a risotto and Irene a cassoulet.

'Because I'm starving,' she said. 'I can't remember when I was last this hungry. Years and years ago. I could eat two meals.' And it was true; she felt a cavernous hollow inside her; her hands shook with hunger. Hunger or some other mysterious emotion that gnawed at her insides.

While they were waiting for the meal to arrive, she phoned her answering machine. No messages. She pictured her house, drab and empty, dust gathering in corners, dead flies on the window sills, a musty smell in the folds of the curtains, teddies propped on the pillows, dressing gowns hanging from the hooks on the door, slippers in pairs, the alarm clock by her bed still clicking its green numbers round. In three, four days' time, she would be home again, waiting for her daughters to return, the dead spaces to fill up with sound, and this strange period would be over, a dream in bright colours.

They ate their meal very slowly. Small mouthfuls, sips of red wine. Other tables emptied, filled up again with new arrivals. He asked about her work and she told him. She tried to describe dyslexia, the wrongly wired brain, the treachery of words and how they sprang shut like traps, the looming fog that children experienced, stumbling helplessly through the intricate lexicography of the world. She told him about her time in Africa, heat and decay and glittering sunlight, how she had felt free there, independent, and herself at last. She talked—because suddenly the memory returned to her, a bright fragment, like a stone shining in a rock pool—about an evening when she had sat outside her house, after the sun had abruptly set, and listened to children dancing just out of her sight: the soft thud of their bare feet on the baked mud; the rhythmic clap of their hands; the mingling coo of voices. About her mother's stroke that had recalled her to England in November, fog settling. Her mother's vain struggle for words. She drank more wine and said—she heard the words she spoke with surprise—that Adrian was right to have gone. They'd trapped each other into a version of themselves that they didn't want; their marriage had hardened into a kind of hollow shell. Luke listened intently. It was like unpacking small, cherished objects and laying them before him.

She liked him because he didn't speak. He didn't try and charm her, or fool her. Because there was nothing flash about him, nor vain. Because he was private and self-contained and cool and he didn't need saving. Because when she left, in two days' time, he wouldn't suffer and neither would she, not really—not with that terrible, burning regret and the forlorn sense that she had lost something that she would forever want to recapture. Women are always wanting to go backwards, she thought; the tug of nostalgia and desire are hopelessly mixed. But she wanted to go forwards, and Luke was simply on her journey, just as she was on his. This watery, landlocked journey that was taking her home.

So, mid-sentence, she stopped, leant across the table, pushing aside her plate. She put the tips of her fingers on his cheek. He didn't move, sat quite still and never took his eyes from her. She traced the line of his thick eyebrows; felt how his hair was bristly velvet, springing back in the wake of her touch; followed the shape of his chin with the faint dimple in its centre, softly touched his lips. She drew his face with her fingers, taking her time. Then she sat back again, liquid with desire.

'Tell me about Mary,' she said.

'Mary,' he said. It wasn't a question, just a word, an echo. She waited and he stared past her, his face wiped of expression.

'Sorry,' she said. 'You don't need to tell me.'

'She wanted children.'

'You didn't?'

'No.'

'It's not really something you can compromise over.'

'No. So—' He shrugged. 'We called it a day.'

There really was something rather scary about him, she thought to herself happily.

'And then she met David?' she pressed him.

'Three months later they were married and she was pregnant.'

'Oh.'

'She's very happy.'

'What about you?'

'Me?'

'Yes.'

'I'm happy for her, too. And I'm fine. You can't plan everything in life. Things don't work like that. Well: do you want pudding?'

296

'I certainly do. That chocolate tart looks tempting.'

They ordered and then he said, 'Right. Tell me about your children.'

'Do you really want to hear?'

'Yes. I like other people's children.'

'You're not just being polite?'

'No!' He smiled at her at last. 'It's not that sort of evening.'

'OK.' She slid a mouthful of tart into her mouth and chewed. 'The eldest is Sasha. She's eleven now. Very pretty, or I think so anyway, with long light-brown hair that she wears in plaits; grey eyes. A bit like a storybook picture of a little girl, if you know what I mean. Very neat; you should see her room. Very serious, very responsible—she worries about other people. She's a daddy's girl really—she's the one I worry about most now. It's hit her hard. I don't know what's going on under the surface. She steals things. Lies, I think. Clem's the opposite—small, fierce, strong, looks like a boy, considers she *is* a boy really. Picks quarrels with the whole world, and especially with Sasha and Aggie—Aggie's three.' She grinned and twisted her glass round by its stem. 'Like Katherine, except Katherine doesn't have tantrums or eat garden snails and jellyfish and whole bars of soap.'

Irene looked down at the table, where her hand rested; her nails were growing back and the white stripe where her wedding ring had been was gone. She looked at the knots of wood where her fingers pressed, a swirl of honey-coloured patterns. Then traced the golden spiral with her finger. She looked up into Luke's brown eyes and said softly, 'And then . . .'

She stopped dead. A thick snake coiled in her throat and she couldn't swallow. Beads of sweat gathered on her forehead. The air was like a blanket around her. 'Then . . .'

'Yes?'

'Let's go now.'

'You haven't finished your tart. Or your sentence. Are you all right?'

'I need to get out.'

He asked for the bill in bad French and insisted on paying—'I'm a single man; what else should I do with my money?'—and they walked out into the soft night.

'Better now?'

'Mmm. Shall we go down to the lake? Or do you want to go back?'

They walked down the narrow street that opened out into the town's main square, then to the pebble beach where earlier Katherine had paddled. From here, they could see their boat, moored among the others. There was enough of a breeze to stir up small waves that slapped gently onto the shore.

Irene bent down and found a flat stone. She crouched and threw it over the water.

'I can never do it more than once or twice.'

Luke picked up a stone. It skimmed lightly across the lake's surface: one, two, three, four . . .

'It's a man's thing.'

'That's what Adrian always used to say.'

'Adrian.' He had this strange habit of saying a word and letting it settle between them like an object they both had to stare at.

'At least now I feel alive again. Though that can hurt, can't it, feeling alive?'

'Why do you feel alive again?'

'You know.'

'Tell me.'

'No, I won't tell you.' She smiled at him. 'I feel a bit odd.'

'In what way?'

'Light-headed. Trembly.' She held out a hand and it shook slightly. 'As if I could blow away.'

'You sound like you're still hungry.'

She giggled. 'Hardly.'

'Are you tired?'

'Tired? No, not at all. Is it late? Do you want to go back?'

'No.'

They stared at each other.

'That's good,' she said softly.

'Mickey . . .'

'Nothing.'

'Nothing?'

'Nothing,' she repeated firmly. 'Nothing, nothing, nothing.'

They started to wander slowly along the shore, away from the boat and the town. Irene took off her sandals. Holding her skirt up with one hand, she walked through the shallows, the pebbles shifting under her feet, the water cool and silky against her calves.

'I hope Juliet'll be all right.'

'Yes.'

'Look at the moon low over the water. It's huge this evening.'

'If you took a photograph of it, it wouldn't look like that. It would look much smaller, just like it does when it is high in the sky—that's just an optical illusion. Your brain's tricking you.'

'Can that be true?'

'It's true.'

'I never knew that.' She walked in a bit deeper. The water soaked into the dipping hem of her skirt. 'Everything seems so far away,' she said dreamily. 'London, the kids, everything that's happened.'

'I know.'

'And in a couple of days this'll seem far away too . . .'

Then Luke was walking towards her, in his light summer trousers and his thin cotton shirt, as if he didn't notice that he was in a lake. Calmly wading into the water, looking at her. She let her skirt fall, so that it spread for a moment like a flower around her, and backed away from him. He followed. The water was up to their hips now.

'You're mad,' she said. 'Crazy. Like standing in the thunderstorm drinking whisky. And they all think you're the sensible, practical one.'

'Quiet Uncle Luke?'

'Something like that.'

He'd reached where she stood, and stood smiling down at her. Then his smile suddenly vanished.

'I'm tired of being good,' she said. 'I'm so very tired of everyone thinking that I'm good. Good old Irene. I'm not fucking good. Not inside me, where no one can see.'

He put one hand on her shoulder; she could feel the wet imprint of his fingers through her shirt. Then he bent his velvet head and kissed her. His cheek scraped her skin; heat coursed through her and the dark water lapped around her. She closed her eyes and put both arms around his wet, solid

300

body, under his sodden shirt, pulled him closer to her. They fell back into the lake, still wrapped around each other, and for a brief moment were under the darkly glinting surface in a drowning embrace.

They came up gasping and without saying anything, sloshed their way towards the shore weighed down by their drenched clothes.

'Look at you,' said Luke, pulling out a few sodden euro notes from his pocket and grimacing.

'Look at both of us.'

'Irene?'

'Mmm.'

'What were you going to tell me? In the restaurant.'

She could feel desire changing, like a cloud changes as you watch it, into something else. A mountain becomes a valley; an arrow becomes a dragon.

'Nothing.'

'OK then.' He picked a trail of weed out of her hair. 'It's up to you.'

Irene picked up another stone and turned it over in her hand. It was smooth and round, like a gull's egg, with a little vein of light grey running through it. There were words that she carried with her like stones—rolling around in her skull, lodged in her heart, embedded in the lining of her empty womb. Why were they so hard to speak? She took a deep breath.

'After Aggie . . .' she said. She was starting to feel cold now. Her skirt dragged down and dripped on her feet. Her wet hair stuck to her cheek. 'After Aggie . . .'

After Aggie they hadn't wanted another. They'd

had enough of sleepless nights, nappies, tetchy quarrels, mounting debts, British holidays in the drizzle, dead-end jobs to make ends meet, doors slammed shut on plans they'd made. Of course she should have read the familiar signs and known earlier, early enough to have made a difference—and maybe she had known, keeping it quite secret and safe even from herself.

Not a grain of rice any more; not even a pea, a broad bean. No: a scrunched-up body, a prehistoric face, thready arms that stretched out and legs that kicked.

'After Aggie there was Felix.' She spoke the name to the little black waves that slapped on the shore, to the dark riffle of wind around them. 'After my grandpa.'

There—she had said his name out loud. That secret word, hauled out of the icy cellar.

She heard Sasha's high, clear voice: 'I'm going to have a little boy and call him Felix. That means happy. He's going to be big and strong and have blue eyes and live to a hundred.'

A little boy: the shock of seeing his swollen genitals. Hearing him give his quaint, reedy cry, like a curlew's lonely call, and falling in love all over again, hurtling off that cliff: loose downy skin, hard gums against her nipple, almond eyes, thin grasping fingers that clutched at her and lost her all over again. She had gathered him to her as if she could take him back inside her and keep him safe for ever. If she closed her eyes she could feel the pouched shape at her breast, breathe his smell of sweet grass, mustard seed, sawdust, clean puke.

'I used to lie there in the dead of night and listen to his breathing.'

Sometimes it was so quiet she had to lean close to hear it; tiny light breaths. He was just a few inches away from her, lying on his back in the Moses basket they'd had with the other three. She would wake time and again in the night and lie with her eyes wide open but her breath held, straining to hear the feathery sounds. She would lean over and make out, in the dimness, the shape of his pale face, his mop of dark, cow-licked hair. Sometimes, as she watched, he would raise his hands like a conductor asking for silence before he began to summon music. She would hover above him, suspended in that frozen moment. His blistered lips puffed in and out.

How could it be, that she missed it, the moment when his breathing stopped and he lay in his own utter silence? For the first time in months, she and Adrian had made love, quiet and careful, and then Irene had turned over on her side, away from the basket and towards her husband, and had slept through the night, her hand against Adrian's hip, her thighs sticky. She woke up feeling wonderfully refreshed, sun flooding through the curtains. Then she turned towards her silent son.

'He died,' she said to the lake.

Clenched fists that didn't uncurl when she touched them; faint blue around his lips.

Six weeks old. Sudden Infant Death Syndrome. SIDS. Cot Death.

'I don't talk about it much.'

She didn't talk about it at all, and gradually everyone around her had stopped talking as well; it was fenced off like a shaft that went down and down, you didn't know where the bottom was. People thought it just got better after a while—

he'd only been a few weeks old; she had three lovely daughters. But the silence he left was a roar inside her head.

'I think it made me a bit mad for a while. I never used to be scared of things. Now I'm scared of almost everything.'

Leaning over her daughters' beds night after night, standing outside their doors, gripping their hands so tightly when they crossed the road that they'd cry out in pain, phoning home each day to make sure their plane hadn't fallen out of the sky or their skin hadn't exploded in a sinister rash, waking up at night from dreams of them drowning, falling, bleeding, calling out her name . . .

'And angry,' she added.

Anger like a hurricane raging through her, a forest fire crackling through lines of great fragile trees. If she opened her mouth it would come gushing hotly out. Dragon's breath: stand clear. She could scorch a person just from opening her mouth and screaming, screaming, screaming . . .

'There you are,' she said.

A calm elation filled her. She waited.

'It's a nice name, Felix. Unusual.'

'D'you think so? My father didn't think much of it. But maybe that's because he was named after Mum's family.'

'Do you have a photo?'

'I'll show you sometime. If you'd like.'

'I'd be most honoured,' he replied formally.

'Honoured?'

'Honoured,' he repeated gravely, ridiculously, dripping in front of her like some mad medieval knight.

She took his sodden head between her hands

again and kissed him. Reeling back the years. Far from anywhere, empty of anger, empty of fear. Blithe at last. What a journey this had been, after all.

Behind them were trees, a darker darkness, where they could breathe in the sharp scent of resin and dry compacted earth. They could lie on the hard ground, her skin pricked by needles, her tangled lake-hair full of dirt and insects, her damp skin soaking up the powdery skim of top soil.

She lifted his hand and laid it across her breast.

'Oi!' they heard. 'You two!'

Mickey was standing on the deck of the boat, flickering a torch in their direction. They stared at him, then at each other.

'Oi!' he called again. 'What are you doing there?'

'Tomorrow,' said Luke.

CHAPTER THIRTY

The boat's engine woke her and she lay looking through the clear strip of glass at the clouds and sky passing overhead. Soon she heard Katherine singing a snatch of song over and over again: 'We're off to see the Wizard, the wonderful Wizard of Oz . . .' And then Mickey, joining in heartily, rolling out a parody baritone. She smiled and stretched. Lorrie's voice drifted past, saying something to Neil. Someone laughing. Plates chinking. The sound of a kettle whistling on the gas stove. She pulled the sheet over her head, trapping herself in a cave of grainy white light, and stretched out her tired limbs. This was her last day; tomorrow she would be gone.

There was a knock at her door and Lorrie came in with a mug of tea.

'Morning.'

'Hi. We're on our way then.'

'We thought you'd like a lie-in. We're motoring right down to the other end of the lake and Luke says we should get to the start of the Canal du Midi before midday.'

'I'll get up in a minute.'

'No hurry. There's breakfast up on deck. It's a perfect day, very warm but breezy.'

'Katherine sounds all right.'

'She's completely all right—she keeps telling everyone rather proudly that she dived into the lake. And Mickey says he's starving.'

'Yeah—I saw him last night and he seemed fully recovered then. Not to say hyper. He kept us up till all hours.'

There was a slight pause. Lorrie looked at the knot of wet clothes in the corner. 'Good evening?'

'Fine, thanks.'

'I didn't hear you come in.'

'I think you were asleep.'

'Yes. OK then.'

She pulled the door shut. Irene drank her tea and then had a shower, washing her hair and then towelling it dry vigorously. She put on her shorts and the last clean shirt, then washed two pairs of knickers, to last her till she got home. In the tiny mirror in the shower room she saw herself, a plumply triangular face covered in golden freckles, her drying hair a streaked coppery cloud. She put up a hand and touched her speckled lips, smiled.

Was it possible she was a woman in her thirties, with three children, a divorce pending, a job, a mortgage, debts, a car, a washing machine, pots and pans and an array of wooden spoons, a grown-up set of cutlery that included a cake slice, a shelf of recipe books, a filing cabinet for bills and receipts . . . ? She felt like a lovesick teenager, just starting out.

'*Weeeeee're off to see the Wizard,*' shouted Katherine.

'The wonderful Wizard of Oz,' bellowed Mickey. 'Come on, breakfast, Kath. I've made eggy bread.'

'Yuck.'

'You won't say that when you've tasted it. I'm the grand master of eggy bread—that's what my kids say anyway, and you'd better believe it.'

'Here, I'm putting sun cream on you.' Lorrie's voice.

'Don't want it.'

'I'm putting it on anyway. Don't wriggle.'

'I want Daddy.'

'He'd put it on just the same. No escape.'

'Here. Coffee for you, Lorrie.'

Luke's voice. In a few minutes, she'd walk up the steps to the deck and he'd be there. He'd look up and their eyes would meet . . . Irene rubbed moisturizing cream into her skin and brushed out her hair. Perhaps, passing near him, their hands would touch and secret currents of desire would bolt through both of them. Perhaps they'd find themselves alone in the galley just for a few seconds, reach out furtively. Later, maybe, they could sneak away like two guilty adolescents, push up against each other in a back street with shutters swinging above them and the smell of frying garlic and peppery herbs . . .

So this was what Adrian had felt. She pushed her feet into her sandals, reached for her dark glasses. He'd felt electrically alive like this: new and brimful of a quivering, weepy, sentimental gladness and every sense charged up so the world became impossibly beautiful and pulsing with meaning. On the one side there was his wife, his daughters, his friends, his house, his well-worn sense of himself, and on the other nothing but transfiguring desire. Which was everything, because it obliterated all the others.

'I never stood a chance,' she muttered. Then added 'bastard' in a satisfyingly vituperative hiss to keep her anger alive.

On deck she said good morning cheerily, not looking over at Luke. Katherine, strapped tightly into her life jacket, was throwing scraps of eggy bread over the side at the gulls that swept untidily down to bag them. Luke was steering—he raised a hand to her and then turned back to his task. That was all.

'Hello, gorgeous,' shouted Mickey. 'Let me slice you a cold peach.'

'How nice of you. Are you still feeling fine?'

'Yup. But I'll never eat oysters again—don't you dare say anything, Neil, or I'll push you in the water and wipe that smug look off your face.'

'I'm not saying anything.'

'How about you after plunging in the lake again yesterday evening?'

Irene felt a blush burning its way up her body. 'Fine,' she said.

'You must have been pissed.'

'Maybe.'

'They fell in the lake,' Mickey bellowed to Lorrie and Neil. He was behaving as if he had drunk half a bottle of whisky.

'Really,' Neil said drily.

'Both of them were wet through.'

'It was a warm evening,' said Irene. 'It seemed like a good idea at the time.'

She spread apricot jam over half a croissant and stood up.

'Can I look through your binoculars?' she said to Luke.

'Sure. Here.'

She sat beside him on the bench and he handed her the binoculars. His fingers brushed hers. Their knees touched. Irene held her breath, tried to stop the fool's grin cracking her face into a gargoyle. She put the binoculars to her eyes and stared blindly across the glare of water.

'Sleep OK?'

'Couldn't,' he said, not looking round at her.

'Me neither.'

'Here,' called Mickey. 'You'll be able to see the mouth of the Canal du Midi through those. Bring them over here, Irene. Come on! Hey, Lorrie, come and have a look too.'

'You should clearly be sick more often. I haven't seen you this cheerful since—oh, I dunno,' said Lorrie, joining them at the bow of the boat.

'Since Sandy left.'

'Maybe.'

'I dreamt about her last night. I dreamt I was chasing her with a big tub of salt, trying to pour it over her heels and the kids were running after me holding on to my shirt tails.'

'Obvious. You want to kill her,' said Neil, from above them.

'What?' said Katherine, her attention snagged. 'Who are you going to kill?'

'No one.'

'Sometimes I do want to kill her. Taking my children away from me. Children need their fathers too, you know. Research shows that.'

'What do you think should happen then?' asked Irene.

'What?'

'Do you think they should be with you most of the time?'

'She was the one who left. Went off with another man.'

'I know. But what should happen now to the children, what's best for them? That's what matters.'

'Salt,' said Neil. 'That's how to kill sea monsters—put salt on their tails.'

'I miss them, that's all. It's not right. Fathers are important too.'

'Of course they are.'

'What happens then?' asked Katherine.

'Do you think they should spend most of their time with her? Just because she's a woman? It's easy for you to say that.'

'I don't know what I think. I really don't. I think each case is different.'

'They curl up and die, that's what.'

'Who wants more coffee?' asked Lorrie.

'They'll forget me. They'll think of him as their real dad, not me.'

'I'm sure that's not true.'

'Why are you sure? How can you be?' He

seemed to genuinely want an answer.

'Children love even bad parents. You're a good one.'

'Or some juice maybe?' continued Lorrie. 'Kath, how about a lolly?'

'Am I? Why do you think that?'

'Is anything left of the monsters afterwards?'

'Just a puddle.'

'Yuck!'

'The way you talk of them; the way everyone talks about you. You won't lose them.'

'I feel I already lost them.'

'I know. It can't be the way it was.'

'Is that what you feel?'

'Kind of. Look. There it is.' She pointed. 'We're going through there.'

The broad canal lay like a road ahead of them, tranquil and straight, shaded with vast plane trees. Mickey grabbed Irene by her forearm and leant towards her. His white smile hardened into something like a snarl.

'Did you two get off together then?'

'What?' She shook him off and stepped back. '*Get off!*'

'I'm not an idiot, you know.'

'Mickey, please.'

'Why not me? Hmm? Why him and not me? What's he got that I haven't?'

'Listen, this is ridiculous. You know it is.'

'You knew how I felt. So did he. You're humiliating me.'

He was aggressively unhappy, bellicose with self-pity and loneliness. His holiday was ending and he was returning to his empty life. She touched his hand pleadingly.

'Mickey, please. No one's humiliating you and nothing's happened, OK? And today's my last day. Tomorrow I'm going home.'

'Whatever.' He shrugged and picked up the binoculars again. 'But don't think I don't notice. That's all.'

Irene climbed back up the steps and sat beside Luke once more, laying a hand on his back for an instant. Even when she moved apart, she could feel the heat radiating from him. Katherine followed, sucking on a lolly that stained her lips and tongue a deep red. She picked up her book from the table and squeezed her body between them.

'Read to me,' she demanded.

'OK.'

'Once upon a time, there were three little pigs,' she began. Katherine squirmed happily and drops of red flew over Irene's legs and bare feet. She read the book once, then again, making the huffing and puffing more dramatic; Luke steered nearer to the canal's opening. Katherine put a sticky hand on each of their thighs.

'If I'd seen a picture of this, a year ago,' said Irene, 'I would have thought I'd gone completely bonkers.'

He just smiled and pushed his foot against hers.

'Again!' said Katherine. 'Again again again!'

'Once upon a time . . .'

*　　　*　　　*

She lay on the deck and Lorrie rubbed cream into her back. She could feel his eyes on her. She read *Great Expectations*. She was near the end now, and would never read or think of it again without

312

associating it with these two weeks. There were smudges of oil on its thin, densely printed pages, making them translucent, and its spine was cracked. She'd pressed a small scarlet flower on its inside cover.

She biked along the towpath with Neil, Katherine and Mickey. Wind in her hair and on either side of the civilized water lay smooth hills, golden vineyards, far-off chateaux. The boat lay far behind them, a white shape reflected in the still water. Remember this, she thought to herself: remember.

They reached a small town, moored up beside all the other boats, had lunch in a café that sold slices of pizza and salads. Irene slid off her sandals and laid her dusty soles on Luke's calf. He looked at her; gave her a funny half-smile that turned her stomach liquid. She prodded at her Mediterranean salad, drank two tumblers of water.

'It's Irene's last night,' said Lorrie. 'It's gone too quickly.'

'What time do you have to leave?' Luke asked neutrally.

'I haven't really decided,' said Irene. 'I want to feel on holiday till the very last minute. But not too late. I think it's easiest to get a taxi from Béziers to take me to my car. It'll only take a couple of hours or so for me to get back to the place we set off from three days ago.'

'And then, straight back?'

'I'll have to stay somewhere tomorrow night. But with luck, I'll be sleeping in my own bed the night after tomorrow.'

'Let's take her out for a slap-up meal,' said Mickey, draining his beer mug and reaching over to take some of Lorrie's.

'Don't be daft. You've been incredibly generous to me already, letting me join your holiday like this. I haven't paid my share of the boat yet.'

'It was just a place that would have gone empty anyway.'

'I'm paying my way.' She pushed aside thoughts of debts, overdrafts, the leaking roof, school shoes for the new academic year . . .

'How about a meal then an all-night game of poker? Bottle of whisky and blackjack, like we used to do. Remember, Neil? Mary used to beat all of us, didn't she? Brilliant liar, my big sister. Isn't she, Luke? You know her best; all her secrets. Maybe she didn't lie to you but I wouldn't bet on it, I wouldn't bet a single penny. Most women are liars—except Juliet couldn't bluff anyone. Still can't, come to think of it; she's the most honest woman I ever met. That's why it took her so long to get hitched. You on, Luke? You owe me about twenty quid from the last game.'

'I'll see,' said Luke cautiously.

'Boring. Just say yes.'

'What does Irene want to do?'

'Irene, what do you want to do?'

'I'm easy,' she said.

'Easy? Oh no, I don't think so.'

'What's that supposed to mean?' said Lorrie.

'Irene knows. Don't you, Irene? Anyway, that's decided. Dinner and gambling. We'll see the sunrise together.'

*   *   *

She sat beside him at the front of the boat, their

314

legs hanging over the edge. She was conscious of Neil and Katherine a few feet behind them, doing a puzzle together, of Mickey out of sight on the deck above.

'Tell me about clouds,' she said.

'Clouds.' He took her hand and held it in his lap. She shifted so they were touching. 'What do you want to know then?'

'Just tell me something. Anything. What's that one?'

'Cumulus,' he said, smiling.

'I suppose I knew that.'

'You probably did.' Their bare feet pressed together. 'People used to think they were all different, that there was no way of categorizing them. They were God's mystery.'

'How many kinds are there then?'

'Just the three—cumulus, cirrus and stratus. Though of course there are subsets.'

'Ah,' she said vaguely. 'Go on.'

'Let's see. I belong to the Cloud Research Group.'

He stroked her wrist with a calloused thumb and she shifted her body ever so slightly so that their legs touched.

'Do you?'

'Mmm. That's why I'm taking a sabbatical in America next month. We're attempting to find out what the effects of global warming are on clouds.'

'Are there effects?'

'It's hard to measure though NASA does have a fancy new device. But it looks likely that clouds will become lower, thicker—that's important, because perhaps they will reflect the sunlight back into the atmosphere and counteract the effect of warming.'

'Like the earth protecting itself.'

'Sort of—on the other hand, they might also trap the heat, like a blanket.'

'Scary.'

'Yes. Your freckles have all merged together, you know.'

'I know. How did you get that scar?'

'I cycled into a branch.'

'So many things I don't know.'

'Ask me.'

'What food don't you like?'

'Avocados. Tomato ketchup.'

'I'll remember not to give you those.'

'You're going tomorrow,' he said.

'I know.'

'Do you have to?'

'Yes.'

'Irene.'

'Mmm?'

'We need to be alone for a bit.'

'We do.'

He lifted her hand and swiftly bent his head to kiss her palm. Behind them, Neil and Katherine were still clicking wooden pieces into place. On the deck above Lorrie was saying something to Mickey.

'Tonight Mickey's going to make us stay up all night. I know that manic gleam in his eyes.'

'They'll go to sleep eventually.'

'And you won't.'

'No. I won't.'

'Good.'

*   *   *

316

She lay on her bed, not moving, naked, her book laid spine down across her stomach. A warm breeze blew through the open window. She watched the blue sky and the clouds rolling past. Small, plump pillows; a child's drawing of summer. Cumulus. She touched her skin with the tips of her fingers. Tomorrow she would be gone, but there was still tonight.

CHAPTER THIRTY-ONE

Almost all her clothes were dirty. She just had the scruffy jeans and creased tee-shirt that she would travel in tomorrow. She took her orange dress from its hanger and buried her face into its soft brightness; it still smelt new. When she dropped it over her head, it fell in light, whispery folds down her body so that she felt naked in it, libidinous. It stroked her skin when she moved.

'You look nice,' said Lorrie as she came out of her cabin.

'My last night—I thought I should dress up.'

'I'll put a dress on as well, as soon as Neil and Katherine are out of the shower. But are you sure you can't stay longer? We've only got a couple of days more ourselves.'

'I'd love to, Lorrie—but it wouldn't feel right. The girls are coming home in a few days and I don't want to risk anything going wrong. I need to be ready—'

'I know, I know. Well, we'll miss you.'

'I'd like to keep in touch.' Irene felt suddenly shy.

'Of course we'll keep in touch. Actually, we're coming to London in November. Neil's got some meeting on fishing quotas he's going to and Katherine and I are tagging along with him.'

'Good, we can see each other then—I'd like that. And Katherine and Aggie can meet each other. I could take—'

She stopped for a moment as words rolled back down her throat; Luke had come from the deck, swinging from the steps, and was standing near her. Cropped hair, wide-set brown eyes that gave him the look of an alert, slightly anxious animal, thick brows, strong forearms, long fingers, scar on his lip. If she lifted a hand, she could touch him. Desire flooded her body.

'I could take you places,' she finished feebly.

'Great.'

'Shall we open that sparkling wine?' said Luke. 'Before we go out.'

'Definitely. Take it all up on deck and I'll get changed.'

'Where's Mickey?' asked Irene as Lorrie opened the door to her cabin, offering a glimpse of Neil, naked and pink shouldered.

'Having a fag on the towpath. You look nice,' said Luke.

'Do I?'

'Yes. Lovely.'

'Thank you.'

He lifted a hand to touch her. Katherine barged out of the cabin and took Irene's skirt, tugging it.

'Read me my book now.'

'Just once. Then we're all going to have a drink on deck before supper. Aren't you tired?'

'Read me the story about the duck.'

'OK.'

'Do the different voices, like before.'

'I'll try.'

'I'll get the drinks then.'

*   *   *

She felt drunk before she took a sip, bubbles prickling in her nostrils. They sat on the deck in the golden evening light, a baked landscape on either side of them, rosy clouds on the horizon, the smell of thyme in the air. Store this away, lay it up for winter days.

'A week ago, we didn't know each other,' said Irene.

'Juliet's half-sister-in-law. That's what we called you.'

'Did you? I was partly dreading you arriving.'

'Why? You don't seem like someone who's easily intimidated.' Mickey was drinking more quickly than the others, gulping the sparkling wine as if he was quenching his thirst.

'I don't know. You were this big group and I was just me, I suppose. And I'm not used to that—being just me, I mean. Whatever being me means.' Why was she talking like this? She took another small sip; light bounced off the water and the world tipped and wavered. 'I've been part of a group for so long—a pair, Irene-and-Adrian or Adrian-and-Irene, a family group—and suddenly I was trailing around on my own. You don't know until you're without it how used you get to someone else speaking for you, finishing your sentences, filling in silences.'

'I don't like people doing that to me,' said

Lorrie, not looking at Neil and speaking in a deliberately neutral tone. 'It makes me feel I've lost my identity.'

'I know. You don't like it until you don't have it, and then you miss it. Or at least, you feel cast off and adrift somehow.' She turned to Mickey. 'Do people match-make for you?'

'People not too far from where I'm sitting now have been known to, not to mention any names, Lorrie.'

'I do not!'

'Ha! What about that woman with that strange hairstyle last month?'

'I thought you two . . . Don't eat too many of those, Kath, you won't want your supper.'

'I don't want supper.' She picked up a handful of crisps and stuffed them into her mouth, glared round the group with bulging cheeks.

'It's awful,' said Irene. 'You feel such a self-conscious fool. And you know at once if you don't like them in that way, which of course you never do, so you have to sit through an evening knowing that there are these expectations—it's like buying a house.'

'What!' Neil laughed incredulously. 'A house?'

'It is. It's like when you visit a house and you can tell as soon as you pull up outside it that it's not for you, but you have to go through all the motions of being interested—in fact, the more you don't want it, the more you have to pretend that you do, going from room to room complimenting them on their sash windows or their kitchen units or airing cupboard or whatever.'

'First time I've been compared to an undesirable property,' said Mickey. He pulled the bottle towards him and poured himself a splash more wine.

'You know what I mean though.'

'We should go. I booked that restaurant for eight and it's a good ten minutes' walk from here.'

'Did you fall in love with your house?'

'That's not really what I was talking about.'

'No, but did you?' Mickey drank what was left in Luke's glass and leant towards her pugnaciously.

'It was the best we could do at the time.'

'So sometimes you just have to take what's on offer.'

'With houses, maybe.'

'Not with people?'

'No.'

'Come on,' said Lorrie, standing up. 'Enough of this. I'll wash Kath's face and then we'll be off.'

They walked along the towpath. Irene hung back to walk with Mickey.

'Are you all right?'

'Why shouldn't I be?'

'You just seem a bit—angry about something.'

'I'm OK. I just don't like being made a fool of.'

'I already told you that nothing . . .'

'It's none of my business what you choose to get up to. But when you said to me it was the wrong time for you, I thought you were telling the truth.'

'I was telling the truth.' She tucked an arm through his. 'Let's go and have our meal and then play poker.'

'Don't fucking patronize me.'

'OK.' She pulled her arm free again and quickened her stride. 'Like you said, it's not really any of your business.'

'So you are?'

'Leave it, Mickey.'

'I'm the gooseberry now? Perfect.'

'Don't be an idiot.'

He muttered something under his breath.

'What's that?'

'Nothing.'

'I thought . . .'

'Nothing,' he repeated.

'OK. The others are waiting for us.'

*   *   *

They hung back at the restaurant door. The tips of their fingers brushed. He trailed a finger down her arm and she shivered in the warmth.

'Get a move on!' called Mickey, who arranged it so that Irene and Luke were at opposite ends of the table.

They smiled across at each other. Irene lifted the glass of cold white wine and pressed it against her forehead. Waiting.

*   *   *

By two o'clock, Lorrie had retired exhausted, twenty-five euros up and with smudges under her eyes. At three-thirty, Neil, breaking even, joined her—they heard him pulling off his shoes, cleaning his teeth, murmuring something to Lorrie, then the cabin light went off.

'The whisky's finished,' said Mickey, lighting another cigarette and dealing again. The smoke drifted in spirals past his flushed cheeks and glittering eyes. 'How about some brandy?'

'I think I'm about to drop,' said Irene.

322

'You're winning. You can't pull out now.'

'I have to leave early tomorrow.'

'All the more reason to stay up now. The last fling.'

'No, really, Mickey.'

'Party pooper. You go then. Luke and I will continue. OK, Luke? We'll raise the stakes, make it matter. It has to hurt if you lose.'

'I'm all in too,' said Luke, looking across at Irene. He'd hardly touched his drink.

'Oh fuck this. We're on holiday here. You can sleep all day tomorrow.'

'I don't want to sleep all day tomorrow.'

'No wonder Mary left you.'

'Mickey—'

'What's fucking happened to everyone, that's what I want to know? Live a little for once, hey?'

'I'm knackered, that's all.'

'You don't look it to me. Maybe you just want to be somewhere else. Or you want me to be somewhere else.'

'I don't know what you're going on about.'

'I'm not blind, you know.'

'One last hand, if you insist, and then we should all turn in.'

'I'm not blind and I'm not stupid and I'm not a child either—I'll stay up until I want to go to bed.'

He poured himself a large glass of brandy and threw it expertly down his throat. The expression on his face didn't alter, but Irene saw there was a vein throbbing in his temple. He sloshed more brandy into the glass and over the table, then started sloppily dealing cards. Several slipped from the pack and scattered onto the floor.

Irene bent to pick them up. Then she stood up.

'Goodnight then. I'll see you tomorrow.'

'Night,' said Luke softly. 'Time for me, too. What about you, Mickey?'

'I'm staying right here. Bang in the middle. Not moving. Not going anywhere.'

'You're not going to bed?'

'Nope.'

'Do you want a blanket?'

'I won't be sleeping.' He looked from one to the other and grinned. 'I'll just sit here with my eyes wide open and wait for morning to come. Not long now.'

'OK,' said Luke evenly.

CHAPTER THIRTY-TWO

Irene went into her cabin and shut the door. She stood for a few minutes, listening to the sounds next door, Luke's muttered goodnight, Mickey's drawled response. Footsteps and a door opening, closing. The clink of a bottle's neck against glass. You imagine something so hard it almost becomes real. She had spent the day letting herself melt into the warmth of Luke's body, feeling his mouth against hers and his fingers touching her, opening her up. In her mind, she had been an anonymous body arching in the darkness, pale skin glimmering like a fish under water, a stranger and free from herself at last.

She rubbed at the creased silk of her dress, listened to the rustle of the trees on the towpath. She could feel, behind her eyes and in the Velcro scratchiness of her throat, that she was tired. If she lay down now, sleep would swamp desire. That would be the end of it all.

She straightened her shoulders and opened the door again. She could hear Katherine coughing in the cabin next door.

Mickey was slumped on the sofa. His eyes were closed, though his fist was still curled around an empty tumbler on the table. Irene walked softly across the floor, her bare feet sticking on the plastic. She raised a hand to tap on Luke's door.

'Where going?'

Mickey's red eyes stared out of his slack face. She stared back.

'Where do you think I'm going?' she said.

'Gonna fuck Luke?'

'Yes.'

He stood up and lurched towards her, grabbing her by the shoulder and wrenching her round to face him. All his features seemed to have slipped.

'Stop it,' she said.

'Bitch,' he hissed between his strong white teeth. 'You bitch.' He shook her so her head wobbled and pain sloshed behind her eyes.

'Let go.'

Luke's door opened and suddenly there were three of them wedged in the small space between the cabins, and the air was thick with the sound of breathing. Irene felt as if she was trapped in some strange dream—a fatuous comedy, a surreal disaster. Then Luke pushed Mickey backwards, so that he stumbled and had to stop himself from falling.

'Get your hands off her.'

'I'm not the one who's got his greedy, grubby hands on her,' said Mickey, staggering forward like a punch-drunk boxer. 'Thief!'

'Oh for God's sake,' said Irene. 'This is mad.'

But even as she spoke, Mickey was flailing a fist towards Luke, and following after it so his whole body swung wildly. In a weird slow motion Irene saw Luke jerk back, hands coming up to his face, and at the same time saw Mickey toppling sideways and down, carried by the momentum of his cartoonishly mis-thrown punch. Behind her, Neil was saying, 'What the fuck . . . ?' and behind him, out of their cabin, Lorrie's voice came plaintive and befuddled: 'What on earth's going on, Neil?'

And then Luke was on his knees beside Mickey, calling his name, as bright scarlet blood dripped from his jaw. But Mickey didn't answer.

Irene stood quite still. She stared at Luke's blood, dripping onto Mickey's shirt, and at Mickey's face, suddenly chalky under his tan. A blue bruise was spreading across his temple.

'Here,' said Lorrie, pushing her aside. 'Let me look.'

She was naked except for a pair of stripy knickers, and she leant over Mickey with her pendulous breasts just a few inches from his closed eyes. As she laid her hand on his forehead, he stirred and muttered something thickly. His eyes flickered open and shut.

'Give me a cushion or something,' she said to Neil, hovering behind them. 'And a tee-shirt for me while you're at it. What happened?'

'He fell over,' said Irene. Neil passed over a grubby towel, which Lorrie tucked tenderly under Mickey's head, lifting a thread of hair off his sticky skin. 'He'd drunk too much and got quarrelsome, and then he—well, he lashed out at Luke and kind of fell over. I don't know really.'

'Mummy? Mummy?'

'Go back to bed, Kath. Neil, take her back to bed.'

'Is he dead?' she asked in an interested voice.

'Don't be daft.'

'He looks dead.'

'He's coming round now,' Lorrie said softly to Luke.

'Mickey?' said Luke. 'Mick?'

'Sappen.'

'What's that, mate?'

He half struggled up. 'What's happened?'

'You hit your head.'

'Aches.'

'You will.'

'I feel strange,' he said. 'Not right. Strange. Ugh.'

'Don't move for a bit,' said Lorrie.

But Mickey writhed into a sitting position. His face was a dull, scummy grey; there were beads of sweat on his forehead.

'Sorry,' he said. 'Sorry sorry sorry sorry . . .'

Irene squatted beside Mickey while Lorrie pressed the pads of her fingers against his temple.

'How do you feel now?'

'Sick. You must be a lovely nurse. Lovely. Like being a baby again.'

'Let's get you on the sofa.'

'Can't—need to . . . Sorry.'

'It doesn't matter.'

'No—I mean for being such a wanker.' Tears started streaking the grime on his cheeks. Irene wiped them away with the back of her hand.

'Here, take our hands and pull yourself up,' said

327

Lorrie. 'That's the way. Lie down over here. Irene, get a glass of water for him, will you? Can you remember falling?'

'Falling—no. Remember grabbing Irene. Remember that. Sorry.'

'You've got a bit of concussion, that's all. Nothing to worry about. Best keep an eye on it for a bit—you shouldn't go back to sleep for a few hours, OK?'

'Haven't slept yet.'

'You can sleep all you want tomorrow. Though of course it's been tomorrow for ages, hasn't it?'

Luke glanced at his watch. 'Nearly five. It's pretty much light outside. I'm going to put some other clothes on.'

'I'll make everyone tea,' said Irene, suddenly aware of how cold she was in her grubby orange dress and her sticky, bare feet. She wanted a hot bath and a large bed and no one else near her. 'Mickey, tea for you?'

He nodded, grimacing. The bruise that spread from his left temple and up his forehead was violently blue, as if he'd been dyed.

'Luke? Tea?'

For the first time, he and Irene looked at each other. 'That would be very nice,' he replied formally.

'I'm hungry,' Katherine said from the cabin in her piping voice. 'Is it breakfast?'

'No,' they heard Neil reply. 'It's the middle of the night still. Go back to sleep.'

'How can it be night if it's blue outside?'

'It just can. Sleep.'

'But I'm hungry. I want Weetabix.'

'We don't have Weetabix, you know that.'

328

'Weetabix.' Her voice was getting higher all the time. 'I want Weetabix. I want Lambie.'

'Lambie's at home. Here's Teddy.'

'Don't want Teddy. Want Lambie. Want my red chair. Want my *Maisie* book.'

The door was shut sharply and her voice ebbed to a far-off whine. Lorrie stretched her arms, her tee-shirt riding above her knickers and her bare tanned midriff.

'It's going to be a long day,' she said.

'Yeah.'

Irene struck a match, turned the gas nozzle till it hissed, then lit the stove. She swilled out the teapot. Down the corridor they could hear the asymmetrical splatter of Luke's shower.

'Especially for you. You're leaving in a few hours.'

'Mmm. Only if everything's OK here.'

'Of course it will be—won't it, Mickey?'

'Sure,' he said groggily, his eyelids fluttering.

Lorrie looked at him. 'This is hopeless. Tell you what, Mickey, you can sleep for a bit and one of us will just wake you every half an hour or so. Though I don't know that that's any better—sounds like torture to me.'

'I don't need to sleep,' he said, but his eyes were already rolling back and his mouth opening as he spoke.

'You get back to bed,' said Irene. 'I'll keep an eye on him. It was my fault anyway.'

'Is that so?'

'He was jealous.'

'Of Luke?'

'Mmm.'

'In what crappy alternative world is that your

329

fault?'

Irene shrugged.

'He's wretched, that's what,' said Lorrie in a half-whisper, glancing over at Mickey sprawled slackly on the sofa. 'And drunk. And he's been antagonistic to Luke ever since he started going out with Mary, and then even more when he stopped.'

The kettle started a stuttering whistle; Irene lifted it off and poured boiling water over the tea bags. Behind them, she could hear Katherine saying: 'I want Lambie *now*. I want my Teletubbies video. I want Weetabix. I want my yellow nightie with the flower on front . . .'

'I'd better go and sort her out in a moment,' said Lorrie. She hesitated. 'You and Luke . . .'

'Nothing really,' said Irene dreamily, drearily. 'A holiday might-have-been. Something lovely in the air. Here, take this tea to Neil and give your daughter a hug. I'm going to put on my jeans. There's tea for you,' she called through Luke's door. 'On the side.'

She went into her cabin, and sat on the itchy blanket, drinking her tea. Then she took off her dress. The shower was cold when she stepped under it, but she washed herself vigorously in its chilly dribble, and dried herself with a thin, skimpy towel. There were goose bumps all up her arms; her bones ached.

For the first time in the holiday, she dressed in jeans and trainers, and bundled all her dirty clothes into her bag. Her grey skirt and ruffled top, still a bit wet and faintly braided with salt; her orange dress that was torn on the shoulder and smelt of brandy; her grimy shorts, her leather

330

sandals, her swimsuit, her sun cream, her absurd floppy hat.

She cleaned her teeth and put her sponge bag on top of her clothes, along with her books, and then zipped up the case. She slid her passport and wallet into its side pocket; pulled a comb roughly through the knots in her hair and put that in too.

'There,' she said. 'Finished.'

*   *   *

Back in the living space, she sat on the corner of the sofa and laid a hand on Mickey's shoulder. She shook it gently, then more firmly.

'Mickey? Mickey, you need to wake up.'

'Whooris?'

'Mickey, wake up. Talk to me.'

'Talk.'

'Count to ten.'

'Whar?'

'Count to ten.'

'What for?'

'Just do it.'

'One, two, three, four, five, six, seven, eight, nine, ten . . . Irene?'

'Fine. You can go back to sleep now.'

'I was an oaf.'

'Oh Mickey, it doesn't matter. It's all in the past. Are you all right?'

'Headache thundering like the Niagara bloody Falls. Never been there. Never been anywhere. Dublin. France.'

'You can still do it. You can go anywhere.'

'I called you bitch.'

'You were drunk.'

331

'No wonder Sandy left me.'

'Hush. Don't say that.'

'You're going today?'

'In a few hours. An hour's motoring away is where I can get a taxi. Though I might have to borrow some euros from Lorrie and Neil to get me back to my car.'

'I'll lend you . . .'

'No. It'll be fine.'

'Irene, you and Luke . . .'

'Leave it. Go back to sleep now.'

'Sleep's gone away. Feel like shit but couldn't sleep now.'

'I'll get you a cup of tea, shall I?'

'Why don't I do that?' Luke came out of his cabin, in a fresh white shirt and baggy jeans with a rip across one knee. His feet were bare. His skin was swollen around the cut on his jaw and he looked tired and subdued. His eyes were dulled, like lead. He was impossibly far away from her now.

'Luke?' she asked politely.

'Mmm?'

'Maybe we could get going in a bit, since we're all awake—it's probably a good idea for me to be on my way as soon as possible. I've got a long drive ahead.'

'I was just being an idiot,' said Mickey. 'Just an overgrown crappy idiot.'

Luke looked at his watch. 'The lock ahead doesn't open for an hour or more. We'll get going as soon as it does—how about that?'

'Fine. Thanks.'

Lorrie came out of the cabin. 'Did I hear you talk about leaving?'

332

'Yeah, as soon as we get to Béziers.'

'Why don't we all have breakfast on deck, one last time? I bought all those blood oranges yesterday which I'll squeeze, and there are a few croissants which'll be fine if we sprinkle them with a bit of water and warm them in the oven.'

'There are some peaches in the fridge which need eating. And the yoghurt.'

'Perfect.'

'How's Katherine?'

'She's cheered up now that Neil's reading to her. But God knows what she'll be like for the rest of the day. You're lucky you'll be out of it. How're you doing, Mick?'

'There's a drum banging in my head. And I feel sick. And a fool.'

'You are a fool.'

'Thanks. Apart from all that I'm fine.'

'Good. Take it really easy for the rest of the day, OK?'

'I should clean myself up.'

But he didn't move, and a few minutes later he fell asleep again. His mouth opened slightly and a snore wheezed from him every time he breathed out.

*　　　*　　　*

She just needed to be gone now, to be alone in her small, rusty car, music playing loudly and the road lying straight and grey in front of her. The sun rose in the sky, ribboning orange clouds on the horizon. The air was already warm and dry; it smelt of sheets that have been ironed, baked earth. She pictured the dry, dusty earth going down and down; no moisture anywhere; layers of light, friable grit with insects tucked into its open pores. She wanted wet mornings, muddy afternoons, saturated green fields, swollen ditches, grey chasing clouds, lonely starless nights. She wanted to be with her family again.

She looked across at Luke as he cut up the peaches with his Swiss Army knife, running the blade through the rosy flesh in a complete circle, easing the two halves apart, carefully prising out the stone, cutting the halves into segments and laying them on the plate. A little nostalgic shudder of lust passed through her. She wouldn't see him again, nor feel his hands on her. He was already part of her past, something that might have been. He felt her gaze and looked up. His face was grave, attentive, a bit remote. She attempted a small, rueful smile; he laid down the knife and then, in front of Neil and Lorrie, reached over and put his warm, broad hands over hers.

In her mind, she was standing up, pulling him to his feet and leading him down the ladder, past sleeping Mickey, to her cabin; she was closing the flimsy door, closing the thin curtains and lifting her crumpled shirt over her head . . . Lorrie leant forward and poured coffee for them all; Luke lifted his hands away from hers to cradle his mug. Irene sipped the acrid brew, slid a segment of cold, ripe peach into her mouth.

'OK,' she said.

Luke stood up. 'Time to get moving then.'

'I guess.'

'I'll start the engine.'

'Are you all packed?' asked Lorrie.

'Yes. There wasn't much anyway.'

334

'It won't be the same without you,' said Neil, his chin on his daughter's head as she ate her croissant, and she looked at him with surprise. He'd been a dry, pale presence for her—Lorrie's husband, Katherine's father, a half-sketched figure in the background, hidden by her over-coloured emotions.

'Thank you,' she said awkwardly, feeling as if she was making a speech but had forgotten to bring the notes. 'It's been lovely. You've been lovely—all of you. I was a stranger and you made me welcome. I feel restored.'

'You make it sound as if we won't see you again,' said Lorrie, as Luke disappeared from their view.

'You have to say goodbye to Mickey for me,' said Irene.

'Where are you going?' asked Katherine, suddenly lifting her head and staring at Irene with suspicious, reddened eyes.

'I'm going home.'

'I want to go home, too. Mummy, I want to go home.'

A moment later the engine coughed into life. Lorrie, Katherine by her side, took the wheel; Irene and Neil scrambled off the boat and, practised now, untied the ropes from the bollards and then, at a call from Luke, pushed the boat away from the bank and jumped aboard. In the early morning, everything was clean and absolutely still; only the motion of their boat broke up the glassy water, stirred the perfect reflections of dappled plane trees and streaked blue sky. Through the grey hoops of bridges, half mirror and half real; past the vineyards with their turning leaves and bursting grapes; under low branches

335

which brushed their deck.

'Lock ahead,' called Lorrie. 'Béziers, Irene!'

Irene went and fetched her bag. As she passed Mickey, she leant forward and touched her lips to his clammy forehead. 'Take care,' she whispered, and he groaned and shifted his position; he stank of alcohol and sweat and his clothes were stained. He looked like the tramp who sat with his trolley outside Irene's work.

On deck, she kissed everyone on their cheeks, except for Katherine who she picked up and hugged until she wriggled and asked to be put down. As the boat slowed, she clambered up onto the bank. Luke passed her her bag and she smiled at him, waved her hand at everyone else, and walked down the hill towards the town. When she looked back, she couldn't even tell which was their boat among all the others queuing up for the lock. They all looked the same.

CHAPTER THIRTY-THREE

He stepped right out in front of her, a thumb raised, and she jammed on her brakes and stopped a few feet from him. He slung his canvas bag over his shoulder and walked towards the car as if there was nothing more natural than that he should be hitching a lift from her an hour after they'd self-consciously said goodbye. She watched him coming in the rear-view mirror, and for a moment, she thought of driving away in a spray of gravel, leaving him standing there.

'Where are you trying to get to?' she asked as

she leant over and pushed open the door.

'You, damn it,' he said.

He was panting slightly and there were circles of sweat under his arms. He must have run, she thought with satisfaction. She felt like a cat that's got the cream; anticipation licked its way over her body, and a shivery thrill went through her.

'I can take you some of the way,' she said. 'Climb in then.'

'You sure you want me to?'

'Yes.'

He threw his bag over the back seat and slid into the seat beside her. They sat there not looking at each other, not saying anything, grinning like two schoolchildren who've got away with something.

'What did you . . . ?'

'I said I'd meet them at Montpellier airport, tomorrow evening.'

'Oh.' A day, she thought. We have one day together.

'I thought I wasn't going to make it in time.'

'What now?'

'Let's go. You need to get home. I'm just keeping you company some of the way.'

She put on her dark glasses and slid a tape into the machine. He leant back in his seat. She could feel he was looking at her but she didn't look back; she kept her eyes on the road ahead as it streamed past her and the sun rose in the sky, tearing through the last of the gauzy clouds.

'When are we going to stop?' she asked at last.

'You decide.'

'Are you hungry?'

'No.'

'Thirsty?'

'No.'

'Luke?'

'Mmmm?'

'I feel nervous, all of a sudden. Maybe I've forgotten how to do this.'

'I think the trick is not to think about how to do it.'

'It's been so long.'

'For me too.'

'Really?'

'Really.'

'You haven't touched me yet.'

'I'm waiting till I can't wait any longer.'

*   *   *

An hour later, he laid her down on the baked earth. There was a rock against one shoulder, digging into her. Her hair was full of moss and dust, and twigs snapped against her skin. Insects crawled over her. The sun crashed through the branches of the trees and shattered on her eyelids. Her skull was flooded with blazing sky and fractured light. He pulled off her shirt; his hands were full of her soft, pale breasts and his mouth was against the pulse in her neck. He peeled off her jeans. She flung her arms out wide, crucified and gasping on the stony ground, and when he put his hand between her legs she shuddered. She kissed the corner of his mouth, bit into his soft lips till she tasted blood, dug her fingernails into his back and listened to the groan of pleasure that she ripped from him. She felt his weight and wanted to be crushed; she gripped his moleskin head and stared into his murky eyes and watched him

338

watching her as she broke apart again and again, hearing herself cry out with a voice she'd never heard before. She was a stranger at last. A stranger in a foreign land.

Later, they lay facing each other, damp with sweat, and he very delicately picked bits of wood and dry leaves out of her hair.

'Thanks,' she murmured, blinking up at him.

'I'm hungry now.'

'Mmm. Me too.'

'We can buy a picnic and stop somewhere.'

'What time is it?'

'Midday.'

'I've got to get at least halfway there today.'

'Let's find a good point on the map where we can stop for the night. Then tomorrow, you go on to Calais and I'll get a train to Montpellier.'

'A night together, that'll be nice.' She ran a thumb over his lip. 'Isn't this weird?'

'Is it?'

'I think it is.'

'You're possibly right.'

'Do you do this kind of thing often?'

'I don't think so. What kind of thing is this kind of thing?'

'Sex, I suppose.'

'Not often.'

'Are you still in love with Mary?'

He didn't move or reply for several moments, just lay staring up at the shiny blue sky.

'Probably,' he said at last. 'It doesn't matter any more though.' He sat up and looked around for his clothes and she watched him: how the sun gleamed off his pale stomach and his tanned legs; how a line of hair ran down his stomach. Grit and dead leaves stuck to his sweaty back.

He didn't ask about Adrian, but she squinted up at the brightness and considered. If Adrian had died, instead of leaving her, then she would certainly be in love with him still. Their story would have had a beginning, middle and end; a clear shape and an obvious meaning. She would fill her memory bank to the brim with all their happy and intense moments, replay the times he'd told her he loved her, allow herself to picture them making love to each other, let his tender face lodge in her mind, remember anniversaries, speak to him though he was no longer there, feel understood by his looked-for ghost. She would forget the squabbles and the irritations, the way he crushed her and the way she resented him; the way they both pushed each other into narrower lives. Sorrow would be noble and fulfilling, and death would give their marriage a splendid afterglow; her mourning would be official and respected. It would give her life a kind of resonance. She would bring up the girls with vivid stories about their beloved, lost father and support herself with the knowledge that she had been his chosen one, his best-beloved.

But he had left her and she wasn't his best-beloved, she wasn't anyone's best-beloved, and their shared story was ragged and partial and unglamorous, full of nasty loose ends that flapped about in her mind. Not an unimpeachable tragedy, but a kind of ordinary, everyday failure; not a sealing up of the past perfect, but a horrible, frantic untying of it so that everything she'd taken for granted flew out from it and tumbled around her.

'Lunch then,' she said.

In the early evening, they stopped at a narrow, gloomy hotel set back from the busy road, with a tall, sculpted hedge around its garden and a small fountain in the courtyard. Their room, at the top of the building, was bare, cool and dim, and overlooked the red-tiled roofs of the town and, beyond that, the station where Luke would take his train at 11.05 the next morning. Steam from the kitchen curled through the open window; they could smell garlic and ginger and hear the muted gabble of voices rising, falling. There was a large fan in the ceiling which, when they turned it on, clicked lazily round, its blades blurring.

Irene had a shower and, while she was waiting for Luke, dozed off on the firm bed, wrapped in the thin towel and with the starched bolster under her head. She dreamt she was at home again with Adrian and the girls; nothing happened in the dream, she was simply sitting at the table in the kitchen and living the life that she had once had. When she woke with a jerk, she couldn't remember where she was; she looked up at the flick of the fan's blades and waited. Even when memory returned, filling up the blank attics in her head, it felt unreal. The dream of the familiar past, and the oddity of the present, scrambled together in her tired mind. She stared dazedly at Luke, sitting naked at the bottom of the bed, towelling himself dry.

'Sleep some more, if you want,' he said. 'It's still quite early—we don't need to eat at once.'

'If I sleep now, I'll be awake all night.'

She sat up and stretched, letting the towel slip from her body. She felt his eyes on her and smiled and held out her arms.

*   *   *

They ate soup that tasted of cabbage, then fish that tasted of chicken. The brie was rubbery and the wine sharp. They barely spoke, although their knees touched under the small table that separated them, their hands met. They didn't talk because there was no need any more. They were in each other's past now, a few days of summer. Tomorrow, they would take their different roads. They wouldn't meet again. He would go to America, where he would think about Mary and lose himself in the clouds; she would return to her daughters and she would pick up her life where she'd abandoned it just two weeks ago. Because there aren't really endings, she almost said out loud. You just go on as best you can. That's all.

In the darkness, they held each other. She could make out the glow of his open eyes. Very quiet, very slow, very kind. The fan clicked past. The watch on his wrist ticked in her ear. Two strangers, saying goodbye.

*   *   *

At half past five, she woke. A cock was crowing somewhere, and between the half-open shutters, over the gables of the roof, the day was beginning to brighten. She lay for a while listening to the sound of Luke's breathing. He murmured something and shifted, clamping a forearm over his eyes to keep out traces of light. She'd read in a book that when you share a bed with someone, you change positions at the same time as each other through the night. She'd always found it strange and touching to think of the hours she and Adrian had spent, unconscious and yet together—alone in the grip of their dreams, and yet hands, legs, bodies touching each other, consoling each other.

After a few minutes she swung her legs cautiously out of the bed and stood up. She padded to the small bathroom, washed her face and cleaned her teeth. Her face was pale and her hair a tangle. Then she found her clothes and put them on noiselessly. She had nothing to pack. Almost everything was in the car.

She hesitated, looking at the sleeping Luke; leant over and kissed his warm, damp forehead.

'Thanks,' she whispered, and crept from the room.

CHAPTER THIRTY-FOUR

Irene was home by five, and although she'd barely been away a fortnight her memory played strange tricks on her. The house seemed smaller, the ceiling lower than she'd thought. The staircase turned away at a sharper angle. She dropped her luggage inside the kitchen door, stuffed her first load of washing inside the machine, noticed that there was a vase of dead roses standing in green, smelly water. Then she went upstairs slowly, breathing in the musty air, seeing how the small pane of glass at the top of the landing was smeared and how the carpet was grimy and threadbare.

She opened the window in Aggie and Clem's room, sat on the nearest bed, picking up Aggie's teddy and holding its prickly, balding body against her cheek. She went into Sasha's room and unnecessarily straightened the duvet, then drew her finger across the sill, gathering up a smirch of dust. From the window, she saw that the grass on the lawn was long; the yellow roses had bolted and dropped their petals in little heaps on the ground. The misshapen pears on the tree were weighing down its branches and a few had already fallen.

Next, she wandered into the box room, that was to have been Felix's and that since his death had stood unused, just boxes of hand-me-down Babygros and tiny, stained cardigans that he never got to wear, soft crocheted blankets that had never been unpacked. Irene pulled a handful of clothes from a bin bag and pushed her face into their pastel folds. They smelt of talcum powder. The Moses basket stood in the corner, with a small sheet folded neatly inside and on top of that a white, fluffy seal, the girls' present to him when he'd been born. They'd all crowded round him and Clem had touched his button nose with her grubby forefinger, looking embarrassed, and Aggie had started to cry because his fragile head was against Irene's breast and suddenly that was where she wanted to be. Sasha had just stared, as if she was trying to learn his face, his tiny features. Then with a cautious smile she'd put the seal at his feet and said, 'Hello, Felix.'

Irene picked a framed photograph out of the box near the door and held it. It had been taken a few days after his birth, when he was asleep. His

344

eyelids were slightly swollen; his face smooth. He had a button nose and a small mouth already with a milk blister on the upper lip. She had called him tadpole, poppet, pigeon, honey-bun, muffin, my dearest sweetest love. There was a faint red stork mark between his eyes. She held the photograph against her chest and stared around. A boy called happiness.

'Clem can sleep here,' she said aloud, noticing how her voice bounced round the empty room. 'I've decided I don't want to move again, after all.'

It was small and run-down, in an unlovely street, and a poor, neglected neighbourhood, another world from the airy detached properties her friends lived in, but suddenly she felt fond of the house, protective of its shabby honesty. It was in the heart of the city, among the throng of ordinary, unprivileged lives, and it held so many of her stories. It told her who she was. Like her skin protecting her outrageous heart, it hemmed her in and held her safe.

She went downstairs and put the photo among all the others. Her family, the one she'd been given.

*　　　*　　　*

At the twenty-four-hour supermarket, she filled a trolley with familiar things—chicken drumsticks and pork sausages, hot chocolate and miniature marshmallows to go with it, caramel ice cream, green apples, unwaxed lemons, porridge oats, pudding rice, lime cordial, milk chocolate digestive biscuits, raspberry jelly, tea bags, baking potatoes, fish fingers, Marmite. She let herself imagine spooning food onto the girls' plates, their faces turned towards her, and felt a stab of fear. They weren't all hers any more. They belonged to another world as well, and would be looking at her with the judging eyes of people who had left. She would feel self-conscious with them, and would worry about what they thought of her.

She sat at the kitchen table, as she'd done in her dream the evening before, and drank a cup of mint tea. She rang Karen, who was surprised two weeks had gone by already; they arranged to meet once the girls returned. They would go to the zoo together, or maybe the aquarium; giant rays and mean-eyed sharks would glide past the faces that they squashed against the glass.

Irene said nothing to her about Luke. She would tell no one and he would be her secret, like a walled garden only she knew about. There were good secrets and bad, she thought; the ones that slowly poison and the ones that give solace. This secret was good; it had blue skies and a healing sun, and in its enclosed space she could recover the self she had thought she had lost.

She called Jem, but there was no answer. She imagined the phone ringing in their small house, echoing through the rooms where the evening sun would be slanting in through the windows, laying its fingers across the cool tiles. It seemed such a very long time ago, another world, that she'd danced in their garden in her orange dress. Everything was like a dream, unreal and preternaturally bright—not just her summer, but her life, episodes strung like gaudy beads in her memory. The little girl who longed for her father; the teenager who listened to her mother weep; the young woman who let herself fall in love as if she was jumping off a cliff and had nothing to break her fall, but it didn't matter because she knew she would fly; the mother standing over her dead son, unable to weep, because when you weep, the thaw has set in, and the great freeze is over; the betrayed wife standing at the foot of the bed where her treacherous husband lay and hurling abuse at him while he laughed at her.

She was all of these, and yet they felt like strangers to her, far removed from this woman standing in front of the cracked mirror in her bedroom, where she saw herself full length for the first time in weeks, and liked what she saw for the first time in years. She looked slim, strong, sturdy, healthy. Ready for life.

*   *   *

At half past four the next afternoon, when Irene was in the kitchen peeling potatoes for supper, the doorbell rang. Nervous happiness jolted through her; her knees shook, and she pushed her hair behind her ears, wiped her hands against her sides.

Adrian stood at the threshold, a half-smile already in place. He wore a bright blue shirt, which was rolled up over muscled brown arms. His hair was long and his cheeks stubbly. He kissed Irene chastely, carefully, on both her cheeks so she felt his bristles and smelt his old familiar smell. And then he looked at her, the new Irene who had miraculously become the woman he'd fallen for so long ago, wearing a loose yellow dress that he remembered from years back, with soft, bleached hair and honey-coloured skin and bright eyes in a freckled face. She knew by his expression that she was lovely to him once more, after so many years of being invisible. For a second, she thought she would reach out and take his hand in hers, hold it against her cheek for the comfort of it.

She looked so small and solitary, standing in the doorway with the light falling across her face. Adrian wanted to take her by her thin shoulders and look into her grey eyes and say to her: we fucked everything up, didn't we? I fucked up and at last I'm sorry. This wasn't the way it should have been. I should have cherished you. But what was the point, after all? Everything was done and their story was finished.

'There was no space,' he said instead. 'I've parked the car down the road. Aggie's asleep in the back, and the girls are just getting their things out of the boot.'

'Good.'

She smiled at him and tears filled both their eyes.

'They're wretchedly tired after the flight. They might be a bit . . .'

'Yes. It'll be all right.'

She looked over his shoulder towards the road. There was Sasha and, several feet behind her, Clem, struggling towards her, herded by Frankie. Who had, she saw, an unmistakably rounded tummy and, as she came nearer, the secret bloom of pregnancy on her face.

'I should have said; I know I should have told you but . . .'

'It doesn't matter. I think I knew anyway.'

'Irene . . .'

'It doesn't matter.'

She walked towards her daughters, then broke into a run. Sasha wore jeans and a new tee-shirt, with a picture of a kangaroo on the front. Her hair was neatly plaited, and a brightly patterned sun hat was perched on her head. She looked fresh and tidy, though as she approached, Irene saw little purple smudges under her eyes. Irene opened her arms and Sasha walked daintily into them, putting one hand onto her hat to keep it in place. Irene felt her daughter's rib bones, her tiny breasts, pressed like buds against her. Her skin smelt of soap and after-sun lotion.

'Hello, Mummy,' said Sasha.

'Hello, honey. You're so . . .' So what? So thin, so precious, so grown up, so terrifying. 'You're so welcome home,' she made do with. Over Sasha's shoulder, she saw Clem break into a jagged run, her backpack dragging on the pavement behind her. Her face was a ruddy brown, her hair stood up in spikes; a chocolate smear ran from cheekbone to jaw.

'Clem! Clemmie!'

'Look!' Clem stopped short and, bending down, opened her backpack in a frenzy of impatience. 'Look at what I've got.'

She pulled a chunky wooden box out and pulled open the stiff lid. A shell fell out and rolled onto the pavement; its pink spiral broke into gritty fragments as they watched.

'Clem,' said Irene squatting down beside her. 'Shall we look at that inside, rather than here?'

'No! Look! Look! It's somewhere here. Oh here, my ostrich feather. I held a koala; you have to see.'

The contents of the box spilled onto the tarmac. A film canister rolled onto the road. A small carved wooden crocodile bounced under the hedge. A blurred, underexposed photograph of Clem holding a sleepy koala bear spread at their feet.

'She's exhausted,' said Frankie, apologetically, as she approached them. 'She's been so looking forward to seeing you she didn't sleep on the plane. Did she, Adrian?'

'Hardly.'

'It's getting dirty!' shouted Clem. 'It's all ruined.'

She bounded after the crocodile, crouching her frantic little body under the hedge to gather it up.

'Clem,' said Irene, her voice wobbling with love. 'Darling Clem, it's fine. I want to see it all as soon as we get inside. Here, let's put everything back in the box.'

'Leave me alone. You don't care.'

She was pushing things back into the box, then she stood up, holding the box to her chest, and started running back down the pavement, away from them all.

'She's overexcited,' said Sasha in a reassuring voice. 'She's glad to be home really.'

'I know,' said Irene. 'Hang on, I won't be long.'

She caught up with Clem, who'd slowed to a stumbling walk.

'Show me the photo then,' she said.

'You said we had to look at it inside,' Clem said in a sullen voice. Tears streaked her dirty, mutinous face.

'I was just being stupid. I want to see it now.'

'I held it.'

'Was it soft?'

'Soft but a bit smelly.'

350

'It looks very comfy in your arms; it must have trusted you. Was it heavy?'

'Really heavy, but I didn't drop it or anything.'

'We'll put it in a proper frame and you can have it by your bed.'

'That's good.'

'Shall we go inside now?'

'OK.'

They walked up the road hand in hand and stopped by the car, where Frankie stood, shifting from foot to foot, jingling the car keys, anxious to be gone. Irene hardly glanced at her. Aggie was slumped in the child seat, fast asleep. Her head was tipped to one side, and saliva trickled down from her slackly open mouth that was still faintly swollen from the jellyfish sting. Irene saw by the pulse in her eyelids that she was dreaming. She opened the back door and, leaning forward, hauled her straw-headed daughter out like a sack of potatoes, settling her weight on her hip and on her shoulder. Aggie half woke, smiled, murmured something incomprehensible, and snuggled into her mother. Her cheek was damp with sweat.

'Hello,' Irene said into the top of her head.

Clem held her skirt tightly in her grubby fist as they walked to the house. Sasha was waiting at the door with Adrian.

'I didn't want to go in without you.'

'Why not?'

'I don't know. I'm worried you'll have made it all different.'

'Hardly!'

'Is my hamster alive?'

'He certainly is.'

'I thought he was dead.'

351

'Come on, let's go and see him.'

She turned to Adrian. Aggie's head lolled heavily against her; her legs dangled clumsily down.

'Goodbye,' she said.

'Goodbye.'

He hugged Sasha and whispered something in her ear, lifted Clem high in the air, laid a finger against Aggie's cheek. Her eyes snapped open and she stared beadily at him.

'I'll call,' he said.

'Fine.'

For a moment he hesitated, poised between his past world and his present one. Then he turned on the pathway. Frankie, sitting in the car with one hand laid across her plumpening belly, turned on the engine as he came towards her. Irene stood in the doorway with the girls, watching him leave.

CHAPTER THIRTY-FIVE

'Once upon a time,' said Irene, lying on Aggie's bed with a book on the pillow between them.

'What time is it?' asked Clem.

'Nearly eight o'clock.'

'I don't mean here, I mean in my body.'

'I suppose it's early morning in Australia—but in your body it's probably not just Australia any more. Lots of times are crashing into each other.'

'Like cows.'

'What!'

'Go on with the story,' said Aggie. Then she put her thumb in her mouth and spread her fingers in a

352

chubby lattice across her pink face.

'Once upon a time, in a far-off land, there was a giant who was very sad because no one . . .'

'Not from a book,' said Clem. 'Tell us a story from your own life. Tell us about when you were young.'

'Yes,' said Aggie, unstoppering her mouth. 'Tell us.'

Sasha appeared in the doorway. She had had a bath and was already in her night clothes. She sat cross-legged on the floor between the two beds and put the damp end of one of her plaits into her mouth. Irene put a hand on her warm head and Sasha gave her a cautious smile.

'Let me see . . .' said Irene, casting her mind back. It was always easier to remember sad stories than happy ones, the times when things changed, not the times they remained the same. 'There was this one time when I found a baby bird, lying in the garden. It was really young, it had only just grown its feathers, and it was completely helpless. It was making these pitiful piping sounds, and its mother was calling back to it from the tree above, but of course she couldn't do anything for it. It was going to die. We decided we would try and save it.'

'We?'

'Me and your granny.'

'And Grandpa,' said Clem.

'Well,' Irene hesitated. 'Grandpa wasn't really there when . . .' She saw the tearful gleam in Clem's bloodshot eyes and changed her mind. 'Grandpa too. We decided to try and save the baby bird. It was a blackbird—you know, the ones with bright yellow beaks and a beautiful song. We've got a blackbird that sings in our garden, hour after hour. I'll show you tomorrow morning when you wake up. Anyway, we very carefully picked up the bird—it was so terrified that its heart was thundering in its tiny body and I remember I was scared it would just break apart—and put it in a shoebox, with cotton wool in it. And somehow Granny got hold of this teat pipette . . .'

'Whassat?' muttered Aggie, half asleep, thumb back in her mouth.

'It's a little pipe you can squeeze liquid from. Like in Clem's bottle of ointment, remember, when we had to squeeze drops into her eyes for conjunctivitis? So every day, I fed it warm milk, and then bread mushed up in milk—and then, as it got bigger, we dug worms up from the garden and fed him that. Someone lent us a bird cage and he lived in that.'

'What was he called?' asked Sasha.

'Reepicheep. After the mouse in Narnia—I'll read you the stories soon, Clem. He needed to be fed every hour or so, and my teacher said I could bring him to school with me. He became like a class pet. He'd even sit sometimes on your finger, like a budgerigar. He got bigger and stronger and soon he was flapping his wings. He was almost ready to let go.'

'Why couldn't you keep him?'

'Because he was a wild bird; it wouldn't have been fair. So one day we took him into the garden, and I stood on the step ladder with Reepicheep in my hand, and I threw him up in the air. And he flew away. Free.'

'Did he stay in your garden though, and sing?'

'Yes,' said Irene firmly.

It was a lie, of course. What had happened was

354

that one night the bird had suddenly died, there in the cage, and by the time Irene had found him the next morning there were maggots on his feathery body. But you can change your stories, she decided. They don't have rules; you can let them pull you in whatever direction they suddenly decide to take, out of the shadows and into the sun.

'He sang from the tree, day after day,' she said, smiling at the three faces. 'And I sat and listened to him. I thought he was singing to me.'

*   *   *

Once upon a time, there was a woman who fell in love with a man and she really thought that, as in a fairy tale, they would live happily ever after. She believed that they would grow old together, and she wouldn't ever be alone or lonely again. But the book doesn't close there. Marriage is not the end of a story, just its beginning. Now she knew she was glad Adrian had left her, glad of the tunnel of grief she'd travelled through, glad she had no idea of where exactly she was going and what would happen to her next. Who was she going to become, over the next page?

'Goodnight,' she said softly.

She kissed Sasha on the top of her head and watched her pad like a cat from the room. She hugged Clem tight, noting her hectic cheeks, her sour breath. She bent over Aggie and gathered up the soft, squashy loaf of her, holding her close, breathing in her fresh baked smell.

'Mummy,' said Aggie, her eyes half opening.

'Mmm?'

355

'I love you.'

'Me you too.'

'How much do you love me?'

'More than it's possible and then some.'

'Well, I love you—I love you like an owl on the moon.'

'What!'

'Like an owl on the moon.'

*   *   *

Irene went downstairs. Everything was quiet, but the quality of silence felt entirely different, now that her daughters had come home to her. She looked out of the window and saw the pink clouds in the darkening sky, and smiled to herself, remembering. Already the young moon was floating low among the chimney pots and London trees.

Like an owl on the moon, an owl on the moon. Her heart skipped a beat, for where would she rather be than here, in this small and run-down house where three girls slept peacefully, knowing that she was standing guard over them till the morning came? And who in the whole wide world was as lucky as she was, to be loved like an owl on the moon?